Praise for Lisa Gardner

THE PERFECT HUSBAND

'A nail-biting chase novel packed with tension and fiery sex, building up to a terrific denouement'

Good Housekeeping

'A pacy and gripping story'   *Essentials*

THE SURVIVORS CLUB

'Bestselling author Lisa Gardner is a force to be reckoned with. Her writing style is punchy and fast moving, and there's a rich vein of black humour running through her breakneck prose. Dialogue is crisp, descriptions concise and to the point . . . the complex plot rattles along at a fair old lick. It's all good stuff and cements Gardner's place as a writer of great suspense tales'   *Crime Time*

'Both clever and engrossing, this is a heart-stopping read that will grip you with every page'   *Good Book Guide*

THE KILLING HOUR

'Gardner's sixth high-octane page-turner . . . With tight plotting, an ear for forensic detail and a dash of romance, this is a truly satisfying sizzler in the tradition of Tess Gerritsen and Tami Hoag'   *Publishers Weekly*

'The storytelling is sharp and there are enough plot twists and red herrings to satisfy most readers eager for a sizzling thriller'   *Crime Time*

D068102E

Lisa Gardner sold her first novel when she was twenty years old and has since been published in over a dozen countries. Now living in the New England area with her husband and daughter, she spends her time writing, travelling and hiking. Her latest novel, *Say Goodbye* is published in hardback by Orion.

Visit her website at www.LisaGardner.com.

By Lisa Gardner

Say Goodbye
Hide
Gone
Alone
The Killing Hour
The Survivors Club
The Next Accident
The Third Victim
The Other Daughter
The Perfect Husband

the perfect husband

LISA GARDNER

An Orion paperback

First published in Great Britain in 1998
by Orion
This paperback edition published in 1999
by Orion Books Ltd,
Orion House, 5 Upper St Martin's Lane,
London WC2H 9EA

An Hachette UK company

Reissued 2007

Copyright © Lisa Baumgartner 1998

The right of Lisa Gardner to be identified as the author of
this work has been asserted by her in accordance with the
Copyright, Designs and Patents Act 1988.

All rights reserved. No part of this publication may be
reproduced, stored in a retrieval system, or transmitted, in
any form or by any means, electronic, mechanical,
photocopying, recording or otherwise, without the prior
permission of the copyright owner.

A CIP catalogue record for this book is available
from the British Library.

Printed and bound in Great Britain by
Clays Ltd, St Ives plc

The Orion Publishing Group's policy is to use papers that
are natural, renewable and recyclable products and
made from wood grown in sustainable forests. The logging
and manufacturing processes are expected to conform to
the environmental regulations of the country of origin.

www.orionbooks.co.uk

Acknowledgments

Writers have a tendency to view their craft as a solitary occupation. In fact, it takes many people to create a book and I'm indebted to quite a few. I would like to express my deep appreciation and gratitude to all the people who helped me in this process, including:

Jack Stapelton, Bristol County assistant district attorney, who generously and patiently answered a multitude of questions about crossjurisdictional investigations and arrests.

Steve Belanger, corrections officer, who shared with me enough details about life in a maximum security prison to convince me never to commit a crime.

Chris Fuss, college buddy and dear friend, who not only provided his experience in orienteering and the Revolutionary War reenactment, but also let me play with the rifles.

Aaron Kechley and Valerie Weber, two Williams alumni, who told me so much about quaint, beautiful Williamstown, I just had to use it for murder.

And to the remaining police officers, FBI agents, and other corrections officers who kindly agreed to answer my questions but asked that their names be withheld.

These people gave me their knowledge. In some cases, I did take artistic license. Any mistakes, of course, are mine alone.

Finally, special thanks to my agent, Damaris Rowland, for believing in my talent even more than I did; to Nita Taublib for being willing to take a risk on this book; to Beth de Guzman, whose razor-sharp editing made this manuscript come alive; to my family and my friends Heather, Dolly, Michele, Terry, Lori, and Betsy for their support and endless supplies of chocolate; and to my fiancé, Anthony Ruddy, for sharing it all with me and showing me a beautiful future. Words aren't enough.

THE PERFECT
HUSBAND

Prologue

The first time he saw her, he simply knew. He watched her red and white pompoms bounce in the air. He saw the long, golden ribbons of her hair wave across the blue summer sky. He memorized her gleaming white smile as she cried her cheerleader chants and pranced with the other girls around the freshly mowed football field. Once he'd been hungry, now he looked at her and was full. Once he'd been barren, now he studied her and felt his insides burst.

He knew everything about her. He knew her parents were well respected in Williamstown, a unique position for nonacademics in this liberal arts college enclave. He knew her family came from good German stock, four generations of fair-skinned blonds running the local store, Matthews', and living out their years without ever traveling more than four blocks from their place of birth. They had a tendency to die peacefully in their sleep, except for Theresa's great-grandfather, who'd died of smoke inhalation at the age of seventy-five as he'd helped free horses from his neighbor's burning barn.

He knew Theresa rushed home from cheerleading practice every afternoon to help her parents at their store. She tidied small shelves packed with imported olive oils, spinach nutmeg pasta, and local-made maple candies molded to look like oak leaves. During late September and early October, when Williamstown was overrun by people oohing and aahing over the golden hills and scarlet underbrush, Theresa was allowed to slice Vermont cheese and fresh creamery fudge for the tourists. Then the season would pass and she would be relegated to housekeeping once more, dusting the blue-checkered shelves, sweeping the one-hundred-year-old hardwood floor, and wiping down unfinished pine tables. These were the same duties she'd had since she was twelve and he'd listened to her father tell her half a dozen times in a single afternoon that she would never be smart enough to do anything more.

Theresa never argued. She simply tightened her red-checkered apron, ducked her blond head, and kept sweeping.

She was a popular girl in her high school class of nearly one hundred, friendly but not outgoing, attractive but demure. While other seventeen-year-old girls at Mt. Greylock High School were succumbing to the star fullback's urgent groping or the forbidden lure of cheap beer, Theresa came home every Friday and Saturday night by ten.

She was very, very punctual, Theresa's mother told him. Did her homework the way she was supposed to, went to church, attended to her chores. No hanging out with dopers or druggies, not their Theresa. She never stepped out of line.

Mrs. Matthews might have been as beautiful as her daughter once, but those years had come and gone quickly. Now she was a high-strung woman with faded blue eyes, dirty-blond hair, and a doughy body. She wore her hair pulled back tight enough to stretch the corners of her eyes and crossed herself at least once every two minutes while clicking together her rosary beads. He knew her kind. Prayed to the Lord to deliver her from all sorts of evil. Was glad at her age she was no longer required to have sex. And on Friday night, when Mr. Matthews drank a whole bottle of Wild Turkey and smacked her and Theresa around, she figured they both deserved it because Eve had given Adam the apple and women had been serving time ever since.

At fifty years of age, Mr. Matthews was pretty much

what he'd expected as well. Steel-gray hair, buzz cut. Stern face. Trim waist. Huge arms that bulged as he hefted hundred-pound bags of flour and seventy-pound tanks of pop syrup. He sauntered through the tiny store like an emperor in his domain. While his family worked busily, he liked to lean across the counter and shoot the breeze with the customers, talking about the falling price of milk or the hazards of running a small business. He kept a loaded gun beneath his bed and a rifle in the back of his truck. Once a year he shot one deer legally and – according to local rumors – bagged a second illegally just to prove that he could.

No one told him how to live his life, mind his store, or run his family. He was a true bull-headed, narrow-eyed, dumber-than-a-post son of a bitch.

Jim had spent just two afternoons in the store inspecting father, mother, and daughter, and he'd learned all he needed to know. The parents would never cut it in high society, but they had no genetic defects or facial tics. And their daughter, their beautiful, quiet, obedient daughter, was absolutely perfect.

Jim opened the door of his car and stepped out. He was ready.

Above him the spring sky was pure blue. Before him the Berkshire hills framed Mt. Greylock High School with pure green. Below him the unbroken valley spread out like a verdant buffet, endless fields spotted by faint dots of red barns and black-and-white Holsteins. He inhaled the scents of spicy pine, fresh mowed grass, and distant dairy farms. He listened to cheerleader songs. 'Go fight win, go fight win.' He watched Theresa's long, limber legs kick at the sky.

'We're from Greylock, no one can be prouder. If you can't hear us, we'll shout a little louder.'

He smiled and stepped into the full brilliance of the spring sunshine. He caught Theresa's eye as her lithe body dropped into the splits, her pompoms victoriously thrust into the air. She smiled back at him, the gesture reflexive.

3

He took off his sunglasses. Her eyes widened. He unfurled his charming grin until she blushed becomingly and finally had to look away. The other cheerleaders were now glancing from her to him with open envy. A few pouted prettily and one overdeveloped redhead pushed out her perky breasts in a belated attempt to redirect his attention.

He never took his eyes off Theresa. She was the one.

He turned slightly and the sunlight glinted off the police shield pinned to his young, well-toned chest. One hundred feet from him, behind the chain-link fence, Theresa's gaze fell to his badge. He saw her instant nervousness, her innate uncertainty. Then her beautiful brown eyes swept up his face, searching his eyes.

He knew the moment he had her. He registered the precise instant the wariness left her gaze and was replaced by vulnerable, tremulous hope.

And the power that filled him was unimaginable.

In his mind he heard his father's voice, low and soothing as it had been in the beginning, before everything had gone to hell. His father was reciting a parable: There was once a tortoise and a scorpion faced by an incoming flood. Fearful, but wanting to do the right thing, the tortoise had told the scorpion he would carry the deadly creature across the raging waters to the opposite shore if the scorpion would agree not to sting him. The scorpion gave the tortoise his word and climbed onto the tortoise's back. They set out, the tortoise's short, strong legs churning powerfully, fighting to bring them to shore. The waves crashed over them, sending them reeling back. The tortoise swam and swam, struggling to bring them forward even as the water swept them back. The waves grew fiercer. The tortoise became tired. Soon, even the light weight of the scorpion began to seem like a heavy chain, threatening to drag him under. The tortoise, however, refused to ask the scorpion to jump off. He swam harder, and finally the shoreline appeared in view. It looked as if they would make it.

4

And then the scorpion stung him. Just dug in and jabbed the poison deep into his flesh. The tortoise looked back in shocked bewilderment, the poison burning his blood, his legs turning instantly to lead. He could no longer move. They both began to drown. At the last minute, with the salty brine filling his mouth and nostrils, the poor tortoise cried, 'Why did you do such a thing? You have killed us both!'

The scorpion replied simply, 'Because it is my nature.'

Jim liked that story. He understood. It was his nature too. He could not think of a time when he hadn't known that he was better than everyone, smarter than everyone, faster than everyone, colder than everyone.

What he wanted, he got.

Now he smiled at beautiful seventeen-year-old Theresa Matthews. He let her see the Berkshire County badge he'd worked so hard to earn. And his hand lovingly stroked the billy club hanging at his waist.

Look at me, Theresa. Look at your future husband.

In the beginning it had been that simple.

In the beginning . . .

I

Five years later

J. T. Dillon was drunk.

Outside, the white-hot desert sun was straight up in the sky, bleaching bones and parching mountains. Saguaro cacti seemed to surf waves of heat while sagebrush died of sunstroke at their feet. And all over Nogales, people hid in darkened rooms, running ice cubes down their naked chests and cursing God for having saved August's apocalypse for September.

But he didn't notice.

In the middle of the cool green oasis of his ranch-style home, J. T. Dillon lay sprawled on his back, his right hand cradling the silver-framed picture of a smiling woman and gorgeous little boy. His left hand held an empty tequila bottle.

Above him a fan stirred the air-conditioned breeze through the living room. Below him a Navajo print rug absorbed his sweat. The room was well maintained and tastefully decorated with wicker furniture and sturdy yucca soap trees.

He stopped noticing such details after his first day of straight tequila. As any marine knew, true binge drinking was art, and J.T. considered himself to be Tequila Willie's first Michelangelo. Shot number one seared away throat lining. Shot number two burned away the taste of the first. Half a bottle later, no man worth his salt even winced at the sensation of cheap, raw tequila ripping down his esophagus, into his stomach, and sooner or later, out his bowels.

By the end of day one J.T. had been beyond conscious thought. The ceiling fan had become a prehistoric bird, his wicker sofa a tiger lying in wait. The toughest, meanest marine in the world had developed a bad case of the giggles. When he closed his eyes, the world had spun sickeningly, so he'd spent his first night with his eyelids propped open by his fingers, staring at the ceiling hour after hour after hour.

Now, on his fourth day of straight tequila, he'd gone beyond thought and surrendered most of his body. His face had gone first. He'd been sitting by his pool, swigging some great Cuervo Gold, and abruptly he'd realized he could no longer feel his nose. He tried to find it with his fingers – no dice. His nose was gone. An hour later his cheeks disappeared as well. No rasp of whiskers, no sting of sweat. He had no cheeks. Finally, not that long ago, he'd lost his lips. He'd tried to open them and they hadn't been there anymore. No lips.

It made it damn hard to drink, and he had twenty-four hours of serious boozing left.

He rolled slowly onto his side, discovering he still had arms and a remnant of a pickled brain. He squeezed his eyes shut and hazy images clustered behind his eyelids. He'd been a champion swimmer and percussion rifle shooter once. He remembered the welcoming smell of chlorine and the heavy weight of his black walnut rifle. He'd been a marine with 'raw talent, lots of potential' before he'd been asked to leave.

After the marines had come the stint as a mercenary, doing work he never told anyone about because then he'd have to kill them. The next image was more hesitant, still raw around the edges, as if it understood that even after four days of straight tequila, it had the power to bruise. He was back in the States. Rachel stood beside him. He was a husband. His gaze dropped to the little boy squeezing his hand. He was a father.

Now he was a drunk.

His manservant Freddie arrived, taking the silver-

7

framed portrait from J.T.'s hands and replacing it in the safe where it would remain until next September.

'How are you doing, sir?'

'Uh.'

His iguana crawled into the room, its four-foot tail slithering across the red-tiled floor. The tequila screamed, 'Red alert! Godzilla attacks!' The sane part of him whispered through parched, rubbery lips, 'Glug, go away. I mean it.'

Glug pointedly ignored him, settling his plump body in a sunbeam that had sneaked through the venetian blinds and making himself comfortable. J.T. liked Glug.

'Water, sir?' Freddie inquired patiently.

'What day is it?'

'The thirteenth, sir.'

'Then gimme another margarita.'

In the distance a phone rang. The sound made J.T. groan, and when the noise had the audacity to repeat itself, he crawled painfully toward his patio to escape.

The sun promptly nailed him like a ball peen hammer. He swayed onto his feet, squinted his eyes from long practice, and oozed straight tequila from his pores.

Dry heat, they'd told him when he first moved to Arizona. Sure it's hot, but it's dry heat. Bullshit. One hundred and twenty was one hundred and twenty. No sane man lived in these kinds of temperatures.

He'd spent enough time in jungles, pretending he didn't notice the water steaming off his skin or his own pungent odor. He'd learned to block out some of it. He'd simply inhaled the rest. The jungle lived inside him now. Sometimes, if he remembered Virginia plantations and the way his father had sat at the head of the table, clad in his full Green Beret uniform, his trousers bloused into glossy black Corcoran jump boots, his shirt pressed into razor-sharp creases and ribbons pinned ostentatiously to his chest, the jungle took up its beat in his veins.

Then J.T. would laugh. It was the one valuable lesson

he'd learned from his father. Women cry. Men laugh. Whiners moan. Men laugh. Wimps complain. Men laugh.

When Marion had called to tell him the colonel was dying of prostate cancer, J.T. had laughed so damn hard, he'd dropped the phone.

Freddie emerged on the porch, austere in his neatly pressed linen suit. 'Telephone, sir.'

'Is it still the thirteenth?'

'Yes, sir.'

'Tell 'em to go away.'

Freddie didn't move. 'It's Vincent, sir. He's called four times already. He claims it's important.'

J.T. plopped down on the deck and dangled his fingertips into the pool. He'd dreamed of owning a pool like this most of his life. He half-hated it.

'Sir?'

'Vincent always thinks it's important.'

'He refuses to hang up, sir.' Freddie placed the phone on the patio. His indignant sniff indicated what he thought of Vincent. J.T. rolled over on his back. Neither Freddie nor the phone appeared to be willing to go away.

Grudgingly he lifted the receiver. 'I'm retired, Vincent.'

'No kidding, old man.' Vincent's booming voice made J.T. clutch his forehead. 'I got a live one for you, Dillon. Right up your alley.'

'It's the thirteenth.'

'All over half the globe.'

'I don't take calls until the fourteenth, and I don't take your calls any day. I'm retired.'

'Dillon, wait till you hear about the money –'

'I don't need money.'

'Everyone needs money.'

'I don't need money. I don't need business. I'm out. Good-bye.'

'Hey, hey, hey! Hold on! Come on, J.T. Hear me out,

9

for old time's sake. Listen, I met this woman. She's really terrific –'

'Good fuck?'

'That's not what I meant –'

'Blond probably. You always were a sucker for blondes.'

'J.T., buddy, don't be such an ass. I wouldn't have called you about just anyone – I know you're retired. But this woman needs help. I mean, she *needs* help.'

'Yeah? Grab a phone book, look up St. Jude, dial the number. If anyone answers, let me know. I might try dialing it myself someday. Bye.'

'J.T. –'

'I don't care.' J.T. hung up the phone. Freddie was still standing there. A bead of sweat traced his upper lip. J.T. shook his head.

'What were you so worried about?' he chided his manservant. 'That I'd say yes? That I'd give up all this for a thirty-second adrenaline rush? Freddie, I thought we knew each other better than that.'

'I'll bring you another margarita, sir.'

'Yeah, Freddie. We understand each other just fine.'

J.T. let his head fall back against the heat-proofed patio. The sun pierced his eyelids until he could see the red veins zigzagging his flesh.

Freddie reappeared with a salt-rimmed glass and set it by J.T.'s head.

'Freddie?' J.T. said.

'Yes, sir?'

'Let another call come through, and I will fire you.'

'Yes, sir.'

'Even if it's the colonel, Freddie. Do you understand?'

'Of course, sir.'

'Good.'

Freddie pivoted sharply and left; J.T. didn't bother to watch.

He tipped into the pool fully clothed. He sank all the way down. He didn't fight it, he'd never had to fight water. From the beginning, Marion had been able to do anything on a horse and J.T. had been able to do anything underwater.

His feet touched bottom. He opened his eyes and surveyed his kingdom, the sides of the pool formed by jutting red stone, the bottom that looked like strewn sapphires.

The tickling started in the base of his throat, the instinctive need to breathe. He didn't fight that either. He accepted it. The need, the panic, the fear. Underwater, he could accept anything. Underwater, the world finally made sense to him.

He ticked off the seconds in his mind, and the tickling in his throat grew to full-fledged choking. *Don't fight it, don't fight. Ease into the burn.* He passed the two-minute mark. Once he'd been capable of four, but that wouldn't happen today.

Two minutes forty-five seconds. That was it. He rocketed to the top. He broke water with a furious gasp, swallowing four gulps of air at once. His jeans and T-shirt were plastered to his skin, the tom-toms pounded against his head.

The memories were still in his mind. Rachel and Teddy. Laughing. Smiling. Screaming. Dying.

Every year he had his bender. Five days of remembering what he couldn't stand to forget.

Five days of blackness rolling over him like a fog and choking out the light.

After a minute he began to swim. Then he swam some more. Above him the air was dry, and the crickets began to sing as the sky turned bloodred.

'Are you alive?'

'Whuh?' J.T. groggily lifted his head. He'd passed out facedown on the patio. Something clammy was sticking to his skin. Wet clothes.

'Mr Dillon? Mr J. T. Dillon?'

He squinted his eyes, his pupils refusing to cooperate. Somehow everything seemed red, red and shadowed and ugly. He tried focusing harder. A human being appeared before him. She had black hair, which reminded him of an Elvis wig. He let his forehead sink back down.

'Are you all right?'

'That's always been subject to some debate.' He didn't bother to look up again. 'Lady, I don't buy Avon products or Girl Scout cookies. On the other hand, if you have any Cuervo Gold, I'll take two cases.'

'I am not the Avon lady.'

'Tough break.' He had to be dying. Not since his first day at West Point had he felt this ill.

'Mr Dillon –'

'Go away.'

'I can't.'

'Stand up, pivot one hundred and eighty degrees, and don't let the gate hit your ass on the way out.'

'Mr Dillon . . . please, just hear me out.'

He finally pinned her with a bleary gaze. She sat on the edge of a deck chair, perched like a scrawny dove and framed by the mesquite tree. Young. Really bad haircut. Even worse dye job. She tried to appear nonchalant, but her white knees were shaking. He groaned.

'Lady, you're out of your league.'

'I . . . The . . . I . . .' She stood up stiffly and squared her shoulders. Her face was resolute, but the rest of her ruined the impression. Her too-white suit was wrinkled and ill fitting. She'd lost a lot of weight recently, and the shadows beneath her eyes were too dark to speak of sweet dreams.

'Mr Dillon –'

'Freddie!' he called out at the top his lungs. 'Freddie!'

The woman's lips snapped shut.

'He went out,' she said after a moment. She began to methodically shred her right thumbnail.

'Went out?' He moaned again, then shook his wet hair. Water sprayed out, a few drops hitting her silk suit, but she didn't flinch. He sluiced a hand through his hair, wiping long strands back out of his face, and looked at his unwanted guest one more time.

She kept a careful distance. Close enough not to show fear, but far enough to be prudent. Her stance was solidly balanced and prepared for action, legs wide apart with one foot back, chest out, arms free. It gave him a sense of déjà vu, as if he should know something about her. But the intuition came and went too fast, and he didn't feel like pursuing it.

'Your friend left,' she said. 'I watched him climb into a sedan and drive away.'

'Huh.' He sat up reluctantly. The world spun, then righted. Considering that his blood had to be ninety percent tequila by now, his vision was much too clear. How long had he been out? How much alcohol had he sweated from his pores? He was sobering up too fast.

He ripped off his T-shirt and dropped it on the deck. Then his fingers went to work on his jeans.

'I want to hire you.' The woman's voice had gained a slight tremor.

He stripped the clinging denim from his legs and tossed the jeans onto the deck. 'Better.'

'I . . . I'm not sure this is appropriate,' she said.

J.T. turned on her with a scowl, hands on his hips. Buck naked, he looked her straight in the eye and wondered why the hell she hadn't smartened up enough to disappear by now. 'Lady, does this villa look like a convent to you? This is a private residence and I'm the beast in charge. Now, get the hell out of my sight or do something useful with your mouth.'

He gave her a sardonic smile, then walked away. Freddie had left him a margarita on the poolside table. It was melted, but he didn't mind. He downed half in a single gulp.

'Vincent sent me,' the woman whispered behind him.

'That son of a bitch,' J.T. drawled without any real emotion. 'I'll just have to take him off my Christmas card list.' He downed the second half of the margarita.

'I'm counting to five. Be gone before I'm done, or heaven help you.'

'Won't you please just hear me out?'

'One.'

'I'll pay you.'

'Two.'

'Vincent did not tell me you were a pigheaded drunk!'

'Three.'

'I need a professional!'

He turned, his arms crossed over his bare chest, his expression bland. 'Four.'

Her face grew red. Frustration animated her body, bringing up her chin, sparking her eyes. For a moment she was actually pretty. 'I'm not leaving!' she yelled. 'Goddammit, I have no place else to go. If you'd just stop feeling sorry for yourself long enough to listen –'

'Five.'

'I won't leave. I can't.'

'Suit yourself.' J.T. shrugged. He placed the empty margarita glass on the table. Then, naked as the day he was born, all one hundred and eighty pounds of muscle and sinew, he advanced.

2

Sweat beaded her upper lip. Her eyes took on a dangerous sheen. Her gaze shifted from side to side. She jammed a hand inside her purse.

J.T. pounced, hurtling his full weight upon her. They went down with a thunder, the contents of her purse spilling, a silvery gun skittering across the patio. She bucked like a bronco and attempted to scratch out his eyes with her ragged nails.

He slapped her wrist down hard. He lay on top of her, trying to keep her still while protecting the more sensitive parts of his anatomy from her lashing feet. She grabbed a fistful of his hair and yanked.

'Shit!' He jerked his head free, snapped his fingers around her wrist, and slammed it down.

She winced, but when she looked at him, her eyes still contained fire. He was bigger than her, stronger than her, and a helluva lot tougher than her. She wasn't going anywhere, and they both knew it.

She made one last futile attempt to jerk free.

'Come on,' he goaded unkindly. 'Try it again. Do you think I'll suddenly change my mind and let you go? Look at me, sweetheart. Vincent didn't do you any favors by giving you my name. I look like the devil and I am the devil. Genetics decided to play truth in advertising.'

'I have money,' she gasped.

'Who cares.'

'One hundred thousand dollars.'

'Ah, honey. That's much too cheap for me.'

'Funny, you don't look like the expensive type.'

He arched a brow at her unexpected barb. She wasn't struggling anymore, so she wasn't totally naive. He took the time to give his uninvited guest a more thorough inspection. This close, he could see that she was truly ragged around the edges. The back of her neck was whiter than the front, as if it had been recently protected by long hair, then ruthlessly exposed by desperate scissors. The roots of her dull black hair appeared blond. Her fingernails seemed to have spent quality time with a cheese grater. She had the peaked look of the anemic. For chrissake, she probably had a large target tattooed on her back.

'Little girl, don't you have enough to worry about without picking fights with me?'

'Probably,' she said gamely, 'but I have to start somewhere.'

She lashed out with her foot. He shifted and stopped the blow in time. Just as he began to grin smugly, she sank her teeth into his forearm.

He paled. His neck corded and pain shot through him, sharp and deep, as her tiny white teeth found a nerve.

Rage, primal and ugly, rose up inside him. The need to lash back. The need to return the pain inflicted upon him. He felt the jungle drums in his veins and suddenly he was hearing his father's boots rapping against the hardwood floors. His grip on her left wrist tightened. She whimpered.

'Fuck!' He yanked his arm from her mouth. Blood dewed the dark hairs and made him even angrier. With a heave he was on his feet, fists clenched, eyes black, anger barely in check. *Control, control.* He hated men who took it out on women. *Control, control.*

The silver Walther .22 semiautomatic that had been in her purse now lay just six inches from his feet. He kicked it into the pool. It wasn't enough. Once he got good and pissed off, nothing was ever enough.

'What the hell were you thinking?' he roared. She was still lying on the patio, her skirt hiked up around her thighs and revealing slender legs badly in need of muscle tone. She held her wrist against her chest. It obviously hurt, but she didn't make a sound.

He swore again and contemplated leaping into the pool. He needed a drink.

'You don't draw down on a marine,' he muttered fiercely. 'What kind of idiot draws down on a trained professional?'

'You were going to attack me,' she whispered at last. She clutched her wrist closer, the harsh red imprint of his hand staining her pale skin. It shamed him.

'I was going to carry you out of here!'

She didn't say anything.

He thrust a finger at her. 'This is my home! You shouldn't go barging into homes uninvited, unwanted and . . . and . . .'

'Untrained?' she supplied.

'Exactly!'

She didn't argue. She merely worked on getting to her feet. She swayed slightly when she stood. She didn't seem to be aware of it, smoothing down her skirt and clutching her jacket shut as if that would somehow protect her.

'I know you don't want me here. Vincent's been trying to call you, and you were never home. And I . . . I couldn't afford to wait, so I got your address and I just . . . well, I just came here.

'Train me,' she said abruptly. 'Just train me, that's all I want. One month of your time. I'll give you one hundred thousand dollars and you teach me everything you know.'

'What the hell?'

'One month, that's all I'm asking. You never have to leave the villa, you don't have to do anything other than lounge around and tell me what to do. I'm stronger than I look. I learn fast. I don't whine.'

'*Who* are you?'

She hesitated. 'Te – Umm . . . Angela.'

'Te-um-Angela? Uh-huh. Well, just for the sake of

argument, why does a happy homemaker like you need training, Te-um-Angela?'

'I . . . I'm being stalked.'

'Of course. Who?'

'Who's what?'

'Who is stalking you?'

She fell silent. He shook his head. 'You don't need a mercenary, you need a shrink.'

'A man,' she whispered.

'No kidding.'

'My . . .' She seemed to debate how much to admit. 'My husband. Ex-husband. You know how it goes.'

She spoke too quickly. She glanced at him to see if he believed her or not.

He shook his head again, this time in disgust. 'You came all the way here just because of a domestic disturbance? Lady, you track a man like me down and the least you could do was have half the Medellin cartel after your hide. Jesus Christ. Go get a restraining order and leave me alone.'

She smiled wanly. 'Do you really think a piece of paper scares away a monster?'

'It beats hiring a professional. What did you do, run into Vince at a Tupperware party? You're looking at stay-fresh seals, he's hawking his connections with retired reprobates —'

'We were introduced. By a mutual friend who understands that I need real help.'

'Real help?' he snorted. 'You've seen too many Sunday night TV movies. Go to the Nogales police. I'll draw you a map.'

'The police are the ones who lost him,' she said quietly. 'Now, I'm turning to you.'

He shook his head. He tried his best scowl. She remained standing there, somehow dignified in her ugly white suit, somehow regal with her bruised wrist held against her stomach. And for once in his life, J.T. couldn't think of what to say.

The night grew hushed, just the sound of the water

18

lapping against the edge of his pool and the lonely cry of the crickets. The mesquite tree fluttered with a teasing breeze behind her, while white rocks at her feet glittered in the porch light. The night was warm and purple-black, deceptive in its softness.

'J.T.,' she whispered, 'did you save the orphans in Guatemala?'

'What?' His heart began to beat too fast.

'Vincent told me about the orphans. Did you do that? Did you really do that?'

'No, no. You can't blame that one on me.' But his denial was too sharply spoken, and they both knew it.

'One month,' she repeated. 'One month of intensive training. Self-defense, shooting, evasion, stalking –'

'Population control, intelligence gathering. Ambushing and counterambushing. Sniping and countersniping. Evac and evade, infiltration and penetration. All SpecWar goodies –'

'Yes.'

'No! You don't get it. Do you think killing machines are made overnight? Do you think Rambo rose up out of the ground? It takes *years* to learn that kind of focus. It take decades more to learn not to care, to sight a human being in a scope and pull the trigger as if the target really is nothing but the watermelon you used in practice.'

Her face paled. She looked ill.

'Yeah, you're just a lean, mean killing machine. Get outta here and don't come back.'

'I . . . I . . . I'll give you me.'

'What?'

'I'll give you my body, for the month.'

'*Chiquita*, you were better off sticking with the money.'

She smiled, her expression apologetic, resigned, knowing. Before he could stop her, she dropped to her knees. 'I'll beg,' she said, and raised imploring hands.

'Oh, for God's sake!' He crossed the patio and

grabbed her shoulders, shaking her as if that would rattle some sense into her head.

'Please,' she said simply. 'Please.'

He opened his mouth. He tried to yell and he tried to snarl. Hell, at this point he'd settle for gnashing his teeth. But the words wouldn't come out. So many years of dirty living, and still he could be thwarted by such a simple thing as the word *please*.

'Goddammit, it's September thirteenth and I'm sober. Would someone please get me a drink!'

She took a step to comply, but then she swayed like a laundry sheet, her knees beginning to buckle.

'That's it. To bed,' he commanded, furious as hell. 'Just pick a room, any room with a bed, and lie down in it. I have a couple of hours of tequila left, and I don't want to see you again until the fourteenth unless you're bringing me a bottle and have a lime in your navel and salt on your breasts.' He pointed toward the sliding glass door. 'Out of my sight!'

She took an obedient step forward and tottered dangerously.

He had no choice. With a muttered oath he swung her up in his arms. She went rigid, her hands balling as if she would fight him, but her run-down state defeated her before he did. She sank into his arms like a balloon that had just had all the air let out. He could feel her rib cage clearly, as tiny as a bird's. He could smell her, the clear scents of exhaustion and fear and a warmer, mysterious odor. Then he pinpointed it – baby powder. She carried the scent of baby powder.

He almost dropped her.

He didn't want to know. He refused to know.

The closest bedroom was neat and tidy, thanks to Freddie. J.T. dumped her unceremoniously onto the double bed. 'Got any stuff?'

'One bag.'

'Where?'

'The living room.'

'Freddie will bring it in. Car out front?'

'Took a taxi.'

'Used a fake name, *Angela*?'

'Yes. And I paid cash.'

He grunted. 'Not bad.'

'I'm learning,' she told him honestly. 'I'm learning.'

'Well, learn how to sleep. It's as good a skill as any.'

She nodded, but her brown eyes didn't close. 'Are you an alcoholic?'

'Sometimes.'

'What are you the other times?'

'A Baptist. Go to sleep.'

She murmured, 'I know why you saved the children.'

'Yeah, right. Good night.'

'Because you missed your family.'

He jolted to a stop in the middle of the room and shuddered. *Rachel and Teddy and the golden days of white picket fences and four-door sedans.*

She was wrong, of course, his family had come after the orphans. And yet her words cut close. 'You don't know what you're talking about.'

'I have to.' She sighed and her eyes drifted shut. 'My daughter and I need you. You're the only hope we have left.'

'Shit,' J.T. said again, and made a beeline for the margarita mix.

Midnight. In downtown Nogales, some bars were just opening. It wouldn't be uncommon for J.T. to be heading out the door at this hour, dressed in jeans and a chambray shirt, pocket full of money and hands desperate for a beer. He'd stumble home at three or four, a couple of six-packs beneath his belt and a woman in his arms. The nights ran together.

This was the first time the man could recall a woman sleeping in the guest room with her own suitcase. The first time he knew a woman was in the house but not in J.T.'s bed. Instead, J.T. was facedown in the living room, the iguana keeping him company.

The house was still, quiet, almost stagnant. And yet

the man knew that everything had changed. After three years, the pattern had been broken. His instructions on this point were clear.

He crept through the darkened hall. Moonbeams bathed the living room in silvery light. In one corner a small, yellow-glowing heat lamp illuminated the iguana and J.T.'s bare feet. Neither creature stirred.

The man turned away and moved carefully down the hall to the study. He picked up the telephone, years of practice making the motion soundless. He dialed from memory, already cupping his hand over his mouth to muffle his voice.

'There's a woman,' he said the moment the other end picked up.

'A woman?'

'Vincent sent her.'

'Damn.' A long pause. 'Her name?'

'Angela, that's all. Not her real name.'

'Obviously. Vital statistics?'

'Mid-twenties, five feet two inches, one hundred pounds, brown eyes, fair complexion, originally a blonde.'

'Armed?'

'A Walther .22 semiautomatic.'

'Huh. Child's toy. ID?'

'Nothing.'

'She must have something.'

'There was nothing,' he insisted. 'I checked her suitcase – the lining, hair-spray canister, hairbrush, shoe soles, everything. Plenty of cash but no ID. She has an accent. I can't quite place it. Northern maybe. Boston.'

'A professional?'

'I don't think so. She doesn't seem to know much.'

'Given the company J.T. generally keeps, she's probably an ax murderer who hacked up her husband and children.'

'What should I do?'

A frustrated sigh. 'He's back in business?'

'She's here, isn't she?'

'Damn him. Never mind, I'll take care of it. You just hold tight.'

'All right.'

'You did the right thing by calling.'

'Thank you. How . . . how is he?'

The silence stretched out. 'He's dying. He's in a lot of pain. He wants to know why his son isn't here.'

'Does he ask for me?'

'No, but don't worry. He doesn't ask for me either. All he's ever cared about was J.T.'

'Of course.' His voice was appropriately apologetic. He'd given his loyalty to a hard man a long time ago. His loyalty had never wavered; over the years he'd simply grown accustomed to his place. 'I'll call you if anything changes.'

'You do that.'

'Good night.'

'Yeah. Good night.'

He cradled the phone carefully. It didn't matter. The overhead light snapped on.

He turned slowly. J.T. lounged against the door-jamb. His arms were crossed over his bare chest. His eyes were bloodshot, but they were also intent.

'Freddie, I believe it's time we talked.'

3

Tess Williams awoke as she'd learned to awaken – slowly, degree by degree, so that she reached consciousness without ever giving herself away. First her ears woke up, seeking out the sound of another person breathing. Next her skin prickled to life, searching for the burning length of her husband's body pressed against her back. Finally, when her ears registered no sound and her skin found her alone in her bed, her eyes opened, going automatically to the closet and checking the small wooden chair she'd jammed beneath the doorknob in the middle of the night.

The chair was still in place. She released the breath she'd been holding and sat up. The empty room was already bright with midmorning sun, the adobe walls golden and cheery. The air was hot. Her T-shirt stuck to her back, but maybe the sweat came from nightmares that never quite went away. She'd once liked mornings. They were difficult for her now, but not as difficult as night, when she would lie there and try to force her eyes to give up their vigilant search of shadows in favor of sleep.

You made it, she told herself. *You actually made it*.

For the last two years she'd been running, clutching her four-year-old daughter's hand and trying to convince Samantha that everything would be all right. She'd picked up aliases like decorative accessories and new addresses like spare parts. But she'd never really escaped. Late at night she would sit at the edge of her daughter's bed, stroking Samantha's golden hair, and stare at the closet with fatalistic eyes.

She knew what kind of monsters hid in the closet. She had seen the crime scene photos of what they could do. Three weeks ago her personal monster had broken out of a maximum security prison by beating two guards to death in under two minutes.

Tess had called Lieutenant Lance Difford. He'd called Vince. The wheels were set in motion. Tess Williams had hidden Samantha safely away, then she had traveled as far as she could travel. Then she had traveled some more.

First she'd taken the train, and the train had taken her through New England fields of waving grass and industrial sectors of twisted metal. Then she'd caught a plane, flying over everything as if that would help her forget and covering so many miles, she left behind fall and returned to summer.

Landing in Phoenix was like arriving in a moon crater: Everything was red, dusty, and bordered by distant blue mountains. She'd never seen cacti; here roads were lined with them. She'd never seen cactus; here they covered the land like an encroaching army.

The bus had only moved her farther into alien terrain. The red hills had disappeared, the sun had gained fury. Signs for cities had been replaced by signs reading:

STATE PRISON IN AREA.
DO NOT STOP FOR HITCHHIKERS.

The reds and browns had seeped away until the bus rolled through sun-baked amber and bleached-out greens. The mountains no longer followed like kindly grandfathers. In this strange, harsh land of southern Arizona, even the hills were tormented, methodically flayed alive by mining trucks and bulldozers.

It was the kind of land where you really did expect to turn and see the OK Corral. The kind of land where lizards were beautiful and coyotes cute. The kind of land where the hothouse rose died and the prickly cactus lived.

It was perfect.

Tess climbed out of bed. She moved slowly. Her right leg was stiff and achy, the jagged scar twitching with ghost pains. Her left wrist throbbed, ringed by a harsh circle of purple bruises. She could tell it wasn't anything serious – her father had taught her a lot about broken bones. As things went in her life these days, a bruised wrist was the least of her concerns.

She turned her attention to the bed.

She made it without thinking, tucking the corners tightly and smoothing the covers with military precision.

I want to be able to bounce a quarter off that bed, Theresa. Youth is no excuse for sloppiness. You must always seek to improve.

She caught herself folding back the edge of the sheet over the light blanket and dug her fingertips into her palms. In a deliberate motion she ripped off the blanket and dumped it on the floor.

'I will not make the bed this morning,' she stated to the empty room. 'I choose not to make the bed.'

She wouldn't clean anymore either, or wash dishes or scrub floors. She remembered too well the scent of ammonia as she rubbed down the windows, the door-knobs, the banisters. She'd found the pungent odor friendly, a deep-clean sort of scent.

This is my house, and not only does it look clean, but it smells clean.

Once, when she'd taken the initiative to rub down the window casings with ammonia, Jim had even complimented her. She'd beamed at him, married one year, already eight months pregnant and as eager as a lap-dog for his sparing praise.

Later, Lieutenant Difford had explained to her how ammonia was one of the few substances that rid surfaces of fingerprints.

Now she couldn't smell ammonia without feeling ill.

Her gaze was drawn back to the bed, the rumpled sheets, the covers tossed and wilted on the floor. For a

moment the impulse, the sheer *need* to make that bed –
and make it right because she had to seek to improve
herself, you should always seek to improve – nearly
overwhelmed her. Sweat beaded her upper lip. She fisted
her hands to keep them from picking up the blankets.

'Don't give in. He messed with your mind, Tess, but
that's done now. You belong to yourself and you are
tough. You won, dammit. You *won*.'

The words didn't soothe her. She crossed to the
bureau to retrieve her gun from her purse. Only at the
last minute did she remember that the .22 had fallen on
the patio.

J. T. Dillon had it now.

She froze. She had to have her gun. She ate with her
gun, slept with her gun, walked with her gun. She
couldn't be weaponless. *Defenseless, vulnerable, weak.*

Oh, God. Her breathing accelerated, her stomach
plummeted, and her head began to spin. She walked the
edge of the anxiety attack, feeling the shakes and
knowing that she either found solid footing now or
plunged into the abyss.

Breathe, Tess, breathe. But the friendly desert air kept
flirting with her lungs. She bent down and forcefully
caught a gulp by her knees, squeezing her eyes shut.

'*Can I walk you home?*'

*She was startled. 'You mean me?' She hugged her
schoolbooks more tightly against her Mt. Greylock
High sweater. She couldn't believe the police officer was
addressing her. She was not the sort of girl handsome
young men addressed.*

'*No,' he teased lightly. 'I'm talking to the grass.' He
pushed himself away from the tree, his smile unfurling
to reveal two charming dimples. All the girls in her class
talked of those dimples, dreamed of those dimples.
'You're Theresa Matthews, right?'*

*She nodded stupidly. She should move. She knew she
should move. She was already running late for the store,
and her father did not tolerate tardiness.*

27

She remained standing there, staring at this young man's handsome face. He looked so strong. A man of the law. A man of integrity? For one moment she found herself thinking, If I told you everything, would you save me? Would somebody please save me?

'Well, Theresa Matthews, I'm Officer Beckett. Jim Beckett.'

'I know.' Her gaze fell to the grass. 'Everyone knows who you are.'

'May I walk you home, Theresa Matthews? Would you allow me the privilege?'

She remained uncertain, too overwhelmed to speak. Her father would kill her. Only promiscuous young women, evil women, enticed men to walk them home. But she didn't want to send Jim Beckett away. She didn't know what to do.

He leaned over and winked at her. His blue eyes were so clear, so calm. So steady.

'Come on, Theresa. I'm a cop. If you can't trust me, who can you trust?'

'I won,' she muttered by her knees. 'Dammit, I won!'

But she wanted to cry. She'd won, but the victory remained hollow, the price too high. He'd done things to her that never should have been done. He'd taken things from her that she couldn't afford to lose. Even now he was still in her head.

Someday soon he would kill her. He'd promised to cut out her still-beating heart, and Jim always did what he said.

She forced her head up. She took a deep breath. She pressed her fists against her thighs hard enough to welt her skin. 'Fight, Tess. It's all you have left.'

She pushed away from the dresser and moved to her suitcase, politely brought to her room by Freddie. She'd made it here, step one of her plan. Next, she had to get J.T. to agree to train her. Dimly she remembered mentioning her daughter to him. That had been a mistake. Never tell them more than you have to, never tell the truth if a lie will suffice.

Maybe J.T. wouldn't remember. He hadn't seemed too sober. Vincent should've warned her about his drinking.

She didn't know much about J.T. Vince had said J.T. was the kind of man who could do anything he wanted to but who didn't seem to want to do much. He'd been raised in a wealthy, well-connected family in Virginia, attended West Point, but then left for reasons unknown and joined the marines. Then he'd left the marines and struck out solo, rapidly earning a reputation for a fearlessness bordering on insanity. As a mercenary he'd drifted toward doing the impossible and been indifferent to anything less. He hated politics, loved women. He was fanatical about fulfilling his word and noncommittal about everything else.

Five years ago he'd up and left the mercenary business without explanation. Like the prodigal son, he'd returned to Virginia and in a sudden flurry of unfathomable activity he'd married, adopted a child, and settled down in the suburbs as if all along he'd really been a shoe salesman. Later, a sixteen-year-old with a new Camaro and even newer license had killed J.T.'s wife and son in a head-on collision.

And J.T. had disappeared to Arizona.

She hadn't expected him to be drinking. She hadn't expected him to still appear so strong. She'd pictured him as being older, maybe soft and overripe around the middle, a man who'd once been in his prime but now was melting around the edges. Instead, he'd smelled of tequila. His body was toned and hard. He'd moved fast, pinning her without any effort. He had black hair, covering his head, his arms, his chest.

Jim had had no hair, not on his head, not on his body. He'd been smooth as marble. Like a swimmer, she'd thought, and only later understood the full depth of her naiveté. Jim's touch had always been cold and dry, as if he were too perfect for such things as sweat.

The first time she'd heard him urinate, she'd felt a vague sense of surprise; he gave the impression of being above such basic biological functions.

Jim had been mannequin perfect. If only she'd held that thought longer.

She'd stick with J. T. Dillon. He'd once saved orphans. He'd been married and had a child. He'd destroyed things for money.

For her purposes, he would do.

And if helping her cost J. T. Dillon too much?

She already knew the answer; she'd spent years coming to terms with it.

Once, she'd dreamed of a white knight. Someone who would never hit her. Someone who would hold her close and tell her she was finally safe.

Now she remembered the feel of her finger tightening around the trigger. The pull of the trigger, the jerk of the trigger, the roar of the gun, and the ringing in her ears.

The acrid smell of gunpowder and the hoarse sound of Jim's cry. The thud of his body falling down. The raw scent of fresh blood pooling on her carpet.

She remembered these things.

And she knew she could do anything.

4

J.T. was up at the crack of dawn. He didn't want to be. God knows, it was stupid for a retired man to be up with the sun, but he'd spent too many years in the military to shake the routine from his bones. Oh-six-hundred: Soldier gets up. Oh-six-hundred-fifteen: Soldier does light calisthenics. Oh-six-hundred-thirty: Marine swims fifty laps, then showers. Oh-seven-hundred: Retired man pops open a beer in the middle of his living room and wonders what the hell he's doing still getting up at oh-six-hundred.

Now it was after nine on the fourteenth of September. He'd survived another year, hung over, dehydrated, and sick of his own skin. No more tequila. He drank beer instead.

He was drinking his third when Rosalita arrived for the annual post-binge cleanup. Born into a family of eleven children, Rosalita had used her survival instincts to become one of the finest whores in Nogales. J.T. had met her the first week he'd moved to Nogales, picking her up in the usual manner. Over the years their relationship had somehow evolved to something neither of them dared to label. As a whore Rosalita had absolutely no morals and no shame, but as a business-woman she had rock-solid ethics and the aggressiveness of a tiger. She was one of the few people J.T. respected, and one of even fewer people he trusted. Perhaps they'd become friends.

She straddled his lap wearing a red gauzy skirt and a thin white top tied beneath her generous breasts. J.T.

31

cradled her hip with one hand. She didn't notice. Her attention was focused absolutely on his face.

She'd spread an old green hand towel over his naked chest. Now she whipped the shaving cream in the small basin on the right and lathered it generously over his face. Rosalita believed a man should be shaved the old-fashioned way – with a straight razor and plenty of devilish intent.

He had enough respect for her temper to hold perfectly still.

He sat there, watching the world take on the warm, fuzzy hue he'd come to know in the last few years, and even then, even then he knew when *she* walked into the room.

Her feet were bare and silent on the hardwood floor, but she broadcasted her arrival with her scent. He'd been six when his father had taught him to air-dry his clothes, wash with odorless soap, and rinse his mouth with peroxide so the deer wouldn't smell anything as he crept up behind. In those days he'd accepted such teachings with reverent awe. His whipcord-lean, ramrod-straight, rattlesnake-tough father was omnipotent in his eyes, the only man he knew who could bag a six-point buck with a single shot. The colonel had had his talents.

Rosalita sighted Angela hovering in the doorway. Her fingers instantly dug into his chin.

'*Hijo de puta!*' she spat out.

J.T. gave her a small shrug and lifted the Corona bottle to his lathered lips.

'Angela, Rosalita. Rosalita, Angela. Angela is a current guest at our high-flying retirement resort. As for Rosalita . . . what shall we call you? An international hostess and entertainer?' He glanced at Angela. 'Every year on September fourteenth Rosalita cleans me up. You might call it her frequent flyer program.'

Angela nodded, her gaze going from him to Rosalita to him with open discomfort. The tension in the room was unmistakable. 'Nice to meet you,' Angela said at last, her voice unfailingly polite.

Rosalita froze, then began to smile. Then began to laugh. She repeated the words back to J.T. in Spanish, then chuckled harder. *Nice to meet you* wasn't something other women generally said to whores. Only a good girl would feel compelled to say such a thing, and at this stage of her life, Rosalita knew she had nothing to fear from 'good girls.'

She picked up the razor, shoved J.T.'s head back, and exposed his throat. She pressed the straight edge against his jawline and slowly rasped it down, her dark eyes gleaming.

Angela sucked in her breath nervously.

'She can't kill me yet,' J.T. volunteered conversationally. 'I'm one of the few men who can pay her what she's worth.'

Four forceful strokes, and his neck was clean. Rosalita shoved his head to the side and turned her attention to his cheek.

Angela finally entered the room; she wore an old white tank top and frayed khaki shorts that had probably fit her once. Now, they hung on her frame. In daylight, her coarsely dyed, badly whacked hair looked even worse – as if she was wearing a bad wig. For no good reason, it annoyed him tremendously.

'Your wrist?' he barked, startling Rosalita and Angela both.

'My wrist? Oh, oh, that. It's fine. Just a bit bruised.'

'I have some ice. We'll put that on it.'

'No, it's not necessary. It's not even swollen.' She moved along the side of the room, up on the balls of her feet, her back to the wall. As he watched, still searching for something to do that would make him feel better, she took a careful inventory of all the exits. Someone had at least told her a thing or two.

Her gaze fastened on his iguana, a frown marring her brow.

'Real,' he supplied.

33

'What?'

'The iguana. That's Glug. He's alive.'

'Oh.' She looked at Glug for several seconds. The creature didn't move.

'Where's Freddie?' she asked.

'I gave him the day off.'

'*Gave* him the day off?'

'Yep.'

'So there's no one here?'

'Rosalita probably doesn't like to be called no one.'

'But she doesn't live here, does she?'

'Nope.'

'So only you'll be around today?' She was clearly nervous. Her stance went from relaxed to prepared. Legs apart, shoulders back, hips rotated for balance. Just as it had last night, it tugged at his brain.

Abruptly recognition came to him.

'Cop.'

She froze.

'Uh-huh. I noticed it yesterday – you stand like a cop. Feet wide, chest out for balance. Left leg slightly back to keep your holster out of reach.'

She looked cornered.

He frowned, angling his head more so Rosalita could attend better to his cheek. 'You're not a cop though. You can't even hold a gun.'

'I'm not a cop,' she muttered.

'So just who are you, *Angela*? And what about your daughter?'

'What daughter?' Her voice had gone falsetto.

'Oh, give it up. You can't lie worth a damn.'

She smiled tightly. 'Then you'll have to teach me how.'

'*Idiotas*,' Rosalita interjected. She grabbed the hand towel and rubbed the remains of the shaving cream from J.T.'s face with more force than necessary. '*Hombres y mujeres? Bah. Perritos y gatitas.*'

With another shake of her head she flattened her

palm on J.T.'s chest and tried to launch herself from his lap. He clamped one hand over Rosalita's wrist.

'Wait.'

He twisted her lush form on his lap, bringing her ample hips intimately against his groin. Angela had gone still, as if expecting some new form of attack.

'Look at her,' he said, pointing at Angela. 'Look at that haircut, Rosalita. We can't have her running around like that.'

Rosalita raked Angela up and down with a scathing eye. She was clearly unimpressed.

'I can't take it any more, Rosalita. With that do, she might as well pin a "fugitive" sign on her coat. Fix it for me, will you? We'll consider it my good deed for the decade.'

'You're too kind,' Angela murmured.

J.T. continued focusing on Rosalita. 'I'll pay, of course.'

Payment was the magic word. Rosalita started out asking for twenty but settled for ten. J.T. took the money from a highly skeptical Angela, pointing out that Rosalita certainly couldn't do any worse than Angela had. Moments later Rosalita had Angela positioned in J.T.'s chair, the green towel wrapped around her neck. While she washed Angela's hair and set about snipping with expert flair, J.T. propped himself up on the edge of the couch and opened a fresh beer despite Angela's disapproving frown. He could see her wrist, now on her lap. It was badly bruised.

So now you're beating up on women, J.T. Just how low do you plan on sinking?

In the disconcerting quiet of his living room he didn't have an answer. He'd never considered himself a great man, not even a good man. But he had his few principles and they gave him comfort. Don't lie and don't pretend. Don't hurt people weaker than yourself – there are enough SOBs out there who deserve it. Never, ever hurt a woman.

If Rachel could see him now, she would be ashamed.

He crossed over to the sliding glass door and watched the sunlight dance across the rippling surface of his pool.

'*Terminé!*' Rosalita announced.

Reluctantly, J.T. turned to inspect Angela's new look. He froze, too stunned for words.

Rosalita had hacked off most of Angela's hair. Now intricately layered strands darted before her ears, wisped at the back of her neck, and fringed around her eyes. The short-cropped hair should have made her look like a teenage boy, except teenage boys didn't have cheekbones that high, noses that small, or lips that full. Teenage boys didn't have saucer-shaped eyes of liquid brown, framed by thick, lush lashes.

'Jesus Christ,' he murmured. 'Jesus H. Christ.'

He started pacing. Even then he felt the tension curling up inside his belly.

'It's . . . it's a start.' Angela sounded a little stunned by the transformation herself as she gazed into the hand mirror.

Rosalita bustled away with the basin of soapy water, leaving them alone in the living room. A taut silence descended. Angela's fingers began to fidget on her lap.

'Want a piece of advice?' J.T. said all of a sudden. 'It's free.'

'Doesn't that make two good deeds in one day? I thought you'd already met your quota for the year.'

'You caught me at a weak moment. Now, do you want the advice or what?'

'Okay.'

'Dye your hair,' he said flatly. 'It's the trick of a disguise – come up with something that looks even more you than the real you. I'd recommend a dark brown or auburn, something that fits your natural coloring. Then you'll have a new look that's subtle. Right now you're too obvious.'

'Oh.'

'So there you go. Visit a pharmacy, buy some hair dye, and thirty minutes later you'll be all set.'

'Thank you.'

He grimaced. 'Advice wasn't that good.'

'J.T., about yesterday. I need to talk to you, will you –'

'Hungry?' He turned to face her. 'You need to eat more. I can make oatmeal.'

She hesitated, clearly wanting to return to the original topic. 'That makes three good deeds,' she pointed out.

'Blame it on my upbringing. I certainly do.'

'Breakfast would be nice, I guess.' She nodded toward the nearly empty beer bottle dangling from his fingertips. 'Looks like you've already had yours.'

'Yep.'

'Do you always drink so much?'

'Only to excess.'

'Vince didn't say you were an alcoholic.'

'I am *not* an alcoholic. Prissy teetotaler.' He thumped the bottle against his thigh. She had an accent. A northern accent. Well educated. What had brought a well-educated northern woman all the way to the Mexican border, exhausted, malnourished, and obviously terrified?

His gaze fell to her thighs.

Shit.

He took a step toward her. She stiffened. It didn't matter.

He walked right up to her even as she leaned way back, sinking into the chair. Her eyes were wide and fearful. He ignored her distress, reaching out and swiping a finger down the vicious scar marring her pale thigh. Broad. Shiny. Many snaking tributaries, the kind that would be made by a bone snapping and tearing through flesh.

'He do that?'

She didn't answer.

'Dammit, did he do that?'

She opened her mouth, then gave up and simply stared at him.

'Who the hell are you, Angela?'

'A woman who needs help.'

'Your husband was that bad?'

'No,' she said bluntly. 'He was worse.'

J.T. turned away. He was angry again. That was always his problem. He was too good at getting angry and not good enough at fixing anything. *Control, control. It's not your problem, it's not your business.*

But he hated the sight of the scar on her thigh. It made him think of things he'd dedicated the last few years to forgetting. And it made him want to find her ex-husband and slam his fist through his face.

He forced himself to relax and took a swallow from his beer. He didn't speak again until he trusted himself completely.

'I'll make oatmeal.'

'Thank you.'

'Honey, you haven't tasted it yet.'

Angela followed him into the kitchen. He was proud of the kitchen – Rachel had designed it. He knew a lot about pools, and in the last couple of years he'd become a good landscaper. He didn't know much about decorating though. In the marines you stuck a girlie poster above your bed and that was considered the finishing touch.

Rachel had had a natural flair, so she'd designed the house they were going to build in Montana, where the sky was endless and they would always feel free. He was going to learn about horses. She was going to study interior decorating. Maybe they would have a second kid, give Teddy a little sister to play with. And Teddy and his little sister would be raised right, without any bad memories to keep them awake on dark nights later in life.

Those dreams were gone. J.T. just had Rachel's kitchen, a large, cool room with a red-tiled floor and eggshell-blue counter. The stove was big and accented with a wreath of jalapeños. A huge collection of brass pots and pans hung from a wire rack suspended from the ceiling. He'd placed each one just where he figured Rachel would have, having listened to her excitedly describe the kitchen night after night as they'd lain together in bed and dreamed like children.

'It's a nice kitchen,' Angela said from behind him. 'Do you cook a lot?'

'I don't cook at all.' He moved to the sliding glass door, which Rosalita had left slightly cracked. The heat seeped in like a tentacled beast. He shut the door.

'You aren't going to lock it?'

'Lock what?'

'The door.'

'No.'

There was a small pause. He contemplated the pots and pans, trying to figure out which to grab. It had been a long time since he'd tried cooking anything; that was Freddie's job.

'Do you lock your front door?'

'Nope.'

'Could . . . could I do it?'

He looked at her. She stood by the wood table, her hands twisting in front of her, and her gaze fastened on the sliding glass door.

'Sweetheart, this is Nogales, the outskirts of Nogales. You don't have to worry about anything here.'

'Please.'

He was really starting to hate how well she used that word. 'You're scared,' he said flatly.

She didn't bother to deny it.

'You think he followed you here? This big bad ex-husband of yours?'

'It's possible. He's very, very good at that.'

'You said you paid cash, used fake names.'

'Yes.'

'Then you're fine.' He turned back to the stove, but he heard her move behind him, then heard the click of the sliding glass door lock sliding home. Whatever. He didn't feel like telling her about the small arsenal he kept in a safe and the fact that even dead drunk he

39

could shoot the Lincoln head out of a penny at two hundred yards. If she wanted the doors locked that badly, he wasn't going to argue.

He boiled water. He opened a canister of oatmeal and wondered how much he was supposed to dump in. He dumped in half and figured what the hell. If he could rig explosives, he ought to be able to manage oatmeal.

'Generally people measure it out,' Angela commented, returning to the kitchen.

'I like to live dangerously.'

'I want my gun back.'

'The water-logged .22? You'd be better off with a slingshot.'

'I want my gun.'

It irritated him. Too many people thought guns fixed things. They didn't. He ought to know. There wasn't anything he couldn't do with a rifle and yet everyone he'd ever loved had been destroyed. Guns didn't fix anything.

'First let's get through breakfast.' He dumped the oatmeal into two bowls. It had the same consistency as mud. He sprinkled the bowls with raisins for more iron and poured two glasses of milk. Angela looked at the oatmeal as if it were an unrecognizable life-form.

'Eat,' he said. 'Tough guys never turn away from a nutritious meal. Hell, if we were outside, I would've topped it with bugs. They're almost pure protein, you know.'

'I didn't know,' she confessed, and finally, gingerly, scooped up the first spoonful and thrust it into her mouth. Her eyes were closed. She looked like a little kid and he found himself thinking of Teddy again with a sharp, bittersweet pang.

'Yugh,' she said.

'Told you I wasn't a cook.' He took in three spoonfuls at once. 'Don't chew. It goes down easier.'

She looked horrified. She pushed the bowl away. Just as fast, he pushed it back in front of her. 'Eat,' he ordered. 'I wasn't kidding before – soldiers eat what

40

they're given. And you need your iron, Rambo, so stop dreaming about room service.'

For a moment it appeared that she would defy him. But then she picked up her spoon and eyed her oatmeal as if it were a summit to be scaled.

'I can do this.' She dug in.

'It's oatmeal, Angela, not Armageddon.'

She ate the whole bowl and cleared the dishes without saying a word. Then she began washing them with the smooth movements of someone who'd done chores all her life.

J.T. wasn't used to having someone else around who wasn't Freddie or Rosalita. He felt uncomfortable and, worse, self-conscious. Virginia etiquette crept up and tapped him on the shoulder. He should put on a shirt. He should put on shoes. He should pull out a chair for the nice young lady, offer her lemonade, comment on her beauty, and talk about the weather.

'Why move to Arizona?' Angela asked. She stacked the rinsed dishes noisily beside the sink. Her bruised wrist didn't seem to bother her.

'No helmet laws.'

'Oh.' She'd run out of things to say. He'd run out of them a long time ago himself. He began ticking off the seconds in his mind. He'd hit only six when she shut off the water and pinned him with a determined look.

'I'm not going to leave,' she announced. 'I need your help. Sooner or later you'll realize that.'

'I'm not going to realize any such thing. You're lying to me through your teeth.'

Her lips thinned. 'You don't want the truth. I know men like you. You don't want to become involved. You think you're happy living in a self-pitying vacuum.'

'Self-pity, that's what's wrong with me? First, it's drinking, now self-pity. Do you watch a lot of Oprah?'

'You think you'll be better off if you never care again.'

'Can you prove otherwise?'

'I don't need you to care, Mr Dillon. I don't need you

41

to give a . . . a rat's ass about me. I want you to train me anyway.'

'You want me to be a lap dog,' he corrected her. 'You want me to listen to your lies, do as you ask, and never question a thing. I know how it works. I've seen Oprah too.'

He kicked back his chair and crossed the alcove. He passed the barrier of the counter. He kept advancing, his eyes dark slits. He saw her mouth open, but no word of protest emerged. She took a step back, but was brought up short by the kitchen sink. She was trapped.

He flattened her against the counter. Her breath came out more rapidly, but she didn't back down. She brought her chin up defiantly and met his gaze. He leaned into her, flattening her breasts against his bare torso, pressing his body against hers so she'd know exactly what he was capable of. He lowered his head until his breath whispered across her cheek, and she sucked in her breath in an attempt to put distance between them.

'I don't believe you,' he said softly, dangerously. 'I don't believe a woman abandons her daughter and comes halfway across the country to a mercenary's house just because her ex-husband is stalking her. And I don't like being lied to and used.' He planted his hands on the countertop.

'Why shouldn't a woman hire a trained professional?' She licked her lips nervously, then caught herself and stated more fiercely, 'Husbands, boyfriends, fathers, kill women all the time.'

'Hire a bodyguard.'

'I don't want a bodyguard! I want to know how to fight. I want to know how to protect my daughter. I am so sick and tired of running scared. You' – her finger jabbed his chest – 'you probably don't know anything about being vulnerable, being frightened. But I know. And I'm sick of it. I want my life back.'

She grabbed one of the porcelain bowls and shattered it against the sink. She raised one jagged shard and wielded it like a knife. 'I might have been slow once. I might have actually thought that if I was just good enough, just obedient enough, just *sweet* enough, it would keep me safe. Well, I don't do "sweet" anymore and I don't do "obedient" anymore. So don't mess with me, Mr Dillon. You have no idea what I am capable of.'

She pressed the sharp edge against his bare chest with enough force to line his skin. The edge ran against the scar that zigzagged furiously down his sternum. That scar had been inflicted by a man known for his sharp temper, fast hands, and utter lack of remorse. J.T. explored Angela's eyes now to see if she had that in her.

He wouldn't grant her speed. He wouldn't grant her skill. But in her gaze he found something better: dispassion.

'Jesus, you are a dangerous woman.'

'I'm learning.'

A sound split the air, startling them both. High, shrill. Sirens. Wailing sirens approaching his house. He took a step back.

His first thought was Marion, but then he noticed his house guest. She'd frozen. And she appeared terrified. Why would the cops frighten a woman running from her husband? Then he knew, positively knew, that he'd been used.

'What have you done?'

'Nothing. Absolutely nothing,' she muttered.

The sirens wailed closer. Three cars, he figured. Three police cars pulling into his driveway and shattering his peace.

'Why are you so afraid? What are you hiding?'

Her eyes were no longer so certain. She tried to push away, but his grip was too strong.

'Let me go. I didn't do anything. I just don't want anyone to know I'm here. Especially not the cops.'

'That shy, *Angela*?'

'It's not safe. He has contacts –'

'*He*? Sure, Angela, this omnipotent he. The mystery man who may or may not be stalking you, who may or

43

may not have injured your leg, who may or may not even exist. I am tired of *he*, Angela. You want my help, you'd better do a helluva lot better than that.'

'I'm not lying! Jim wants me dead. No, he wants me to suffer horribly. I saw the pictures. I saw what he did . . .' Her voice trailed off. Then she went wild, beating at him furiously. She tried to jab his shoulder with the porcelain shard, but he deflected the blow, knocking the makeshift weapon from her hand.

'Let me go,' she cried.

The sirens came to a screeching halt on his driveway.

'Oh, my God,' she whispered. 'Maybe he's already found me.'

His hands gripped her shoulders, but suddenly he wasn't so sure. Her fear was too genuine, her panic too real. He could feel the tremors beginning now, snaking down her delicate frame.

'Talk to me, Angela, tell me the truth. Come on.'

'He was a cop! Don't you get it? He was a cop!'

He stepped back in shock, automatically letting her go. He was surprised but didn't know why he should be. There was no rule saying cops had to be good guys, just as there was no guarantee that well-respected army colonels didn't torture their families as a hobby.

Angela moved into the middle of the kitchen. Her arms were wrapped tightly around her thin waist. 'I need my gun back. Give me my gun.'

'I can't do that.'

'Oh, what are you so afraid of? Do you think I'm going to try to shoot my way out with a peashooter?'

'A gun won't help you.'

'It's the only thing that has.' She paced a dizzying circle. 'I'm leaving. Tell them what you want. I won't let them see me here. I thought confidentiality meant something in your line of work.'

'Wait –'

'I don't have time.' She kept moving.

They both heard the first of several car doors open and then slam shut.

Angela didn't turn around. Seconds later he heard the door of her room shut, then the telltale sound of the bolt lock sliding home. He had visions of little Angela flipping over the bed and hunkering behind it like the last man at the Alamo.

He was left alone in his kitchen, with the disorienting feeling that everything had slid out of control. What if this ex-husband had actually arrived? What was he prepared to do these days? How could he stand aside?

Then he heard the voice over the bullhorn. His shoulders relaxed. His lips twisted. No big, bad, evil Jim.

It was just his sister, summoned by Freddie, and riding to the rescue.

He squared his shoulders and prepared for the real war. Whoever had written that blood was thicker than water, had never met the Dillons.

5

Marion Margaret MacAllister had committed only two sins in her life. One, she'd been born the second child. Two, she'd been born a female.

She'd done her best to rectify these sins over time. In the men's locker-room world of the FBI, she could outshoot, outfight, and outthink her fellow agents. With her cool blond looks, she'd earned the nickname Iceman. She liked it.

Until two weeks ago, when her world had started falling apart.

She'd just turned thirty-four and had been passed over for promotion again, ostensibly because she was too young. William Walker, who did get the post, was only thirty-six – and balling the deputy director's daughter. Her father was dying of prostate cancer, a death that was taking a long time coming, and her husband of ten years had left her for a twenty-two-year-old cocktail waitress.

Then last night she'd gotten the call from Freddie. J.T. always had impeccable timing.

She motioned for the Nogales police to stay back and approached the house on her own. She wore her favorite navy blue pants suit. It was sharp and one hundred percent business. It was also too hot for Arizona. She focused on the cool feel of her gun pressed against her ribs while the dusty air stung her eyes.

'Good morning, Marion,' J.T. drawled. He lounged against the doorjamb, half naked and rumpled, as if caught mid-fuck. 'How kind of you to visit.'

'We received a report of an intruder. I came to investigate.'

'All the way from D.C.?'

'Nothing's too good for my older brother.' She smiled with brittle sweetness and had the rare satisfaction of seeing her barb strike home. 'Step out of the way, J.T. The officers here will secure your house.'

'I don't think so.'

'Jordan Terrance –'

'Freddie call you from town?' He shifted, crossing his ankles and getting more comfortable. She knew from Freddie that he drank a lot. She'd expected the alcohol to have taken a greater toll, but J.T. had always been a lucky SOB. Not even booze had thickened his waistline or sagged his middle. He was still the lean, fit man she remembered. The kid who'd won all the swimming trophies. The son whose uncanny shooting had made their father so proud. She wanted to strangle him.

'Freddie filed the report,' she replied stiffly.

'Ah, and here I thought he and I had reached an understanding.'

'What do you mean?'

J.T. made a great show of examining his fingernails. 'I know he calls you, Marion. I know he's Daddy's little spy. You're both so afraid that someday I'll get drunk enough to speak the truth. Don't worry, I've been speaking it for quite some time now, and nobody's interested.'

'I don't know what you're –'

'I sent him away. Told Freddie to take a few days off – I didn't think my visitor wanted an audience. As for myself, well . . .' He shrugged. 'Freddie makes a fine margarita. Of course now I'll have to reconsider his return. Calling the police about an intruder – that was pretty clever. I think he's a lot more clever than either of us suspect.'

'So there *is* an intruder! Step aside.'

'No.'

'Goddammit, J.T., I know there's a woman inside.

47

And what do you really know about her? Look at your track record –'

'Leave my past out of it.'

'We're going to search the house, J.T. I want this woman gone.'

'Got a search warrant?'

'Of course not. We're responding to a report of an intruder –'

'And I'm telling you as owner of this property, there is no intruder. Now, take your little blue men and find another party to crash.'

'You stubborn, drunken, son of a –'

'Marion, you never did learn how to play nice.'

'J.T., as your sister –'

'You're ashamed of me, embarrassed to have me in the family, and on really good days you wish I was dead. I know, Marion. These open exchanges of family sentiment always leave me feeling warm and fuzzy all over.'

'So help me God, J.T., if I find so much as a BB gun on your property –'

'It's Arizona. Lax gun laws. You gotta love that in a state.'

'I'm here to try to help you, J.T. –'

'No, Marion, you're not. You're still doing Daddy's bidding, and we both know it.' His voice grew suddenly soft. 'Why don't you ever stop by just to visit, Merry Berry? Why, with you, is it always war?'

Marion grew suffocated beneath the neck-high buttons of her suit, and for a moment she was beyond anger.

J.T. straightened away from the doorjamb.

'Send the cops away. Daddy never approved of outsiders nosing around in family business. Is he dead yet?'

'No.'

'Too bad. Well, it was nice talking to you. We should really get together more often.'

'I'm not leaving.'

48

'I'm sorry, Marion. You know I care about you, but I have this strong allergic reaction to federal agents. No, I'm afraid I have a strict No Cops/No FBI Agents policy for my property.'

'You are such a bastard!'

'I used to pray that was the case, but I probably have too much of the colonel in me for it to be true. What a shame.'

J.T.'s implacable grin told her he wasn't budging. He always had been a stubborn ass. But then, she could be stubborn too. And she had her orders. Straight from the colonel.

'Fine. I'll check my badge at the door.'

'And your backup band?' J.T. nodded toward the cops.

'If you can assure us that there's no intruder inside, I'll send them on their way.'

'Oh, the intruder's inside all right. I think the boys in blue should go on their way anyhow.'

He smiled at her. Then he walked inside and shut the door.

She was left standing in the broiling sun with three state troopers looking at her for guidance. She wanted to scream and she wanted to curse, but most of all she wanted to forget she'd ever met her husband.

'Go home,' she said to the troopers. 'I have the situation under control.'

Then she knocked on the door of her brother's house and prepared for round two.

Tess sat on the floor of her room, her ear pressed against the door. She'd locked it but knew from experience that the lock was too feeble to hold. She still didn't have her gun and wasn't sure what she'd do if she did. It was imperative that no one know she was there, but was she desperate enough to shoot an FBI agent to keep her identity secret?

When she found herself thinking that she could just

49

wound the woman, she realized she was desperate enough.

She'd listened to the exchange in the front yard. Now she heard the woman's voice echo down the hall from the living room.

'All right, J.T., where is she?'

'She stepped out for a moment. I got the impression she didn't much care for the police.'

'Oh? Doesn't that tell you something right there, *brother dear?*'

'Only that she's spent some time in L.A.'

'Give it up, J.T. If Lizzie Borden were alive today, she'd come to you for help.'

Tess wanted to resent that comment but couldn't; too many newspapers had referred to her as the Bride of Frankenstein. The tabloids had even carried her supposed biography under the headline

SO I MARRIED AN AX MURDERER.

The late-night talk show hosts had gotten in a few stingers as well.

She didn't like to think about Jim. She wanted definitive answers and the clarity of hindsight. She didn't have that. Even after all these years the images were murky and disjointed in her mind. The press could package her story as neatly as they wanted. She'd lived it and the truth did not allow her that luxury.

Jim Beckett had been handsome. He'd been strong. He was a highly commended police officer and a lonely man who'd been orphaned as a child. His mother had been frail, sickly, he'd told her. She'd collapsed when he was eight and his father had died in an automobile accident rushing to her side. With no surviving relatives, he'd been placed with foster parents. He'd grown close to that family, but tragedy had struck again. When he was fourteen, his foster father had been killed in a hunting accident. His foster mother had fought to keep him, only to succumb to breast cancer while he was in college. Jim Beckett was alone in the world, but then he'd seen her.

On their fourth date he sat with her on the porch swing at her father's house and took her hand. 'Theresa,' he whispered somberly. 'I know about your father, how he treats you and your mother. I understand how afraid you must be. But you're not alone anymore. I love you, baby. We're alike. We each have no one. But now we'll be together forever. No one is ever going to hurt you again.'

She believed him. She cried that night while he rocked her against his chest, and she thought, *Finally, my white knight has arrived.*

Six months later she became Jim's bride in one of the largest weddings Williamstown had ever seen. She moved from her father's house and watched Jim hang a blown-up wedding portrait above the mantel of their new home. It was the first thing anyone saw when they walked into the Beckett house: a huge glossy photo of the most beautiful blond couple in Williamstown. People nicknamed them Ken and Barbie.

On their honeymoon Jim sat her down and explained that there were a few rules she would need to follow. She was a wife now. A police officer's wife. The rules were straightforward. Always walk two steps behind him. Always ask his permission before buying anything. Wear only clothes he'd approved. Always keep the house immaculate and always cook his steak rare. Never question him or his schedule.

She nodded. She was confused, but she promised to try. She was an eighteen-year-old bride, she wanted to be perfect.

She made mistakes.

The second night after they returned from their honeymoon, Jim burned her wedding dress to punish her for buying note cards without asking. She begged him not to, so he burned her veil as well. She wasn't supposed to question him. She must remember not to question him.

51

She struggled to remember that. She struggled to adapt. In the first few weeks she lost most of her personal belongings to the fire. Her cheerleading outfit. Her baby blanket. Her yearbook. For a change of pace Jim cut up her childhood teddy bear into little pieces, then burned the pieces when she didn't have dinner on the table in time. Jim told her she must be stupid to lose so much stuff, so she tried harder.

She didn't want to fail the only person who claimed to love her. And he didn't hit her. He yelled sometimes. He was strict, he told her she was stupid, but he never, ever raised his hand.

She was so grateful for that.

She learned. She ran out of stuff for him to destroy. Then she discovered she was pregnant and life settled down. Jim couldn't wait to be a father. When she gave birth to Sam, he showed up at the hospital with the most ridiculously expensive strand of pearls. He told her she was beautiful. She'd done well.

And she thought everything would be all right.

Two months later Jim announced it was time to have a second child. She sat at the dinner table, breastfeeding Samantha and feeling so exhausted, she could barely keep her eyes open. She made a mistake. She forgot about the rules and said no, she couldn't handle two babies and maintain a spotless, perfect household. Jim grew quiet. He set down his fork. He pinned her with his overbright blue eyes. 'You can't handle it, Theresa? Do you think of hurting Samantha? Is that what you're telling me? Do you think of beating my baby? I know it's in your blood.'

She cried. She said no, she'd never do such a thing. She could tell he didn't believe her. Later that week she committed her first act of blatant rebellion: She bought a diaphragm and hid it under the bathroom sink. The week after that she pulled it out and discovered a pin resting delicately on top. Jim stood behind her, his face implacable. She couldn't take it anymore. She hadn't slept in two and a half months. She was exhausted, overwhelmed, and frightened she would fail as a mother. She began to sob. Jim finally moved. She cringed, but he just took her in his arms. He stroked her hair, touching her gently for the first time in months, and told her everything would be all right, he would help her. He lowered her to the bathroom floor. He pushed up her skirt. He took her while she lay there, too exhausted, too shocked, and too much in pain to move.

Afterward, he told her he wanted a boy this time. A boy to name Brian, after his father.

Jim's absences grew longer, and his returns crueler. Whatever she did, it wasn't good enough. She was a bad wife, a horrible mother. She was a stupid, stupid girl who should be grateful he'd agreed to marry her. A handsome, charming, well-respected man like him could certainly do better.

One day he sat her down in the living room and told her he was going out. He would be gone for a while. Maybe he'd return. Maybe not. He hadn't decided yet. No matter what, she was not to go down into the basement.'

'The basement? Why would I go into the basement?'

'Because I told you not to go there, so now you're thinking about it. And you'll think about it the minute I leave. "What is in the basement? Why shouldn't I go into the basement? What is he hiding in the basement?" I've planted the suggestion in your mind, you won't be able to rest until you go into the basement. I know you that well, Theresa. I can control you that much.'

'No. I won't go into the basement. I won't.'

But the minute he left, her eyes fell on the basement door. She put her hand on the doorknob. She twisted. She opened the door and stared down into the gloom—

Tess quickly cut off the rest of the memories. She pressed her fingers against her temples, already tasting bile.

Some days she could recall things objectively. She could distance herself, analyze the scenes as if they'd happened in somebody else's life. Some days she couldn't. Now she concentrated on breathing and the feel of the warm Arizona sun.

Down the hall, Marion and J.T. continued to war.

'He is dying, J.T. It's not some twisted ruse.' Marion's voice was brittle. 'Our father is dying.'

'Our father? I don't think so. I gave him to you when you were fourteen. We were playing poker, as I recall, and I was beating you quite badly. You threw a fit. So I said fine, what was the one thing you really wanted –'

'Fuck you, Jordan Terrance.'

'– and you said you wanted "Daddy" all to yourself. So I gave him to you lock, stock, and barrel. To this day I believe you got the bad end of that deal. Or tell me, Marion, did you forget that as well?'

'I didn't forget anything, J.T. I just choose to remember happier days.' There was a long pause, then Marion said, 'It's because of *her*, isn't it?'

A second pause. 'She had a name, Marion. She was a human being.'

'She was a lying, manipulative prostitute who caught Daddy in a weak moment. He'd just retired, he was vulnerable to . . . to female attention.'

'Mom will be happy with this analysis.'

'Mom has more bats in her belfry than a gothic church.'

'Finally we agree on something.'

'The point is, Daddy made a mistake –'

'A mistake? He got a seventeen-year-old girl pregnant. Our father, the pedophile.'

'He took care of her.'

'Is that what you call it?' J.T.'s voice dropped to a low tone that prickled the hair on the back of Tess's neck. Marion didn't recover quickly this time, but when she did, her retort was sharp.

'Oh, that's right. Daddy is the root of all evil. Hell, he was probably the one standing at the grassy knoll.'

'I wouldn't put it past him. Have you ever watched the JFK tapes closely?'

'Grow up, J.T. Daddy needs you right now, though

God knows why. Maybe you don't like him, maybe you're never going to see eye to eye with him, but for chrissake, he gave you life. He put a roof over your head. He raised you and gave you anything you ever asked for – the sports car, West Point, military appointments, *cover-up* – you got it all.'

'And it still burns, doesn't it, Marion?' J.T. said quietly. 'Though Roger was hardly a shabby consolation prize.'

'Roger left me, J.T. But thanks for asking.'

'What?' J.T. sounded genuinely surprised, perhaps even stunned. 'Marion, I'm sorry. I swear to you, I'm sorry –'

'I did not come here for your pity. You utter those words one more time and they'll need Super Glue to put your face together again. No, don't say anything more. I'm sick of this conversation – it never gets any better. I'm staying seven days, J.T. Seven days for you to see the light. Then I wash my hands of this whole mess.'

'Merry Berry –'

'Don't call me that! And tell your "guest" that if I catch either one of you doing anything remotely illegal, I'll arrest both your asses. Got it?'

'You don't have to scream for me to know how much you care.'

'Oh, go knit yourself a Hallmark card.'

Tess heard the sharp, ringing sound of heels against hardwood floors. The fast, furious footsteps grew closer and Tess held her breath. But the sound passed her by. Marion stormed to the end bedroom, where her arrival was punctuated by the sound of the door slamming shut.

Tess released her breath. Her body sagged against the door. Everything was okay. This Marion was an FBI agent, but she was also J.T.'s sister and was here for reasons that had nothing to do with Tess.

She was safe, no one knew who she was, and she was still in Arizona.

She couldn't take any more. It was still afternoon, but

her exhausted body demanded rest. She crawled into bed, pulled the covers over her head, and welcomed slumber.

6

It was cold in the basement. She could feel a draft but couldn't identify the source. The light was feeble, just a bare overhead bulb that lengthened the shadows. Beneath her feet she felt hard-packed dirt.

What was that leaning in the corner? A shovel, a saw, a hammer. Clipping shears and two rakes. Had she ever seen Jim use any of those things? There was a baseball bat as well. A long, golden baseball bat. She'd thought he kept his bats in the coat closet. Why in the basement? They hardly ever went into the basement.

She smelled fresh dirt and turned toward the scent. In the far corner she saw a mound of dirt perfectly shaped as a fresh grave.

No. No, no, no.

A hand clamped over her mouth.

She screamed. She screamed and the palm shoved the sound back down her throat. She was pinned against a body, struggling and squirming wildly. *Dear God, help me.*

Thick fingers dug into her jaw and pinned her head into place. 'I thought you wouldn't come down here, Theresa. I thought you said you wouldn't.'

She whimpered helplessly. She was trapped. Now he was going to do something awful.

She felt his arm move behind her. A black scarf slid over her eyes, shutting out the light, cutting her off from everything.

She moaned in terror.

He tied a rolled pillowcase over her mouth, the cloth

pressing against her tongue and digging into the sensitive corners of her lips like a horse's bit.

He released her and she fell to the ground.

'I told you not to come down here, but you had to, didn't you, Theresa? You had to know. You shouldn't pry if you don't want answers.'

He dragged her to her feet and pulled her across the dirt floor. The pungent odor became stronger. The smell of dirt and something else, something astringent. Lime. Fresh lime to cover the scent of decaying corpses. She gagged against the pillowcase.

'That's right. You're standing at the edge of a grave. One push and you'll tumble right in. Fall into the grave. Want to know what you'll find there?'

He pushed her forward into empty space and she screamed in her throat. He jerked her back against him and laughed softly in her ear. 'Not quite yet. Let me show you everything else.'

His fingers dug into her hand, forcing it to reach out. She begged, her words muffled, gasping sobs behind the pillowcase. He was going to make her touch something. Something she didn't want to touch.

Her hand was buried into a glass jar. Round, firm, and moist shapes slid around her fingertips. 'Eyeballs,' he whispered. 'I saved the eyeballs from all my past wives.'

He yanked her hand back and plunged it into something else. Hair. Long and smooth and sickeningly damp at the ends. 'Scalped 'em too,' he hissed.

Again he yanked her hand back and plunged her fisted fingers into something else. Squishy and tangled and oily. Caught on her fingers, twisted around her fingers.

'Guts. Lots and lots of guts.

'And here, baby, is my crowning achievement. Her heart. Her warm, pulsing heart.'

Her hand was forcefully closed around the mass. His fingers curled around her throat. Tightening, tightening,

tightening as his breathing accelerated with excitement in her ear.

'You have no idea who I am, Theresa. You have no idea.'

And just as the spots formed before her eyes, just as the abyss opened before her and she knew she could fall right in and never have to think again, his fingers let her go and the air rushed into her oxygen-starved lungs.

The blindfold was snatched from her eyes. She was staring down at blood, so much blood. She turned, too horrified to run.

She saw his face clearly. His leering, cold face.

J. T. Dillon smirking down at her with coal-black eyes.

Tess woke up harshly, the scream ripe on her lips, her heart pounding in her chest. She clutched her fist to her throat, gasping for breath. Sweat trickled down her cheeks like tears.

A pause, then she scampered out of the strange bed and turned on every light she could find. The room had hardly any lamps. She needed more light, lots and lots more to dispel the shadows lurking in the corners.

She found herself in front of the closet doors, securely blockaded by a chair. *Open the damn doors. Know that he's gone, that you won, you won.*

Suddenly with a cry of rage she kicked the chair away, grabbed the handle, and yanked the door open.

'Come on, where are you, you bastard?'

Only empty hangers stared back at her. She took a deep breath, then another, until her body stopped shaking.

You're in Arizona. You're safe. There is no blood on your hands.

It was a cow's heart. A cow's heart, linguine in olive oil, silk threads, and peeled grapes. Stuff from a grade-school haunted house.

'Look around you, Theresa,' Jim had said after he'd snapped on the basement light. 'Look at what you're so terrified of. If you're willing to believe peeled grapes are eyeballs, no wonder you look at me and see a monster.'

She collapsed on the ground.

He squatted down until he was eye level. 'I told you not to come into the basement, but you did. You're so determined to think I'm doing something wrong. Why do you think so little of your husband, Theresa? Why are you so determined to be afraid of me?'

She wasn't able to summon an answer.

'You know what I think? I think you have really low self-esteem, Theresa. I think your father and his abusive behavior taught you to think of yourself as nothing. And now you have this handsome, charming, decorated police officer who loves you and you just can't believe that, can you? Rather than accept that a good man loves you, you wonder what's wrong with me. You obsess that there must be something wrong with me. I suggest you stop focusing on my problems, Theresa, and spend a little bit more time contemplating yours.'

He left the basement.

She remained on the floor actually wondering why she questioned her perfect husband.

Jim had been that good.

Then other memories, other images overwhelmed her. Jim's hands around her throat, squeezing, releasing, caressing, soothing, choking. The baseball bat arching up, looking like a fairy's wand in the moonlight. Whistling down. Her thigh cracking . . .

She ran for the door, undid the lock, and made it to the bathroom just in time to be violently ill.

'Was it something I said?' J.T. stood in the doorway.

Her eyes squeezed shut. She remained hunched over the sink, her arms trembling, her legs shaky. She tasted bile. She tasted despair, by far a more savage flavor.

'Please go away,' she whispered.

'Sorry, but there isn't a Virginia man alive who can walk away from a puking woman. Consider it our southern charm.'

She heard the patter of his bare feet against the

60

bathroom floor tiles and caught the faint odor of chlorine as he approached. His torso pressed against her. She stiffened and his chest rumbled with a growl of disapproval.

He said, 'Just turning on the water. Tastes like the rusty pipe it uses to visit us all the way from Colorado, but last I checked, it was better than vomit.'

He stepped away. With a sigh she scooped the water over her face and neck, letting it pour through her mouth. It did taste metallic and rusty.

'Better?' he said after a moment.

She turned off the faucet and faced him. He wore nothing but a pair of swimming trunks, which rode too low on his hips, revealing a faint white line of untouched skin. Water trickled across his shoulders, down into the fine black hair on his flat belly.

He raised a half-filled beer bottle and looking straight into her eyes, polished it off.

'Take it.'

'What?'

'The towel, *chiquita*. You look like hell.'

Belatedly she saw the hand towel he was holding. She took it gingerly from him. He hadn't done anything, but she was scared anyway. In her experience, men – and particularly muscled men – were a clear threat to women. She couldn't picture her father without seeing his fleshy face turn beet red as he raised his thick fist. She couldn't picture her ex-husband without seeing his cold blue eyes dispassionately returning her stare as he fed her wedding gown to the flames.

But J.T. came highly recommended. Surely mercenaries didn't kill their clients. That had to be bad for business. What about a policeman murdering taxpayers? That was bad for business too.

But she'd been in J.T.'s house for forty-eight hours without incident. He fed her breakfast. He shielded her from the police. Surely if he had violent tendencies, she would've seen some indication.

Of course, it had taken her two years to recognize the violence in Jim.

Her hands came up and rubbed her forehead. She wanted to own herself, she wanted to trust herself. Two and a half years after putting Jim in prison, she still wasn't sure that had happened. She was stuck somewhere between the old Theresa Beckett and the new Tess Williams.

'Rough night for the *Better Homes & Garden* lady?'

'It's that knit one purl two,' she murmured. 'I keep having nightmares of dropping the stitch.'

'Yeah? And here I keep dreaming of blowing up churches. Come outside, the cool air does a body good.'

He turned and she realized that he expected her to follow. She looked down at her legs uncovered by her purple Williams College T-shirt. Generally she didn't follow half-naked men around while wearing only a T-shirt. Her mother had had strong feelings about women showing too much flesh. Only bad women did that, and they went straight to hell, where little devils did horrible things to them every night to punish them for being so wanton.

The image of herself as a wanton was so absurd, she had to smile. She'd never been a femme fatale, never sparked hidden flames. She'd been the dutiful, confused wife. Now she was the scared, emaciated mother. All signs indicated that J.T. found her about as attractive as an animated skeleton. She was fine with that. She just wanted him for his semiautomatics.

She followed him out to the deck, shivering as the night air hit her. J.T. didn't seem to notice. He plopped down on one of the chairs and picked up a gold cigarette case. A six-pack sat on the glass table.

Her arms wrapped around her middle as she stared up at a rich blue sky dotted with stars. The nights in Williamstown would be cool and clear by now, but the air would be scented with the rich, musty odor of drying leaves and aging pine, the refreshing tang of wind sweeping down from the Berkshires. She wondered what her daughter was doing just then. Probably fast asleep, tucked in bed with her pink flannel nightgown and her favorite talking doll. If she closed her eyes, she could almost capture the scent of No More Tears shampoo and baby powder.

Baby, I love you.

'You eavesdropped, didn't you?' J.T. asked.

'Yes.'

J.T. flipped open the slim cigarette case, banged out a cigarette, and lit it. He stared at her as he dragged deeply. 'Filthy habit. Would you like one?'

He held out the case, then snatched it back. 'Wait, I forgot. You can barely walk as it is – no cigarettes for you.'

He exhaled, leaning back and crossing his ankles.

'I didn't know you smoked.'

'I'd quit.'

'You went out in the middle of the night to buy cigarettes so you could start again?'

'Nope. I stole Marion's cigarettes. I was the one who taught her how to smoke, you know.' His lips twisted. 'At least that's what I recall. You'll have to ask her what she remembers.'

'There seems to be little love lost between you and your sister.'

'I've never been a fan of revisionist history.'

Keeping her voice neutral, she asked, 'She's really an FBI agent?'

'Yes.' Briefly his chest puffed out. 'A damn good one.'

'I heard her say she's staying for a week.'

'She is. So if you are a crook, don't tell her. She'll drag you in.'

'And you would let her?'

'If you're a crook.'

'Very good,' she acknowledged. 'You've covered all the bases. If I stay, I must be legal. If I'm gone in the morning, well, I've saved you a bunch of trouble.'

'Don't let my good looks fool you, sweetheart – I'm no dumb bunny.'

She nodded, her gaze returning to the night sky. She was cold. She wanted to go inside and sleep. She was terrified of the nightmares that would find her again.

'One month of training,' J.T. said all of a sudden. 'I'll do it.'

'I know.'

'Don't be so smug. We start first thing in the morning, oh-six-hundred. Physical fitness, self-defense, small firearms, the works. I'll burn your butt into the ground and turn you into a whole new woman.'

'All right.'

'Do you want to know why I changed my mind?'

'It doesn't matter.'

'But it does matter, Angela. It matters to me.' He waved his hand around the villa, the garden, the pool. 'I don't own this. Not really. Every square inch of this place, every pebble, every cactus, was paid for by my father. You could say I'm still on allowance. I can keep this, I can live this way forever in return for only two things. The first doesn't concern you. The second is that I never return to "the business." I take you on, I train you, I lose all this. Do you think I should do that for you, Angela?'

'No,' she told him honestly.

'Then we agree. I'm doing it for me. Because I want to. Because I've got the worst case of orphan envy in the whole wide world.'

He grabbed a beer, climbed off the chair, and walked toward her.

She could feel the tension in him. He was not a man who played by the rules – he probably *had* blown up churches. He had anger and dark moods she didn't understand. He was unpredictable, raw around the edges. When he moved, he didn't make any sound. And after the marble-smooth facade of Jim, he seemed unbelievably real. If this man had a problem with you, he wouldn't poison your dog or burn down your garage. He'd tell you about it to your face. He'd let you know. If he discovered a father beating his daughter, he wouldn't rig a stockroom ladder to fall, breaking the father's leg. He'd walk up to the man and slam a fist through his face.

He stopped so close, she could feel the faint heat of the cigarette.

'You dreaming about him, Angela?'

'Sometimes.'

'When was the last time you slept through the night?'

'I . . . I don't know.'

'Fixed yourself a good meal?'

'A long time.'

'Well, stop it.' He ran a finger down her arm. She flinched and he shook his head. 'There's nothing to you, Angela. You've let yourself go. Now you're just bones with shadows rimming your eyes. A good stiff wind could blow you over.'

'It's hard,' she said. 'We've . . . we've been on the run. There are problems –'

'Tough. You have to learn to compartmentalize. From here on out, you separate. You're scared, sleep anyway. You're anxious, eat fruits and vegetables. Get some mass on those bones, then we'll talk muscle. And stop shredding your nails. If you won't take your body seriously, how is anyone else supposed to?'

'Strange advice coming from you.'

'I just preach, never practice.' His fingers lingered on her arm. The pads of his fingertips were rough and warm. He doodled a lazy pattern she felt down to her toes. She stepped back.

'You don't like that?'

'I . . . no, I don't.'

He chuckled. 'Liar.'

'I'm looking for a teacher, not another mistake.'

'Ah, and that's how you see men.' He tapped the beer bottle against his forearm, then lifted it for a deep swig.

'We'll start in the pool,' he said. 'Try to get you in shape without hurting anything.'

'I'm not a good swimmer.'

'I thought you said you didn't whine.'

She brought up her chin in defiance and he laughed. 'You're good. You have spirit.'

'Oh, that's me,' she muttered. 'I'm just plain *spunky*.'

He chuckled again, then his gaze grew speculative, caressing her cheek. He raised the cigarette. The end glowed red as he inhaled. Several seconds passed before he released the smoke.

She found herself watching the small O formed by his whiskered lips. She watched the long strands of his silky black hair brush his collarbone. The porch light flickered over him. She wanted to touch his skin, see if it felt as warm as it looked.

She glanced down immediately, caught off guard by her own reaction.

'Scared?' he murmured huskily, his voice too knowing.

'No,' she said instantly.

'You're shaking in your boots. And I haven't even tried anything. Yet.'

'I'm not scared!' But she was, and they both knew it. She was uncomfortable, and her thoughts were muddled. Should she trust him, should she not trust him? Should she run, should she play it tough? Should she step closer, should she step away? She was sick of the doubt.

She made her decision. Before she lost her courage, she grabbed the beer bottle and yanked it from his grasp. She crossed to the white gravel bed bordering the cactus garden and dumped the beer out.

'No more. I hired you. I want you sober.'

'A marine shoots better drunk,' he said curtly, no longer amused.

'Well, J.T., you're *not* a marine.'

'Big mistake, Angela. Big mistake.' He stalked toward her.

She stood her ground. 'You getting mean?' she said haughtily. 'Do you miss the beer that much already?'

'Not the beer. Sex.' His arm whipped out, faster than

66

she could have imagined. One hand palmed her head, his fingertips rubbing her scalp.

'You still haven't moved. Maybe you want to kiss me. If you do something that dangerous, will you feel strong?'

He bent over her. This close she could see the feral gleam in his eyes, could see the individual hairs of his twenty-four-hour beard.

Facial hair. Genuine facial hair to go with the hair on his chest. He had no idea what those things meant to her. No idea what it was like to be confronted by a man who was anything but cold.

'Come on, Angela, kiss me. I'll show you the third thing I'm very, very good at.'

He leaned closer still but didn't touch her lips. They both knew he wouldn't. He wanted her to do it.

She reached up and carefully, hesitantly, touched the prickly rasp of his beard. It was softer than she imagined. Her fingertips tingled. He sucked in his breath. She was holding her own. She followed his jaw, learning its strong, solid line. Her fingers tangled in his hair.

'For God's sake, don't you know how to kiss a man?' He yanked her closer.

And she punched him in the shoulder.

He grunted, more with surprise than pain, and fell back a step.

'That's what I'm supposed to do, right?' she stated firmly. 'I'm supposed to take a stand. Well, I did. And while I'm at it . . .' She yanked the cigarette from his lips. 'I hate smoking.'

'Too late. You should've run, Angela, exited stage left while you had the chance.'

He caught her easily and pulled her against him hard. One minute she was standing by the cactus garden, the next she was pressed against a burning body, her legs cradled by muscled thighs, her torso clamped by sinewy arms. She opened her mouth to protest, but he merely took advantage and captured her lips.

He was not bashful or calculating. His tongue plunged in deep, hot, knowing, and tasting of tobacco. He filled her, stroked her, grazed her teeth, and challenged her. She squirmed in his arms. The kiss deepened and ripened, never painful, but insistent until she felt something unfurl in her stomach.

She wanted to melt a little. She wanted to dig her fingers into his shoulders and hold on to him.

With a harsh cry she hammered her fists against his chest. He let her go.

'Bastard!'

'Absolutely. And I warned you.'

She wiped the back of her hand over her mouth. She felt raw and exposed all over. She wanted to beat the crap out of him.

He didn't step back or come closer. He just stood there, challenging her. She couldn't overpower him. He was stronger – men were always stronger – and she didn't know how to fight yet. Her eyes began to sting. Dammit, she was going to cry.

'Don't,' he said.

'Leave me alone.'

'Oh, come on, Angela, you were doing so much better than that. Don't give up on me now.'

'You arrogant son of a –'

'Much better. It's the spirit that will keep you alive, Angela. Don't lose the spirit. Now go to bed.'

'And yourself?' she fired back. 'Are you going to stay out here all night, ignoring your own advice?'

'Probably.'

She cocked her head to the side, sizing him up. 'I see,' she said casually. 'Your sister's only been here twelve hours and you're already falling apart.'

'Shut up, Angela.'

'Why? You can mess with my mind but I can't mess with yours? I might not be very strong and I'm probably a lousy shot, but I can connect the dots. You and your sister have some different opinions on your father. You seem to want to have a relationship with her. She seems to want to burn you at the stake. How am I doing so far?'

'Go to bed,' he warned.

'Not when I'm on such a roll. What did your father do anyway?'

'What didn't he do? Good night.'

'Did he hit you? I know about that kind of thing.'

'Your father beat you?'

'All the time,' she stated flatly. 'I still hate him for it.'

'Huh. Now, see, I think that kind of hatred is healthy. I'm a firm believer in it myself. Marion disagrees. She says our father was merely a little strict.'

'But you don't agree?'

He grunted. 'The colonel thought child rearing was a fucking blood sport.' He walked to the table, lit a new cigarette, and inhaled. His hands trembled slightly.

'Go away, Angela. Surely you got bigger things to worry about than my twisted family.'

She didn't go away. They had a connection now, and it mattered to her. 'And the woman?'

'The woman?'

'The prostitute who had your father's child.'

'My, my, you really did eavesdrop.'

'Yes,' she said shamelessly.

He continued smoking and she decided he wasn't going to answer her. Then just as his cigarette burned down to the nub, he said, 'My father took a seventeen-year-old prostitute as a mistress. He liked to do that kind of thing. She got pregnant. So the colonel tossed her out. She stood on the doorstep and begged for her clothes. He told the butler to turn the dogs loose. She left.'

'That's it?'

'Of course not. The girl tried going to Marion next. She didn't want money for herself, but for the baby.'

'But Marion . . .'

'Turned her away. Marion's whole life is about selective memory. Daddy is her darling. Whatever he does must be all right or the universe will cease to exist.

If Daddy says the girl's some lying whore he's never met, then the girl's some lying whore he's never met.'

'So she came to you?'

J.T. cocked one brow. 'You mean you haven't figured it out?'

She shook her head.

'The girl's name was Rachel. Her son, my half brother, was Teddy.'

'Oh,' she breathed, her eyes wide as the pieces clicked.

'That's right,' J.T. said softly. 'I married her. And she was the best thing that ever happened to me.'

J.T. dropped his cigarette on the patio and ground it out with his heel. He saluted her mockingly and she still couldn't think of a response.

'Get some sleep. Oh-six-hundred, at the pool. And keep clear of Marion, Angie. She doesn't like you, and Marion knows how to eat a person alive, then pick her teeth with the bones. We're damn proud of her.'

He left her alone on the patio, listening to the water lap against the pool while somewhere in the distance a coyote bayed at the moon without ever getting a response.

7

This is Jim Beckett interview number one, conducted by Special Agent Pierce Quincy with assistance from Lieutenant Lance Difford of the Massachusetts Crime Prevention and Control Unit. Location is Massachusetts Correction Institute Cedar Junction at Walpole. Date is November 11, 1995. Jim Beckett has been incarcerated approximately three months. With his approval, this interview is being audiotaped and filmed. Do you have any questions?'

BECKETT: Quincy? As in the coroner on TV?
QUINCY: Medical examiner.
BECKETT: Did you watch the show as a child? Was it your favorite show?
QUINCY: I saw it a few times.
BECKETT: What did your father do?
QUINCY: He's a plumber.
BECKETT: Not nearly as exciting as a coroner. I see your point.
DIFFORD: Cut the crap, Beckett. We're not here to watch you head-shrink the FBI. Quincy's only read about you, but I know you, Beckett. Don't forget that.
BECKETT: Lieutenant Difford, charming as always. The part I enjoyed most about being a police officer was reporting to dumb fucks like you. The big bad police lieutenant whose experience and street savvy will keep everyone safe at night, when all along it's your own man who's going out there, pulling over sweet blondes, and dicing them up. How's your insomnia, Lieutenant?
DIFFORD: Fuck you –

QUINCY: All right, let's get down to business. Lieutenant Difford's right, I've never personally met you, Jim, but I know all about you. I also saw all the files you pulled from our Investigative Support Unit, so I know you're familiar with serial killer profiling techniques. As we've discussed, this interview is strictly voluntary. You don't get anything in return, except a break in what must be a very monotonous routine here at Walpole. Would you like a cigarette or anything?

BECKETT: I don't smoke. My body is my temple.

DIFFORD: Jesus Christ –

BECKETT: I want to see my profile.

QUINCY: We're not into swaps, Jim.

BECKETT: Afraid I'll be able to refute it, see all the flaws? Or are you afraid I'll be able to someday use it to my advantage?

QUINCY: You have an IQ of 145. I don't underestimate that, Jim.

BECKETT: *Laughter*. You're not half bad, Special Agent Quincy. I may just come to like you.

DIFFORD: Shit, are you two gonna exchange love letters or can we get on with it?

BECKETT: Wait a minute. I get it. You two are playing good cop/bad cop. The smooth, sophisticated FBI agent and the blue collar, illiterate street cop. Have I mentioned yet that the FBI and local law enforcement agencies haven't had an original thought since 1975?

DIFFORD: Maybe, Beckett, we're just being ourselves.

QUINCY: Jim, I'd like to start by having you describe yourself in your own words. If you were profiling yourself, what would you say?

BECKETT: I don't think so, Quincy. You're the professional here. You go first. I'll tell you if you're getting warm.

Pause.

QUINCY: All right. The FBI entered the case with the discovery of the third body outside of Clinton, Mass. Later it was determined that this was the sixth victim, but at the time there were only two other crime scenes for comparison. The victim was a twenty-three-year-old mother and cocktail waitress returning from work. Her car was found pulled over on the side of a secluded back road, the windows rolled up and the doors locked. Inside, the glove compartment was open, her keys were in the ignition, and her purse was sitting in the passenger seat. Her clothes, covered with debris from the nearby woods, were found neatly folded and stacked in the trunk. There were no signs of struggle.

A quarter of a mile from the car, the body was discovered in the ditch. The victim had been stripped naked and placed faceup, arms and legs spread-eagle. A tree branch was stuck in her vagina. Clearly the body had been arranged for shock value. The victim had been sadistically tortured and sexually assaulted. Exact cause of death was difficult to determine. The victim's own pantyhose had been tied around her neck for ligature strangulation. In addition the victim's head had been savagely beaten with a blunt instrument – later determined to be the same tree branch that was inserted in her vagina.

Bruises around the victim's breast, buttocks, and inner thighs revealed the unsub [unidentified subject] had spent a significant amount of time torturing the victim before killing her. The extensive amount of postmortem mutilation, combined with the precise posing of the body, indicated that he'd probably spent at least an hour with the victim after the murder. The unsub had also taken the time to clean up the crime scene. There were no prints, no body hair, no semen samples, or torn clothing left behind. The victim had some defense wounds on her hands, indicating a struggle, but she'd been quickly subdued. We could find no traces of skin cells or blood beneath her fingernails.

We theorized that the unsub had utilized some credible ruse to lure the victim from her car. He'd then controlled the victim, tortured her, raped her, and killed her with particular fury. Afterward he'd arranged the body, vented further rage in postmortem piquerism, then returned to her vehicle, where he stored the clothes in the trunk and locked the car doors.

Several aspects of this crime stood out. First the fact that the unsub had lured the victim from the safety of her automobile versus using a blitz-style attack suggested that the unsub appeared to be a safe, credible person with advanced communication skills. The amount of time spent with the victim indicated the unsub was comfortable and confident in his abilities to execute the crime and escape. Lab tests revealed traces of spermicide and latex in the woman's vagina, indicating that the killer had most likely worn a condom for the sexual assault, then removed it from the crime scene. Most likely, the unsub was already at the stage where he traveled with a 'murder kit' containing such items as condoms, gloves, perhaps disguises, anything to assist him with his attack. Finally, the level of sheer violence and cruelty, combined with the vicious and shocking postmortem mutilation, indicated a man with unbelievable rage toward women.

We were dealing with a psychopath.

BECKETT: Please continue, you're finally getting interesting.

QUINCY: The unsub was most likely a white male in his late twenties to early forties. Age can be difficult to determine, but given the elaborate nature of the crime and mutilation, we estimated that the homicidal rage had been developing for quite some time. The unsub was already refining and perfecting his technique. His use of a ruse indicated the foresight and planning of a more experienced man, leading us toward an age of early- to mid-thirties. We predicted he would be outwardly charming and charismatic. A man of above-average IQ, socially adept, a capable employee, and either married or involved in a significant relationship. He was physically fit, good with his hands, and probably working in a 'macho' job. His car would be a middle-class dark sedan, possibly an old police cruiser. He had spent time in the military, but his egocentric personality and arrogance made him a poor fit – he was discharged under less than honorable circumstances. He probably has a past record of assault and/or minor sex offenses. Perhaps DWI arrests. Also, the style of ligature was similar to what you see in prison rapes, indicating that this man had probably served time.

He obviously considered himself a sophisticated killer. All three women were young, beautiful, and blond. Also, all three were risky victims for him to choose – these were not prostitutes or strippers, but mothers, daughters, and college students who had families to miss them and pressure the police for further investigation. The killer probably spent a great deal of time patiently driving around, waiting to find the right woman in the right place –

BECKETT: He's disciplined?

QUINCY: Well, as disciplined as a homicidal maniac can be.

BECKETT: It's discipline, Quincy, trust me. When the urge to kill is that strong, it takes strength and willpower to wait for the right one. You wouldn't know that. I doubt you've ever had a strong, passionate impulse in your life. What about trophies?

QUINCY: Generally serial killers take trophies. From looking at a crime scene, it's impossible to know what's missing. Maybe the unsub took a ring to give to his wife so he can experience a cheap thrill every time he looks at her. Maybe it was just a lock of hair. He'll take something though, to help him relive the crime later.

BECKETT: See, you're wrong. I didn't take anything. Why put something in my possession that would link me to a homicide? Bundy, Kemper, they thought they were smart, but they were really just animals, furious, savage animals who were slaves to their own hunger. I'm not a slave, Quincy. I controlled my impulses. I limited myself to my pattern.

QUINCY: Pattern?

BECKETT: You've never figured it out, have you?

QUINCY: Patterns are a favorite with Hollywood. Lunar

cycles, numerology, astrology – they rarely have any-thing to do with it.

BECKETT: I agree entirely.

QUINCY: Then what do you mean by pattern?

BECKETT: You're supposedly the expert, Agent. You figure it out.

Pause.

QUINCY: What about visiting the graves of your victims?

BECKETT: Never.

QUINCY: You never visited a grave site? Not even a memorial service, a vigil, anything?

BECKETT: Discipline is the key.

QUINCY: What about returning to the crime scene? You could pretend to be there as a police officer.

BECKETT: I am a Berkshire County cop. What would I be doing at a Clinton, Massachusetts, crime scene? I insist, discipline is the key. I'm not toying with you, Agent.

DIFFORD: Bullshit. The omnipotent guise is how you get your rocks off, Beckett. If you were so fucking smart, so fucking disciplined, so *controlled*, you wouldn't be sitting in jail right now.

BECKETT: Have you ever thought of going on a diet, Difford? Look at you. You're hitting the doughnuts much too hard these days.

DIFFORD: You came back for Theresa, Beckett, just like she said you would. A smart man would've skipped town, but not you. You couldn't let it go, not after what she did. You weren't so disciplined then, were you, asshole?

BECKETT: And where were you, Difford? When I wrapped by hands around my lovely wife's neck and began to squeeze the life out of her flailing body, where was her police protection? Where was your fat, lazy ass?

QUINCY: Gentlemen . . .

BECKETT: The agent's right. This exchange of pleasant-ries isn't advancing science. But I have to say I'm not impressed, Agent Quincy. At this point you might as well have been reciting a textbook. Come on, *Special Agent*. Dazzle me.

Pause.

QUINCY: Your first murder wasn't planned.

BECKETT: Elementary. What killer has ever planned his first murder? You have desire, then in a fraction of a moment of time you realize that you have opportunity. You either act or you don't. That's what separates the men from the boys. Me from you.

QUINCY: You pulled her over for speeding. You had every intention of writing her a legitimate ticket. You were on duty at the time. Stop me if I'm wrong, Jim. Then you see her. She's blond, beautiful, and sitting so trustingly in her car, ready to hand you her driver's license and vehicle registration. You've been under pressure for some time. You've been drinking –

BECKETT: I don't drink.

QUINCY: But you've been under stress, even more stress than you're used to. You realize no one's around, the road is deserted, and this beautiful woman is looking up at you and smiling apologetically.

BECKETT: She wanted me.

QUINCY: You were sloppy, weren't you, Jim? You thought it was about control, but you had none. You followed instinct and the next thing you knew, you'd raped and killed a woman with your oh-so-identifiable police cruiser parked behind her car.

BECKETT: I didn't panic.

QUINCY: Your uniform was ripped, wasn't it? You'd left semen in her body and were vulnerable to DNA matching. People had probably seen you pull her over. What to do next?

BECKETT: I wrote her ticket, of course.

QUINCY: Yes, that was good. You got into your car. Gave a status report and said you were continuing on. But you didn't continue on. You hid your police cruiser, then you returned to the scene. You dressed the victim, you placed her in her car, covering her with the blanket from your trunk so it looked like she was sleeping. You needed to hide her body, but you can't drive too far away because how will you get back? So you drive her car into the nearby lake, knowing the water will do your dirty work for you. If she'll just stay in the water four, five days ... It's hard to gather evidence from a floater.

BECKETT: Particularly after a year.

QUINCY: You got a good break, didn't you? The woman is listed as missing, your superiors call you in to ask since you gave her a ticket. You handle it cool as a cucumber, all paperwork appropriately filed –

BECKETT: I already said that half the fun was reporting to shit-for-brain lieutenants who never suspected a thing.

DIFFORD: Son of a bitch, we caught you in the end!

BECKETT: Ten bodies later ... that you know about. But, Quincy, I'm still not impressed. So the first murder was unplanned. So the body was dumped in a lake to cover the crime. That's all logic. Tell me something cool. Tell me something that will send goose bumps up my spine.

QUINCY: The night you killed the first victim, Lucy Edwards, your wife was in the hospital, giving birth to your daughter. That was the stress you couldn't handle, Jim. The birth of your daughter.

Pause.

BECKETT: Too easy. You have the date on the ticket, so you know she disappeared that day.

QUINCY: That doesn't mean she was killed the day she was last seen. You know it's impossible to accurately pinpoint the time of death of a body that's spent a year underwater.

BECKETT: It's still just logic.

QUINCY: No, it's statistical odds, Jim. All killers have a triggering event. For disorganized killers, it's generally the loss of their job or a major confrontation with their mother. For organized killers like you, birth of their first child rates right up there. The new addition to the family, the financial strain – particularly for a police

78

officer who was already living beyond his means. Your arrogance is your Achilles' heel, Jim. You want to think you're unique. You want to think you're the best, but really, you're just like all the others. And we can profile you the same way we profile them, by looking at what the others did.

Pause.

BECKETT: Then you don't need to talk to me, do you?

QUINCY: It's not the *what* we're trying to figure out, Jim. It's the *why*. You killed ten blond women, beautiful, loving, caring women. What drives a man to do such a thing?

BECKETT: You mean watch a woman beg for her life, snap her neck, then go to the hospital to see his newborn daughter? That was a good night, you know. Have you ever met my daughter, Samantha? She's a beautiful little girl, bright too. Tell him, Difford. You know Sam. Sam is the best thing that ever happened to me.

DIFFORD: And if the world has any justice, she'll never know who you are, Beckett. Theresa told her you were dead. She even bought a grave marker. You have a pink marker, Beckett. What do you think of that?

BECKETT: You're bitter, Lieutenant.

QUINCY: Jim, why did you kill those women?

BECKETT: They were immoral, godless sluts who deserved to die.

DIFFORD: He's lying. He doesn't have a religious bone in his body.

BECKETT: *Laughter.* For a change, Difford's right. But I get so bored with the my-mother-toilet-trained-me-at-gunpoint excuse.

QUINCY: Did you hate your mother?

BECKETT: Which mother? Adoptive or biological? Actually, it doesn't matter. Neither of them was worth hating.

QUINCY: They told me you've been exchanging letters with Edward Kemper III.

BECKETT: Sure. Ed's a big guy. Six nine and three

hundred pounds. That's a hell of a lot of psychopath. I work out everyday here, you know. I'm up to bench-pressing three-fifty. [*Beckett pulls up sleeve and flexes for camera.*] Impressive, huh? But I still got a ways to go to catch Ed.

QUINCY: Ed's IQ is also 145, did you know that?

BECKETT: He's a real Renaissance man.

QUINCY: He killed ten people as well. Is that why you decided to write to him? His victims were closer to home though – his grandparents, his mother, and her best friend . . .

BECKETT: Yeah, Ed's read a little too much Freud. All he talks about is how much he hated his mother. For God's sake, he attacked her with a claw hammer, decapitated her, then raped her corpse. It's time for him to move on. Have you heard about the larynx?

QUINCY: I read the interview notes.

BECKETT: Now, is that irony or what? Poor, bed-wetting, traumatized Ed is jamming his mother's larynx down the garbage disposal as a last symbolic act, and the disposal jams and throws the bloody voice box back up at him. Ed says, 'Even when she was dead, she was still bitching at me. I couldn't get her to shut up!' That's one of my favorite stories.

QUINCY: Did your mother bitch at you? Was she demanding?

BECKETT: My birth mother was a weak, pathetic hypochondriac without an intelligent thought in her head. When she dropped dead, she merely fulfilled her own prophecy.

QUINCY: Your father?

BECKETT: My father was a good man, don't bring him into this.

QUINCY: Would he be ashamed of you now, Jim?

BECKETT: For what?

QUINCY: I think he would be, Jim. I think you know that. I think Jenny Thomson really got to you.

BECKETT: Who?

DIFFORD: You know who the hell he's talking about,

Beckett. Little Jenny Thomson. The seventeen-year-old from Enfield. The girl whose head you cut off.

QUINCY: You didn't decapitate anyone else, Jim. Only her. You also let her get dressed after you had raped her. I think she shamed you. I think she told you that she was driving home from visiting her dying father in the hospital. That he needed her, she was his last reason to fight for life. That she loved him very much. But she'd seen your face. You had to kill her. So you did, but you didn't feel good about it, not like the others. The others you looked in the eye, but not Jenny. She was manually strangled from behind, but even then you didn't feel right about it. You were troubled and you were angry because you didn't want to be troubled. So you cut off her head, classic depersonalization. You hid it under a pile of leaves, not able to look at her. You left her body covered, not exposed like the others. But you still felt shame, didn't you, Jim? Every time you think of her, you feel shame.

BECKETT: No.

DIFFORD: You're shifting in your seat, Jim. You don't look so comfortable anymore.

BECKETT: My leg's fallen asleep.

DIFFORD: Sure, Jim.

BECKETT: I saw Jenny's father in the hospital.

QUINCY: What?

BECKETT: The nurses never put it together, did they? I went to the hospital. I wanted to see if her father was really there, if he was really dying. You can't trust what a woman says, particularly once you have her. They'll say anything if they think it will save their life. So I checked up on it.

I found him in an oxygen tent in intensive care, *Mister* Quincy. He wasn't allowed visitors, but I told the nurses I was working on his daughter's case and I had good news for him. Of course they let me in. Young nurses. One of them was quite beautiful but she was a brunette.

I leaned over until I could press my face against the

81

oxygen tent. And I told him how beautiful his daughter was and how wonderfully she'd screamed. I told him she'd begged for her life and she'd prayed to God, but God hadn't saved her. She belonged to me and I took her. He died the next day.

You want to know what makes me, Mister Quincy? If you want to understand me, forget the mommy-hating or the bed-wetting, animal-torturing, fire-starting triad you guys developed. It's so much simpler than that. There's power in the world, and that is me.

It's the power of being alone with a woman and having her plead for her life. It's the power of having her on her knees and watching her implore God to intervene. He doesn't. She's mine. I am the strongest, I am the best. I used to not understand the Nazi officers and what they did during the Holocaust – I respected their discipline, but I didn't quite get them. Now I do. I've held a beating pulse between my fingers and I've squeezed. And it's the best goddamn feeling in the world.

DIFFORD: You're sick, Beckett. You are fucking sick.

BECKETT: Get over it, Difford. It's guys like me who keep you employed. You were just a backwater no-name county lieutenant until I came along. I was the best thing that ever happened to your career. You should like me.

QUINCY: Jim –

DIFFORD: You're wrong, Beckett. You're not the most powerful person in the world. Theresa is.

BECKETT: What?

DIFFORD: You heard me. Who brought you down, who put you in jail? Face it, you married a sweet eighteen-year-old girl you thought you could control, manipulate, and terrorize to your heart's content. But instead of simply rolling over and playing dead, she figured you out. She learned you, she fought you. She toppled the omnipotent Jim Beckett.

BECKETT: Theresa is a weak, stupid woman who

couldn't even stand up to her own father. All you had to do was raise your voice and she cowered in the corner.

DIFFORD: She kept a log on you. All the times you said you were on duty when you weren't. All the times you came home with unexplained scratches and bruises.

BECKETT: She was a jealous wife.

DIFFORD: She tracked the mileage on your odometer. She kept a whole little book of evidence against you, writing in it secretly every night until she finally had enough to call the police. And you never suspected a thing.

BECKETT: Theresa is not that smart!

DIFFORD: She turned you in, Jim. You terrorized her, you traumatized her. You burned everything she owned, told her day in and day out that she was worthless, and still she stood against you.

BECKETT: I made her pay. Every time she takes a step now, she thinks of me.

DIFFORD: And every time you hear the cell doors slam shut, you can think of her.

Pause.

QUINCY: One last question, Jim –

BECKETT: Do you know what I dream of, Difford? Do you know what I think about every night? I dream of the day I see my wife again. I picture sliding my hands around her neck and feeling her hands flail against my chest. I envision choking her to the edge of unconsciousness. And then, while she's lying there, staring at me helplessly, I pick up a dull Swiss Army knife and hack off her fingers one by one. Then her ears. Then her nose. And then, then I cut out her beating heart. I'll do it someday, Difford. And when I do, I'll mail her heart to you.

Lieutenant Richard Houlihan walked to the front of the debriefing room and shut off the film projector. At his signal the lights came back on and sixty-five police officers and federal agents blinked owlishly. The room held the largest task force Massachusetts had ever seen.

The second largest task force had been assembled two and a half years ago for the same purpose – to find former police officer and serial killer Jim Beckett.

'Now you know what we're up against,' Lieutenant Houlihan said without preamble. 'Jim Beckett has always prided himself on his superior intelligence, and last week he demonstrated again what he can do. At nine A.M. two corrections officers escorted Beckett from 10 Block at Walpole to the Multipurpose Room where he had signed up for time to conduct legal research. The corrections officers had followed proper protocol – Beckett's hands were cuffed behind his back, his legs were shackled, and they were with him at all times. Yet somehow he managed to slip free of the cuffs – we believe he may have fashioned a home made lock pick – and the moment they entered the Multipurpose Room he turned on the two officers. In two minutes he beat both men to death with his bare hands. One officer managed to activate the red alarm on his radio. When Walpole's security officers descended upon the room ninety seconds later, they found Beckett's handcuffs and leg shackles on the floor and two dead men – one missing his uniform and radio. Immediately all units were locked down, the lieutenant in charge issued a red alert, and a full-fledged search began. Somehow in this time period Beckett entered central command dressed as the guard. In full sight of the main facilities he knocked out the lieutenant and sergeant running central command, seized the master key, and unlocked the system, opening all cell doors and blocks.

'In the ensuing prison riot, Beckett simply walked away, still dressed as a corrections officer. It took eight hours to determine that he was missing.

'An eight-hour headstart. Nobody has seen him since.

'I won't lie to you, people. The weeks ahead will be the toughest weeks of your career. The Walpole's IPS [Inner Perimeter Security] Team searched the immediate area for forty-eight hours. They called in the town, county, and state police for support. The National

Guard helped search for Jim Beckett. Nothing. The state's Fugitive Squad took over from there. For the last week they have combed Beckett's old neighborhoods, quizzed former associates, and turned the state upside down. The man has no remaining family other than his ex-wife and daughter, no community ties, and no friends. In the NCIC a national warrant has been listed for the man without results. In short, the Fugitive Squad found no leads and now it's up to us.

'You will work harder than you've ever worked, under more pressure than you've ever felt. The governor is watching this case. The state police colonel will receive daily briefings. Some of you have been through this before. Some of you were part of Task Force 22, assembled two and a half years ago also to catch Jim Beckett. That time he eluded capture for six months, then finally surfaced inside the house we were supposed to be protecting. Theresa Beckett almost died that night, and that, people, was our fault.

'In this room we have three task forces assigned to cover three eight-hour shifts. Do not think that because your shift is up you will simply go home. This case is front-page news – the crime hotline is currently logging two *thousand* calls a day. You do not leave until the leads generated on your shift have been recorded, classified appropriately, and followed up as indicated. Friday night Beckett will be featured on *America's Most Wanted*, and we're bringing in truck-loads of volunteers to help man the hotline. He's also listed on the FBI's Web site of America's most wanted – FBI agents will pass along any leads generated there.

'Yes, the work will be long, tedious, and grueling. Yes, morale will be low and tempers high. But we will do this, people. Beckett was once a police officer. He used his shield to lure young women away from their cars and kill them. He has attacked fellow officers, he has brutally murdered two prison guards. There is no case more personal and more important than this one.'

Lieutenant Houlihan shifted back a step, allowing his

words to penetrate. When the officers began to lean forward, waiting for the next word, the plan that would catch this particular son of a bitch, he continued.

'Historically Beckett has operated in four states. Those other states have organized smaller task force teams, and they will coordinate their efforts with ours. From New York we have Lieutenant Richardson – please stand. From Vermont is Lieutenant Chajet, and from Connecticut is Lieutenant Berttelli. If you receive calls from these men or their officers, do everything in your power to assist them. They will be happy to return the favor.

'Most of the crossjurisdiction investigation will be coordinated through VICAP [Violent Criminal Apprehension Program]. This system is run by the FBI and is designed to collect, collate, and analyze all parts of the investigation through computer and communications technology. If Beckett strikes in another state, the computer will recognize the MO entered by that state into the system and notify them to contact us. You guys don't have to understand it. Your supervisors have been trained in the system and they will assist you. The big trick is, should you come up with a lead, don't sit on it. Bring it to your supervisor immediately. Speed matters.

'In addition to VICAP, the FBI is providing profiling support. Here with us today is Special Agent Quincy, who you just saw on film interviewing Jim Beckett. He's going to tell us what to look for. Agent.'

Lieutenant Houlihan stepped away from the podium. No one stirred. Police briefings could be rowdy affairs, punctuated by gallows humor and good-natured ribbing. Not this morning. Every officer sat quietly, feet flat on the floor, eyes forward. The seriousness of the matter was etched into every face and the fresh lines creasing each forehead.

Special Agent Quincy stepped up to the podium. He could identify with the officers staring back at him; he'd served as a homicide detective in Chicago and then with the NYPD before getting his doctorate in criminology and joining the Investigative Support Unit at Quantico. Now he worked over one hundred cases at a time, traveling two hundred days a year to profile unsubs, advise local law enforcement agencies on how to catch the unsub, and aid with interrogation of the caught unsub. It was stressful work. One wrong piece of advice and the investigation could head in the wrong direction, costing lives. It was hard work, logging eighty hours a week and thousands of miles. Even when he was back in Quantico, he was shut up in a windowless office sixty feet belowground. Ten times deeper than the dead, they said.

It took its toll on everyone's life. First his wife had complained about the travel. Then she'd complained about his hours. Then one Saturday, when he'd made a point of being home, she'd accidentally sliced off her finger while chopping carrots. She'd walked into the living room, carrying her index finger and appearing one step away from fainting. Quincy had looked at her bloodied hand and severed digit, and he'd thought of the Dahmer crime scene, the Vampire Killer, Kemper's victims, and he'd heard himself say, heaven help him, 'It's only a scratch, dear.'

The divorce papers had arrived last week.

But Quincy still couldn't give up his work. Jim Beckett had been wrong in the interview; FBI profilers did understand about passion, obsession, and compulsion.

Quincy began: 'Jim Beckett is a pure psychopath. Most of you out there probably think you know what that means. I'm here to tell you that you don't. Forget what you've read in the papers. Forget what you've seen in the movies. I'll tell you what to look for and we want you to focus on that. We know this man. We knew him when he killed the first victim, and we knew him when he returned six months after his first disappearance to kill his wife. We knew him in prison and we know him now. Working together, we're going to get him.

'Beckett is a master of disguise. His high IQ and

natural charm enable him to blend into almost any situation. Two and half years ago he successfully hid from one of the largest manhunts in New England history for six months. We still don't know where he hid or how he did it. The bottom line is, forget what he looks like. From here on out, he's the unidentified subject, the unsub. And like any unsub, we can catch him without a physical description. We can catch him because of who he is. That's the one thing the unsub can't change.

'All right. Our unsub is a thirty-six-year-old pure psychopath. This means he is highly compartmental-ized. On the one hand, he is perfectly aware of community standards and norms. He knows how to fit in, how to be successful, and how to make people like him. He's charming, outgoing, and self-assured. On the other hand, he considers himself outside of societal norms and above anyone he meets. He has no feelings of guilt, remorse, or obligation. He lies easily and is obsessed with appearance. He has a powerful sex drive and in fact, for all his outward disdain toward women, he is dependent on them for his identity and self-esteem. He can't stand to be alone. He will maintain at least one female companion at all times.

'This may not sound like much, but it gives us a lot to work with. First, this is not an unsub who will hole up. His need for companionship, sex, and interaction means he's out there right now, moving among us. He could be the security guard applying for a position at a small Vermont college or the new hire of the Connecticut Highway Department. His disguises will be "macho" – look out for firemen, construction workers, security guards, cowboys, etcetera. He lies easily, which means sooner or later he may trip up and give himself away.

'Second, he is highly materialistic and image-obsessed. Before, he maintained his perfect house, perfect clothes, and perfect car through supplementing his cop's salary with credit card fraud and theft. He'll utilize those skills now, probably stealing cars, wallets, etcetera. Remember, Bundy was first pulled over in Florida on suspicion of auto theft and stolen credit cards. If you receive calls of a middle-aged white male or pretty blond female involved in auto theft, jump.

'Third, we have Beckett's need for women. In prison he hooked up with a young blond groupie named Shelly Zane from the Walpole area. She hasn't been seen since the day of the prison break. Most likely she's his accomplice. In your files you'll find copies of all the letters he sent her. Mostly your generic pornographic prison stuff, but searching Shelly's apartment has already given us our first big break. If you'll turn to the section marked "Possible Aliases" in the binders on your desk . . .

'We assembled this list based on researching Shelly's last two weeks in Walpole. According to her phone records, she made calls to several medical supply stores, different states' motor vehicles departments, and various county records offices. We believe she was helping Beckett create a new identity by researching how to get a new birth certificate. One option, of course, is to order blank certificates from a medical supply store, then forge a doctor's signature and county stamp. That level of forgery would probably hold up to get a license and a social security card.

'However, Beckett will eventually need to leave the country, and birth certificates are checked out when someone applies for a passport. As anyone who's worked fraud here knows, there's only one good way to get a "real" birth certificate. You go to the local library and on microfiche, read the obituaries until you find a kid who was born the same year as you but died in a different county or state several years later. As long as the counties don't cross-reference birth and death certificates, the birth certificate will still be on file. You simply request a copy of that birth certificate from the county and assume it as your own.

'Sure enough, the local librarian told us Shelly had

spent four days reading the microfiche of old newspapers. Going through the same newspapers, we found only four names that would fit the criteria for Jim Beckett: Lawrence Talbert, Scott Hannah, Albert McDougal, and Thad Johnson. We've notified the passport office to contact us should anyone request a passport for those names. There's a good chance Beckett will want that passport sooner or later. When he does, we got him.'

A hand came up in back. 'Why are you so sure he'll leave the country?'

'Good question. That brings us to the unsub's last major weakness: his ex-wife, Theresa Williams. As you heard on the tape, Theresa played the key role in Jim's identification and capture. He's never forgiven her for that. Each day in prison he wrote her a letter and in each letter he described exactly how he was going to kill her.

'The women of New England may be terrified now and they may be locking their doors, but frankly they're pretty safe. Beckett is going to kill again, yes. And most likely, Shelly Zane will be his first victim, once she is no longer useful to him. But his real target, his ultimate goal, is Theresa.

'He'll kill her. He'll find their daughter, Samantha, whom he seems to genuinely love. Then he'll get the hell out of Dodge. Through VICAP we track most of the United States and Europe. Jim knows that. It's our guess, given his fascination with the Nazis, that he'll head south to either Brazil or Argentina.'

A new hand went up. 'Which part of the task force is watching Theresa Williams?'

The powers that be exchanged glances. Special Agent Quincy stepped aside and Lieutenant Houlihan took over the podium. 'Ms. Williams has opted against police protection.'

'What?' Murmurs broke out. Lieutenant Houlihan raised his hand to settle things down. His reaction had been the same when Difford had called him and outlined the ridiculous plan.

'She knows she's in danger. She decided her best odds lie with her being on her own.'

'We must have at least a few feds on her. He could get to her and no one would even know it.'

'People, her location is given out only on a need-to-know basis, and no one in this room needs to know.'

More grumbles. 'What about the daughter?'

'She is in protective custody with her own guards. None of you need to concern yourself with that.'

Even more grumbles. Cops hated to be left in the dark.

'What about the pattern Beckett mentioned?'

'We're working on that. Any other questions?'

Some people shook their heads. Others exchanged dubious glances. To a person, they already looked stressed.

Lieutenant Houlihan tapped the podium with his fist. 'People, that's a wrap.'

The front doors released a small flood of blue-uniformed officers. They poured into the bright fall sunlight, blinking their eyes and readjusting to daylight. Some walked in pairs, others in small groups. All walked fast, men and women with a lot of work to do.

At the end of the block, one man peeled off from the group, casually waved good-bye, and disappeared down a side street as if his cruiser was parked there.

He didn't get into a car.

He walked down that block, then another, then another. He doubled back, then finally, when it was clear no one was following him, he disappeared into the woods. He stripped off his uniform, revealing the orange construction uniform beneath it. From behind a boulder he produced the hard hat he'd hidden earlier. Shelly had been in charge of securing uniforms, following his instructions, of course. She'd done that part of her job well.

He tucked the police uniform into a paper bag and reentered civilization. His face was already expertly made up – a bit of padding here, the skin tucked there – to give himself a whole new look. After a fifteen-minute walk he arrived at the motel where Lola Gavitz had a room.

'Honey, I'm home.'

Whistling, he locked the door behind himself, then checked the curtains. He didn't bother turning on a light. He tossed the paper bag onto the single queen-size bed and walked through the gloom to the bathroom.

Shelly hung naked in the shower.

Duct tape covered her mouth. More tape bound her wrists and ankles. A small hand towel protected the tender skin of her neck from the clothesline he'd wrapped around it. The other end of the clothesline was attached to the shower head, suspending Shelly three inches off the ground. Classic autoerotic asphyxiation setup. One did learn so many useful things as a police officer.

Shelly could keep the clothesline from strangling her by looping her arms over the showerhead and holding herself up. Or she could swing her feet onto the edge of the bathtub. Of course, then she ran the risk of her feet slipping off and the sudden fall snapping her neck.

Her arms must have gotten tired though, for now she did have her feet on the edge of the tub. As he entered the bathroom, she raised her head wearily, her long blond hair sliding back from hollow eyes.

He looked at her feet. He curled one hand around her ankle. One push, that's all it would take.

She rolled her eyes in terror.

'What do you think, Shelly? Do you want to live?'

She nodded as furiously as she could with a clothesline around her neck.

'The police predicts that I'll kill you once you're no longer useful to me. Are you still useful to me?'

More nodding.

He reached up and slowly loosened the clothesline.

She collapsed into the tub like a sack of grain. He studied her for a moment, noting the silky cascade of blond hair over white skin. He stroked that hair for a bit. Then he undid his construction overalls and let them fall to the floor.

Shelly stirred in the bathtub, recognizing her cue. She lifted her face and he ripped off the duct tape with one quick tear.

'That's a good girl. Remember, you have to be useful, Shelly. You have to be useful.'

Her mouth closed around him. He let himself relax by degrees into the frantic sucking. His hands continued to stroke her blond hair, lifting it in fistfuls and releasing it. For one moment he indulged himself in the fantasy that it was not Shelly on her hands and knees in front of him, but Theresa. His stupid wife, Theresa.

He'd never made her perform like this. He'd never made her do any of the things he'd had the others do. She was his wife, the mother of his child. He'd considered her separate. Now he saw the error of his ways.

Now he dreamed of all the things he would have her do when he saw her again.

He closed his eyes and his hands curled around Shelly's/Theresa's neck.

'I'm coming for you, baby. I'm coming for you.'

8

She was fading on him. Her strokes had long since passed the fluid point. She did little more than beat at the water, and he could see her chin trembling. Twenty laps, that's all she'd done. Barely over four hundred yards, when he could swim three thousand. Jesus, they were in trouble.

He'd started her with calisthenics. She couldn't do a single push-up. Fine. Arm muscles were a problem for some women, and she had a particularly slight build. They'd moved on to stretching. Her flexibility was pretty good. She did a solid twenty sit-ups, survived twenty jumping jacks. He'd moved her on to squats, and she practically keeled over on him. No arm muscles, no legs.

The woman was beyond out of shape. She simply had no muscle mass. And skin and bones didn't fight very well.

'Another,' J.T. commanded.

'No,' Angela said, but was too tired to put any force behind her word.

He scowled at her, she turned sluggishly into another lap. 'You call that form?' he barked out. He needed a whistle.

'I told you, I'm not a good swimmer.'

'No kidding. And no push-ups, no squats. Honey, how have you gotten through life?'

'Housewives don't do the Iron Man,' she snapped. Well, it was something. If all else failed, maybe she could verbally spar Big Bad Jim into the ground.

She reached the end of the pool, and without his

permission clung to the wall. Her shoulders were shaking. She placed her cheek against the patio as if finding a pillow.

She looked like a worn-out child. She looked like someone ought to pick her up, curl her in his arms, and rock her to sleep while stroking her hair.

J.T. stalked away from her in a hurry.

'Know what your problem is?'

'No, but everyone seems to have a theory.' Her lips twisted into that enigmatic, too-old smile that meant she was referring to her husband and the suitcase of secrets she wouldn't share.

'You think too much.'

'I've heard that before.'

'I mean it. You're clinging to the patio and you're thinking, I'm tired. You're thinking, My legs hurt. Tell me I'm wrong, Angela.'

Her eyes finally opened, her lashes spiky with water. 'All right. I'm tired, my legs hurt.'

'You have to find the zone.'

'The zone?'

'The zone. You ever play sports?'

'Sports?'

'Sports, Angela. You know, football, basketball, hockey, swimming, whatever. We can look it up in the dictionary if you'd like.'

'I . . . I was a cheerleader.'

'Now, why didn't I guess that?'

'It's not as easy as everyone thinks,' she retorted immediately. 'It takes a lot of flexibility and discipline. Have you ever been able to kick above your shoulder? I don't think so. We practiced very hard and it was brutal on the knees.'

'I'm not arguing. Must take some strength too, building pyramids, all that.'

'Yes. But I was one of the smaller girls. I was the top, not the base.'

'Ever fall?'

'All the time.'

'Get back up?'

'All the time.'

'Why?'

'Because that's what you were supposed to do.'

'Exactly. So you didn't think about it. You didn't say, "I hurt too much." Or "I'm afraid." Or "She'll drop me again." You just got back up because you were supposed to.

'That's what you do here, Angela. You swim and you keep swimming without a thought in your head because that's what you have to do. And you do the push-ups and you jog and you do all the things beyond exhaustion because you have to. Then one day you'll discover you're in the zone and you don't feel your legs anymore, you don't feel your arms anymore. You exist just as motion. That's the zone. Then you can do anything.'

She looked fascinated, she looked awed. He wasn't comfortable with her looking at him like that. He was just telling her the facts, not revealing the laws of the universe.

People thought soldiers and jocks were brutish men. It wasn't true. A lot of the Navy SEALs or Green Berets or Force Recon Marines looked more like accountants. Some of them were small enough to be nicknamed Mouse. Others were six four and so stringbean skinny they could barely walk through a strong wind. Extreme performance was not physical but mental. It was focus and concentration. It was finding that internal zone, where you could zero down the universe to one act, one motion, one goal. You could plow facedown through mud in the pouring rain because you were not thinking of the weight of your pack or the cold sting of the rain or the taste of the mud. You were not thinking of the two hours' sleep you'd had last night or the twelve miles you'd run this morning or the two hundred push-ups and two hundred pull-ups you'd done the minute before. You thought only of the next inch you had to crawl and then the inch after that. The world became a simple place.

And for a moment you could do anything.

SpecWar superstuds were not Arnold Schwarzenegger. They were Buddhist monks.

And former Force Recon Marines like J.T. were the men who realized the zone couldn't last forever. Sooner or later, training ended, combat ended, everything ended, and you were the same man you always were, lying on your bunk with the rage bunching your shoulders and the unrelenting memories racing through your mind.

Then you poured yourself a drink.

'I'll do another lap,' Angela volunteered. Her eyes had narrowed. His pep talk must have worked, because she looked fierce.

'You do that.'

She pushed off with more force than grace. She didn't have a swimsuit, so she wore an oversize T-shirt and shorts. The excess material created a lot of drag and quickly slowed her down. She slogged forward anyway.

Toward the end she faltered badly, and he thought he might have to drag her out by the scruff of her neck to keep her from drowning. Her flailing hands found the patio as he took the first step forward.

'No zone,' she gasped. 'God, this is horrible!'

He sat on the edge of the pool beside her and stuck his feet in the water. 'You want it to be simple. It's not.'

'Oh, how the hell would you know! Look at you!' She waved her hand at him. 'You probably catch rattlesnakes by hand. How hard has any of this ever been for you? How hard?'

'Not very,' he agreed calmly. 'I was born for this shit.'

'I hate you.' She rested her forehead against the pool edge.

He let her feel sorry for herself for a minute. Why not? There was a world of difference between the two of them. The colonel was a mean, lean bastard and he'd passed his genes to his children. In contrast, Angela had a small, slight build and no natural hand-eye coordination. She would have to fight for every lap, war with every shot. Nobody said life was fair.

'Your daughter, she's for real?'

Angela stiffened instantly, so he took that as a yes.

'Think about her, then. Don't think about yourself, focus on her.'

'What do you think has gotten me this far?'

'Huh.' They sat in silence. 'How old is she?'

Angela couldn't seem to decide how much to tell him. 'Four,' she said after a moment. 'She's four.'

'You have her someplace safe?'

'As safe as can be expected.'

'Huh.'

'Okay, it's time for another lap.'

He was surprised. '*Chiquita*, you're pretty beat.'

'I have to learn how to do this. If I'm weak, then I'd better get strong. Two more laps, all right?'

'You are stubborn.'

She appeared startled. 'I'm not stubborn.'

'Of course you're stubborn. You made it here, didn't you? What do you call that?'

'Desperation,' she said frankly.

He shook his head. 'No, trust me, you're stubborn.'

'Really?' She looked pleased. 'I'm stubborn. Good. I'm going to need that.'

She pushed off while he remained sitting there, blinking his eyes and wondering if he would ever understand her. The woman had spirit. He would've liked to have met her before the world had run her into the ground. He had the feeling that she'd been beautiful once. A petite, smiling woman with long blond hair.

Jesus, J.T. Give it up.

Behind him, the screen door slid open.

'So where's the mystery intruder?'

J.T. pointed toward the pool.

'Oh, for God's sake,' Marion said as she walked over to the edge. 'She looks like she's drowning.'

'That's her version of the doggie paddle.'

'You're kidding me.'

'Nope. Still think she's a fugitive?'

Marion finally appeared skeptical. 'I don't know,' she hedged. 'She doesn't look like much, but given the company you usually keep . . .'

'Gee, thanks, Marion. That's kind of you.'

They watched as Angela reached the end of the pool and struggled her way back. It was a long, painful process for everyone.

J.T. shook his head. 'I don't think one month is going to be enough.'

Angela finally reached J.T. and Marion, her face beet red. She clung to the edge of the pool while introductions were made. The two women showed about as much enthusiasm as could be expected.

'You can call me L.B. for short,' Angela said.

'L.B.?'

'Lizzie Borden.'

'Oh.' Marion had the good grace to flush. 'I'll confess, you're not what I expected.'

'I'm not a criminal.' Angela tried to pull herself out of the water, but her exhausted arms wouldn't cooperate. J.T. grabbed her shoulders and lifted her as if she were a featherweight. She returned her attention to Marion. 'In fact I've worked with the FBI before.'

'Whatever problems you have, I'm sure I can recommend a good law enforcement agency –'

'No, you can't. I've been through it all. I've worked with them all. And I know for certain that law enforcement can no longer help me. What I need is someone like your brother. J.T. is going to help.'

'Wait a second.' J.T. took a quick step back, waving his hands in defense. 'I'm just training you!'

'Exactly. That's the help I need. So tell me, *sensei*, what's next on the list?'

He looked at her for a moment, then at Marion. His sister was mutinous and disapproving. In fact, the only calm person on the patio was Angela.

'What's your name?' Marion prodded. 'If you have nothing to hide, you won't mind giving me your name.'

'I have nothing to hide and I do mind giving you my name. It's none of your business. Besides, if I remember correctly, you told J.T. you were here as his sister, not an agent.'

'Ignore her, Angela, Marion can't help herself.'

'I'm trying to offer help.'

'Then thanks but no thanks. Now, if you'll excuse me, I can afford only a month of J.T.'s time and I have a lot to learn. Is it time to eat yet? I'll make the oatmeal. J.T. is too dangerous with a saucepan.'

She headed for the house without another word. Marion released her pent-up breath in a low hiss. 'Jesus Christ, J.T., what have you gotten yourself into now?'

'I'm just training her on how to protect herself, Marion. How bad can it be?'

'With you, J.T., pretty bad. But that's okay, I'll keep my opinions to myself for now. Why don't you go and pour yourself another beer.'

'I can't.'

'You can't?'

He scowled. 'I agreed to stop drinking for the month.'

She arched a brow. 'Of course, J.T.'

'Dammit, I am *not* an alcoholic!'

'Of course, J.T.'

She smiled sweetly and walked away.

J.T. squeezed Angela a glass of fresh orange juice; that gave Marion her first opportunity. A cold drink created condensation on a glass, ruining fingerprints. A hot drink suffered the same due to steam. A room-temperature drink was perfect. She joined them for the end of breakfast, behaved admirably by making polite conversation, and offered to do the dishes. She set Angela's glass and spoon to the side. Later, when J.T. took Angela outside for a walk, Marion got out her fingerprint kit and went to work. One full thumbprint and two partial indexes later, she called the lab.

'The Nogales police will be faxing you some prints this afternoon. I want you to run them for me immediately. Call me here as soon as you know. Talk only to me. Are we clear? No, no, I have to go through the police – I don't have a fax machine here. It's not a big deal. They're just backwater cops, they'll cooperate. We can trust them.'

9

Nightfall. J.T. stood over the barbecue wearing a Red Hot Cajun Lover apron and grilling boneless breasts of chicken. Marion was tossing a salad and downing beers as if she were determined to pick up where her brother had left off.

Tess didn't cook anything. She didn't help with anything, and J.T. and Marion seemed fine with that. It had been seven years since she'd had someone cook for her. She found she wasn't very good at letting go. Her fingers twitched at her sides while the anxiety built in her belly. She was supposed to look perfect for dinner, hair done, makeup done, dressed to the nines. She was supposed to have Samantha fed ahead of time so she would play quietly in the bassinet, where Jim could admire his child without being bothered by her. The table had to be set a certain way, candles lit, flowers fresh, forks on the left, dessert spoon above, knife and spoon on the right. Their three-bedroom house should be spotless, the old hardwood floor smelling of lemon wax while the area rugs were freshly vacuumed and cleared of children's toys.

Jim had chosen their house because of the beautifully carved wood trim around the fireplace and windows. In other old homes, some generation always made the mistake of painting the trim white or cream or olive green. Fine old wood latexed out of existence. Not in their home. Jim had turned the original oak trim over to her like a precious gem. It had survived one hundred and twenty years. It gave their home the class and elegance befitting a decorated police officer. Nothing had better happen to the mantel or the banister or the doorjambs on her watch.

When Samantha was one year old, she'd gotten her hands on a spatula covered in spaghetti sauce. She'd waved it with glee, promptly splattering red dye no. 5 all over herself, the walls, and the oak windowsill. Two drops on the hundred-and-twenty-year-old wood and Theresa couldn't get them to come all the way out. She tried Formula 409, she tried mayonnaise. She set a plant there on a lace doily and hoped Jim would never figure out that she'd failed in her mission. Two weeks later he'd dragged her out of bed at two A.M. He took her down to the kitchen. He handed her sandpaper and stain. And he stood over her until seven A.M., supervising her sanding down and restaining the window frame, his arms crossed and his face grim. Samantha began to cry upstairs.

Jim made her continue to work while her arms ached, her eyelids dragged down, and her daughter sobbed her name in the little room above.

Tess curled her fingers into the lounge cushion to get them to stop shaking. Those days were gone. She could rest if she wanted. She could wear old shorts and a T-shirt to the dinner table. She could play games with her daughter in the living room without worrying about a piece of Lego hiding under the sofa and getting her in trouble later. She could abstain from makeup. She could simply be herself.

If she could ever figure out who that person was.

She rolled onto her stomach and carefully stretched out her back. She hurt. J.T. had led her through a tough regimen of swimming and weight lifting. She figured she must have some muscle after all, because surely bone couldn't hurt that much.

J.T. had done most of it with her. He'd stretched. He'd done fifty push-ups and two hundred stomach crunches. Then he'd stood on his head with his back to the wall and lowered his straight legs until his toes touched the ground. Up and down. Up and down. Her stomach had hurt just watching.

'Take a couple of Advil before you go to bed,' J.T. advised from the grill. 'You'll be grateful in the morning.'

'If I live that long,' she muttered. She rolled over onto her side. She was sore around her ribs. She hadn't realized muscle existed there.

'Food's ready. Eat up. We'll take a walk after dinner. It's important you don't get stiff.'

She said, 'Aaaagh.'

'Remember, no whining.'

'For God's sake, J.T. Give the woman a glass of wine and ease up before you kill her.'

Tess looked at Marion with surprise, then gratitude. Marion had remained in the house most of the day. Tess could pinpoint her location by following the smell of chain-smoked cigarettes. Now the agent was dressed in fine linen slacks and a classic cream-colored silk blouse with billowing sleeves and graceful cuffs. With her hair pulled back in a French twist, delicate gold hoops winking at her ears, and more gold accenting her narrow leather belt, she belonged in an upper-class garden party. Her face, however, ruined the impression. Her delicate features were frozen into a hard look, her blue eyes perpetually narrowed into a stern, suspicious stare. When she walked, she had the fast, determined footsteps of a woman who would mow you down if you didn't get the hell out of her way.

If Marion MacAllister had met Jim Beckett, Tess was sure she would have fired her gun first and asked questions later.

They ate out on the patio. Marion served a salad with a light raspberry vinaigrette. J.T. barbecued chicken accompanied by dirty rice and beans. She needed protein, he told her, and dumped an extra spoonful of rice and beans on her plate.

She ate everything, discovering an appetite that was powerful and foreign to her. She started out with silverware and delicate movements. Then she gave up and followed J.T.'s example, greedily tearing the chicken into strips and popping them into her mouth with her fingers.

'Is Freddie coming back?' she asked between mouthfuls.

J.T. and Marion exchanged glances. 'No,' J.T. said, his gaze never leaving Marion's.

Marion simply shrugged. She ate only the salad and half a chicken breast. After warring with herself for a full minute, Tess helped herself to the other half.

'Go easy,' J.T. commented.

'I know how to eat.'

He raised one brow but shut up. For all his words of caution, he ate two whole chicken breasts and three helpings of rice and black beans. He chewed voraciously, chasing down his food with long gulps of iced tea.

And every now and then she saw his gaze slide to Marion's beer with barely tamped hunger.

'So what did we learn in fugitive training camp today?' Marion asked at last. Done with her meal, she sat back and lit up.

'Swimming and weights,' Tess volunteered.

'She has a ways to go,' J.T. supplied.

The conversation drifted. They listened in silence to the distant sound of crickets singing in the dusk and the occasional whir of hummingbirds among the cactus.

'Do you swim?' Tess asked Marion.

'A little.'

'She rides. Dressage.' J.T. pushed his plate away. His gaze rested on his sister. 'At least she did when we were younger.'

'I stopped.'

'Hmm.'

'There was no point to it,' she said sharply. 'No one rides horses in real life. It's not a usable or marketable skill. Really, it was a waste of time.'

'You think?' J.T. drawled neutrally.

His fingers roated the empty glass in front of him, sliding up the condensation on the side, then twirling the base again. 'I used to watch you ride. I thought you were pretty good.'

'You watched me ride?'

'Yeah. I did. Could never figure out how you managed it. Such a tiny thing commanding a twelve-hundred-pound beast around the ring. I used to think you belonged to the horse more than you belonged to us.'

'I never saw you at the arena.'

'I didn't want to interrupt.'

'Huh,' Marion said. There seemed to be a wealth of suspicion in that grunt.

J.T. turned to Tess. 'What did you do?'

'Who, me?'

'I assume you had a childhood, unless that stork story's true after all.'

The question caught her off guard. She wasn't used to anyone asking about herself. 'I did Girl Scouts,' she answered finally. 'I didn't have hobbies or things like that. I worked after school. My parents owned a general store with a small deli. Cheese, fudge, gourmet foods. It was a lot of work.'

'Working-class parents?' Marion asked. 'New England, right? You have a northern accent.' She was obviously taking mental notes.

'Down, girl,' J.T. said lightly. He offered Tess a crooked grin. 'Forgive Marion. Unlike you, we never worked as children – our father did the smart thing and married money. Now Marion is hell bent on overcoming this stigma by turning into a workaholic. We can't take her anywhere anymore. She's liable to arrest the host for income tax evasion.'

'One of us had to have follow-through. You certainly don't.' Marion stubbed out her cigarette and reached for another. She said to Tess, 'You want to know a little bit about your hero? Well, let me tell you.'

'Uh-oh,' J.T. said.

'J.T. at seventeen. He's into orienteering. Do you know what orienteering is?'

Tess shook her head. Tension swept over the table. J.T. hadn't moved, but his expression was tighter. Lines had appeared at the corners of his mouth. Marion leaned forward and plunged on.

'Orienteering is a sport from Scandinavia, developed during one of the world wars. Basically you're turned loose with a detailed topographic map of an area and thirteen controls –'

'Flags,' J.T. supplied.

'Flags to find. You have a compass, you have a map, and you have three hours to find however many flags you can find.

'It can be brutal. The courses are rated for difficulty and the truly advanced ones – the red and blue courses – aren't even forest trails, they're just flags left in the forest. You get to plow through the underbrush, hike up mountains, cross teeming rivers. People get lost. People get injured. You have to know what you're doing.'

'I knew what I was doing,' J.T. said. 'I made it back.'

'Barely!' Marion returned her attention to Tess. 'So here's J.T., seventeen years old and already arrogant. You think he's insufferable now? You should've known him then.'

'I was a saint.'

'Get over it. These competitions, class A meets, are a big deal. You compete by age group and prizes are given out. Our father always dominated the blue course, the hardest level. He always won first prize. Then we have J.T. He's still too young for the blue course. He's seventeen and the toughest course for him is the red, and he's good. Everyone thinks he'll win it and everyone's talking about how the father will take blue and the son will take red. The colonel's already choosing the spots on the mantel.'

Her jaw set, her gaze hardened. 'Morning of the meet. *Morning of the meet.* Does J.T. register for his category in the red course? No. He registers for blue. A seventeen-year-old kid registering for blue.'

'I'd already done red,' J.T. said. 'I wanted something new.'

'You would've won!'

'Trophy's nothing but cheap metal that gathers dust.'

'So what happened?' Tess demanded to know.

'Einstein here,' Marion supplied in a low growl, 'goes running off in his orienteering suit. Three hours later he's nowhere to be found. Two hours after that they're arranging the search parties, when all of sudden from the underbrush comes this huge commotion. Thrashing and cursing and swearing. Mothers are running to cover the ears of their children, and lo and behold, it's J.T. Half of his face scratched off, both of his hands mutilated, and his ankle in a twig brace. He'd fallen off the side of a hill.'

'It happens.'

'It wouldn't have if you'd stuck to red!'

'It did. And I made it back.' He turned to Tess with a wicked grin. 'Walked two miles on a broken ankle. How's that for *cojones*?'

'More like stupidity,' Marion muttered.

'The colonel was impressed.' J.T.'s voice was deceptively innocent, but Marion flinched. 'That was the kind of thing Daddy liked,' J.T. continued, his eyes fastened on Marion's face. 'Enduring pain. Having balls. Walking on broken bones. Being an m-a-n.'

Marion remained silent. Between her fingers, the cigarette trembled.

'He was wrong, you know,' J.T. said. His fingers spun away the glass in front of him. 'He should've let you compete, Marion. The orienteering, the Civil War Reenactment Society. I taught you how to read the compass, do you remember that?'

'No.'

'What about my percussion rifle? You watched me carve out the stock from the black walnut during the afternoons. Do you remember that, or did you block

108

that out too, Marion? Did you leave all the memories behind?'

Marion remained mutinously silent.

'I remember,' J.T. said softly. 'I remember you watching me forge the barrel and locks. Took me a year to carve out that damn rifle and you watched every day. I remember you trying to pick it up – you must have been ten or eleven. But at four and a half feet long and a front-heavy twelve pounds, it was too big for you. You couldn't get the end of the barrel off the ground. So you poured the powder in it instead and rammed down the patch and ball with the rod. Then I lifted the rifle waist-high so you could half cock it, place the percussion cap, and move it to full cock. All that was left for me was to raise it to my shoulder, aim, and fire. Do you remember that, Marion? Do you remember any fucking thing?'

'You're lying.'

'Why, Marion? Why would I lie about that?'

'Because that's what you do, J.T. Invent fantasies.'

'About percussion rifles?'

'You can't stand the truth. You can't stand knowing just how much Daddy gave you, just how much Daddy favored you, and just how badly you fucked up anyway.'

J.T.'s knuckles whitened. Then abruptly J.T. pushed away. 'Sure, Marion, that's it.' He stood and began gathering dishes. 'Everything happened the way you imagined and Daddy's only crime was shutting you out. You do have follow-through. If you'd done orienteering, you would've won the trophy.'

'We'll never know, will we?'

'No, we won't. At least you have trophies from dressage.'

'Who the hell cared about dressage?'

'You did, Marion.'

Marion rose. She wouldn't look at J.T. She grabbed three plates, creating more noise than necessary, then stalked through the sliding glass door.

J.T.'s gaze remained on the door. His hands held two glasses in midair.

'You'll have to forgive her,' he murmured after a bit. 'She can be very intense.' He gathered more dishes, his movements short and choppy. 'Wanna hand me that bowl?'

'I'll help.'

'You don't have to – you must be sore as hell.' He wouldn't look at her. His gaze fixed on the table, his voice brusque. Still, she could see the darkness rolling upon him, bunching the muscles on his neck, rounding his shoulders. The patio lights washed over his face but couldn't penetrate the shuttered look masking his expression. Just his hands moved, long, callused fingers reaching, grasping, stacking. Thrusting, lifting, slamming, rapping out a staccato beat of frustration and anger that ran all the way through him and deep into the ground. 'Take some Advil,' he commanded crisply. 'Get some rest. You got a helluva lot of work ahead of you, Angie. None of it's going to be easy.'

'All right.' She still didn't move.

'Get in the house, Angela.'

'I could carry something in.'

'I don't need any help.'

She remained standing beside him, not sure what she wanted and not sure why she stayed. She studied his face, looking for something that eluded her. His expression didn't offer her any miracles. 'You . . . you and your sister, you grew up doing this stuff, didn't you?'

'What stuff?' He finished stacking all the plates and bowls. Now he gathered silverware.

'Orienteering and the Civil War reenactment. Horses and hunting. Swimming.'

'*I* did it, not Marion. The colonel was more interested in his son than his daughter. It worked for a while. Then I got too old and stubborn, stopped winning the trophies, got sick of shooting Bambi. And maybe the colonel stopped trusting me with a gun in his presence. The colonel wasn't stupid.'

Tess shivered.

'No more father-son outings,' J.T. announced. 'I joined the swim team and became the one-mile freestyle champ for Virginia instead. The colonel thought swimming was for sissies. I think he had something against men shaving their legs.' He gathered up the glasses.

'I wish I'd learned all that,' Tess said softly. 'I wish my family had been into those kinds of things. That I'd had an older brother or uncle or anyone to teach me about guns or self-defense or survival. Even how to read a compass. I wish I'd *known* it sooner.'

J.T. turned toward her. His eyes were empty and spiritless. 'Yeah, Marion and I, we're tough. We're just so damn tough.'

He carried dishes to the house. 'Tomorrow we start with handguns.'

Tess slept and, as always, Jim found her again in her dreams. In the shadows of the night she was back in Williamstown, lying in bed, the covers pulled up to her chin.

He's going to come out of the closet, she thought. Her mother had told her there was no such thing as monsters, but her mother had lied because her mother hadn't wanted to believe in such people as Jim Beckett.

He's going to come out of the closet. Run, Tess, run.

But she couldn't run. She had no muscle. She was a shapeless blob, a weak, defenseless feather pillow.

In the distance she heard a baby crying. She knew she had to move. *You must protect Sam. You have to protect Sam.*

It was too late. Her closet door slid open and he stepped into the room, grinning and golden and hefting the baseball bat.

'Did you miss me, Theresa? I missed you.'

She whimpered. She heard the plea bubble in her throat and she knew she was going to die. Samantha had stopped crying, maybe she sensed the danger. Please let her remain quiet. If she would just remain quiet long enough . . .

Jim leaned against the wall and bounced the baseball bat off his ankle. 'Where's Sam?'

'Gone,' she whispered. *Don't cry, Sam. Don't cry.*

'Tell me. I'm her father. I have rights.' He lifted the bat and stalked toward the bed.

'I am going to kill you, Theresa. Samantha will be all mine, and you're too pathetic to do anything about it.'

The bat lifted and she whimpered and she remained frozen, watching it arch.

The house was silent, her baby was silent. No more crying.

'Discipline is the key,' Jim whispered, and the bat whistled down.

Tess woke up, terrified and already reaching for the phone. She wanted to call Difford and hear Samantha's voice. Her fingers clenched convulsively around the receiver as she lay in bed, her chest heaving, the sweat rolling down her cheeks.

Slowly she forced her fingers to relax. It was dangerous to call Sam at the safe house, dangerous to do anything that would connect her daughter to her. If you really want to keep her safe, Difford had told her, you have to let her go.

So Tess let her go. Tess hugged her baby, kissed the top of her sweet-smelling head, and let her go.

And now she curled up in her bed, hugging her pillow as if it were her daughter, and thirsting for the scent of baby powder. Six A.M. Massachusetts time. Sam would be at the waking edge of slumber. Did she sleep well at the safe house, or did she have nightmares the way she sometimes did? During those times Tess would crawl in bed beside her and whisper the story of Cinderella with Sam cradled in her arms and smelling like Johnson & Johnson's No More Tears shampoo. They would both make it through the night and in the morning, like any child, Sam would smile and be happy once more.

Tess wanted so much more for her daughter than running from city to city and living in fear. She wanted Sam to grow up feeling smart and strong. She wanted her daughter to know she was beautiful and loved because Tess's parents had never told her any such thing.

She wanted Sam to be happy, and the desire made the darkness sweep over her like a wool blanket, stifling her. She wasn't sure how to give the gift of joy. She wasn't sure how to be a good parent. She had no examples to follow.

Four A.M. She crawled out of bed, shaking and shivering and feeling her leg throb. She saw Jim stepping out of the closet and heard the crack of the baseball bat connecting with her leg.

I'm going to kill you, Theresa. Sam will be mine.

Tess padded through the silent house. Not knowing what else to do, she followed J.T.'s lead. She jumped into the pool and started to swim.

Edith Magher took pride in her garden. She'd lived alone all her life, never having found Mr. Right, and by the time she was forty she knew she was destined to be a childless spinster and that was that. She adopted her garden instead, each flower, stalk, and leaf becoming precious to her.

She worked outside every day, spring through fall. In the narrow six streets that served as her tiny neighborhood, she was widely regarded as having the best yard, and even that new couple who bought the house on the corner kept their big, pawing Labradors at bay.

She was outside now, preparing her flower beds for winter. Late September was generally beautiful in Lenox, Massachusetts, the trees turning a rich gold, the sky an unbelievably bright blue. This year, however, the weather was turning cold unusually fast. On the news they were already issuing frost warnings, and even the diehards who vowed never to turn on their furnace until the first of November were beginning to think twice.

Edith hadn't decided whether she was prepared to turn on her heat yet, but she was definitely tending to her garden. She believed firmly in being prepared, which was why she'd been able to retire from her bank teller job at the age of sixty instead of slaving away until sixty-five, as so many others had. This afternoon was perfect for gardening; the huge maple tree in her yard reflected a dozen shades of gold and the slowly sinking sun made the leaves even deeper. When Edith breathed in deeply, she caught the rich odors of drying leaves, fertile earth, and mulled spices. Some people worked on their gardens in the morning, but Edith had always preferred dusk.

Yesterday she'd gotten word that her dear neighbor Mrs. Martha Ohlsson was finally returning from Florida. Given the news that that horrible serial killer – Jim Beckett, that was his name – had just escaped from Walpole, Edith was looking forward to Martha's return. Living next to an empty house no longer seemed safe.

Edith reminded herself every night as she locked up her tiny two-bedroom bungalow that she had nothing to worry about. Her community was a small one, a quiet one. The heart of Lenox boasted old, beautiful Victorian houses that had once been the summer homes of Boston's elite. Edith Wharton had given Lenox its claim to fame by building her mansion on the outskirts of town. Neighboring Tanglewood spread its lush green grounds and unbelievable mountain view for people who appreciated the Boston Symphony's fine music and mother nature's even finer grandeur. Between Tanglewood and the Wharton mansion, Lenox saw a fair amount of tourists during the bright summer months and brilliant fall.

Now, thanks to the unexpected cold spell, Lenox was already taking on its winter rhythms, tranquil and slow. Nothing much had happened in Edith Magher's community since a few years before, when the Joneses' oldest son had broken his arm in a car accident.

Every now and then, however, Edith had these spells. Not often – it had been years since the last one. But she was having them now, and sometimes at night she found herself lying awake just listening to the sound of her own heartbeat. She looked over her shoulder more too, as if expecting to see something awful.

Her great-great grandmother Magher supposedly had had the gift of sight. Edith didn't believe in such things. She trusted only the earth, the power of mother nature, and the beauty of her garden.

Which was why when she looked up now and saw the ephemeral image of a thin blond girl standing at the base of the old oak with blood on her face, Edith shook her head and said, 'Don't you do that to me.'

The vision politely vanished.

Edith went back inside her house and brewed a strong cup of black tea.

10

'Don't stand there.'

'Why not?'

J.T. grabbed her arm and dragged her toward him.
'Because that's a jumping cholla.'

Tess glanced at the stubby, fuzz-covered cactus then
gazed at his long, tanned fingers still wrapped tightly
around her upper arm. 'So?'

He shook his head, massaging his temples with one
hand. His eyes were bloodshot, his cheeks thick with
beard. For a change, his black hair was pulled into a
ponytail and he'd donned a worn T-shirt and a pair of
sandals. They were his only concessions to civility,
however. He'd gone twenty-four hours without alcohol
and was hell on wheels. '*Jumping* cholla, Angela. See all
those tiny, furry spurs? Trust me, you won't think
they're so tiny and furry when those glochids leap onto
your arms and hook into your skin.'

'But it's just a plant!' As she said this, however, she
was eyeing the cactus with suspicion and taking a step
closer to J.T.

'It's a particularly talented plant.'

He released her arm, then stepped away. He was
definitely cagey.

In contrast, she felt optimistic. She didn't care how
much oatmeal J.T. made her swallow or how many laps
she swam, she'd never be able to compare to a man's
strength.

But a gun . . .

As J.T. lifted the small, silvery semiautomatic out of
the case, she nodded. She was going to become a master

marksman. That would be her advantage. Jim might be stronger than her and he might be faster than her, but not even the omnipotent Jim Beckett could outrace a bullet.

In the hot, dusty desert of Nogales, Tess was going to become the next James Bond – licensed to kill.

And she would stand there in the shadowed room, watching Jim step out of the closet like the real-life monster no one wanted to imagine. She wouldn't cower anymore. She wouldn't shake. She would not beg for her life and she would not fear for her daughter. She would stand, tall and regal, her face as cool and composed as Marion's. She would point her .22, watching Jim suddenly freeze, suddenly pale, and suddenly realize that now she was the one in control.

'Can I hold it?' she asked quietly.

J.T. lifted up the gun, then froze when he saw the gleam in her eye.

'It's not a toy,' he said sharply.

'I hope not.'

'Keep the safety on, never place your finger on the trigger until ready to shoot, and don't *ever* point it at a person, even in jest. Those are the rules.'

'Yes, sir.'

J.T. shook his head. 'You just don't get it. You ju –'

'Is that the target?' She turned away from him, her veins humming with heady adrenaline. Twenty-one feet from her, two bales of straw sprouted from yellow Arizona dust. Red and white ringed targets were attached to the front of each bale by thick nails in the corner. The targets weren't that far away. They were good-sized. She thought she could take them.

J.T. didn't say anything, but she felt his gaze on her as he gave her the semiautomatic. She held it out and practiced looking down the sight. She'd held a gun a few times before. Fired one a few times. Hit a man.

She knew more than J.T. suspected. She liked it that way.

'When can I take the safety off?'

'Take the safety off? A – you're not wearing earplugs nor eye protection. B – the gun's not loaded. C – where did you learn that awful stance?'

His harsh words briefly dimmed her euphoria, but she nodded. She was there to learn. He would teach her.

J.T. tossed her earplugs and eye goggles, shoved a box of bullets in his pocket, and wrapped his body around hers.

'Here, like this.' His arms sandwiched hers, bringing her arms up straight and adjusting her grip. His groin cradled her hips and his thighs burned into her legs. Something hard and unyielding pressed into her left buttock. The box of bullets, she thought. Her stomach felt hollow.

J.T. adjusted her arms and legs as if she were a mannequin. 'We'll start with the Weaver stance which uses two hands for better control while twisting your body so you make less of a target. Face to the side, feet slightly apart for balance. Now extend your right arm toward the target, using your left to pull your arm against your chest and secure your grip. There you go. Now look down the barrel. Don't squint. You've been watching too many Dirty Harry movies.'

He withdrew. She almost fell.

'What do you see, Angela?'

'Straw?'

'No shit. Pick a ring, any ring.'

'The bull's-eye,' she said fiercely. She made the mistake of moving and lost her stance. He arranged her once more, looking impatient.

'Shoulders down, arms straight. Tuck the butt of the gun in the V between your index finger and thumb. Grip it firmly. Now, see the front notch on the gun?'

She nodded.

'That's your front sight. You want to align it perfectly between the two rear sights. Then you want to aim at the target so the bull's-eye sits right on top of your aligned front sight, like a full moon. Got it?'

She nodded vigorously. 'Can I take off the safety?'

'Fine. We'll do a dry run first so you can get used to the feel of the trigger.'

'All right.' It took her four tries to push the safety down.

'Okay,' J.T. continued crisply. 'You have a Walther .22 semiautomatic pistol there, just like the one you were carrying. It's not a powerful gun and it's not super accurate, but it's small, easy to conceal, and reliable. If you're at close range, you'll hit something. So for you, that means let the attacker get in close, aim for the chest, which is the biggest target, and once you start firing, don't stop. You wing someone with a .22 and it's like grazing a charging lion – you'll only piss him off.'

'How reassuring.'

'Align your sights. Find the target. Take a deep breath, exhale slowly, then hold the rest of the air in your lungs, and pull back the trigger *steadily*. Okay. Fire.'

She squeezed the trigger. The first pull was long. Her arms bounced up and her elbows locked, but the trigger came back easier than she'd expected. The trigger mechanism clicked dully in the silence, gutless without bullets. With more enthusiasm she followed up with quick, short jerks of her index finger, all that was now necessary for the double-action pistol.

'Congratulations,' J.T. informed her. 'You just killed a cloud.'

He taught her how to load the magazine, then showed her how the gun locked open when the last shot was fired. With a push of a button the old magazine was released and she could pop in a new one. Simple. Easy. Foolproof. The gun held six bullets in the magazine plus one in the chamber, giving her seven tries to get things right.

She put in the earplugs, donned her goggles, and leveled the loaded gun at the sacrificial bales of straw. She fired the gun, then leapt like a scared jackrabbit at the noise.

'Let me be more specific,' J.T. drawled beside her. 'Before you pull the trigger, open your eyes.'

'I did.'

'Uh-huh. Try again. Hammer's already cocked back from the first pull, so you don't have to squeeze too hard. Remember to actually hold your breath while squeezing the trigger. Otherwise, your arm automatically jerks up when you inhale, and down when you exhale. You want to minimize your arc of movement. If it helps, picture my head on the target.' He smiled sweetly.

She pulled the trigger six times. She finally hit the hay bale. The target remained unscathed.

'Sugar, I didn't know you cared.'

'Shut up.' She no longer felt cocky or triumphant or ready for battle. How could anyone miss with seven shots?

She tried thinking of the zone thing. She tried picturing her daughter. She thought of that night in the basement, her hand wrapped around the cow's heart, thinking it was a real heart, a real human heart.

She swayed on her feet.

J.T. caught her elbow.

'Maybe you want to try again tomorrow,' he suggested quietly.

'No. No, I have to be able to do this.'

'It's not such a great thing to know how to do, shooting a gun.'

She pulled herself together. 'It's the only thing.'

He was silent for a moment. He shrugged. 'Suit yourself. I'm just the teacher.'

His hand slipped off her elbow. She stood alone. He rammed a fresh magazine into the gun and handed it to her.

She fired the first bullet. Her trigger pull was jerky, and she missed the hay bale altogether. Furious and frustrated, she bobbed the gun down and pulled back the trigger with vengeance. She finally hit the edge of the bale, then she hit it again.

Four more shuddering shots, each more difficult than the first, and she still didn't hit any red rings on the target.

The gun emptied. Her ears were ringing. She continued to pull back the trigger until J.T. removed the gun from her grasp. Her face was ashen, her eyes dry. She couldn't look at him. She stared at the hay bales and wondered how she could do so badly.

'*What are you going to do, Theresa? Hit me, beat me, shoot me? We both know you're not that tough. You couldn't even stand up to your father. You couldn't protect your mother. You're nothing, Theresa. Absolutely nothing, and I own you.*'

Stop it, stop it, stop it. She wanted him out of her head!

'Angela,' J.T. said sternly, 'you're thinking too much.'

'I swear I'm not thinking!'

'Find the zone. Whatever is going on in your head, block it out. Just block it out.'

'I don't have a zone!'

He shook his head, suddenly furious. 'You want to do this, Angela? Are you serious about this? Forget the damn gun, grow a backbone instead. You're tough, I've seen it. But you're an endurance tough, and that's not enough. I bet when this Jim guy hit you, you took it. I bet when anyone threatens you, you curl up in a little ball and you survive.

'Well, that's fine if survival is all you want. But you came to me. You said you wanted to do more than wait, more than endure. You wanted to fight. So learn how to fight. Stop squeezing your eyes shut and open them wide. Stop flinching at the sound and open your ears. I don't care what your mama told you, the weak will *not* inherit the earth. It'll go to the people who can run the distance and still stand at the end.'

'Like you,' she said bitterly.

'You think I'm still standing? *Chiquita*, you are *not* looking close enough.' He popped the empty magazine out of the gun and in one clean motion replaced it. His arm extended. He glanced once; one second was all he seemed to need. Then his head swiveled back to her and he pulled the trigger. She flinched at the noise, but he didn't. He kept squeezing, bam, bam, bam, bam, the concrete man in action. The gun emptied.

His hand dropped to his side.

The center red circle of the target had just been annihilated.

'My God,' she whispered.

He slapped the gun into her palm. 'Stop flinching, stop jumping. Start focusing. Maybe you gotta learn to hate. I know it works for me.'

'All right,' she said. She could hate. She hated her father for every time he pulled back his arm in rage. She hated Jim for letting her believe he would save her, then plunging her into a hell deeper than even her father could imagine. And she hated herself because she'd let both of them hurt her, because it had taken her twenty-four years to figure out she had to fight, and she still wasn't any good at it.

She assumed the opening stance. Picture Jim, she thought. Picture the police photos. Remember every single thing that he did.

She gagged. She started firing. Tears were on her cheeks.

You're blind, you're stupid. You didn't see who he was. You didn't stop him sooner.

But I figured it out before anyone else! I stopped him eventually. I fought, dammit.

Too late, not good enough. How could you have let him use you like that?

I was just a kid, a mixed-up kid, and he chose me for just that reason. Because he knew how much I wanted someone to love me, how much I needed anyone to love me.

He knew you were weak. He knew you were malleable. You didn't disappoint.

J.T. grabbed the gun from her hand. 'Stop it!' he barked. 'What the hell are you doing?'

She blinked her eyes rapidly. Slowly he came into focus. Her ears were ringing from too many gunshots. Red dust was glued to her cheeks. She looked at him. She looked at the hay bales. Straw had flown in all directions from the top of the bales; she'd finally hit the white fringe of the target with a couple of shots. The red rings remained intact.

'You're not paying attention,' J.T. raged. 'You're pulling the trigger like Dirty Harry and your mind isn't even on it. And that's blasphemy, lady. Pure, simple blasphemy!'

'I'm trying, dammit!' She was furious, not at him, but he was available, so she chose him. She stabbed her finger against his chest. 'I hired you to teach me, dammit. If you're so great, teach me how to fire this thing.'

'Fine,' he said tersely. 'Fine.'

He stepped behind her without foreplay. She was flattened against his body, her shoulders molded to his chest, her hips against his groin, her thighs against his thighs. His chin settled on her shoulder and his breath whispered across her neck.

'Point,' he ordered.

She brought the gun up.

'Aim.'

She sighted the target.

'I said aim, Angela! What are you trying to shoot? The dirt? The sky? A cactus? Two hay bales aren't enough for you?'

'I am aiming!'

'Look down that barrel, woman. Picture your husband,' J.T. muttered in her ear. 'Picture his face as that bull's-eye, sugar. And give him hell for what he did to you.'

Her body stiffened. Her arms leveled and her eyes narrowed. Suddenly she felt very calm and very cold. She sighted the target, steadied her grip, and with a triumphant flood of adrenaline, yanked back the trigger.

The bullet sailed so far wide of the target, it was going to have to catch a train to get back to Arizona.

She stood there, shocked and appalled.

'Shit,' J.T. murmured, then shook his head and rolled his shoulder. He stepped back. 'We'll try again tomorrow, Angela. You have three and half weeks.'

She looked at the target again, then at the gun in her hand. It had betrayed her. The gun was supposed to be her advantage. If she couldn't shoot, how could she win? If she couldn't outfight, outrun, or outshoot Jim, how was she going to win?

'But I hit him once before.'

'You shot your husband?'

'I hit him. In the shoulder. It was solid.' She shook her head in a daze. 'He was moving at the time. Maybe he ran into the bullet.'

'You shot your husband?' J.T.'s brows knit into a single dark line.

'What else was I supposed to do? Let him beat me to death with a baseball bat?'

'*What*?'

She wasn't paying attention to him anymore. She threw the gun to the ground.

J.T. snapped his hand around her wrist. 'Don't do that. A gun isn't a toy. If it had been loaded, you could have shot us both.'

'Well, then at least I would've finally hit something!'

'Don't take it out on the gun and don't take it out on me, Angela. It takes time to learn these things. Did you think the money would buy you a sharpshooter's badge?'

'You don't get it,' she cried. Her gaze went to his fingers, tight and strong around her thin wrist. Those fingers could snap her bone the way Jim's fingers had wrung her neck. 'You don't know, you don't understand the things he did.'

Her voice cracked. 'I lied to you, J.T. I lied.'

He went rigid. 'I don't like lia –'

'I thought if you taught me it would be enough. But let's face it, three and half weeks won't be enough. You have to help me,' she whispered. 'You have to –'

'Don't tell me what I have to do.'

He released her wrist. One quick movement and he'd brushed her off as if she were nothing but a clinging cholla glochid.

'You don't under –'

'Shut up!'

She realized then that she'd been wrong. She'd thought him unaffected, but he was overaffected. His face contorted, his fists clenched at his sides. There was anger and there was rage, and then there was an emotion too potent to describe. Something that had been poured into him at creation and he was consumed by it from the inside out.

He took two steps forward and she shrank back.

'What is it with women? Can you tell me that, Angela? You come here, you barge into my life, and what the hell, I let you stay. I tell you who I am, I tell you what I can give. And maybe I'm hard and maybe I'm crude. Maybe I want a beer so badly I'm waking up in a sweat in the middle of the night. But I haven't touched one, sugar. I told you what I could give, you told me what you wanted, and we struck a deal. And now you want to change the rules?

'Now you suddenly want more and *I'm* the bastard for not giving more? Lady, I've been down the hero path, and let me tell you, the laurels don't fit. I know they don't fit. I don't try to get them to fit. I don't give a damn that they don't fit. I will *not* play that game again. You hear me? I will not play that game!'

His hair slipped free from its band and flew around his face. She could feel his hot breath on her cheek, the strength of his body bending over hers.

She said, 'Liar.'

He stiffened as if struck. 'What?' It was daylight and the sky stretched out blue and unchecked as only a desert sky could spread. But he squeezed her view down to just his presence, just his black, glowering, threatening presence.

She brought her chin up. She couldn't shoot a gun so she might as well talk smart. 'You can say what you want, but I know more about you than you think. You're not as cold as you pretend. You care about your sister very much. You obviously loved your wife and son.'

'Oh, those are great credentials. My sister hates me and my wife and son are dead. I'm going back to the house.'

'Wait.' Her hands reached for him. He slapped them down.

'I thought you didn't trust anyone, Angela? I thought you said you were going to take care of yourself!'

The word stung. 'I'm not as good as I thought.'

'Learn to be better.' He yanked open the gun case, stuffed the gun and spent shells back in, and walked away.

II

'Tough day at work, darling?' Marion called out with mocking sweetness as J.T. stalked back into the pool area.

'Women are the root of all evil,' he growled, then stormed into the house, tossed the gun case into his safe, and locked it up tight. That detail attended to, he walked back across the living room, unbuttoning the fly of his jeans as he went.

He thrust open the sliding glass door just in time to encounter Angela about to do the same. They both froze. He scowled first. 'Rosalita will dye your hair. Three o'clock. Go eat lunch.'

'Coward,' she said, and shouldered her way past him. He stood stock-still for a moment longer, flexing and unflexing his fingers.

'Lovers' quarrel?' Marion asked innocently, and took a long sip of an icy cold beer. One of his beers. One of his favorite beers.

'Shit.' He ripped his T-shirt off over his head in a single yank. Two quick jerks, and he kicked his jeans across the patio. Clad only in boxers, he made a beeline for the pool. He clambered up to the low diving platform and assumed a runner's stance.

'Cannonball?'

'Watch and learn, little sister.' He bolted down the slim board, energy harnessed, focused, then unleashed with the force of lightning. Bam, bam, bam, leap . . . and soar through the air like an eagle. Free, suspended, graceful. Fuck them all.

He dove clean and arrow-straight into his deep blue pool, firing all the way to the bottom.

And the crowd goes wild.

J.T. didn't come up right away. He drifted along the beautiful blue tiles, suspended like a stingray as his lungs began to burn. He rolled over on his back, fighting to remain down, reveling in the feel of oxygen-starved tissue.

Semper fidelis, baby. Once a marine always a marine.

God, sometimes he missed those days, treading freezing cold water next to his buddy as part of the hydrograph survey team. They'd do a neat over-the-horizon insert, navigate to the beach, and hide the craft. Then, while two guys directed, they'd extend the chem-light rope out three hundred meters into the ocean, a pair of marines treading water every twenty-five meters in order to analyze the gradient and consistency of the ocean floor, information that would be used for a major beach campaign. It could take eight hours to get all the info. Eight hours of dark silence, treading water and feeling your legs go numb. Basic biological functions happened in the course of eight hours. New guys got embarrassed or ashamed. Old guys simply accepted the warmth of urine suddenly passing through cold water as a kind of camaraderie, a kind of sharing that made your team-mates closer to you than your wife or mother or sister. You couldn't explain that to women. They just didn't get it.

Being a marine made you part of something, linked you to something noble. He'd gone out there with guys, good guys who did good work and never offered excuses. He'd recognized the look in their eyes because it was the look he had in his own. He'd known the set of their jaws, the sheer determination of their will. They'd sat up there on planes, prepared to make midnight jumps down to drop zones they couldn't see, and no one had bitched and no one had moaned. They'd shared their fear quietly, in the steam fogging up their goggles. Then when the command came, they'd risen as one, stood in line, and each hit the butt of the guy in front of him in the universal signal of 'Jump, and God go with you.'

He'd liked it. He'd thought he'd finally found something he could do, a place he belonged. But even marines had to take orders, and the first time he'd had to deal with a hypocritical, shit-for-brains, wife-beating senior officer, he'd lost it. He'd tried to hold his temper. He had. But then he was thinking of Merry Berry and all those nights he'd listened to his father's jump boots clip down the hall to her room. And he was thinking of all the times he tried to tell someone of what really went on in their house at night and all the times he was beaten by the colonel for 'spreading ugly, foul rumors.'

You got a problem with me, boy? You fight like a man, you take me on, hit me if you think you can. But don't go spreading lies, boy. That's the way a wuss fights, a weak, pussy-whipped mama's boy.

One night his CO had pulled back his hand to smack his wife, and J.T. had stepped over the edge. He'd beaten the man to within an inch of his life and would've beaten him more. Would've like to pulverize his head, smash the man into the ground until nothing remained. Four guys had to pull him off. And the wife called him a brute and ran back to her mushy-faced husband, throwing her arms around his neck and burying her black eye against his shoulder.

That had been the end of the Marine Corps for J. T. Dillon.

At last he saw what he'd been waiting to see – Marion peering down over the edge of the pool.

He pushed himself off the bottom and rocketed toward the top. He emerged in a flurry of water, shaking his head like a Labrador and spraying his sister liberally.

'Now, that's a dive!' he exalted, and shook his head again.

'Oh, for God's sake.' Marion took a step back and stared at him in disgust. Then she looked down at her water-spotted silk tank top. 'Look what you've done, J.T.! Christ, it's like you're six years old or something.'

'Loosen up, Marion. Wanna swim, or are agents too tough for that?'

He got what he wanted in under thirty seconds. Marion was as predictable as a wind-up doll. She might as well walk around with a sign reading

EGO – PUSH HERE FOR BEST RESULTS.

'I can fucking swim.' She jabbed the air with her bony index finger. 'Suicides.'

'Suicides? I don't know, Marion. Pretty serious for a woman.' He continued treading water and smiling at his little sister.

'Oh, you're going to pay for that, J.T. First one who cries uncle loses.'

She grabbed the bottom of her tank top and to his amusement, stripped it off. He had her mad and he had her wired. He would feel bad about it, but she was an adult; she should know better than to take up the gauntlet without thinking it through. Suicides involved swimming the length of the pool, jumping out to do five push-ups, diving back in, and repeating the process. They required serious upper body strength, giving the man the clear advantage. Not that Marion would ever admit to something like that.

Not perfect, ambitious Marion.

Her linen shorts puddled onto the deck. He discovered that even his sister's underwear was businesslike – practical pink Lycra bra and panties that were less revealing than a bathing suit. Had Roger gotten tired of efficient underclothing? Even J.T. wasn't self-destructive enough to ask his sister that question.

He swam to the end of the pool, hefted himself out, and stood.

'Ready?'

Marion had that gleam in her eye and that tilt of her chin that said she was more than ready. She was going to wipe the deck with his ass. His sister had been keeping in shape too. No fat on that body and no glimmer of weakness in that gaze.

He was looking forward to the competition.

'Go.'

They sprang in unison, firing into the pool like serious seals.

J.T. made it to the other end first, but he had length on his side. It also took him slightly longer to pull his entire six-foot frame from the water. Two steps forward and he dropped squarely onto his flattened palms. He was aware of Marion right beside him. One, two, three, four, five.

Up and into the water we go.

He was adrenaline and he was energy and he was delighted.

The first ten laps were easy. Then lungs started to burn more, motions took on a rubbery, slow-motion-like feel. He heard Marion's labored breaths as she fell down for more push-ups. Then again, maybe he was just listening to his own.

They both stumbled a bit upon rising, jostled into each other, then like punch-drunk fools exchanged glares and dove back into the pool for more.

After fifteen laps they definitely weren't seals any-more. Not even walruses. More like corked bottles bobbing in the water and reaching desperately for shore. His chest seemed to have been invaded by an army of stinging red ants and his biceps were as obedient as overcooked spaghetti. Marion's push-ups made her look like a tepee swaying in the breeze.

But she didn't cry uncle. Not Marion.

And he didn't cry uncle. Not J.T.

He decided they had more in common than they appreciated. They were both stupid beyond words, weak, ugly children determined to prove that they weren't.

Fuck you, Colonel, sir.

He hefted himself out for number twenty. His hand slipped and he went splashing back in. Marion was still in the water beside him. She seemed to be beating at the deck more than using it to pull herself up.

'You're never going to say it, are you?' he gasped.

'Bite me.'

'Such language, Marion.'

'Bite me.'

She gave a last lunge and managed to beach herself on the patio, flailing on her stomach like a dying fish. He had no choice but to follow.

'We'll say it together.'

'Youcryuncleifyouwanttocryuncle!' she expelled in one breathless rush.

'Yeah? Then let's see your next push-up, Pocahontas.'

Her eyes closed, she groaned but didn't move and didn't cry uncle. He decided two could play that game. He beached himself beside her and concentrated on enjoying the warm, solid feel of his patio.

Idly, in the hazy world of the oxygen-deprived, he thought that he felt the best he'd felt in days. Like liquid gold.

He was going to hate himself in the morning, but then, he could say that about innumerable things he'd done the night before. At least suicides weren't likely to come after him with a shotgun or give him a hangover.

Marion was moving. She planted her hands on the deck and prepared to lift her quivering body.

'You just don't quit, do you?' he asked with genuine awe.

'No.' She gritted her teeth and with a determined grunt heaved her body up. Her arms shuddered like leaves. Slowly, so painstakingly he had to grit his teeth to watch, she lowered herself to the patio and touched her nose to the surface. Even good form.

'One,' she gasped, triumphant.

So he was forced onto his arms to do five more.

Oh, well, he thought philosophically. Sooner or later one of them was bound to drop dead.

An hour later they were both collapsed on the patio

chairs. Not moving. Not talking. Just lying – and lying suddenly felt like hard work.

Through the sliding glass door J.T. could see Rosalita bent over Angela's seated form, massaging suds through her short-cropped hair. Angela had changed into a pair of old khaki shorts and a white tank top. From his vantage point he could see her legs clearly, the way her thighs curved into rounded kneecaps, which gave way to slender calves, which tapered to delicate bare ankles.

He'd always loved bare ankles. Exposed ankles and bare feet. Feet could be incredibly sexy, especially small, dainty feet sporting red-painted toenails.

Rachel had painted her toenails. Sometimes, if he'd been a very good boy, she'd let him paint her toenails. He remembered late Saturday nights when she would lie back on their down-covered bed and place her small white foot on his dusky chest. She would relax, talking, laughing, giggling over inconsequential things while her long blond hair pooled around her like a halo. His job was to carefully apply the glossy red lacquer to her toenails and enjoy the sound of her happiness. He'd always liked Saturday nights.

Then there were the Sunday mornings when Teddy would crawl into bed with them, and J.T. had finally understood why people loved the smell of talcum powder.

Shit.

He didn't want to think about any of that.

That was always the kicker for him. He didn't have the stamina for the bad memories or the strength for the good.

'You want to talk about Roger?' he asked Marion, apropos of nothing.

'No.'

'I thought you guys had a good marriage, you know – other than the fact that he was Daddy's hand-picked henchman and had absolutely no redeeming qualities of his own.'

'Didn't I just say I didn't want to talk about it?'

'Yeah, but we both know I'm a son of a bitch.'

She snorted at that and they both drifted into silence. 'He left me,' she said finally, her voice flat. 'He found some young cocktail waitress and decided she was the love of his life.'

'Bastard.'

'Yeah. Guess you can say you were right, J.T.'

He nodded but didn't actually say the words. He didn't have the heart to do that to her, not to proud Marion, who he would have sworn had actually loved Lieutenant Colonel Roger MacAllister. 'I'm sorry, Marion,' he said softly. 'I . . . When Rachel died . . . It's tough. I know it's tough.'

She was silent for a moment, then turned toward him. 'I hate him, J.T. You can't imagine how much I hate him for betraying me.'

He wanted to reach over and take her hand. He was afraid if he did, she'd snap it off at the wrist. 'You're better off,' he said, but the words sounded weak. 'He wasn't strong enough for you, Marion. You need a real man, not some army bureaucrat. That's the lowest life form imaginable.'

She returned to staring at the sky. 'Maybe.'

'Have you filed for divorce?'

'I should. It would kill Daddy though. He's already furious with Roger and me for not having produced grandkids.'

J.T. read between the lines. Angry at her *and* Roger? He doubted it. He bet the good old colonel called Marion into his room on a regular basis and screamed that she was a bad wife, disobedient daughter, and an all-round failure as a woman for not giving birth. Yeah, Colonel was probably spitting mad at not having another life to ruin.

'Daddy's already dying, so I'd go ahead with the divorce. If it kills him a little faster, well, there are a whole host of people willing to pay you for that. Of course, I top the list, or I would if I had money. I've lost all that now.'

Her lips thinned disapprovingly, but for a change Marion didn't pursue the subject of the colonel.

'I think Angela is a fraud,' she said, abandoning traditional battlegrounds for new territory. 'She lies through her teeth.'

'No shit, Sherlock.'

'Why, J.T., I thought you hated liars. I thought your twisted moral code did not tolerate such behavior.'

He shrugged. 'I'm getting old, Marion. The world is wearing me down.' He turned to look at the woman in question, her shoulders covered by old towels, and her eyes closed while her hair marinated. He remembered her pounding his chest with those tiny hands that now gripped the chair arms.

She was bright, she was proud, she was determined.

She'd shot her husband. He'd tried to beat her with a baseball bat.

'I want to know who she is,' he said. 'Can you help me, Marion?'

There was a long, long silence. 'What do you mean?' his sister asked carefully.

'I mean, of course she's lying and of course Angela's not her real name. Normally I wouldn't pursue the matter. It's bad for business. But now I want to know. I want to know who she is, who's her husband, and what the hell has he done.'

'You're sure?'

'Yes.'

'You're serious?'

'Yes.'

'I already started.'

'What?'

'I took her fingerprints,' Marion said calmly. 'I faxed them in to be analyzed against the national database. It's already been twenty-four hours. Anytime now I should be getting a call telling me exactly who she is.'

His mouth opened and closed several times. He wanted to be angry but couldn't pull off the emotion. When he'd agreed to let his sister stay, had he really thought she would do anything less? Proud, ambitious, driven Marion?

And he wanted to know the answer.

'You'll tell me what you learn,' he commanded quietly, 'and no one else. If she has done something, Marion, if she is in trouble, you won't handle it –'

'Like hell. I am a federal agent –'

'No! You're my sister. You're here as my sister and that's what I want you to be. Five more days, Marion, is that asking too much? Five days, please just be my sister. I don't mind so much being your brother. I'll try not to embarrass you.'

She was silent. Stunned. He could feel it. For once, cool Marion wasn't so composed. 'All right,' she said, and seemed as shocked as he was by her answer. 'I'll tell you what I find, J.T. And it's up to you to deal with it. For five days.'

'Thank you. I mean, honestly, thank you.'

The sliding door opened. Angela appeared on the patio, looking self-conscious. Her hair had been rinsed and blown dry, though it still looked a little damp around the edges. She raked one hand through the short strands, then knotted her hands in front of her. 'Well? What do you think?'

She looked beautiful. The fading sun sparked the rich brown color, giving it fire. Her face looked pale and lovely, her eyes endlessly deep. He thought she looked nothing like the woman she'd been just hours before.

And that scared him.

He said, 'It suits you.'

'That's what a disguise is supposed to do, right? Suit you.'

'You do learn fast.'

'I do,' she assured him. 'So don't worry about me and my little outbursts, J.T. I will get tough. And I'm going to learn how to shoot that gun!'

Marion shook her head. 'You'll be sorry, J.T.,' she murmured under her breath. 'You'll be sorry.'

Dinner on the patio was a silent affair. J.T. grilled swordfish. Angela and Marion consumed it without comment. As soon as the last bite was taken, Angela rose, cleared the table, and disappeared into the kitchen.

Marion lit a cigarette. J.T. stared at all the stars and wished his throat didn't feel so dry. He could feel sweat bead his upper lip, his shoulders, his arms. He told himself it was the heat, but he was lying. He wanted a beer. He was staring at Marion's and coveting it like a man lost in the desert.

Find the zone, he told himself. Use the zone.

But the phone rang and jarred him back out.

Marion looked at him for one moment, then got up to answer it. He sat there alone with the crickets, his gaze still locked on her beer.

Just one sip, maybe two.

You gave your word.

Ah, Christ, it's just a beer. What's so criminal about a man having a beer? Men shouldn't listen to women anyway, it only gets them into trouble.

You will not be an alcoholic.

Having a beer after dinner is not alcoholism, it's enjoying a beer. Just one. I drank all the time in the service, we all did. And could we perform? We always performed. It helps take off the edge. Christ, I want to take off the edge.

Find the zone.

Fuck you, J.T. You know you're a liar, you know there's no real zone. Only time you find it is when you're in battle, and rifle shots crack the air and adrenaline buzzes in your ear. The only time you're calm, you're centered, you're at peace, is when someone's trying to kill you. And that's just plain twisted.

His hand reached out on its own. His fingers curled around the base of the cold, wet bottle.

God, he was so thirsty. His fingers were trembling. He wanted, he wanted, he wanted.

The sliding glass door slammed back and he leapt guiltily, stuffing his hand beneath his thigh.

137

Marion stood on the patio with the lights golden around her. The picture shook him back to other times. Marion standing at the foot of his bed in her long white nightgown, her blond hair cascading down her back, her hands twisting in front of her. Marion begging him to save her, while the colonel pounded at his locked door and demanded his children let him in.

J.T. searching for a place to hide his sister. The colonel taking the door off its hinges.

He bit his lower lip to contain the memories.

She took a step forward, then another. Slowly her face became visible. She was uncommonly pale.

'Angela isn't in the kitchen,' she whispered. 'She isn't anywhere in the house.'

J.T. nodded dumbly.

'That was the Information Division. I know who she is, J.T. And, my God, I think I may have screwed up. I may have really, really screwed up.'

12

Lieutenant Lance Difford was getting old.

He was unbearably conscious of it these days. His hair had thinned considerably; it was harder to get up in the mornings. Coffee was starting to hurt his stomach and he was actually contemplating giving up doughnuts and prime rib.

Now the weather was getting colder and yeah, his insomnia was growing worse.

He wasn't actually that old – fifty was hardly one step away from the grave in this day and age. He'd never planned on leaving the force until he was sixty. He was a good lieutenant, a decent cop, a respected man. Once, he'd thought he'd spend his days investigating death, helping the Hampden County DA prosecute homicides, and eventually retire to Florida to visit baseball's spring training camps.

Then a girl was found outside of Ipswich, her head beaten in and her own nylons wrapped around her neck. Eight months later they had another girl in Clinton and calls from the DA in Vermont wanting to compare their crime scenes with homicides from Middlebury and Bennington.

Virtually overnight Difford went from low-key police work to one of the highest-profiled cases Massachusetts had ever seen. At the end he could summon unbelievable amounts of manpower just by snapping his fingers, from county resources to state resources to the FBI. Everyone wanted to help catch the man who'd probably killed four women in three states. Except then it became five women, then six women, then ten.

Difford had aged a lot those days. Six task forces operating around the clock and the most manpower logged on a single investigation in the state's history.

What we have here, boys, is the worst serial killer New England has seen since Albert DeSalvo in '67. And you know how many mistakes he's made? Zero.

Special Agent Quincy had them staking out grave sites and memorial services without avail. They'd arranged with columnists to profile the victims, keeping their names and tragedy fresh in the public mind. Maybe the guy would contact a loved one to brag. Maybe the guy was actually the bartender at the local police hangout, pumping officers for details. They'd executed the case like a textbook study, and still more blond daughters/wives/mothers went out for a drive and never came home.

Then one night Difford had gotten the phone call, not on the hotline but at home. The woman's voice had been so muffled, he could barely discern her words.

'I think I know who you're looking for,' she whispered without preamble. Difford had the image of a woman crouched in a closet, her hand cupping her mouth, her shoulders hunched in fear.

'Ma'am?'

'Is it true it's a blunt wooden object? Could it be a baseball bat?'

Difford gripped the phone tighter. 'That could be, ma'am,' he said carefully. 'Would you like to make a statement? Could you come to the station?'

'No. No, no, absolutely not. He'd kill me. I know it.' Her voice rose an octave before she cut it off. Difford listened to her deep, steadying breaths as she tried to pull herself together. 'I know who it is,' she said. 'It's the only explanation. The bats, his temper, all the unexplained hours . . . The look I sometimes see in his eye. I just didn't want to believe –' Her voice broke. 'Promise me you'll protect my daughter. Please promise me that. Then I'll give you anything.'

'Ma'am?'

'This man, this killer you're looking for – he's one of you.'

Difford felt the chill shudder up his spine, and he knew then that they had him. The Hampden County DA had become involved in the case at the request of the Berkshire County DA – the minute the Berkshire County team began to suspect a Berkshire County cop might be involved.

The next morning Difford arranged with the Berkshire County DA to keep Officer Jim Beckett busy that afternoon. Then Difford paid a visit to Beckett's wife.

Difford liked Theresa Beckett. He didn't know why. He'd been prepared to hate her, to think nothing of her. If her accusation was true, then she was the Bride of Frankenstein. What kind of woman married a killer? What kind of police force gave him a job?

Maybe it was the way Theresa sat across from them, so young and scared, but still answering their questions one by one. Maybe it was the way she cradled her two-year-old daughter against her neck when the baby cried, rocking her gently and whispering over and over again that everything would be all right. Maybe it was the way she handed over her life to them. Every small, tortured detail, with her whole face telling them she would do the right thing, she needed to do the right thing.

They stripped her bare that first week. They met with her at prearranged locations every afternoon and dissected her marriage. How long had she known Beckett? Where did he come from? What did she know of his family? What was he like as a husband, a father? Was he violent? Did he ever try to choke her? What about sex? How often? What kinds of positions? Any S&M, choking, sodomy? Hard-core pornography?

And she answered. Sometimes she couldn't look them in the eye. Sometimes tears silently streaked down her cheek, but she gave them everything they asked for and then she gave them even more. She'd kept logs of his car odometer for six months. She'd noted what time he left for work, what time he came home, and listed any inexplicable scratches or bruises on his body.

She told them that Jim Beckett actually wore a wig. Shortly after their marriage he'd shaved his head, his chest, his arms, his legs, his pubic hair, everything. The man was completely hairless, like a marble sculpture. The kind of perp that would leave no hair samples behind at the crime scene.

She told them he was cold, arrogant, and without remorse. The kind of man who would poison the neighbor's dog because he objected to a Pekingese shitting on his lawn. She told them he was relentless, the husband who always got his way. The kind of person who knew instinctively how to make people suffer without even raising his fist.

And each afternoon when they tucked their notebooks away, they told her they needed more conclusive information before they could move against Officer Beckett, and they left her to face her husband alone for another evening.

By the seventh day, they thought they had enough, but apparently so did Beckett. They never figured out who leaked what, but he walked into a sandwich shop on his lunch hour, tailed by two agents, and never came back out. That simply he dropped off the face of the earth.

They moved in force.

Difford still remembered the look on Theresa's face, the way her eyes widened, the way her whole body swayed that afternoon as she opened her door and investigators swarmed her house. They all wore white airpacks borrowed from the fire department, full laboratory treatment suits with hair covers to keep them from further contaminating the crime scene. They looked like creatures from a bad sci-fi flick, weighted down with equipment, moving with an eerie rustle, and descending upon her home.

Samantha had begun to cry, so Theresa called her mother to come take her daughter away.

Then she sat alone on the sofa as the men pulled up her hardwood floor, ripped up kitchen tiles, dug up sections of the basement floor, and chipped mortar from between the stones of her fireplace. They vacuumed all surfaces with a special high-powered vac that picked up hair particles and dust particles. The bags were sent to the Mass. State Police crime lab for analysis. Stains on the carpet were cut out and sent. Ditto with the kitchen tiles. Later, the police crime lab said it had never churned out so many reports on baby saliva and spit-up peaches. One patch of dirt in the basement revealed bovine blood approximately one year old.

Next they brought in the lights. The 500-watt quartz light that helped highlight unseen hair and fibers. The ultraviolet radiation light with a 125-watt blue bulb to fluoresce hair, fiber, and body fluid. The blue-green luma light also to reveal hair, fiber, body fluids, and fingerprints. Finally they even dragged in portable laser lights and infrared. All the toys the CPAC boys never got to play with, never had the resources for, that were now being offered up to them from other states, other agencies, and the FBI.

Half the state police force looked under every stone and twig for the elusive Jim Beckett while the other half dismantled his house in search of evidence of his crimes. Their first discovery was a six-month supply of birth control pills stuffed behind a piece of insulation in the attic, right over the boxes labeled

SAMANTHA'S OLD CLOTHES, TWO MONTHS.

'They're mine,' Theresa told them. Her gaze rested on Difford. 'I got them from a clinic in North Adams. He wanted a second child. I couldn't . . . I just couldn't.' She added without thinking, 'Please don't tell Jim. You have no idea what he can do.'

Then, her own words penetrating, she sank down onto the sofa. One of the officers, a victim trauma expert, sat down next to her and placed an arm around her shoulders.

In the front hall closet they found a family pack of condoms. Theresa said Jim never used them, so the condoms were sent off to the lab for the latex to be analyzed and compared with residue found in the victims. They also discovered five baseball bats and a receipt for an even dozen. Later, analysis of the fireplace ashes revealed wood compatible with the kind used in the bats, plus a chemical compound reminiscent of the glaze finish.

They also recovered four test tubes containing pre-measured amounts of a blue liquid identified as the sleeping drug Halcion, as well as the *Compendium of Pharmaceuticals and Specialties*, a virtual bible of most drugs, their manufacturers, their properties, and side effects.

In the attic, tucked behind a loose board, they retrieved a stun gun and a rubber mallet. But they couldn't find any direct links between Jim Beckett and the victims. Not the trophies serial killers were liable to take, or any traces of blood or hair.

What they did find was copies of files requested by Beckett from Quantico's Training Division. The files contained the profiles and interviews of several serial killers. Beckett had gone through and marked them up with such notes as HIS FIRST MISTAKE. HIS SECOND MISTAKE. THAT WAS SLOPPY.

At the end they found one last summary comment: DISCIPLINE IS THE KEY.

And the week turned into six months without any sign of Jim Beckett.

Now Difford rose off the sofa. He looked out the window of the safe house and identified the unmarked patrol car keeping guard across the street. He checked the front door and then, because he still remembered what had happened that one dark night, would always remember what happened that night Beckett returned for his revenge, Lieutenant Difford checked the closet.

All was clear.

He walked down the hall of the tiny bungalow and opened the last bedroom door. Samantha Beckett slept in a puddle of moonlight, her face soft and smooth and surrounded by beautiful golden hair. Difford leaned against the doorjamb and just watched her.

She looked so unbelievably tiny. She still cried for her mommy. Sometimes she even cried for her daddy. But she must have a lot of Theresa's blood in her, because at four years of age she was also a real trooper. Most afternoons the kid beat the pants off him in dominoes.

Difford sighed. He did feel old, but maybe these were the days for it.

'God, Theresa, I hope you know what you're doing,' Difford muttered.

He tucked the blankets beneath Samantha's chin, then finally closed the door.

'I failed your mom,' he confessed in the hush of the darkened hallway. 'But I won't fail you, kid. I swear, I won't fail you.'

He sat down in the living room, the light on, his police revolver across his knee.

He still couldn't bring himself to close his eyes.

The previous week the media had asked Difford what concerned citizens should do to safeguard their lives now that the infamous Jim Beckett had escaped.

There'd been only one thing he could think of to say. 'Lock your closets.'

13

When it grew past seven and there was still no sign of Angela, J.T. admitted to himself that he was worried. At seven-thirty he gave up memorizing the ceiling fan and pulled on a pair of jeans.

He had only one hunch, but it was a good one. It was cool outside. Fall moving into the desert and bringing some relief. The sky had expelled the sun and now a moon rose waxy and pale. Just enough light to frame the saguaros as frozen soldiers.

The desert wasn't quiet. It hummed and pulsed with the low, rhythmic chorus of the crickets, the eerie cries of the dry wind, and the faint fluttering of Gila woodpeckers whirring among the saguaros. Somewhere far off, a lone coyote mournfully howled.

J.T. left behind the oasis of his swimming pool and headed for the shooting range. He may have locked up his .22, but Angela had reclaimed hers.

He spotted her from thirty feet back, and his footsteps slowed. He didn't call out because he didn't want to startle an armed woman. Then he didn't call out simply because he couldn't think of anything to say.

He stood in the moonlight and watched her point her unloaded gun at hay bales and pull the trigger. Again and again. And then she moved and pointed, trying new stances, practicing moving and shooting.

Over and over.

He could see that her arms shook. He could tell that her fingers had grown thick and sluggish, but she didn't stop. She had set up a flashlight to illuminate her targets and she seemed intent on not wasting the light. She

146

raised the gun and sighted the target and pulled the trigger yet again.

And he could tell that the minute she tightened her finger around the trigger, she dipped the nose of her gun, so that maybe she thought she was hitting the target, but really she was simply killing dirt.

A long time later Tess walked back to the house, her fingers too sore to curl and her arm a mass of knotted muscles. The palm of her hand hurt, her biceps hurt. Everything hurt. But she was trying.

She walked into the yard. And as her hands pressed against the sliding glass door, she knew she wasn't alone.

She turned, the gun empty against her bare thigh, and peered out into the night.

She didn't see him. She felt him.

His gaze washed over her. She felt it touch her face, then move down slowly, caressing the pulse throbbing in her throat, her breasts, her belly, her hips. It traveled back up, settled on her mouth.

A red match glowed in the dark. He brought it up to his lips, cupping it in front of him so that it briefly illuminated his jaw. He inhaled sharply until the end of his cigarette glowed. Then with two quick jerks, he shook out the match.

The darkness settled back between them, no longer calm but filled with a slow-heated pulse. She felt the throbbing rhythm in her blood. She felt the fierce feral pull of his gaze. Her lips parted.

He stepped forward.

'We need to talk.' His arm came up and he dumped a six-pack of beer on the patio table. 'They're for you, Theresa Beckett. Start drinking. And tell me everything.'

'They couldn't find him. They told me they had him under surveillance, that they knew what he was doing at all times, that I was safe. Then one afternoon he entered a sandwich shop and was never seen again. Special

Agent Quincy predicted Jim would be back. Sooner or later Jim would return to kill me.'

You turned on him, Mrs. Beckett, and he didn't see that coming. That's a big blow to a man like him. Now the only way he'll be able to restore his ego, his sense of self, is to kill you. He'll come back. And he won't wait long.

'I made them put Samantha in hiding. We didn't think Jim would hurt her – he seemed to honestly adore her – but we couldn't take any chances. I remained in the house, night after night. Just waiting. For six months.'

She lay in bed every night, covers pulled up to her chin, ears strained, eyes open, and heart stuck permanently in her throat. She chewed her fingernails down to raw nubs. She leapt at small noises. She forgot how to live, how to feel. And winter rolled down from the hills and blanketed Williamstown with snow.

'They searched for him everywhere, but they didn't have many leads. He rarely spoke of the past and the investigators uncovered little. His family was dead, his foster parents dead. His only friends were from the police force, and they were more like acquaintances. There didn't seem to be anyplace for him to go, and yet he disappeared absolutely, completely, as if he'd never existed. I used to wonder if he wasn't just some horrible phantom. I guess the cops began to think the same. Originally there were ten men watching my house. But then one week turned into two months. Then four months. Then six months. Just two plain-clothes officers were still around. And suddenly Jim reappeared.'

Scratching resonated on the roof.

She lunged across her bed, yanked the receiver from the phone, and stabbed the touch-tone buttons.

Lieutenant Lance Difford would pick up, she'd murmur the code, and the police would descend if they hadn't already spotted Jim on the roof.

It would be all right.

Except the phone had no dial tone.

'Waiting for me, wife?'

She looked up.

And her husband stepped out of her closet, wearing his Berkshire County police uniform and looking like a young Robert Redford. He was hefting a baseball bat, and she could see dark smudges and loose hairs matting the end.

She leapt for the nightstand, her ragged fingernails sliding ineffectively across the smooth surface. And with agile perfection Jim lunged forward and wrapped a hand around her ankle.

'No, no!' *she cried, clawing at the mattress, bruising her fingertips on the bedpost.*

He yanked her onto the floor, and she landed hard, the breath escaping her in a painful whoosh. She fought anyway, trying to crawl away as his hand snaked up her exposed calf.

'Where is Sam?'

'You'll never find her!'

'Didn't they tell you what I can do, Theresa? Didn't they tell you exactly how I like to inflict pain?'

His fingers dug into her ankle. Then she felt his breath as he leaned over her back and pinned her neck against the carpet with his forearm. He spoke. His voice drifted over her like velvet, soft, heavy, suffocating her word by word.

'You helped them. Theresa. You told them things about me. Did you think it would go unpunished?'

Jim curved his hand almost lovingly around her exposed throat. Her pulse leapt like a captured mouse against the base of his palm. He slowly started squeezing the air from her lungs.

He told her to fight him. He told her he liked it when they fought him.

She squirmed, her heels searching for traction against the old carpet. She knew he would asphyxiate her slowly, then revive her and do it again, and revive her and do it again. Somewhere along the way, he would rape her and torture her. And then, when he finally tired of the sport, he would pick up the bat and she would be grateful that it was ending.

Her fingers flexed and unflexed above his grip. Her hips writhed desperately.

In her mind, she kept calling for the police. She was so sure they would figure out what was going on. That any minute they'd bang down the front door. They'd save her. No one came.

Spots appeared before her eyes, white and dizzying. She felt herself spinning away, sinking into a dark, whirling vortex of nothing. She was dying and a part of her was too frightened, too overwhelmed to care.

If you don't fight now, she thought dimly, you will die and years from now your daughter won't even remember your name.

'I know what you're thinking,' Jim whispered in her ear. 'You're looking deep inside yourself, trying to find the will to defy me. You don't have it, Theresa. I took it from you. I've known you since the day I met you, and I've turned you inside out and climbed inside of you and now there's nothing left of you. Every bit of you, every last thought you have, really belongs to me. I made you. I'm inside your mind. I own you.'

The lights grew brighter behind her eyelids. The burning spread from her lungs to her whole chest. Her fingers moved feebly, then stilled.

His hands slipped from her throat. And she slammed her fist into his nose.

He fell back with a guttural cry and she didn't wait. Her flailing hand reached for the lower drawer, scrambling with the handle.

'You bitch!' He rolled off her. She heard the heavy swish of air as he raised the baseball bat.

'Please, please,' she whispered hoarsely, and ripped the drawer from the nightstand.

A sharp sound, a whistle. She ducked and rolled, and the floor shook with the force of the bat hitting the carpet.

'I'm going to kill you!'

She was crying and rolling and crying and fumbling with the damn drawer, scrambling through the contents and praying for one last miracle to save her.

Another whistle.

The bat came down on her thigh.

She heard a loud crack, then felt a red-hot bolt of pain fire through her leg. And suddenly she wasn't frightened anymore, she wasn't exhausted. She was just really pissed off.

She tried to leap to her feet, but the blinding pain toppled her. Savage, fierce, stabbing agony that ripped up her leg and brought tears to her eyes. She sensed more than saw the autographed Louisville Slugger arch and suspend.

Her head turned. She stared at him as he stood tall and majestic in an icy sliver of moon, his fake blond hair waving over his forehead, his smooth, hairless chest like sculpted marble.

And she thought that no one had ever told her the devil would be so beautiful.

The bat came down.

Her hand curled around the gun she had sought.

And she moved through the pain, screaming her terror and agony and fury as she rolled over her cracked femur bone and raised her trembling arms.

The bat slammed into the carpet.

She started firing the gun.

'You hit him,' J.T. said at last. She was into the fourth beer now and swaying a bit. Her eyes were flat and glassy.

'Yes.' Her gaze fixed on the shimmering water of the pool. 'I hit him in the shoulder, enough to take him out. The police heard the gunshots, Difford came bursting through. They took him away. It was over.'

'But you never stopped being afraid.'

'No. He was right. I couldn't get him out of my mind. I sold the house, took Sam and we ran. For two years. New names, new towns. I go by Tess Williams now, but

Samantha only calls me Mommy. She can't keep track of the names and she's always scared she'll get them wrong. So she doesn't learn names anymore, she's too frightened. It's a horrible thing to do to a child.'

'You did what you had to do.'

'It wasn't enough. I dreamed about him every night, and every night he was coming after me. A man like that . . . he shouldn't be left alive.'

'No. He shouldn't.'

'He killed two prison guards last week. Beat them to death. He's very strong, you know. I wish Massachusetts had the death penalty.'

'Angela –'

'You might as well call me Tess.'

'No, I don't think I should. You're using an alias to protect yourself. From everything you've just told me, that's an excellent idea. But, Angie, Marion took your fingerprints. She faxed them through the Nogales Police Department to the FBI. That's how I found out your real name.'

She was silent, minute turning into minute. 'Oh.'

J.T. found himself reaching out and taking her hand. It felt cold. 'She was just doing her job. She knew you were lying and she wanted to check up on you.'

'I understand.'

'She knows she screwed up. Given Beckett's background, it's understandable that you wanted to keep your identity secret even from the law. Well, that ship has sailed. Marion would like to bring you in now. She'll escort you back to Quantico personally, set up a safe house, and provide round-the-clock protection.'

'Didn't you just listen to the story I told you?'

'The police made a mistake the first time, but they're smarter now –'

'It doesn't matter!' She yanked her hand from his and stood. 'Don't you get it? He's a cop. He knows their procedures, he thinks like them. As long as I'm with them, I'm not safe because, let's face it, cops operate with rules and Jim has none. He can anticipate them, outmaneuver them, and I'm the one who ends up alone, facing a baseball bat. I won't go through that again. I won't sit around like a stupid mouse waiting for the cat to pounce.'

He looked at her silently.

'I'm staying here,' she stated. 'Even if the Nogales police know who I am, Jim has no contacts in Arizona, right? And the FBI agents in Quantico who called Marion, they can be told to keep their mouths shut, right?'

'I'll speak to Marion about it.'

'Fine, then it's settled. You don't understand, J.T. You think you do. You watch me try to swim and shoot at hay bales and you think I'm helpless. But there is one thing I'm good at. I know how to think like Jim Beckett.' Her lips twisted. Her eyes were shiny with a glaze of tears. She brushed them away with the back of her hand. 'I'm staying. If he does find me here, then I'll deal with him. Or you'll get to deal with him. You may not like it, you may not agree with me, but I was smart when I came here. If there's any person fit to take on Jim Beckett, it's an angry, arrogant asshole like you.'

Christ, she looked like something. She looked strong and she looked fierce. He wanted to yank her down onto his lap and kiss her until her fingertips gripped his shoulders and she roared his name with need. He wanted to feel her quiver as she came.

'We're back on the shooting range tomorrow, Angela. You can put your money where your mouth is then, because, sugar, from here on out, I'm going to push you *hard*.'

'Good!'

'You might want to leave now, Angela, or I'm going to rip your clothes off and take you on the patio.'

'Oh.'

'You're still not moving.'

'It's just the beer,' she assured him hastily as she remained in place. He shifted forward and she finally jolted to life. She scurried across the patio, thrust open the sliding glass door, and ran into the house. He could already picture the lock on her bedroom door slamming shut.

He remained sitting in his garden, listening to the crickets, thinking about her story, and staring at the two unopened cans of Michelob.

14

The sun was straight up, no longer fierce but having gentled through the course of the week to a kindly benefactor. It caressed Tess's cheeks and arms, trying to infuse her skin with a hint of color.

The rest of the desert, however, remained acrimonious. The saguaros looked grim and mocking, the sagebrush shuddered in the breeze. A gray roadrunner darted by. In the distance the bleached-out hills sat glumly, weighted down by rickety shanties and hundreds of lines of drying laundry.

The world was muted gold, dried-out brown, and sun-sapped green. Tess stood in the middle of it, wearing a worn white tank top with khaki shorts and feeling just as insipid and plain as her surroundings.

'Are you going to shoot 'em or sculpt 'em?' J.T. quizzed dryly. He'd stripped off his T-shirt to catch a little sun. Clad in ripped denim cutoffs and beat-up sandals, he looked more like a California surfer dude than a desperado. After two hours of watching Tess miss the targets, he also looked bored.

Marion had stopped by the first hour to lend her expertise. Like J.T., she insisted Tess needed to find the zone.

'Concentrate,' the agent had told her again and again. 'Visualize your hand extending to the target, touching the bull's-eye, and sending a bullet through the brain.'

In case that didn't work, J.T. had been modifying her .22, decreasing the trigger pressure for a smoother pull, and trimming the grip so the gun would fit more comfortably in her hand. There were six fundamentals to shooting: position, grip, breath control, sight alignment, trigger squeeze, and follow-through. Tess was now trying to focus on all of them at once. She had a headache.

Tess adjusted her earplugs and rolled her shoulders. Her hands and forearms throbbed dully. It took a lot of strength to pull a trigger repeatedly. Marion had shown off her own forearms, roped with long lines of wiry sinew. To become an agent, a cadet had to be able to pull a handgun trigger twenty-nine times in thirty seconds. A lot of female cadets couldn't do it, but lean, mean Marion could, and she had the muscles to prove it.

Tess was beginning to believe that there was nothing the Dillon children couldn't do.

She just didn't like the gun. She didn't like its weight, its feel, its noise. In her mind the gun remained inherently evil, too vicious and too powerful. And maybe she feared more than anything that once she became comfortable with it, she would turn a corner in herself and never be able to go back. She'd permanently become part of the violence. She would never escape.

You are part of the violence, she reminded herself. *Your options are to control it or be victimized by it.*

She took a deep breath. She told herself the gun was her friend. She'd used it before and it had saved her. She would master the fear and she would master the weapon.

She adapted the stance J.T. had taught her and leveled her arms.

Okay, Tess. You're a lean, mean killing machine. Align, inhale, hold it, squeeze.

She pulled the trigger. It boomed. She jumped and closed her eyes.

She was an idiot.

She finished out the clip fatalistically. When she was done, she turned to J.T.

He shook his head as he'd been shaking it all

afternoon. 'Tess, why are you so afraid of an inanimate object?'

'There's nothing inanimate about a gun!'

'Then you've been watching too many Disney movies.'

He took a step forward and clasped her wrist. He ran one callused finger up her bare thigh, brushing the bottom of her khaki shorts.

She flinched. She blanched. She blushed.

'What are you doing?' she asked furiously.

'Nice scar,' he said. 'Didn't you learn anything from it?'

'Apparently not enough,' she shot back, unable to meet his gaze. He stood too close to her, and she wasn't prepared for the intense desire to lean forward and press her lips against the scar snaking down his chest.

'How . . . how did you get your scar?'

'Guatemala. I think.'

He was still standing before her. His hand was still on her thigh. 'You think?'

'Could've been El Salvador. After a bit, all jungles look alike.'

'So you were fighting?'

'Over a beautiful woman, I'm sure.'

'Of course.' She had a feeling that with him, there had truly been a lot of beautiful women.

'It's true. I think.'

'I see. After a bit, all beautiful women look alike?'

'Sure. Just taste different.'

She pulled away, trying to cover the motion by retrieving spent casings, but obviously not covering it well enough.

'I offended you?' he said after a moment, his voice emotionless, his arms crossing over his chest.

'After a week of your company? Hardly.'

'Now you're shockless? You're that tough?'

'I'm a fully functional bad ass,' she assured him.

'Good,' he said. 'Then you'll have no problem firing the gun.' He smiled at her grimly. 'Again, Tess. We're not leaving here until you get this right. The gun is a tool. Learn to use it.'

He yanked her around and she came up hard against his chest. 'We're going to try an experiment,' he murmured. His whiskered cheek nuzzled back her hair until his lips were on her ear.

'Okay,' she whispered. She was licking her lips.

'Pick up the gun for me.'

'Okay.'

'Put in a fresh clip.'

'Okay.'

'Sight the target.'

She straightened her arms and assumed the Weaver stance. He smoothed his palms down her arms, encircling her wrist with his fingers. 'Tess, you're getting some muscle tone.'

She started shivering. He misinterpreted. '*Chiquita*, you don't even have the safety off yet.'

'I'm just . . . What are you doing?'

'I'm going to shadow you. You shoot, I'll correct. Relax against me. Come on, sweetheart, relax.' He nudged her arms. She stiffened further. 'Tess,' he murmured. His teeth found her earlobe and bit down gently. 'Relax.'

'Oh, my Lord,' she said, and melted into him.

'I always knew that trick would come in handy.' His body shifted, assuming the correct stance and seeming to mold hers. She let him mold her. She could feel his leg hair and his chest hair, his raspy twelve-hour beard.

'Focus on the target,' he told her. 'Fire.'

She did as she was told. She pulled back the trigger, and her arms leapt spasmodically. He caught them right as they bobbed down and forced them up.

Finally receiving proper guidance, the bullet fired straight and true. It buried itself into the outer ring of the target.

'Oh, my God, would you look at that!'

'See,' his voice rumbled in her ear. 'It's not so hard.'

She whispered, 'Again.'

She emptied the clip. Each time, his body contracted around hers, halting her natural flinch, compensating for her mistake. They went through another clip, and the hay bale took a beating.

'Good,' J.T. said. He stepped back, but his hands remained on her shoulders. After a moment his fingers squeezed her stiff muscles, rubbing her down like a star athlete. She closed her eyes and let her head fall forward. He made her feel relaxed, he made her feel loose. He made her feel as if she could do anything.

'All right,' he said. His hands fell away. She tried not to moan. 'Now it's time to try solo. It's just like before. Stay relaxed. Point and shoot. The gun is just a tool in your hand.'

'A tool,' she repeated obediently.

'A tool. You own it, Tess, you control it. It doesn't control you.'

She took a deep breath and exhaled through her nostrils. She positioned her feet and raised the gun. She closed her eyes.

The gun was a natural extension of her hand. Her tool, for her to control, for her to use. She didn't have to pull the trigger unless she wanted to. That was strength. The power to choose.

She chose to pull the trigger. One, two, three, four, five.

And the paper target went flying.

She stared. She was so stunned, she couldn't even move. And then she turned to him, and she smiled with one thousand watts of triumph.

'Did you see that!' she cried, and pointed with her left hand just in case he'd somehow slept through the occasion. 'Did you see that!'

He smiled at her calmly and nodded. 'You hit it. All on your own, you hit it.'

And then he did something she never would have imagined him doing. He reached over and shook her hand.

She couldn't say a word. She felt his firm, reassuring

grip. She returned it with one of her own. Bad ass to bad ass. She'd done it.

Then she grinned at him and whooped. 'I killed the hay bale! I killed the hay bale!'

She unceremoniously handed him the gun and raced to the long-suffering straw to inspect her work.

J.T. watched her go. She hunkered down beside the bale of straw and promptly stuck her finger in a blackened hole like a little kid. Her hair burned like copper wire beneath the sun. It matched her smile, bright, brilliant, and intense enough to make a man look twice.

She found another hole and poked her finger in that one too. God, the grin on her face!

When had she become so beautiful? She looked over at him and smiled again. Then she rested her head against her big-game trophy and he had to blink his eyes against the tightness in his chest.

In this moment she looked perfect, the way she should have looked from the beginning. She was vital and radiant, earthy and innocent.

It was the kind of moment a man should record on film and carry with him in his pocket to remember on other, darker occasions.

His mind, relentless and ruthless as always, filled in the other snapshots to come. Tess sprawled facedown on a carpet, face bruised and pulpy from a baseball bat. Body outlined in white chalk. Clothes torn and ripped.

He looked away. He focused on the dirt.

No, he thought. It won't come to that. She was tougher than that. The police were smarter than that. Hell, maybe Jim Beckett was already out of the country, sipping planter's punch in the Bahamas.

But he didn't believe any of it.

Goddamn, he wanted a drink.

He thought sobriety was supposed to be good, making a man clear-headed, sharp, focused. For him it was the opposite. He couldn't sleep at night. He was constantly edgy, and his mind was drowning beneath the weight of images he could no longer control.

Maybe a guy like him was meant to be drunk. Maybe a guy like him could only really function with the edge worn off.

He noticed things like Marion's cutting comments. He remembered things like the dreams he'd had when he'd returned to the States five years ago, and the fresh hope he'd found as a newly married man.

He remembered the first time he'd seen Rachel, holding a squalling baby and haltingly telling him she had no money anymore. The colonel had thrown her out, her savings were gone, and men didn't pay much for an exhausted mother. She'd come to him because she didn't know who else to go to. And then the first tear had trickled down her cheek, large and silent, as she'd looked away, clearly ashamed. He'd watched her try to calm her screaming baby and simultaneously wipe the moisture from her face. When he still hadn't given her a reply, she'd walked away, her thin shoulders held with more dignity than he could imagine. He'd known then that he would help her. Whatever the colonel had done to her, she was worth more. She was a better person than he'd made her.

He noticed things like when he lay down at night, the ceiling fan never stopped moving. It hummed and hummed and hummed, and stirred the air against his skin so delicately, it was maddening.

Just that morning he'd fallen asleep enraged by the air and woken up to see Rachel standing by his bed. He would have sworn it was her, and not the early Rachel but the woman who'd become his wife. So beautiful, so lovely. She had smiled at him, soft and serene. His heart had broken in his chest all over again.

Hey, babe, Teddy and I are just going to run to the grocery store. We'll be back in an hour. What would you like for dinner?

And last night he'd had more dreams. This time he was running after the Camaro. He could see it so clearly. The kid, the stupid kid was driving in the middle of the road, swerving from side to side. Up ahead he could see the approaching headlights of Rachel's car. And he was screaming and he was running, but the damn Camaro was going too fast, he couldn't catch it.

At the last minute the kid turned his head, but he wasn't the kid anymore. He was a bald, hairless man with cold blue eyes. Jim Beckett. Beckett was grinning and then J.T. looked through the windshield of the approaching car and saw Tess's screaming face.

'Let's celebrate,' Tess said, trotting back over from the bale of straw. 'What do you do to celebrate?'

He jerked himself back to the present. 'To celebrate a successful kill?'

'Yes. A successful kill. What do you do?'

'Straight shots of Cuervo Gold followed by mad, passionate sex. I'm game if you are.'

She blushed, her breathing accelerated. 'I know,' she said brightly, no longer looking at him, 'let's buy strawberries. Can we get strawberries out here?'

'Sure.' His gaze remained on her face. Her lips had parted. Now her tongue darted out to moisten them. She had very pink lips, like rose petals.

'And fresh whipped cream,' she murmured. 'And shortcake. That's it. I'll make strawberry shortcake with dinner.'

'Tess,' J.T. said hoarsely, 'stop toying with me.'

He grabbed her hand, swung her against his chest, and devoured her mouth. He discovered those pink lips and he thrust his tongue between them, hearing her gasp, then hearing her sigh.

He kissed her deeply, like a drowning man trying to find shore. Her fingers dug into his arms and her grip was strong and urgent, just as it should be. He ate her lips, tasted her, and consumed her. And she opened her mouth for him greedily and drew him in even deeper.

Good Lord, he was drowning and he wanted to drown.

As if from a distance, he heard her moan. His hands found her ass and rotated her hips against his hardening length. Her fingernails welted his skin.

She was hungry. Her leg was already rubbing his thigh. Her fingertips danced up his arms, then his collarbone, and tangled in his hair. She pulled on his head.

'Jesus,' he muttered thickly. 'You take it wild.'

'Okay,' she said, and ground her teeth against him. She split his lip, then jerked back in shock. He touched the cut with a finger and pulled it back wet with blood.

'Didn't realize you were into that kind of stuff, Tess.' He put the finger in his mouth and licked it clean.

'I don't know what I'm doing!' Abruptly she buried her forehead against his chest and her shoulders started shaking. 'I'm sorry. I'm sorry.'

She caught him off guard with her sobs. He stood stiffly, stunned, then some old instinct flared gamely to life.

Slowly he curled one arm around her shoulders. She felt tiny against him. Carefully his other hand palmed her head. His thumb stroked her cheek once, twice.

'It will be all right,' he found himself whispering. 'It'll be okay.'

He brushed the tears from her cheek; he stroked her neck. She felt so unbelievably fragile. Images swamped him: A baseball bat arching up. A man arching the bat over her curled, defenseless body. A two-hundred-pound pumped-up giant about to annihilate his hundred-pound wife.

The rage was instantaneous. He blanked it from his mind and held her closer.

'You wanna talk about it?' he asked at last.

'I'm so humiliated,' she moaned.

'Why?' He shifted her more comfortably against his chest but kept his grip. He suspected the first time he let go, she would bolt.

'Because I'm a twenty-four-year-old mother and I don't know how to kiss. And I don't know what to do and I don't know what to want. Oh, God, it's all so messed up and crazy.' Her shoulders started heaving again.

'Your husband was your first?'

'The only one.'

'And lousy?'

'Yes.' Her arms slid around his waist and she clung to him. He hadn't had anyone hold him like that for a very long time. He'd forgotten about these things. The sweetness of a woman's touch. How much comfort she could give a man. How much she could make him feel whole.

And he felt something inside him rip a little.

He didn't want that. Oh, he didn't want that.

He took her hands in his and as fast and painlessly as possible disengaged her from his body. 'You got time now,' he said stiffly. His gazed bounced all around, landing on everything but her. 'Jim Beckett was a bastard and you left him. Now you got your whole life to figure out the rest. You're starting out fresh and twenty-four's not that old.'

'Was I that horrible?'

God, she was killing him. 'No. No, Tess, you weren't. You just . . . it's like your shooting. You were trying too hard and bringing too many things into it with you.'

'Oh.' Her lips twisted. 'So there's a zone for kissing too? I should've figured that.'

'Yeah. You know those zones.'

'I bet you have them all down.'

'Not all of them. But shooting, swimming . . . fucking. Yeah, I guess I have my strengths.'

She fell silent. He used the opportunity to clear his throat. It felt too dry. He suffered another pang of longing for a beer. Any beer. Dirt-cheap beer, he didn't care.

'We should get back to the house.'

'What are we going to learn this afternoon?'

'Hand-to-hand combat.'

'Not hand to baseball bat?'

He winced. 'We'll cover that too.'

More silence. Then she pulled away. 'All right.'

He heard her footsteps as she moved over to the gun case. Heard the sharp *clack* as she popped it open, then the tinkle of brass casings being poured into their container.

He tried to pull himself together.

He kept seeing that damn Camaro. And his father walking down the hall.

He shook his head. *Push it away, J.T., just push it away.*

It didn't work. He needed a beer.

15

'I know where Jim Beckett is.'

'Yes, ma'am?'

'I've seen him in my dreams. He's with a blond woman and there is the sound of dripping water. Slow dripping-water. Drip . . . Drip . . . Drip . . .'

'Ma'am?'

'I smell fresh snow and pine trees. Yes, he has gone to the mountains. The beautiful, beautiful mountains. There, he will be reborn.'

'Uh . . . yes, ma'am. Which mountains?'

'How should I know that, silly girl? You are with the police. I have given you direction, now you must follow!'

The phone clicked. The operator sighed. 'Yes, ma'am,' she whispered. She hit the reset button on her keyboard and her terminal immediately lit up with a fresh call.

'I've found Jim Beckett!'

'Where, sir?'

'He's living across the street from me. I spotted him last night, through the window. I broke my leg, see, but that doesn't mean I'm helpless. Sitting at my window, I see all sorts of things. And last night I saw him, standing in the window, arguing with a woman. I think he may have killed her.'

'May I have your name, sir.'

'Jimmy Stewart. That's J-i –'

'Jimmy Stewart? As in Jimmy Stewart?'

'That's right.'

'Do you watch a lot of Hitchcock films, sir?'

'Why, yes, yes, I do.'

'Thank you, sir.' She disconnected that call on her own. Her terminal immediately lit up again. Five thousand calls a day and still going strong.

'Jim Beckett is my next-door neighbor!'

'Of course, sir.'

'He just moved in last week. I was suspicious right away. The man's bald, you know. What kind of self-respecting man goes around looking like a bowling ball? He's Irish, isn't he? You can't trust the Irish.'

'May I have your name and address, sir?'

'My name? Why do you need my name?'

'We just need a contact, sir. A police officer will follow up with you and take an official statement.'

'I don't want a cop coming to my home.'

'We can do it by phone, but we need your name.'

'Hell, I don't want a cop coming here. Everyone will think I'm a snitch. I'm not a snitch!'

'Of course, sir, but –'

The caller slammed the phone and the operator winced a little, but there was no time for contemplation. Her terminal lit up again, and with a tired sigh she hit the enter key and started over.

Across the room Special Agent Quincy ran down the log sheets, seeing if anything leapt out at him. He'd been in Santa Cruz working on a series of grave robberies and mutilations. Since many disorganized serial killers started with corpses before graduating to living victims, the local law enforcement had gotten the FBI involved early. The hope was they could catch the guy before young women suffered the same fate as the dead. Unfortunately they weren't having much success. At eleven P.M. Quincy had caught the red eye to Boston. He was exhausted, rumpled, and unshowered. He was used to it by now.

He moved on to the tenth page of the log sheet, but still nothing leapt out at him. Operators took each call, logging the caller, their address, return phone number, and tip. The police officers on duty then sorted through the log sheets, scratching off about eighty percent as worthless, eighteen percent as worth calling back, and two percent as worth checking out in person. From 'Jim Beckett is really Elvis' to reports of grand theft auto, the officers got it all.

Quincy abandoned the log sheet and poured himself a second cup of coffee. Instant. He hated that crap. There would be justice in the world the day police officers had cappuccino machines.

Lieutenant Houlihan spotted him from across the room and approached.

'You look like hell,' the lieutenant stated.

'Thanks. It's part of the new Bureau regulation. All agents must look overworked or they're being paid too much. So how's it going here?'

'The bad news is we still have no sign of Jim Beckett. The good news is we may have found Jimmy Hoffa. Oh, and we've averted two attacks of aliens looking to overrun the U.S. government.'

'Not bad.'

'How's the coffee?'

'Pretty damn awful.'

'Thank you, we take a great deal of pride in that. Notice the economy-size jug of Tums sitting next to it.'

Quincy nodded and finished off the cup. He couldn't help wincing at the end, but at least it was caffeine. He set down the cup, rolled his neck, shook out his arms, and worked on feeling human. He nodded toward the gold medal Houlihan wore around his neck. He didn't remember having seen it before.

'New good luck charm?'

Lieutenant Houlihan shifted from side to side, looking suddenly sheepish. 'My wedding band.'

'Really?'

'Well, it meant a great deal to my wife that I wear a band. I kept telling her, in my line of work you don't want to give that much personal info. Three days ago was our one year anniversary. She had my band melted into this medallion and gave it to me. Now we're both happy. Maybe it is lucky. Luck wouldn't hurt these days. You married?'

'Recently divorced.'

Houlihan pointed to his necklace. 'Third wife,' he confessed. 'She's a trauma nurse, it works out much better. I come home three hours late saying I'm sorry but there was a traffic accident and it took us two hours to find the driver's arm, she just nods, tells me she was held late with a drive-by shooting, and dinner's on the table.'

'I see your point.'

'But I imagine with all the traveling you do, it's still rough. Nothing spells cop – or agent – like d-i-v-o-r-c-e.'

Quincy shrugged. The breakup of his marriage still bothered him. 'Yeah, and then guys like Bundy are getting married and fathering children from death row. I'll never understand women.'

'Not that you're bitter.'

Quincy laughed reluctantly. 'Not that I'm bitter,' he agreed.

'So, Agent, do you have any good news for me?'

'I have news,' Quincy said with a sigh. 'But I don't think it's good.'

He led Houlihan over to the small working space he'd managed to claim. His laptop was already open and running. 'Okay, so Beckett has a pattern.'

'You solved Beckett's pattern?'

'We did, and you're going to like this. We've been looking at numerology, astrology, lunar cycles. I had a friend of mine from the CIA – a decoder specialist – looking up longitudes and latitudes of crime scenes and trying to crack an encrypted message. Computers have been chewing away on this stuff, all because we know how clever Jim can be. And you want to know the answer? I'll show you the answer.'

Quincy turned his computer so Houlihan could see the screen.

'Shit,' the lieutenant said.

'Absolutely. Strictly grade-school stuff. You know

how hard he must have been laughing over this in his prison cell? He's so clever, he makes stupid look good.'

Quincy shook his head. It was all there on the screen and he'd discovered it purely by accident. He'd been listing all the female victims in order in one column. Then he'd listed the crime scenes in order in the next column. He'd glanced at the column. If you took the first letter from each city and scrambled them, they read: Jim Beckett. The bastard had spelled his name in dead women.

'Help me out here, Agent. What does this mean?'

'It means there's method to his madness. It means his talk of discipline isn't completely smoke and mirrors. And, Lieutenant, it means he isn't done.'

'Sure he is, he spelled his name. No letters are missing.'

'These are the dead women, Lieutenant. His past work. Then he attacked his wife in Williamstown –'

'He didn't kill her.'

'Nope, he didn't. But he was sent to jail, and there he killed two prison guards. At MCI Cedar Junction in *Walpole*.'

Lieutenant Houlihan fell silent. Then, 'W. He wanted the letter W. *Jim Beckett w*. What does that mean?'

'It means he has more to say. Maybe *Jim Beckett was* something or *Jim Beckett wants* something. I don't know. But there's a phrase in his head and he won't stop until he's gotten it out. He's not done, Houlihan. He's not done.'

'Lieutenant,' a voice called across the room. 'I have Lieutenant Berttelli from Connecticut on the phone for you.'

Houlihan and Quincy exchanged glances. Houlihan took the call at a nearby table. It lasted just a few minutes.

'They found Shelly Zane. You coming?'

'Yes. What city?'

'Avon. Avon, Connecticut.'

Quincy added it to his column.

It took three hours to drive to the cheap roadside motel outside of Avon. The crime scene photographer had just finished up, and now the Connecticut task force officers were bagging the evidence. Two officers were trying to figure out how to move the queen-size bed, which was bolted to the floor. Finally they decided severing the bolts would disturb the crime scene too much, so they instructed a rookie to crawl beneath the bed and retrieve the victim's fingers.

When Quincy walked in, that was the first thing he saw – some rookie's butt sticking up from beneath the bed as he reached for Shelly Zane's fingers. Those were the games Beckett liked to play. He liked to mutilate his victim's hands and he liked to mess with cops. Somewhere right now Jim was probably driving down a highway and chuckling at the thought of some rookie on his hands and knees recovering bloody fingers and trying not to retch.

Quincy walked into the bathroom, where Shelly Zane's body lay splayed out on the cracked blue-tiled floor between the toilet and the bathtub. Her arms were over her head, her mutilated hands palm up, as if she were caught in the act of surrendering. A pair of nylons were tied so tightly around her neck, they'd almost disappeared into the flesh. Quincy had already spotted the empty package of Hanes Alive Support hose in the wastebasket. Bundy had bragged that they had superior tensile strength, making them the garrote of choice for ligature. Apparently Beckett had paid attention to that part of the Bundy interview notes.

Postmortem lividity was most pronounced in the head, above the ligature line, and in the arms and lower legs, indicating that she'd been hanged. Around the knotted nylons, ruptured blood vessels had turned her neck black and blue. Petechial hemorrhages had darkened the whites of her eyes bloodred.

The back of her head was thick with blood and gray matter. The walls bore the spray pattern. Beckett had strangled her to death, dropped her down, then beaten her with a blunt wooden instrument. Typical homicidal overkill.

Thirteen victims later, Beckett's rage was only growing worse.

Shelly Zane's body was already outlined with chalk, unusual for this early in the evidence-gathering process. Behind him, Lieutenant Berttelli was raking a young officer over the coals for it. Probably the officer who'd arrived on the scene first.

'What the fuck were you thinkin'?' the lieutenant was screaming. 'Didn't they teach you to *never* mess with the crime scene until the photos are taken? What am I supposed to tell the DA now? I got a bunch of fucking photos of a fucking outlined corpse that no fucking judge is gonna admit as evidence.'

'I swear, I didn't do it –'

'Well, it wasn't the fucking chalk fairy.'

'Beckett,' Quincy said calmly. Lieutenant Berttelli shut up long enough to pay attention. 'Beckett knows the rules of evidence,' Quincy continued. 'And he likes to mess with our minds.'

Quincy's gaze came to rest on the note pinned to Shelly Zane's stomach.

'The officers left it for you,' Lieutenant Houlihan supplied.

The note had his name on it. It said in simple block letters: SHE WAS NO LONGER USEFUL TO ME.

Quincy rose. 'He's on the move.'

'You think he's going after Tess?'

'Yes.'

'We should call and warn her.'

Quincy eyed him sharply. 'I thought you didn't know where she was.'

Lieutenant Houlihan shifted. 'I don't personally know where she is, but I know who does.'

'And you would contact this person and he would contact her?'

'Yeah, something like that.'

Quincy nodded. 'Lieutenant Houlihan, absolutely, positively, do *not* do that.'

'What?'

He gestured at the note, and for the first time Houlihan caught the anger simmering in his eyes. 'Don't you recognize those words? Do you think it's mere coincidence that he's using the same phrase I used in the briefing one week ago?'

Houlihan blanched. 'Holy shit.'

'Do you see now how much he's toying with us? That note is a lie, Lieutenant. Because Shelly Zane is still useful to him. You react to her murder. You break the silence, you contact the person, who contacts Tess –'

'Which is exactly what he's waiting for us to do. He's watching us, hiding wherever the hell he hides. The minute we break silence, he'll have her. Holy shit.'

Houlihan looked as if he'd gained ten years in ten seconds. Quincy figured he looked the same.

'Tess was right to go out on her own. We are absolutely, positively, dangerous to her. Beckett's too close for us to see, he hides in our wake. And he's not going to stop until he finds her. He's got his message in mind, but his ultimate target, his ultimate goal, is killing Tess.'

Houlihan looked at the blond corpse on the bathroom floor. He stared at the note piercing her skin. 'God, I hate this job.'

'Me too, Lieutenant. Me too.'

The young, somber-faced man walked into task force headquarters, went straight to the officer on duty, and flashed his badge. 'Detective Beaumont,' he introduced himself. 'I'm from Bristol County and I have an urgent message for Lieutenant Houlihan.'

'I'm sorry, Detective, but Lieutenant Houlihan is currently unavailable.'

'Officer, you don't understand. This is urgent, I mean *urgent*. I just drove up forty minutes from Bristol to make sure Houlihan gets the news. I need to speak with him.'

The officer wavered. Detective Beaumont leaned forward.

'Please. We think we may know where Jim Beckett is. I have to get word to Tess Williams or Lieutenant Difford immediately. Help me out here, Officer. Speed matters.'

She caved in with a sigh. 'See that man standing over there? That's Sergeant Wilcox. He's in charge of the safe house. He can probably help you.'

'Sergeant Wilcox?'

'Yes, that's him.'

'Thank you, Officer. You've been very helpful.'

Edith smoothed a hand over her old blue flannel shirt and tried not to shift too much on the front porch. Last night she'd received a call from Martha, stating that she would arrive first thing this morning – the poor woman had been driving up all the way from Florida over the last few days. That was Martha for you. At sixty years of age, the woman was as proud and independent as they came. She'd moved into the neighborhood only a few years earlier, but the first evening she'd knocked on Edith's door and offered a pint of scotch. The two women had sat on Edith's patio, opened the fifty-year-old bottle, discovered a mutual love of cigars, and spent two hours agreeing that there hadn't been a decent president since Eisenhower.

Edith appreciated such relationships. She was too old for foo-fooing or fussiness. Most women her age started off talking about Jell-O salad and soon fled from the premises when Edith stared them straight in the eye and declared, 'Who the hell cares about Jell-O? It's the rapid proliferation of assault weapons that keeps me awake at night.'

She didn't want platitudes or shoulder-shrugging. Everyone should say what they wanted. It saved time.

Martha spoke tersely. At times she could be imperious, but Edith figured that's what came from living your whole life head and shoulders above the rest. Martha was tall, and that was an understatement. Of Swedish descent, she had her father's impressive height and shoulders, though neither was so attractive on a woman.

Most men were too intimidated to come anywhere near a woman of Martha's impressive bulk, but apparently she'd met an equally impressive Swede in her youth and before he'd died, they'd had one sizable blond son. Edith had never met the son. From the few things Martha had casually mentioned, he was a salesman of some kind and moved a lot. Martha didn't see him often and generally didn't go on and on about him the way some mothers did.

Edith appreciated that. Having spent all her life childless, she got impatient with endless stories about whose son was being promoted to what position and whose daughter was giving birth to how many grandchildren. Good Lord, the world was already overpopulated and overextending the earth's resources. Didn't people give the matter any thought?

An old brown Cadillac turned down the street like an unwieldy boat. Martha had arrived. Minutes later Edith was pumping her neighbor's hand vigorously.

'Lord, Florida was good for you!' Martha's faded blond hair had lightened to a snowy white, which looked natural with her sun-darkened skin. It had been years since they'd last seen each other, but after one glance Edith could tell that Martha was Martha. She still had the same startling blue eyes and smooth complexion; Swedes aged so nicely. Martha's taste in clothes hadn't changed either. Today she sported a huge pair of brown polyester pants and a man's oversize red flannel shirt. A wide-brimmed straw hat perched precariously on her head, smashed there at the last minute.

Martha patted her generous waistline. 'The food was too good,' she drawled huskily, her voice still carrying a

175

hint of Swedish mountains. 'But the weather was too hot. I missed snow.'

Edith shook her hand again. 'It's good to have you back,' she repeated. And it was good. She tried to pretend she didn't see things. She tried to pretend she didn't feel things. But the air in their community was different these days. Edith didn't like it.

And more and more often Edith found herself staring next door and thinking that now was not a good time to live so close to an empty home.

'Let me help with your luggage,' Edith volunteered, already moving toward the trunk and shaking away the shivers creeping up her spine. She had no use for 'feelings' or 'visions.' A person couldn't act on a feeling. 'You travel light.'

'At my age, who needs things?' Martha pulled out two suitcases. 'And the house?'

'Just the same as you left it.' Edith had agreed to take care of the house when Martha had announced she was going to visit Florida for a spell and try her hand at golf. Edith had a key to the place and gave it the once-over every month. Martha called every few months to ask about the house, though generally the discussion turned quickly to politics. Martha didn't like Clinton. Edith couldn't stand Newt. They both enjoyed the conversations immensely.

Edith turned to the front door, already tugging on the suitcase. But then she froze, the hair on the back of her neck prickling up.

The girl stood in front of the door perfectly naked. This close, Edith could see the butterfly tattoo above her left breast. Nothing big or vulgar. The butterfly was small, dainty even, a light flickering of color that spoke of a lonely wish for flight. Blond hair cascaded down her shoulders, of course – all the girls were blondes.

Edith raised her gaze even though she didn't really want to see more. There was nothing, no message, not a plea to give her a hint. The girl just stood there, naked with blood on her face, and her eyes were faintly apologetic, as if she knew she was as unwanted dead as she had been alive.

'Go away, child,' Edith said softly. 'There's nothing I can do for you.'

The girl remained, stubborn. Edith squeezed her eyes shut, and when she opened them again, she'd won and the girl was gone.

Belatedly she became aware of the quizzical look on Martha's face. 'You all right?'

Edith didn't answer immediately. 'Did you hear that serial killer got loose?'

'Huh?'

'Jim Beckett, that's his name. Killed ten women and now two prison guards. Got outta Walpole. That's not far from here.'

Martha didn't say anything, but for one moment Edith saw something flash across those bright eyes. It looked like fear, bone-deep fear. The big woman composed herself quickly, squaring her broad shoulders.

'This is a small community, Edith, a quiet place. Someone like him wouldn't have any cause to come here.'

Edith watched Martha awhile longer, but Martha's expression was blank.

'I'm sure you're right,' Edith said at last.

She didn't believe either one of them though. And it bothered her that they'd each told their first lie over a man such as Jim Beckett. It bothered her a lot.

16

J.T. was on edge.

By nightfall, he paced the living room with enough energy to power a small city. Marion took one look and returned her beer to the refrigerator. She reentered the room with two glasses of water, handing one to her brother.

J.T. downed it wordlessly. He wiped his mouth with the back of his arm. Then he resumed pacing.

'Oh, for God's sake,' Marion said at last, 'you're giving me gray hairs. Sit down.'

He pivoted and headed the other direction. 'Don't you feel it?' he asked.

'Feel what?'

'Tess, go to your room.'

'What?'

'Lock the door. Knit a sweater.'

'Oh, no. If there's something going on, I want to know.'

J.T.'s gaze locked on his sister. Marion shook her head. 'I walked the grounds just half an hour ago, J.T. There's nothing out there but your own dark mood. Stop panicking Tess.'

'She wanted to stay.'

'Would someone start speaking English?' Tess demanded. Her belly had knotted.

'I don't like it,' J.T. repeated. 'Air's different. Something. Shit, we're outta here.'

'What?'

J.T. strode across the room. 'You heard me. Grab your purses, girls, we're blowing this joint.'

'J.T., this is stupid –'

J.T. halted. 'You got friends in the Nogales Police Department, right, Marion?'

She nodded warily.

'Call them. Tell then we're going out for a few hours. Tell them we're worried about the "intruder" returning. Ask them to send a patrol car to cruise around a bit, say half-hour intervals.'

'I don't know . . .'

'Marion, what can it hurt?'

That got her. Marion placed the call while Tess found a light jacket. Tess returned to the living room quickly; she no longer felt like being alone.

Wordlessly they piled into Marion's car, three people staring out at a black landscape, trying to see what was out there.

'A bar?' Tess declared twenty minutes later, staring incredulously at the neon-clad, rock'n'roll-blaring joint. 'J.T., this isn't a good idea. Why don't we go to a movie?'

He kept walking. 'Crowds are good, Tess, and so is a place with five exits.'

Marion and Tess exchanged dubious glances. J.T. strolled inside, obviously no stranger to the establishment.

Located on a busy street in downtown Nogales, it advertised itself aggressively with loud music and rowdy patrons. At the moment Bruce Springsteen was blasting everyone new eardrums with the loudest rendition of 'Born to Run' that Tess had ever heard. Above, a seventies disco ball swirled madly, casting a dizzying array of diamond dots onto a dance floor filled with people who truly knew how to move. The light disappeared at the corners, leaving gaping pools of blackness where she could dimly see couples in various stages of drinking and displaying public affection. Everyone looked Latino.

J.T. cut a clean path through the madness, his gaze watchful. Tess and Marion kept close to him. J.T. raised his hand and pointed to a corner, his lips moving but his words lost in the thundering music. Tess and Marion moved quickly to follow, fading deeper into the hallway, the music receding behind them. New odors assaulted their senses: beer, urine. Sex.

Finally J.T. came to a doorway guarded by tendrils of orange and red glass beads. He held the curtain back and motioned for Marion and Tess to enter. His gaze swept the hall behind them, then he let the curtain drop.

'A video arcade?' Marion huffed. 'You brought us here for video games?'

'They're better than the beer, Marion. Or are G-men too tough for pinball?'

Tess stared. They weren't alone in the room by any means. It was filled with a huge crowd and electronic sounds. She heard a coin machine dispensing change and the glug-glug of some animated character dying. Several men looked up when they entered, appeared a little surprised, then went back to what they were doing before. There were few women in the room. One of them, scantily clad in a crimson skirt and halter top, looked like hell on wheels sitting at a car game. She'd attracted several onlookers and didn't seem to mind.

J.T. went straight to a row of older pinball machines and selected one. DEAD MAN WALKING, it said.

Tess shuddered.

'Come on, ladies. It's hand-eye coordination.'

'I don't have any, thanks,' Tess volunteered.

With another scowl and frustrated sigh Marion gave up on protesting and sized up the machine. 'All right. You're on.'

'Two out of three?'

'Four out of seven. You're obviously not new here.'

'High score is mine.'

'Oh, really? How drunk were you at the time?'

'Stone cold sober,' J.T. drawled. 'Down here, Marion, pinball's serious business.'

'Yeah, well, so is cotton,' she muttered.

'Tess,' J.T. said calmly. 'Watch the doorway, will

you? If anyone white walks in, let me know. I don't think we were followed, but it's been a bit since I played cat and mouse.'

J.T. popped two quarters into the machine. Marion cracked her knuckles and stretched out her arms. The two of them got down to the obviously serious business of pinball, but Tess didn't relax that easily. Her gaze kept darting back to the doorway, just in case Jim Beckett magically appeared.

J.T. was no slouch. He hit five digits before his turn was up, and gave way only after delivering a mocking bow. Marion took over with narrowed eyes and thinned lips. She looked as if she'd gone to war.

She moved too fast, and the first silver ball escaped through the paddles before she'd made much progress. She slapped the machine, earning a tilt sign.

'Relax, Marion. It's just a machine.'

'Fucking machine,' she supplied.

'Have it your way.'

She attacked the second ball, and since she had phenomenal hand-eye coordination and a wicked learning curve, she made the machine sing. A light began to burn in her eyes. And for a moment she looked exactly like J.T.

'She's something, isn't she?' J.T. murmured.

Tess nodded. 'What did your parents feed you?'

'Lies. Pure lies. Taught us the truth of the world early on.' His lips curved into a ghost of a grin. 'See any sign of trouble at the door?'

'No.'

'Huh. Maybe Marion was right. Maybe I just need a drink.'

'J.T. –'

'Shit!' Marion yelled, and hit the machine. 'Piece of junk!'

J.T. jostled his sister aside. 'Easy, honey. Machine can't help it if I'm better than you.'

Marion leaned against the wall next to Tess, but she

no longer appeared relaxed. J.T. settled in at the pinball machine, looking like a captain at the helm of his ship.

'Face it, Marion, you should've joined the marines.'

'No, thanks. I figured one Dillon punching out COs was enough.'

J.T. pulled back the handle and sent the silver ball flying. 'I suppose I could've just enrolled him in the Communist Party, but beating the crap out of his own wife seemed to warrant something more personal.'

'Communist Party?' Tess asked. She wasn't sure she wanted to understand this conversation.

'West Point,' J.T. supplied. 'I enrolled the director in the Communist Party. I *hated* West Point.'

'And that got you kicked out?'

'Nah. That was considered a boys-will-be-boys prank. When he came to call me on it and found me in bed with his daughter, *that* got me kicked out.'

'You seduced the director's daughter?'

'He's a pig,' Marion said. 'Absolutely no self-control.'

'How do you know I was the seducer?' J.T. quizzed innocently.

Marion shook her head. 'Give it up, Jordan. If you were turned loose in a nunnery, by the end of the day they'd all renounce God.'

'Thank you. I try.' J.T. gave Tess a look that was blatantly wolfish. 'Did I scare you?'

'When?' She was having trouble concentrating.

'Earlier. When I asked Marion to call the police.'

'I guess. I have a lot to be scared of.'

'You have both Marion and me here, Tess. It's even legal for Marion to shoot to kill.'

'He's right, you know,' Marion said. 'At least this time. It's not easy to become an FBI agent, and it's even harder for a woman. I'm good. I'll make sure nothing happens to you, Tess.'

Tess didn't answer; she'd been told such things before, and none of the assurance had helped her when

Jim had stepped out of her closet and hefted a bat to his shoulder. She said, 'That was a nice thing you did – putting away the beer. Teetotaling is really getting to him.'

'Yeah, I guess it is. I knew about the annual tequila binges, but they're only once a year and, well, given the circumstances . . .'

'His wife's death?' Tess guessed.

Marion nodded. 'Teddy died instantly. But Rachel . . . She was in a coma for five days. J.T. just kept sitting there in the hospital, holding her hand. He seemed so certain that she would open her eyes and be with him again. He just couldn't let her go. He's weak that way.' Marion pushed away from the wall. 'You have to be able to cut your losses, to move on. But J.T. can't seem to do that. He wants to go back and fix things way after the fact. It's a waste of time.'

J.T. lost his turn and Marion strode forward, leaving Tess to digest this unexpected burst of information. J.T. came to lean against the wall beside her, stretching out his legs and crossing his arms. He already appeared much more relaxed. She moved a little closer to him and joined him in a comfortable silence.

It wasn't until the seventh game that the trouble happened.

Tess never did know who started it. One moment she was watching J.T. volley the silver ball back into the megapoints zone, the next she heard a scream followed by a crash.

Everyone turned at once.

A man, obviously drunk, was towering over the woman who'd been playing the car game. He pointed at her and cursed her in voluble streams of Spanish. Though only half his size, the woman didn't give an inch. She stood to her full height and screamed right back.

The man pulled back his arm. He slapped the woman hard, snapping her head around. She crashed against the machine, falling bonelessly to the ground.

'For God's sake, no!' Marion cried. She lunged for J.T.'s arm, but she was too late. J.T. plunged into the thick of it.

Like a massive tidal wave, the crowd of people surged, some eddying out the door to escape and others moving in closely. More people – muscle-bound, testosterone-pumped men – flooded in, looking for action. Tess saw the woman try to rise, then flounder and fall back. Something dark and wet matted the woman's hair. Blood.

'Damn,' Marion said. She shook her head, then seemed to lose the war with herself and stepped forward.

Tess looked at J.T. He was raising his left arm to block one blow and pulling back his right arm to deliver another. She looked at Marion, striding purposefully ahead.

She took a deep breath.

She set her sights on the fallen woman and stepped into the whirlpool.

It was hot. Sweat-soaked flesh pressed against sweat-soaked flesh until the air seemed to steam. It was loud. She couldn't distinguish any single voice or cry, she just heard the dull roar building to a crescendo. It was thick. She was too short to see over and too small to shoulder her way through. So she pushed and pawed, as if hacking her way through a dense undergrowth, trying to remember where she'd last seen the woman and head in that direction.

She burst into a small clearing and drew in a huge gulp of air. Then, like a swimmer, she held it in her lungs and plunged back in.

An arm caught her in the shoulder and she stumbled. Another arm caught her and tossed her back onto her feet. She lurched forward, her hands fisted at her sides, her jaw clenched. Someone jostled her, and in a spurt of terror she used some of her newly developed muscle to push back. The body gave way instantly. She was amazed.

She pushed herself through and found the fallen woman, who was moaning and clutching her head. Tess hunched down, eyeing the woman anxiously.

A crash resounded above them. Tess and the woman swiveled their heads simultaneously to find the new threat. A man stood beside then, looking not at them but at another charging man. The first man wielded the jagged half of a broken beer bottle in front of him.

'Damn,' Tess swore. Out of the corner of her eye she caught Marion bursting from the crush, her hair disheveled, her blouse ripped. She didn't even glance at Tess or the fallen woman. She went straight after the man with the broken bottle. He tried to bring up his arm to fend her off.

He didn't have a chance. Two smartly delivered chops, and Marion had him writhing on the ground, holding his twisted arm and screaming curses. The charging man hesitated, not sure what to do with a woman. Marion decided the matter for him. Her foot hooked him neatly behind the ankles, and with a fierce yank she toppled him to the ground. A new cry rose up from the crowd.

Tess stopped thinking. She offered her hand to the fallen woman and helped her to her feet. The woman clutched her bloody head.

'Look out!' Marion cried.

Tess froze. The man who'd started it all was there, towering above them, his eyes bright with rage. He carried a chair leg in one hand.

Tess stared at the rounded wood. And she thought, It's not nearly so sturdy as a baseball bat.

The chair leg was raised up into the air.

Then Tess shivered, her gaze locked onto the images suddenly in her head. The baseball bat swinging down. The crack of her thigh. The burning pain. The scent of blood. The knowledge of all the other times the bat had whistled down and connected with human flesh and bone.

How did a head sound when hit by a bat? Like wood cracking? Or more like a melon going *splat*?

A dull roaring filled her ears.

Dimly she heard the chair leg whistle down. Dimly she saw the man tossed forward and J.T. standing in his spot. Then, as if from far, far away, Marion said, 'God, J.T., she's going to faint.'

'Shit.'

Suddenly strong arms were around her, swinging her up. She went wild, fighting and clawing, and she couldn't even remember what she was fighting. She just had to fight.

J.T.'s hand caught hers, trapping them against his chest. 'Shh, *chiquita*, I have you. I have you.'

She buried her face against his shoulder and prayed he wouldn't let her go.

J.T. carried her out of the building and into the cool, night air.

'Are you all right?' J.T. asked half an hour later as he set her down on the sofa.

Marion had dragged the wounded woman out of the bar, entrusted her to the care of the few people in the parking lot, then they'd escaped the scene. Now J.T.'s thumb brushed Tess's cheek, then feathered through her hair. His gaze was intent as he searched for wounds.

'Yes. Yes, I'm fine,' Tess murmured, too embarrassed to meet his gaze. J.T. and Marion had been ready to take on the place. She'd seen one raised chair leg and almost fainted. Some bad ass she was.

'That wasn't how the evening was supposed to turn out.'

'I suppose it's a bad sign when your star pupil almost loses her lunch during her first brawl. Maybe next time Jim shows up, I can vomit on him for self-defense.'

'Tess –'

Marion returned from checking the grounds, snapping on the living room light. She'd already spoken to the police; they hadn't seen anyone lurking in the vicinity.

J.T. moved back. For the first time, Tess noted the scratch running down his cheek and his bruised knuckles.

'You're hurt.'

He glanced at his hands idly. 'It's nothing.' He turned to Marion. 'And you?'

'I'm fine.' Marion leaned against the doorjamb, her silk blouse ripped and linen pants beer-stained. Her hair had come undone, golden waves now rippling down her shoulders. The style took ten years off her age.

'You should leave your hair down,' Tess blurted out. 'You look beautiful.'

'Gets in my way.' The agent was already braiding the strands.

'Forget it,' J.T. told Tess flatly. 'She likes the feminazi style.'

'I prefer the word *professional*. Would you like some ice for your knuckles?'

'Whatever.'

Marion rolled her eyes but went after the ice.

An awkward silence filled the room. Tess didn't know how to break it. She examined her hands. She wished she had bruised knuckles.

'I'm sorry,' J.T. said abruptly.

'For what?'

'Uh . . . the bar fight. They aren't so unusual at that place.'

'You wanted a fight?'

A pause. 'Maybe.'

'All the swimming,' Tess murmured, 'all the weights, the jogging, the shooting, it's not enough for you, is it?'

'I'm an intense kind of guy.'

She looked at him, then she stared at the doorway that led into the kitchen. 'J.T., why are you always so angry?'

'Who, me?'

'Marion has that anger too.'

'Marion has ice in her veins. She likes it that way.'

'Versus you –'

'Who has tequila. It's been a long night, Tess. We all need some sleep.'

'Did you really think someone was watching the house tonight, or was that just an excuse?'

'No,' he said immediately, but then looked troubled. 'I don't know. Maybe Marion was right. Maybe it's just withdrawal. I'm . . . I'm a little on edge these days.' He looked her in the eye. 'Tess, when it comes right down to it, Marion is the one you can count on. I have raw talent, she has follow-through. I get in trouble, she gets things done. Remember that, all right? If push comes to shove, go to Marion. She'll take care of you.'

'You're wrong,' she told him. 'When push comes to shove, you're the one who's going to help me, J.T. You're the only one I know who's intense enough to take on Jim.'

He silenced further declarations with a finger over her lips. Wordlessly he took her hand and drew her off the sofa.

There was no light on in the hallway. It loomed dark and endless, as hushed as a sanctuary. Her footsteps slowed. So did his. When they arrived at her room, she didn't open the door. She leaned against it and stared at his face.

She traced the fresh scratch marring his cheek. 'Does that hurt?'

'No.'

Her fingers curled around his chin, then brushed his lips.

'What are you doing, Tess?'

'Nothing.' She touched his nose, his cheekbone, his eye. Her hand curved around his neck, rubbing the taut, corded muscles there, and she heard his indrawn breath leave him hoarsely.

She liked touching him. She could feel his power,

electric and tantalizing and held precariously in check. She had done the right thing in coming to him.

She'd found the right man.

And she wanted him.

She knew so little about desire. She thought he was the kind of man who could teach a woman all about it. The kind of man who could draw a woman in and wring her out with passion.

She leaned forward.

'Don't.' He grabbed her shoulder and pinned her back. 'Don't.'

'Why not?'

'It's not what you really want, Tess.'

'I'm stronger then you think.'

'Yeah. But maybe I'm not.' He let her go. 'Good night.'

'But –'

His gaze stopped her. It washed over her and stripped her bare. He moved closer. Then closer still. His head dipped. She held her breath and opened her lips, prepared to meet him all the way.

He twisted his head to the side at the last moment, and his teeth caught her earlobe delicately. 'Go to bed, Tess. And lock your door.'

Then he was gone.

17

'*¡Mierda!* You are not even trying!'

'Jesus, lady, you're demanding!' J.T. rolled off Rosalita, lying on his back and staring up at the swirling ceiling fan.

Rosalita propped herself up beside him. 'You are not yourself.'

He cocked a brow. 'You get off twice and you're still so pissed you speak gringo? Rosalita, you are the Antichrist.'

She didn't scowl, she didn't sulk. She looked worried instead. He hated that. God almighty, someone deliver him from the women in his house.

Tentatively she ran one finger down the scar on his chest. He barely resisted the urge to bat it away. 'It's *la chiquita*, no? You like her.'

'I don't like anyone, Rosalita. It's part of my charm.'

No, he was not himself this evening. He was taut and aching. He was screwing the best whore in Nogales and thinking of another woman.

Christ, he wanted her. He wanted to take her until she couldn't walk, she couldn't stand, she couldn't breathe, until all she could do was scream. Then he wanted to take her again.

And afterward? his mind whispered. *What could you give a woman like that out of bed, J.T.? What could you offer a woman like her?*

She was changing, becoming strong, capable. He knew, because he'd seen it before. Seen a woman come into herself and realize that she didn't have just arms and legs but that she could run, fight, give, take. She could reclaim all the pieces of herself that had been stolen by stronger, cruel men and do whatever she wanted.

Rachel had chosen to give herself to him. And he had loved her for that unbearably.

He reached for the nightstand, found a crumpled pack of cigarettes, and pounded one out. He brought it to his lips and lit it. The tobacco seared ten years off his lungs. Gotta hate it. Gotta love it. It was just his style.

Rosalita was still watching him. Now she pressed her body next to his. He could roll her over and thrust into her again and she would only sigh her contentment. He could guide her head down and she would swallow him whole. If he could think of it, she would do it, and she could probably do a few things that defied his imagination as well.

He simply lay there, exhaling smoke and watching it drift languidly up to the whirling fan blades.

'I'll bring you a drink.' Rosalita climbed out of bed, wrapped the sheet around her body. 'You'll feel better then.'

'You should get married,' he said lightly. 'Find yourself a husband and raise a few kids instead of hanging out with the likes of me.'

The look of concern on her face grew. If he did or said one more thing out of character, the woman was going to check his forehead for fever and fetch him a doctor.

She opened the door and trailed down the hall.

Who was she most likely to run into tonight, Tess or Marion? The woman he didn't want to save but seemed to think that only he could save her? Or the woman he'd once tried to save but now seemed to think that he was the devil?

'God does have such a sense of humor,' he muttered to the ceiling. 'Even a worse sense than mine.'

The cigarette burned down to his fingers. He let it drop to the floor, pressing it out with the pad of his thumb. He gave up smoking every morning and started again every night. And tonight it wasn't even dulling his brain the way it was supposed to.

He was still thinking of Tess and thinking of Tess made him remember Rachel. J.T. had married Rachel because he understood that she was an eighteen-year-old mother who wanted the best for her son. He'd married her because if she was as corrupt, twisted, and manipulative as Marion said, then it was the colonel who'd molded her into that shape.

His father had come up to him after the ceremony, pumped J.T.'s hand, and stated, 'Now Teddy will have the family name and I'll get my second son into West Point to redeem my first son's mistakes. I knew you'd do the right thing, Jordan.'

And J.T. had said, 'You touch Rachel or Teddy ever again, and I will kill you. Understand, *Daddy*?'

It was the only time J.T. ever saw the colonel pale.

For the first six months he and Rachel lived together like awkward acquaintances. She had her room in the apartment. He had his. When they talked and interacted, it was about Teddy. But sometimes, late at night, they would sit at the kitchen table, drinking beers and revealing little bits and pieces of themselves.

She told him about the stepfather who made it impossible for her to remain at home. He talked about the first time his father had whipped him and how sure he'd been that he deserved it. She recalled trying to find a job, then realizing homeless fifteen-year-olds couldn't get one. He spoke of the jungle and the endless hours of sitting in steam, waiting for the right moment to pounce and destroy.

One night she told him about the first time she'd sold her body. She'd recited Dr. Seuss rhymes in her mind to block out the act. Afterward she hadn't cried. The man had paid her well, so she hadn't cried. She'd just rocked herself back and forth and tried not to remember the life she'd dreamed about as a little girl.

Neither of their lives made much sense, but somehow, sitting up together late at night, they made the warped, jagged pieces fit. They offered each other the forgiveness they couldn't offer themselves. They planned a future. They built a new life.

Until the little kid who'd been beaten by his father loved her, and the adolescent who'd been rejected by his younger sister loved her, and the man who'd gone off to fight wars because he no longer cared if he lived or died loved her. Until every single deranged, hopeful, frightened part of him loved her.

Then Rachel had gone and gotten herself dead.

J.T. reached over to the nightstand, retrieved another cigarette, and started destroying his lungs all over again.

Rosalita drifted back into the room. She paused at the foot of the bed and smiled.

And just for a minute, in the twisted corridors of his mind he saw Marion, young, vulnerable Marion. And his baby sister's hands were clasped and her face terrified as she ran from the monster they both knew too well. '*Hide me, J.T. God help me, please, please, please!*'

'Shh,' he whispered to his own mind, and squeezed his eyes shut.

When he reopened them, Rosalita was by his side, no longer concerned but triumphant. She held out the icy glass.

Tequila on the rocks with a twist. He looked up at her, and she smiled at him, happy. 'You will be yourself,' she said simply.

'You are the Antichrist,' he whispered.

His fingers curled around the glass.

Marion entered the living room just as a woman in a white cotton sheet disappeared into her brother's room. For a moment Marion thought she'd seen a ghost. She shook her head and crossed to the phone.

She liked the living room late at night. Sometimes she went out there just to sit and watch the moon slide through the open blinds and sift over the wicker furniture. In one corner the iguana slept by a heat lamp. Otherwise she was alone.

She contemplated lighting a cigarette but knew by then that J.T. might appear. Sometimes, as she sat in the shadows, he would emerge from the hall and head straight for the patio. Minutes after he'd slipped through the sliding glass door, she'd hear the muted splash of a perfect dive.

Marion took a deep, steadying breath, picked up the phone, and dialed.

'How is he?' she asked.

'Marion?' Roger's voice was groggy with sleep. It was two A.M. his time. Was he sleeping with his new toy? Had she interrupted something? She hoped so.

'How is he?' She gave up on her earlier good intentions and found a cigarette. Her hand was trembling.

'Marion, it's two in the morning.'

'Thank you, Roger, but I can tell time. Now, how is he?'

Roger sighed. She thought she heard the low murmur of a woman's voice. So the cocktail waitress was there. It hurt. It hurt more than she thought it would.

I loved you, Roger. I honestly loved you.

'He's dying, Marion. Jesus Christ, what the hell do you want me to say? The doctors have given him medication for the pain, but at this point not even that's enough. Maybe another week, maybe two. Or maybe tomorrow he'll die. For his sake, I hope so.'

'Not a very charitable thought about the man you considered your mentor, Roger. But then, we both know just how highly you regard loyalty.'

He was silent. In her mind she could see the way his lips would be thinning right now and his high brow creasing into lines of tension. She'd been married to him for almost ten years. She knew him inside and out. She knew he was slightly weak and spineless. She knew he was smart and ambitious. She knew everything about him – she'd thought that was what marriage was all about.

'All right, Marion,' he said quietly. 'Be bitter if you want to. But you're the one who called me. I'm just the messenger telling you that your father is still in the last stages of cancer. He's in pain, he's delusional. He moans and sometimes he cries out for Jordan and sometimes he cries out for Teddy. If you want him to live like that, fine. I think it's a helluva way to die.'

J.T. and Teddy. She wasn't surprised that the colonel hadn't called her name. He'd never had any use for a daughter.

'And Emma?' she threw in, referring to her mother. Marion didn't like Emma. She considered her a weak bitch more content with fantasy than being a good wife to the colonel. But Roger had always had a soft spot for the demented old bat.

'I worry about her too,' Roger said predictably enough. 'She's quoting Sophia Loren's lines from *El Cid*. I'm half afraid she might actually stick his corpse on a horse one of these days. You know she's always worse under pressure.'

'Pressure? The woman cracks under the strain of what shoes to wear in the morning.'

'Marion . . . why did you call?'

'I wanted make sure nothing had happened.'

Another lengthy silence. This time she knew he was not frowning. Instead, he was painstakingly choosing his words. Roger was a very diplomatic man, a born spin doctor. She imagined his career would continue to advance nicely in the army.

'Marion . . .' His voice was soft. She automatically stiffened her spine. 'I know this is a tough time for you. I know I hurt you –'

'Hurt me? *Hurt me!* You walked out on our marriage!'

'I know, Marion. But –'

'But what? We had respect, we had friendship. We

had ten years of history. My God, Roger, we had a solid relationship.'

'Except that you froze every time I touched you.'

She went rigid, the cigarette burning down to her lips. She couldn't breathe, she couldn't speak, she couldn't move.

'I'm sorry,' Roger said. 'God, I'm sorry, Marion. I know that hurts. But how was I supposed to take that? How was I supposed to live like that? I have needs –'

'It's my job, isn't it? You've always been jealous, haven't you? Thought it took too much of my time, kept me from being the perfect army wife and hostess. And my career is a good career too, one as good as yours – and I'm stronger than you. I shoot better than you. You're . . . you're just an army bureaucrat and I'm the one out there actually making a difference!' Her voice was harsh. It kept her from falling into a million pieces.

'Well, I wouldn't have minded a wife who came home on occasion. A wife who didn't compare me to her boss or to her darling father. Is that so much to ask for?' The carefully crafted words were spinning away from him. She took sublime satisfaction in that.

'You're weak!' she spat out into the phone. 'You're spineless and only half the man the colonel is. You're not a real lieutenant colonel, you just know how to play political games. I'm glad you left. It's better this way. You play with your little child. At least you finally found someone you can be better than!'

'Dammit, Marion! Don't do –'

She didn't hear the rest. She slammed the phone down so hard, Glug flinched. She stared at the lizard, willing it to move so she'd have an excuse to tear it to pieces.

The iguana wisely played dead. She lit a fresh cigarette and inhaled the acrid smoke until tears stung her eyes. Her body was trembling and she hurt, way down deep inside.

For just one moment she wanted to curl into a ball and weep. She wanted to hold out her arms and have someone wrap her in a strong embrace and whisper soothing words in her ear.

It'll be all right, Merry Berry. I'll save you. I'll save you.

The words came out of nowhere, as faint as a dream. She rubbed her cheeks with her fists, swallowing through the tightness in her chest.

To hell with Roger. He was a weak man consoling himself through his midlife crisis with a twenty-two-year-old. She was tougher than him. She was tougher than most men she met. It unnerved all of them. Even in the nineties, men expected a little simpering, a little need. They told her she would have equal opportunity as a female agent, then tried to hide dead bodies from her sight as if she might faint. And then when she bent down and investigated the scene, they exchanged glances over her head as if she were some dyke in disguise.

They told her they didn't mind independence, then looked wounded the first time she didn't cry in their arms because she'd seen a murder. They said they understood her strength, then resented it when she outperformed them on the shooting range.

She was not the one changing the rules. She was not the one saying she was comfortable with one thing and expecting another. She'd married and she was faithful. She'd taken a vow of fidelity, bravery, and integrity, and she was a good agent. She'd promised the colonel she would make him proud and she would be at his side holding his hand when he died. And she'd see to it that he got the best sendoff any man had ever had.

She brushed off her shirt. She patted her hair, which was pulled back into a French twist. She told herself she was composed and together and the strongest thing this side of hell.

Then she walked down the hall to her bedroom.

Her feet slowed by J.T.'s door. The urge welled up so

strongly, her hand actually curled around the door-knob. *Open the door. Go inside. He'll help you, he'll help you. Jordan will save you.*

Then she remembered that day at J.T.'s orienteering match, when their father had come back and he hadn't. She'd stood there while the adults had conferred, holding her stomach against the anger knotting her belly. Jordan had gone and done it. He'd escaped, he'd run away. He'd left her.

Then he was crashing through the underbrush. And instead of being relieved, she hated him all the more. Because he had come back, the dumb bastard, and for just one moment she'd thought that he was free, that J.T. had at least escaped and she wouldn't have to be scared for him anymore.

While the colonel had patted J.T. on the back for walking on a broken ankle, Marion had leaned into the woods and vomited until she dry-heaved.

'I hate you,' she now whispered, the words choked with tears.

She stormed into her room. 'Goddamn everyone in this house,' she muttered. 'Goddamn them all.' She slammed the window open, found a fresh pack of cigarettes, and tapped out one.

That was it. She'd had enough. She'd given J.T. his one week to decide. Tomorrow she would give him his last chance to see the light. Then she was getting out of this hellhole.

The cigarette trembled between her fingertips. She couldn't get it to light. She broke it in half in disgust and stared out the window. She found her arms wrapped around herself, and for an uncanny instant she suffered the sensation she was being watched.

She bolted from the window, grabbed her gun, and returned to the window with it already cocked. Eyes sharp in the night, peering this way, peering that way.

Shit, Marion, what are you doing? Jumping at shadows, ready to shoot at cacti. When did you become so fucked up?

She lowered the gun and hung her head between her shoulders. 'Get some sleep,' she ordered herself. 'Close the window and get some fucking sleep.'

She crawled into bed. The night was quiet and still. Just the crickets, the relentless crickets, murmuring through the night. She wrapped her arms around her pillow, and the exhaustion crashed over her. In two breaths she was asleep.

Merry Berry had some dreams.

The first two were nightmares, making her toss in bed and her lips move in soundless prayer. A tall, dark figure strode into her room. She heard the sound of jump boots against hardwood floors, and the ringing nauseated her.

Then that image spiraled away and she'd arrived in Arizona. She was running around the hacienda, calling J.T.'s name. She had to protect . . . she had to find . . . She rounded the corner and there he was: Jim Beckett's face pressed against the window, his tongue licking the glass.

She murmured in her sleep, trying to push the dream away. She was so tired and she was so afraid. There was never anyone to comfort her anymore. Never anyone who cared.

Sleep took pity on her and dragged her into a softer embrace.

She was little, little and strong. She rode the big gelding effortlessly, feeling his muscles bunch and flex at her command. 'Faster,' she whispered to him. 'Faster.'

Her hair flew behind her, the wind brushing tears from her eyes. Around and around they went. Faster and faster. Until she saw the jump. The big, huge jump looming ahead. They were going too fast, they would never clear the hurdle. Frantically she pulled back on the reins, but her horse fought the bit, his massive head twisting.

J.T.'s voice called out, soft but clear. He'd been there all along, out of sight, but she'd known he was there. She had depended on it.

'You can do it, Merry Berry,' he shouted. 'You can do it.'

She took the jump. She heard him clapping his hands.

And for just one moment she was free.

Jim was ready.

In the dark hours right before dawn he sat naked in the shuttered room and finished his preparations.

On the floor he had lined up two plastic eggs filled with neon purple Silly Putty, a box of clear sandwich bags, two bags of pillow stuffing, four packages of women's nylons, eyeliner, and a fairly expensive black wig guaranteed to make him appear 'ten years younger,' according to the salesman. Last was a large-size Middlesex County police uniform, stolen out of the police locker room from an officer who obviously spent most of his time at Dunkin' Donuts.

Beneath the harsh glare of a bare-bulb desk light, Jim labored over the uniform, his long, lean fingers meticulously ripping stitches and pulling off patches.

In the majority of situations, just the appearance of a uniform was enough; to an inexperienced eye all cops looked alike. But in fact, different departments, cities, and counties had their own distinct patches. Rank was indicated by the colored stripe running down the trouser leg as well as the bars or patches on the collar. Different counties also had different styles – from straight trousers to balloon trousers – and different colors – from brown to navy blue to black. These were all things to consider, since in the next twenty-four hours this uniform would have to withstand the intense scrutiny of people who knew better. Having made it this far, Jim had no intention of being screwed by such a simple thing as the wrong patch or an insignia he couldn't explain.

Beside him, he had a full-color book illustrating all the different uniforms of different state and county law enforcement agencies. He also had a book on police patches as well as his own personal collection he'd compiled during the seven years he'd served as an officer. Some he'd purchased, some he'd stolen. All were useful.

He pulled off the last patch and held the huge dark blue uniform up to the light. It would do.

He set aside the uniform and turned to the items on the floor. He selected the Silly Putty first, pounding it out, molding it, and inserting it into the plastic sandwich bags. When tucked inside the mouth, the pouches would give the appearance of jowls. He cut off the legs of the nylons, filled them with pillow stuffing, and closed the top with a few quick stitches. Instant thunder thighs and Buddha belly. The wig and makeup would be applied at the last minute.

He pulled out an old shoe box and sorted through his collection of badges and name tags until he found what he wanted. He's started stealing badges five years before. Detectives and rookies were the easiest – detectives because they were so arrogant they never thought anyone would rifle their jacket pockets, rookies because they were stupid. Jim had realized such things as authentic badges would always come in handy. He'd built his stockpile carefully. Then, two and a half years ago, when he'd realized his activities were suddenly being monitored and two plainclothes officers were following him, he'd made his final preparations. He'd found the perfect lair. He'd stashed his badges, a fake ID, a ton of cash, and, yes, two passports.

His diligence had paid off. The police never found his cover and he spent two years in prison, knowing that sooner or later opportunity would present itself, and he could pick up right where he left off.

He selected the appropriate badge and went to work sewing on the name patch. God was in the details.

His conversation with Sergeant Wilcox had gone well, particularly once he'd taken the man out to lunch and pumped him full of Halcion. The good old sergeant had slept like a baby as Jim had driven him out of the city, tied him to a tree, and prepared his Swiss Army knife. It hadn't taken long to get all the information he required.

He'd called the sergeant's wife and explained that Wilcox's assignment now required absolute secrecy. Her husband would not be home for a few days, nor would he be allowed to call. By the end of the week they would be able to tell her more.

Then he called the task force, spoke to the officer in charge, and said he was Wilcox's doctor. Wilcox had come down with an extreme case of food poisoning and would be out for the next twenty-four hours. Of course he'd return to duty immediately after that.

Sooner or late the authorities would ask more questions. That was fine. Jim just needed twenty-four hours. It would all be over then.

He rose, stretching out his long, toned body. Three hundred push-ups, five hundred sit-ups a day. Not an ounce of fat on him. Ed Kemper might be bigger, but in an arm-wrestling match, Jim was confident he would win.

He shook out his arms and legs. Four hours of sleep was all he needed nowadays. A deep calm had settled over him. Tonight his plan entered phase two and he was prepared. He had thought of everything, accounted for anything. He was invincible not because that's what he wanted to be; he was invincible because he worked at it.

Two years he'd rotted in Walpole. Two years of living in a six-by-eight cell in maximum security, allowed out for only one hour a day, Monday through Friday. Even then he was placed in handcuffs and leg shackles before being escorted by two guards to the maximum security rec area – really just a new six-by-eight cell outside, enclosed in wire mesh and nicknamed the dog cage. No more than two maximum security prisoners were allowed outside at once, and then they were put in distant cages so even conversation was difficult. Not that it mattered. Walpole was run by the

Latin Kings these days. Like he wanted to mingle with a bunch of fucked up, coked up spicks.

They'd wanted his ass. He had seen it in their eyes sometimes as he was escorted by their cells. He could smell their hatred and blood lust sluicing off their skin, flung toward him with their gang signs and low hisses. He liked to look them in the eye, stare them down, because they thought they were so bad when really they had no idea what it was all about. They clung to each other like weak-kneed bastards, passing drugs in handshakes, murdering over imaginary slights, and figuring it made them men. It meant nothing. The correction officers cracked down. Walpole went to the highest level of security and became a no-contact prison. And Jim found himself sitting across from Shelly in the visiting center with soundproof, bulletproof glass between them because the guards finally figured out girlfriends were swapping more than spit in all those passionate kisses.

Two years of wearing orange. Two years of sitting alone on a cot, listening to stone walls reverberate with unbridled hatred and poorly thought out politics. Two years without sex.

Never again. He'd made his plans carefully, he'd tended to all the details. He would not be going back to jail. And he would have his revenge.

He curled up naked on the bare cot. He slept and dreamed of the feel of Shelly's mouth sucking him dry. And the feel of his hands wrapping around her neck, squeezing, squeezing, squeezing.

'I'm coming for you, baby,' he murmured in his sleep. 'I'm coming.'

18

Tess was ready.

She woke up with the first rays of the sun, stretching out slowly. Newly formed muscles pulled and contracted. She could identify baby biceps, emerging triceps, and infant quads. She ran through a warm-up drill in the middle of her room and was pleased by the smooth, graceful flow of stance into stance.

She was getting there.

Her gaze went instantly to the phone. She wanted to call Sam. She wanted to hear her daughter's sweet voice and tell her everything was going to be all right. Did Difford tuck her in each night, did he read the right stories? Did he watch her eat her fruit, or was she managing to drop it under the table?

God, she wanted to hear her little girl's voice.

And tell her what, Tess? That you'll come home? That you'll save her from her daddy? That you're putting her in jeopardy just by calling?

She turned away, her hands fisted at her sides. Just a few more weeks, then she should be ready to hunt down Jim. The nightmare would end. She would reclaim her daughter. Would they live happily ever after?

Tess wasn't sure she believed in such things anymore.

She got ready for her morning swim. But when she walked into the living room, she froze.

J.T. and Marion faced off with the Navajo rug as their arena, so intent on each other, they didn't notice her. They circled like warring destriers, nostrils flaring, chests heaving, and flanks quivering. Glug served as an unwitting and unlikely centerpiece for the exchange.

'That's right, J.T.,' Marion muttered furiously. 'Daddy's really Darth Vader and I'm Princess Leia. Now step over to the dark side so we can get this show on the road!'

'I already told you I'm not going.'

'I gave you over a week, J.T. How long are you going to carry a torch for a mythical past?'

'Forever is a nice round number.'

Marion threw up her hands in disgust. 'Stop it! Just stop it! What is it with you? No matter what, you have to make a mess of things. Don't you understand that this is your last chance? You walk away from Daddy now, and that's it. He's dying and you will *never* get to wrap up loose ends.'

'You make life sound like an Italian opera.'

'And you like hating him, don't you, J.T.? He's an excuse for you. You get yourself thrown out of West Point, blame Daddy. You punch out your CO, blame Daddy. You drink too much, whore too much, try to kill yourself in godforsaken jungles for causes no one cares about, and what the hell, you blame Daddy. Well, this is it. Tomorrow morning I return to D.C. You can come and redeem yourself, or you can stay here and rot.'

A muscle twitched in J.T.'s jaw. He shook his head. 'I have to train Tess. Even if I was stupid enough to contemplate the trip, I still couldn't go.'

'Coward. You're just using Tess as an excuse.'

'Excuse? What the hell, Marion? Aren't you the one who keeps telling me just how dangerous Jim Beckett is? First you tell me how much help Tess needs, then I'm supposed to just walk away to attend such mundane matters as the colonel's death?'

Marion's face turned several shades of outrage. 'Bring her.'

'Bring her?'

'You heard me, J.T. You don't want to leave her alone, you need more time to train her. Then bring her with you. Take her to D.C. – it's not rocket science.'

'Oh, that's just a great idea, Marion. You're right. I'll bring Tess to D.C. I'll introduce her to the man who beat my sister and raped my wife. And just to see if he's really dead, I'll leave her alone in the room with him. We both know nothing brings the colonel to life like a beautiful, young, defenseless woman.'

'You delusional son of –'

'I hope he's dead!' J.T. declared. Then his voice dropped low. 'Then I *will* go to D.C. just so I can dance at his burial. I'll build a champagne waterfall in the middle of the front lawn and dance around it, singing "Ding-dong, Daddy's dead" for the whole world to hear.'

'You are hopeless! But most of all, you are drunk!'

Tess stared at J.T., waiting for him to deny the accusation, to state once again that he was a man who always kept his word.

Instead, he said, 'I beg to differ. I've had only one drink. That means I am merely myself.'

'But you drank, J.T. And you swore not to. You violated your own twisted moral code. Christ, look at you. Just look! You can't follow through on anything, you can't commit to anything. You are actually a talented human being and yet your life is nothing but a string of failures. And now you're selling whatever future you might have had to the worm in the bottom of the tequila bottle.'

'It was only one drink, Marion.'

'One is all it takes.'

His jaw clenched. 'And you?' he whispered. 'The perfect daughter to the father who beat us as a hobby. And he did worse than that, didn't he, Marion? You can live your life in denial, but I was there too. I know what he did. I heard his footsteps in the hall every night, I saw him go into your room. Don't you think I tried to stop him? Don't you think I . . . I . . . God. I wanted to *kill* him.'

Marion's face had turned to stone. 'Leave me out of your lies, J.T.'

'I'm not the one whose life is a lie. If anything, my life is too honest.'

'Forget it.' Marion threw her hands in the air. 'I wash my hands of you, J.T. You're sick and beyond help. You've destroyed our family, you know that? All of Daddy's hard work, all of his respect, *ruined* because of you. That's it. You're a waste of my time, and I'm outta here.'

She whirled and stepped toward the hall. J.T.'s hand snaked out fast, wrapping around Marion's wrist.

She looked down. 'Keep your hand there one minute longer and you will lose it.'

His grip tightened anyway and he said, 'Don't go.'

'*Don't go?*'

'Stay. Stay right here, Marion. Don't go back to D.C. and don't go back to him. Let him die. Let the colonel just die. And then maybe you and me . . . maybe we can start over again. For God's sake, Marion, you're my little sister.'

Marion glanced up at his face, at eyes that pleaded.

And in a flurry of movement she pivoted, chopped his forearm with her left hand, and yanked her arm free.

'You're a weak, self-pitying bastard, J.T. And there's no way you're dragging me down with you.'

She thundered down the hall like a Sherman tank, pushing Tess aside. Seconds later, the sound of the slamming door registered her departure.

J.T. slowly rubbed his arm where a red welt was rising to life. He looked lost, as if he didn't know what to do with himself.

Tess took a step forward.

'Going to jump in as well? Extract your pound of flesh while the meat's still fresh?'

'No.'

'Why not?'

There was no mockery in his voice. No sarcasm, no challenge. She hadn't thought there would be a time when she would miss that in him.

'It's not fun to kick a man when he's down?' she offered weakly, searching for some reaction in his face.

At long last his lips quirked. 'Yeah, I suppose that's true.'

She took another step forward, but he moved away to the table next to the sofa. He picked up Marion's gold cigarette case, then pulled out a quick ticket to cancer.

'Go away, Tess.' The match flared to life. He brought it to the end of the cigarette and inhaled deeply.

'I can't.'

'Haven't we had this conversation before?'

'Yes, and I won it then too. It's one of the only things I do well – argue with you.'

'Doesn't count. Everyone seems to win at that.'

'You really love Marion, don't you?' She wanted to touch his hand. She wanted to wrap her arms around his shoulders and hold him tight.

It took J.T. a long time to reply. 'Yeah. But I'm getting older and wiser every day.'

'Your iguana,' she reminded him. He always told Marion she couldn't smoke in front of Glug.

His gaze went from her to the pet to her. She could practically see the darkness suddenly bloom in his eyes. The wild self-derision that had been beaten into him by his father and stoked by his sister's rejection. The self-destructive rage that knew his sister was right and he had failed at everything. In fact, he had planned his life just that way.

The darkness scared her. It touched her. It brought goose bumps to her arms and shivers down her spine. Jim's rage had terrified her because it had been so cold. J.T.'s anger moved her because it was so real.

'J.T.,' she whispered, and reached out her hand to him.

'You're right,' he said abruptly.

He lifted the cigarette from his lips. He admired the glowing red tip with mock exaggeration.

He held out his left hand.

'Don't,' she cried, but it was too late. As she watched, he ground out the red tip in his palm.

'What are you doing?' His pain was in her voice.

'What I was taught.'

'J.T.' She took a step toward him.

'Don't do it,' he growled. 'I am a bastard and I am a son of a bitch and I am so on edge, I don't know myself anymore. You step into this room and I *will not* be held responsible for my actions.'

'I'm not asking you to!' she cried. Then she took another step and another step.

She planted herself in the middle of the living room. 'I have seen evil, J.T. I've seen bad and I've seen worse. You are not it, J.T. You aren't.'

'Goddamn you,' he said. 'Goddamn you.' He threw the cigarette case across the room in a fury, and it landed with a ringing thud.

She held her ground.

He flung out his arm and swept the side table clear. The porcelain lamp shattered. The clay coasters cracked.

She held her ground.

'You'll wish you never met me,' he warned. Then right on top of that, 'Goddamn us both.'

He stalked toward her and she was ready.

His hands wrapped around her waist like a vise. Not soft. Not gentle. She didn't murmur one sound of protest as he shoved her back and pinned her against the wall.

If she was going to run, she should've done it earlier. Now she was committed and there would be no stopping.

He lifted his hands and planted one on each side of her face.

'You think I won't take what you offer? You think I'll come to my senses at the last minute and walk away? You think I'm good? You think I'm decent? You haven't listened to a word of what Marion said.'

He caught her lower lip furiously, pulling on it with his teeth.

She wrapped her arms around his neck and bit back. It was rough and crude. He attacked her mouth, she fought back. Her life had been passivity and coldness, fright and rejection. Now she met passion head-on.

His body pressed against hers, his hips showing her exactly what he wanted and exactly what she would give him, because the time for no had come and gone and baby, this was it.

He sank his teeth into the tender flesh above her collarbone. She cried out and he stuck his finger in her mouth like a plug. She bit it, sucking it, rubbing her tongue along its length.

'Christ, you're greedy.'

His fingers slipped up her shorts, dipped into her panties, and thrust into her.

She cried out again, shocked in spite of herself. Unprepared, in spite of him. He slowed. His head came up. He looked at her with glittering eyes.

'You really don't know anything, do you?' he whispered thickly.

'No,' she confessed. 'No.'

'You're too late,' he muttered. 'You're too late.'

'I know, I know.'

His finger slid deeper, penetrating, stretching, seeking. His palm pressed against her, rubbing rhythmically, giving her a tempo she instinctively understood.

She felt the mysteries press against her. She closed her eyes and saw unspeakable colors building behind her lids.

'J.T.' she groaned. 'J.T.'

'Open your eyes. Look at me. I want to see it. I want to see everything.'

Her eyes cracked open, glazed and vulnerable. His finger moved faster and faster. There was no tenderness, just raw, primitive need.

She bit her lip.

And he whispered hoarsely, 'Now.'

She climaxed, screaming and shuddering and melting from the inside out.

She was barely aware of being dragged to the floor. He tore off their clothes, then he was on her, his hands impatiently parting her legs. He rubbed against her, one last second of tantalizing pressure, then he whispered, 'Hold on to me, Tess. This is gonna be rough.'

He thrust inside her, and she was filled. She was annihilated.

She grabbed his shoulders and hung on for dear life.

He pulled back, his arms trembling with the strain. He flirted with her again, rubbing against her, making her squirm. Her legs wrapped around him tightly, and she stopped simply receiving, instead arching to meet each demanding blow.

The climax slammed into them both, screeching through their blood for a long, suspended moment when they could not breathe, could not move, could not feel even the pounding of their pulse.

He pulled away abruptly, the way she knew he would. He rose quickly, as she'd expected. He looked down at her, his face an unreadable mask.

'You don't have to say anything,' she told him. She felt bruised and battered, used and abused. And unbelievably satiated. Wise with the power of the mysteries and sense of her own self.

He strode away from her, already heading for the pool.

'I guess I don't have to ask if it was good for you,' she called out proudly.

He paused, his hand on the sliding glass door. 'Did I hurt you?'

'No.'

'I was rough.'

'I wasn't complaining.'

'Maybe you should have.'

'Already blaming yourself, J.T.? Adding me to the long list of things you beat yourself over the head with late at night? I know you better than you think. I believe in you more than you do. So don't bother hating yourself for showing me the wonders of animal sex. Really, I accept full responsibility for my actions.'

'Tess –'

'J.T., if you apologize now, I'll never forgive you.'

He stiffened. 'Fine.' He walked out the sliding glass door and jumped into his pool.

'Remember, Tess,' she whispered to herself, 'you are strong. You are very, very strong.'

It was a seedy place. Beat-up old trucks and battered blue Chevrolets dotted the parking lot. There might have been painted yellow lines once, but now they were obscured by dust and tumbleweeds. Removed from the nicely paved streets of central Nogales and the all-American McDonald's, the bar sat back in the desert, framed by a distant hill covered with run-down shanties. No smooth adobe walls or cheery red roof. This was wood, gray, beaten wood haphazardly stuck together with gnarled nails and sheer determination. Rusted tin formed a brown-spotted roof. When it rained, the place sounded like a bongo drum.

Now faint sounds of salsa leapt from the cracks, as if even the music was desperate to escape the dreariness. Smoke wafted out, ghostly tendrils curling up to the sky.

A flickering red neon sign pronounced the joint MANNY'S. Just Manny's.

Tired. Dusty. Forgotten.

Marion thought it was perfect.

Her sleek blue rental car looked out of place, but then, so did she. She pushed open the door without apology, entering the joint like the proverbial new gun in town. The music didn't stop for her, but the patrons did. Two men to her left, hunched over a threadbare pool table, looked up from their game. Behind the bar, a short, bald man in a sleeveless denim vest that showed off his serpent tattoos stopped pouring beer from the tap. To her right, small clusters of men and a few women glanced up once, then did a double take.

Marion pushed her way to the bar. 'I want a whiskey. Straight up.'

Serpent man stared at her. She stared back. He still didn't move. 'You got a problem with dollars?' she asked coolly.

'No.'

'Then I think we can be friends.' She pulled out a crisp twenty and slapped it on the counter.

The bartender fetched a bottle of whiskey. As if it had been a signal, the crowd returned to its business.

Marion didn't turn. She didn't look. She sat alone at the bar, listening to the murmurs. She couldn't speak Spanish, but she understood it well enough.

When the bartender gave her her drink, she thanked him with a mocking toast. She raised the glass. She parted her pink lips. And she tossed back the whiskey in one gulp.

She slammed the glass down. She swallowed through the pain in her gut. Then delicately she touched the corner of her mouth with a single French-manicured nail.

'Give me another.'

'*Sí, señorita.*'

'Exactly.'

19

'I want the Apple Jacks.'

'Okay, okay,' Difford muttered, pushing open the door with his foot and balancing four grocery bags with his arms, fingers, and hips. Samantha went barreling in, unmindful of his precarious juggling act. Decked out in her pink winter coat with the hood pulled tightly around her face, she looked like a strawberry version of Frosty the Snowman. Her blond hair peered out around the white furry trim of her hood. Her cheeks were a healthy, happy red. It was probably still too warm for full winter gear, but Difford had never dressed a kid before, so he liked to err on the side of caution.

'Apple Jacks, Apple Jacks,' Samantha sang at the top of her lungs.

Difford grunted, wondered how mothers ever learned how to cope with children, and managed to kick the door shut with his foot. A bit more juggling, and he made it all the way to the tiny brown kitchen, dropping only two oranges.

Samantha chased the fruit down the hall, then came trotting back with the oranges clutched in her mittened hands like trophies. She beamed at him triumphantly. At that moment, despite his best intentions, his chest tightened and he did understand exactly why mothers coped with children.

'Thank you,' he said with somber politeness, and accepted the oranges.

'Okay, the cereal now!' Her smile grew. She was perfectly delighted with herself and her persistent efforts that had finally yielded the sugar-coated cereal. He'd been so careful to buy only healthy things. Tess had given him a list of appropriate grocery items and he'd been plugging Samantha with bowl after bowl of Raisin Bran. But today at the store she'd noticed the Apple Jacks on special display at the end of the aisle and that had been that. She wanted Apple Jacks! Difford discovered he could command a whole police department but not one determined four-year-old. They bought the Apple Jacks. Two boxes. Buy one get one free. He was such a sucker.

'Lunch first,' he insisted. Her face fell, her lower lip jutting out suspiciously. He suffered an immediate burst of panic. 'Oh, no, you don't,' he said, shaking his head. 'Nutrition is important. We have turkey or ham.'

Samantha looked at him, her bright blue eyes keenly intelligent. Her head cocked to the side, and by now he could read the signs. She was determining how hard to push him. This was his own fault; the first few days, he'd given her heaven and earth every time she cried. Samantha had quickly internalized that lesson and become hell on wheels.

He forced himself to stand firm. Think of her as a new recruit, he reminded himself. A cadet who needed a strong guiding hand.

After a minute he won the battle of wills. 'Turkey,' she decided.

Difford grinned, feeling ridiculously proud of himself. He didn't win often. Tess hadn't warned him of a small child's capacity for deviousness.

'Okay,' he said, and put away the groceries. He then laid out the bread, mustard, and mayonnaise. Samantha was in charge of adding the turkey, which she did with true flourish. They sat at the simple wood table and ate in silence.

He figured they'd play dominoes afterward. The kid still kicked his butt, but he was getting better.

He sent her to go get the game while he finished cleaning up. Minutes later he wandered into the living room, where they generally played, sitting cross-legged on the floor. His knees were getting sore.

He was about to push back his reclining chair, when he noticed the pillows. Yesterday he'd tucked them behind his back for comfort as he'd leaned against the sofa. He wasn't much of a pick-up guy. He'd thought he'd left them on the floor.

Now one sat neatly in each corner of the couch.

Samantha walked into the room, carrying the box of dominoes.

Difford said in as calm a voice as he could manage, 'Sam, I want you to go to your room.'

'But I didn't do anything wrong!'

'I know, sweetheart.' His eyes darted around the room as he reached beneath his jacket for his gun. 'We're playing a new game, honey. I just want you to go to your room for a few minutes, okay? I'm ... I'm preparing a surprise for you in the living room.'

She looked troubled. 'I don't like this game!' she cried, dropped the dominoes on the floor, and ran sniffling for her room.

Difford didn't waste any time. Looking across the street, he could see an old green car parked at the corner. He raised his hand. Both of the officers waved back. Okay, his cover car was still present and it was broad daylight. If someone had tried to approach the safe house, the officers would have noticed.

He searched the house anyway, gun drawn and eyes sharp as he went from room to room. Living room was clear. Bathroom, including the shower, was clear. He entered his bedroom slowly, sweeping the space with a steady, level arm, pointing his gun in all corners. Then he pressed himself against a wall and slid the closet door open with his foot. Quick step and pivot, and he faced off against his clothes. Nothing moved, nothing stirred. He brushed his gun through the hangers. Empty.

He started to breathe a little easier. Nerves, he told himself, just nerves. The news of Shelly Zane's murder had gotten to him. The knowledge that Beckett was out there somewhere, gunning for Theresa, was definitely keeping him up at night.

But Beckett was just a man. Tess had stood up to him before. Lieutenant Houlihan and Special Agent Quincy were doing their best to make sure she would never have to again. A lot of good people were working this case. Sooner or later they'd get Beckett.

He finished the sweep of the house, telling Sam it was part of the game as he checked her room, her closet, beneath her bed. He could tell she didn't believe him.

But the house was clear. All was still well. Maybe he'd just forgotten about picking up the pillows. Maybe Sam had done it.

He replaced his gun in his holster. He offered Samantha his hand. She took it without question.

'Dominoes?' he tried.

'I want my mommy.'

'I . . . I know.'

'Do you know where my mommy is?' Her lower lip had begun to tremble.

'Yeah, honey, I do.'

'Make her come home.'

Difford squatted down. 'She wants to come home, Sam, she really does. No one loves you like your mommy does. But she has to take care of some things first. She's, uh, making everything safe, you know? And once it's all safe, she'll come get you and you'll always be together.'

'I want her now,' Sam whispered.

'I know, Sam. I know. Come on, kid, let's play dominoes.' He led her into the living room, not knowing what else to do.

Samantha didn't sit across from him as she usually did. Instead, she sat right beside him, her little shoulder against his side. After a moment he put his big arm around her and patted her awkwardly.

She braved a tremulous smile and opened the domino box.

'My mommy will come home soon?'

'Right.'

'And then we'll always be together?'

'Yeah, honey. Everything will be all right.'

'Can we watch *Jurassic Park* again tonight?'

'Okay,' he said, but couldn't quite stop the sinking feeling in his chest. He patted her shoulder again. 'Okay.'

Tess went to find J.T. The patio was empty, the pool flat. She felt the pinprick of unease.

Gravel crunched. She whirled toward the sound with her hands already fisted.

J.T. emerged from the side of the house, buck naked and wielding his gun. He didn't even glance in her direction. He disappeared around the left side, his gun leading him forward.

She was still standing there stupidly.

J.T. rematerialized on the patio, his gun down by his naked thigh.

'I thought I heard somethin',' he muttered.

'I – I didn't see anything.'

'Yeah, well, you were staring at my butt.'

Her cheeks flushed crimson. 'Just admiring the view.'

'Huh.'

He took two steps forward, one step back, and finally stood still. 'Guess I'm just edgy.'

She contemplated him silently for a moment. 'Did you really drink last night?'

'Yeah. One shot. Tequila. Lord have mercy on my soul.'

'I think it's a little late for that.' She contemplated berating him. She contemplated calling him a fool. She decided in the end that neither was necessary. No one had ever been harder on J. T. Dillon than J. T. Dillon.

She said, 'I need you.'

'Don't.'

'Too late. You know what I'm up against, J.T. Marion's told you enough about Jim. He's going to come after me, and I have to be ready. We've done so well this last week. I can swim farther, I have some muscle tone. I can shoot a gun –'

'Barely.'

'Exactly! I need to learn more. I need you to teach me more. Be there for me, dammit. It's only a few more weeks.'

'I can handle it,' he said stiffly.

'Are you sure? It's not weak to call AA, J.T. It's not weak to admit that you need help.'

'I'm fine! Don't you have any hay bales to shoot?'

'None of them are as much fun as hounding you.' She walked right up to him. She could feel the heat and tension radiating from him, and it made her hot.

'Greedy,' he whispered.

'I learned it from you.'

He was growing hard. She could get him to want her again, get him to take her again. Here on the patio, or maybe beneath the mesquite tree, or maybe on a glass table. Maybe all three.

And then what?

She pushed herself away. His breath exhaled with a hiss.

'Get back on the wagon –'

'I stopped with one,' he interrupted tightly.

'Good. Don't take it any further. Now go after Marion.'

His eyes widened incredulously. 'What?'

'She needs you, J.T.'

He held up his forearm and pointed to the red welt. 'Tess, open your eyes.'

'I have. And I'm telling you she needs you. Why do you think she ran away, J.T.? So that you would follow. So that finally someone would follow.'

'Marion could chew up an armored tank for breakfast, then spit out perfectly formed nails the rest of the day. End of story.'

He strode toward the sliding glass door. 'You still want a teacher, right?'

'Yes.'

'Then stop standing there, yapping at me. This isn't Club Med; get in your damn swim clothes. We'll begin with weights, end in the pool. You got five minutes.'

'She's scared,' Tess whispered behind him.

He said to them both, 'Stop kidding yourself.'

'Can I buy you a drink?'

'I'm not stopping you.' Marion leaned over the pool table, where she was slowly and methodically annihilating all the men in the bar. The sun had gone down. The interior was darker and smokier than before. Her eyes had adjusted hours before, and now she didn't notice the changes.

'Eight ball, left corner pocket,' she called. She lined up the shot, pulled back the stick, and slammed it forward with more force than necessary. The cue ball nailed the eight ball, ramming it into the faded green lip of the edge and forcing it to rocket into the corner pocket with a sharp clatter.

She straightened and raised her cigarette to her lips. Inhale. Exhale. 'I believe you owe me twenty bucks.'

The man grumbled. She hadn't caught his name. She didn't care. He'd been better than the others, but still no match. He coughed up the money. She added it to her stack.

She turned and scanned the bar. She had the tickling in the back of her neck, that sensation of being watched. Of course, the whole damn bar was staring at her. She turned back to the pool table.

Fresh meat arrived with her drink. He smiled at her, trying to be charming, but she wasn't so drunk she couldn't see the predatory intent behind his smile. She accepted the glass, leaning her slim hip negligently against the table and blatantly eyeing him since he was blatantly eyeing her.

He was tall, over six feet. Beneath his red baseball cap, tufts of dishwater-blond hair stuck out like straw. He had a mustache and stubbly beard, and the broad shoulders and muscled arms of a workingman. His stomach wasn't flat anymore though. He'd been a stud once. Now he was going to seed.

'So what's your game?' he asked with a wink.

'Eight ball,' she said coolly, 'I'll give you three-to-one odds. Betting starts at twenty.'

He crossed his arms so that his biceps bulged.

'You really that into pool?'

'You really think you can pick me up with one drink?'

His face reddened. She kept staring at him. Men couldn't stand up to that stare. They all fled like dogs with their tails tucked between their legs. Then they called her a bitch.

'All right,' he said, surprising her. 'I'll play. But I'll warn you now, I'm better than what you're used to.'

'I'll be the judge of that.' She slammed back her whiskey and picked up the cue stick. Her gun was nestled beneath her arm, hidden by her jacket. She liked the feel of it there, comforting and cold.

They got down to business.

Do you miss me, Roger, do you think of me at all? Or am I just a cold bitch to you, one you married for Daddy's connections? How can a cocktail waitress make you so damn happy?

She bent low and broke the balls with a fury. Two solids went in. She inhaled another cleansing gulp of tobacco and contemplated her next shot.

And you, Daddy? Why don't you ever call my name? Wasn't I a good daughter? Didn't I do whatever you asked?

She sank three more, then scratched.

Her opponent took over with a swagger. She was unimpressed.

Then there's you, J.T. Running off and ruining the family name. You're nothing but a drunken loser and then you say I'm like you. I am nothing like you. I am strong.

Her opponent cleared the table. She looked at him, mildly shocked.

'Told you I knew what I was doing.'

'I suppose you did.'

He set down his cue stick while she counted out three twenties and handed them over. He shook his head.

'Haven't you had enough foreplay? Aren't you ready to get down to the real business?'

She contemplated acting outraged. She contemplated feigning ignorance. She set down the money and with a shrug of her shoulders said, 'All right. What did you have in mind?'

'Come with me, darling. I'll fuck your problems right out of your head.'

She stared at him. He was past his prime, but his arms were still lean and hard. He knew how to play pool and was more man than anything else that had walked into the room.

She should tell him no. She was the good daughter who'd only ever slept with Roger. She was the good agent who knew better than to leave with a strange man.

She said, 'All right.'

She picked up her purse and accepted his heavy grip as he led her to the door.

'And you froze up every time I touched you, Marion!'

She still couldn't shake the feeling that someone was watching her, that if she turned around now, she'd find one pair of eyes a bit too sharp, a bit too knowing.

She didn't turn around.

Outside, the air was cool and crisp and her nostrils flared, almost offended by the sweetness after the reeking bar. The sky was pitch black, good for midnight doings.

Her stud led her to his truck. No one was around in the parking lot, but she wasn't worried.

He held open the passenger door for her. She wasn't sure if that was a positive sign or not. She didn't ask where they were going, she didn't contemplate the events at hand. She lit another cigarette and rolled down the window to smoke.

He drove to the middle of nowhere. Had he taken other women there before? Was he married and that's why they didn't go to his apartment? She didn't care. None of it was her business. She was just along for the ride.

'No one comes out here,' he said, looking at her for the first time. 'But it's nice on nights like tonight. You can smell the creosote, look at the stars. Thought you might like it better than some trailer that stinks of beer and socks. I don't clean much.'

'It's fine.'

He opened the door. 'I have a blanket in the back. Ground's soft.'

So he'd come here before. A regular lovers' lane. She watched him in the side mirror. He pulled out a square army blanket and unfolded it on the ground. No iron pipes. No handcuffs. Just a Don Juan after all. She opened her door and stepped out.

The night was chilly, penetrating the haze pressed over her conscience. Then he stepped forward and grabbed her, pushing her against the truck. His mouth swooped down and he stabbed his tongue into her mouth.

The taste hit her hard, the intrusion shattering her apathy until she almost gagged. Then she remembered this was what she was supposed to want. She forced her body to relax. She wound her arms around his neck and tried not to wince as his meaty chest crushed her breast.

He sank to his knees, began to unbutton her jacket.

'Wait,' she said. She didn't want him to find her gun. 'I'll do it. You take off your shirt.'

His eyes were dark with lust. His thick fingers went instantly to his shirt.

'Turn around,' she told him.

'Why?'

'Because I'm fucking shy. Turn around.'

He shrugged and did as he was told. She stripped off her jacket, then unfastened her shoulder holster and placed it on the ground beneath her jacket.

He turned back around and attacked her, tearing off her silk shell. He pressed his teeth against her neck. He spanned her waist with his hands. He brought his fingers up and kneaded her small breasts as if he could force them to be larger, more voluptuous. She stood still, her hands at her sides.

His hands found her bra clasp and undid it, baring her breasts to the night wind. The briskness made her nipples harden and peak. He took it personally, crowing his satisfaction. Hot and wet, his mouth fastened upon a nipple and sucked voraciously.

She looked down. She watched his head bob up and down at her breast. She heard slurping, grunts and groans. His hips were beginning to rock insistently.

He switched to her other breast, his jaw working furiously.

She shivered. She thought in the back of her mind that the stars were very beautiful and that she was very small beneath them.

His hands fastened on the waistband of her slacks and pulled them down along with her sensible panties. She didn't protest.

'Man, baby, you are hot,' he said. 'A real fucking piece of ass.'

She looked at him blankly, wondering if he was even looking at her body. She was not hot. She had flat breasts and almost no hips. She was too thin and wiry. Roger had often complained that there wasn't a single soft spot on all of her body. She was muscle and sinew. There were young boys more feminine than her.

The stud pushed off his pants. His dick sprang out, huge and purple, alien and grotesque. At least Roger had been small.

She took a step back. It was too late.

He dragged her down to the blanket, already snuffling between her breasts, his fingers kneading them painfully.

'Baby, baby, baby,' he muttered thickly. 'Oh, baby, baby.'

She tried to shut her ears against the sound.

'Kiss me. Come on, darling, don't be shy. Kiss me. Touch me. Go wild.'

He placed his lips on hers as if he knew she needed the encouragement. Then he grabbed her hand and wrapped it around his dick. She flinched at the feel of it throbbing between her fingers. It was alive. She should want it, she should revel in it. She should cry, Oh, yes, fuck me.

She wanted to run.

He took her head between his hands. 'Do you nibble? Come on, don't be shy. Swallow me whole, baby. You'll like what I give you.'

Before she could react, he forced her head down. Now his dick was pressing against her cheek, smelling overpoweringly of musk.

'Come on, what are you waiting for?' For the first time, his voice was impatient.

Kiss the willy. Come on, Marion, you know what I want. Be a good girl and open your mouth. Kiss the willy. Kiss Daddy's willy.

She raised her head and vomited all over his lap.

'Jesus fucking Christ!' He sprang back, batting at her furiously. She fell to the side, still vomiting rancid whiskey. Her shoulders trembled. She hunched her small, naked body over her knees and shut out the world until the black void was complete, the memories pushed back and locked up.

She reached frantically for her clothes.

The stud came after her, angry and enraged. She didn't think, she wasn't composed. She fought instinctively, and five moves later he was writhing on the ground without even the breath to curse. Throwing on her clothes, she grabbed his truck keys and told him he'd find his vehicle back at the bar.

Then she climbed in the truck, started the engine, and roared back out onto the long, empty road.

Run, Marion. Run and don't look back. You don't

want to know what's behind you. You never wanted to know what was behind you.

20

J.T. woke up instantly, lying on his back amid the tangled sheets. He stared at the ceiling blankly, blinking his eyes and trying to pinpoint what had woken him.

Then slowly his gaze drifted to the foot of the bed.

She stood there, pale and ethereal once more. Long blond hair tumbled down her back in fat, loose waves. Small hands knotted and unknotted in front of a flowing white nightgown. Her expression tore at him, begging him to save her.

His breath caught in his throat. He told himself again and again that it was only memory: living, breathing memory standing at the foot of his bed. He squeezed his eyes shut, his mind screaming for the demon to go away. He couldn't save her. He hadn't saved her. He was nothing.

He opened his eyes.

She was still there.

And he realized for the first time that she wasn't a child. This wasn't little Merry Berry, stepping from his mind into his bedroom. This was Marion, grown-up, alive, and real.

His hand lifted from the sheets on its own accord, stretching out to her. 'Marion . . .' His voice cracked.

'I came,' she whispered. 'I wanted to see . . . if I'd ever stood here. If it felt . . .' Her eyes squeezed shut. 'No. It never happened! It never, ever happened!'

She grabbed the skirt of her nightgown and fled.

His hand fell to the sheet in shock. He couldn't breathe, he couldn't move. He was suspended someplace between the past and the present and his chest was on fire with pain.

He swung his legs over the side of the bed. He reached the door in two steps, flung it open, and caught a flash of white as she disappeared into her room. He gave chase. He had to. Just once he had to get this right.

Her door slammed shut forcefully, rocking the still house and locking with a definitive click. J.T. beat against it frantically.

'Marion, let me in! Can't we talk about this? Christ, Marion. Just once can't we talk about this?' He pressed his cheek against the wooden door, knowing he was begging and beyond caring.

From the other side of the door he heard a rough, choking sound. She was crying. Cold, perfect Marion was sobbing.

He sank down to the floor.

'Marion,' he called hoarsely. 'Marion, Marion. I tried. I tried so hard to save you. God, I tried . . .'

But there was no reply, just the hoarse sound of his little sister sobbing.

He pressed his cheek against the door. He closed his eyes. Then he banged on the door helplessly with his fist, needing her to let him in, desperate for her to let him in.

Marion, I know I failed you. But I came back. I came back and you'd forgotten everything – all the good moments, as well as the bad – and that failed me. How could we fail each other? How could we serve the colonel like that?

Marion didn't come to the door, nor did she answer his pleas. So he switched to cursing the colonel instead. Thirty-six years old, he cursed his father and wondered how a grown man could feel such fear.

Minutes passed. Her sobbing stopped and silence took its place, reigning in the dark, shadowed house.

'Marion?'

There was nothing. She'd come. She'd left. He was right back where he started except for the pain devouring his chest, the dark, enraged beast screaming and gnashing in his belly.

'It's okay.'

He looked up. Tess stood in the gray-filled hallway, her gaze understanding. She took his hand.

'Give her until morning. She isn't ready to listen to you now.'

'I tried,' he whispered dumbly. *Failure, failure, failure. Pussy-whipped mama's boy.*

'I know.' She touched his cheek. 'It's okay. You were just a little boy, J.T. It wasn't your fault.'

He buried his lips against her hand, squeezing his eyes shut against the unbearable darkness that had lived inside him for so long. He wanted to hate someone; for a moment he even wanted to hate her. But he hadn't enough energy left inside him. He was wrung out and empty.

He felt her guide him to his feet. She led him to his room and tucked him into bed. He simply lay on his back, staring at the ceiling and going insane with the memories. He wanted a drink. Wouldn't someone give him a drink?

Push it away, push it away, Rachel whispered in his mind.

But he couldn't. The memories had been seared into his head and he couldn't get them out of his mind.

Tess pulled out a chair and sat down.

'I'll stay. You shouldn't be alone on a night like tonight. Not with tequila in the house.'

'Stop it,' he muttered. 'Go away. Isn't a psychotic ex-husband enough for you? Can't you just leave the rest of us alone?'

'I've been inside the darkness too, J.T. I know that sometimes the light seems too far away. We all get lost in the dark, and it's such a scary place. Such a lonely place.'

Her words hurt him, looked inside him, and laid him bare. He was thinking of all those nights, listening to the colonel's jump boots ring against the floor. With no one to tell, no one who would help him or Marion.

Night after night, lying there, wanted it to stop, needing it to stop. And always facing it alone.

He gave in with a groan. He grabbed Tess by the hand and yanked her into bed. She fell against him easily, already whispering his name.

'I know,' she murmured against his hair. 'I know.'

He buried his face against her neck.

'I won't leave you,' she whispered. 'I won't leave you'.

His hands dug into her back and brought her closer.

Difford was uneasy.

Long after the sun went down, he and Sam ate their macaroni and cheese dinner. They watched *Jurassic Park* and saw the children survive the monsters. Difford checked out Samantha's room, but there were no demons beneath the bed or in the closet. He tucked her in, brushing back her hair and retrieving her fancy talking doll that did more things than any doll he'd ever heard of. Tonight she had him read her 'Snow White.'

She went to sleep. He prowled the living room and wondered why his nerves were on edge.

The phone rang. He almost jumped out of his skin. He lunged across the living room and caught it before the second ring – he didn't want it to wake Sam up.

'Lieutenant?'

'Yes.' Difford's voice was wary. He waited for the security phrase.

'It rains upon the plains in Spain,' the caller said. 'Difford, it's Sergeant Wilcox. Listen closely –'

'I heard you had some kinda stomach bug.'

'No. I had a bad case of Halcion poisoning.'

'What?' Now Difford paid attention.

'We don't have much time, all right? Some guy calling himself Detective Beaumont showed up yesterday, claimed to be from Bristol County with an urgent message for you. The man spiked my coffee while I was questioning him in the interrogation room.'

'Beckett.'

'Yeah, it was Beckett. He rifled through my note-book, he asked me some questions. Lieutenant, we're pretty sure he knows where you are and that he has a copy of the house key. We have to get you out of the house now.'

Difford was silent. And then, finally confronted by a danger he could act against, he felt calm. 'What is the plan?'

'Okay, the minute you hang up with me, look out your window. Officer Travis is going to get out of the back-up vehicle – he's a big guy, you can't miss him. Just drift casually toward the front door, okay. No sudden moves, Beckett might be watching. Why don't you have a cup of coffee in your hand for the officer. It'll look like the man is just getting his caffeine fix. The minute he's in, shut the door. He'll help you round up Sam. You'll take the car in your garage –'

'Wait.'

'What?'

Difford felt the first beads of sweat pop up on his brow. 'If he, uh, if he has the key to the house, he can get into the garage. I haven't checked the garage recently. I just hadn't thought of it. He could be . . .'

'Shit.' A tense pause. 'All right. I'll tell Officer Travis. Once he's in the house, he'll check the garage, you cover him. If all is clear, the three of you exit the garage. Evasive maneuvers, then come straight to HQ. Clear?'

'Clear.'

Difford hung up the phone. He crossed to the window and pulled back the curtains. The hairs on the back of his neck were up. His breathing had gone shallow.

He saw the car light come on across the street as the door opened. He saw a big, heavyset officer climb out of the front seat. Briefly he saw the second man bent over, as if picking something off the floor. The door shut and the light went out. Officer Travis now looked around. Difford saw the man's hand rest on his unsnapped holster.

'Stay calm,' he murmured to the junior officer. 'Remember, you're just coming for coffee.'

But he could feel the young man's tension from here. Suddenly, in this quiet neighborhood, it seemed the whole world was watching them.

Officer Travis advanced across the street. Belatedly Difford moved to the kitchen to pour a hasty mug of coffee. His eyes were on the garage door.

Beckett turned off the cellular phone and set it on the floor. He'd spent an hour that morning practicing Sergeant Wilcox's voice. The effort had paid off.

He turned, his movements a bit awkward in the heavily padded uniform. His 'partner' had been reclining in the passenger seat, a blanket pulled up to his neck so it appeared that he was sleeping. Knowing the car light would illuminate his form, Beckett leaned over the dead body, straightened the seat, and slumped the man over. Rigor mortis was beginning to set in, so it wasn't easy. Then again, Beckett had gotten used to maneuvering dead bodies. The trick was to bend the man at the bullet hole in his waist.

Beckett looked up. Sure enough, Difford stood in the living room window, waiting for Officer Travis to step out of his car.

'Happy to be of service,' Beckett murmured, and opened the car door.

The knocking echoed through the safe house quietly. Good, Difford thought. Officer Travis was at least thinking of Samantha. Difford approached the door, the steaming coffee clutched in one hand. He had to resist the urge to glance over his shoulder at the garage door.

Keep cool, keep cool.

'Password,' Difford demanded through the dead-bolted door.

'It rains upon the plains in Spain.'

Difford checked out the officer through the peephole. The kid looked young, but then, they all looked young to Difford. He was a big guy who obviously needed to work out more. Christ, how had the Pillsbury Doughboy end up as his back-up? Difford cracked open the door, not amused.

He gave the junior officer another scathing inspection with the chain still on. Difford wasn't about to act stupid now. The uniform checked out, though the kid had no awards to speak of.

'ID?'

Officer Travis dutifully produced his shield. Fine.

Difford unfastened the chain and held out the coffee mug. 'Take it and act calm. Remember, you just came over for a cup of coffee.' His gaze swept the block. The streetlights created puddles of darkness; he'd always hated streetlights. So far, nothing moved.

'All right, come in.'

Officer Travis stepped into the house, looking tense and uncomfortable beneath Difford's scrutiny. 'How long have you been with the force?'

'Two years.'

'Two years and you got this duty?'

'Manpower shortage. The Camarini shooting and this are sucking us dry.'

'Huh. Ever secured a house before?'

'I was part of the Gingham bust. That's why they signed me up.'

Difford finally relented. The Todd Gingham deal had gone badly. They'd thought they had the nineteen-year-old arms dealer holed up in his house in New Bedford. The neighbors had seen him wielding a handgun and looking high as a kite. A SWAT team had been called in. Shot the hell out of the house. Kid escaped out the back and opened fire on a few squad cars. It had taken six officers and a flying tackle to finally neutralize the threat. So Officer Travis had been in the line of fire. He'd functioned beneath gunpowder, adrenaline, and screaming men.

Difford began to relax. He cocked his head and led Officer Travis to the garage door.

'Set the coffee on the table. Take the lead. I already checked out the rest of the house. If he's here, he's in there.'

'No, Difford. He's right here.' Officer Travis moved faster than Difford would have thought a fat man could. He whirled, his arm arched up, and Difford saw his eyes right before the man's fist snapped back his chin.

He went down hard, but his hand got around his gun. *Don't panic, don't panic.*

He pulled his gun out of his holster. *Shoot, dammit, shoot.*

The baton caught him square on the forearm; dimly he heard the crack of his arm breaking. Fingers went numb. Gun flew across the room and hit the wall.

Get his feet. Kick out his feet. Get him down.

His ankle hooked Beckett's. He pulled hard. The baton caught him across the cheek as Jim toppled. Ringing filled his ears. He tasted something rusty in his mouth, blood. Shit, it was pouring down his chin. What had happened to his teeth?

He planted his good arm on the floor and started crawling for his gun. *Faster, faster, faster.*

Tess, I'm sorry. I'm sorry.

He heard the rustle of nylon and knew Jim was beginning to rise. He picked up the tempo, forcing himself to move. The gun was so close, twenty feet, ten. If he could just get his hand out –

Beckett sat on his back hard, slamming Difford to the floor. The breath left him in a giant whoosh and he couldn't get it back. Hands wrapped around his throat and began to squeeze. He fought, he squirmed against the floor. The world spun away and he sank into the blackness.

The void didn't hurt.

And it lasted only a minute. Then the pressure was gone. His lungs instinctively inhaled, his eyes fought to see. Vaguely he felt Beckett rise. He saw his gun kicked far away. Beckett picked up a kitchen chair. He strode down the hall and jammed it beneath the closed door of Samantha's room.

And Difford knew what was going to happen then. The chair told him clearly what Beckett didn't want his daughter to wake up and see.

Beckett walked back down the hall. Difford tried to pull himself away, but his broken arm refused to move and blood and teeth were already pooling in his throat. He shimmied three more feet, then Beckett's hand curled around his ankle, pinning him in place. He couldn't quite stop his own whimper.

'I have a few questions for you,' Beckett whispered in his ear.

A sliding rasp. A knife appeared before Difford's gaze.

'Sergeant Wilcox was too easy,' Beckett murmured. 'Have you ever noticed that cops have the lowest threshold for pain? They spend their whole life studying it and thinking that because they have, they're immune to it. It will never happen to them.'

'Son of a bitch,' Difford gasped.

'Shh. Don't wake Sam.'

Difford's eyes shut. He felt something trickle down, his cheeks. It might have been tears.

'Make it hard, Difford. Give me a challenge. I want a challenge.'

Jim Beckett went to work.

Beckett moved in the moon-shrouded living room. First he picked up the phone and dialed in to the officer on duty.

'Bravo Fourteen,' he intoned. 'Checking in, all's clear.'

'Roger, Bravo Fourteen.'

'Talk to you in an hour.' Officer Travis signed off.

It was now one A.M. At two A.M., the new shift would arrive. Jim had to keep on schedule.

He opened the garage door. He arranged Difford's body in the trunk. Returning to the kitchen, he attended to the mess with paper towels. Blood was oily, harder to clean up than people expected. He'd read of a couple in the Midwest who'd opened a business cleaning up after death. Homicides, suicides, they took care of everything and made a lot of money. While in prison, he'd been tempted to write to them for tips.

Now he didn't have time to be too neat. He got the worst and arranged furniture over the rest. Then he quickly stripped down to the jeans and T-shirt he wore beneath the bulky uniform, tossing the uniform in the washing machine next to the kitchen. He would turn on the washer before leaving. Removing his wig, he also took the time to scrub the makeup off his face – he didn't want to scare Sam. Following that same vein of thought, he found one of Difford's old baseball caps to wear over his bald head.

He'd forgotten Difford's affection for baseball. Had he remembered, he would've killed the lieutenant with a bat just for irony's sake.

One twenty A.M. Jim scrubbed his arms and hands in the sink, then placed the coffee mug inside. He'd left prints everywhere. It was the nice thing about being him now – he no longer had to hide. He could leave fingerprints, hair, blood, wherever the hell he wanted. As an escaped convicted murderer, his job was even easier.

Finally he stood in the hallway before the closed door of Samantha's room. His stomach fluttered with nervous butterflies, a unique sensation. He felt like he was about to ask out a girl for the first time.

He rubbed his hands on his thighs and decided he was ready.

He removed the kitchen chair, not hearing any movement on the other side of the door. Difford hadn't made much noise. Jim had counted on Difford wanting to protect Samantha as much as he did. He twisted the doorknob and very carefully eased the door open.

And the silvery moonbeam illuminated the bed like a

spotlight, accentuating her white-blond hair and spilling over her cheek.

Jim Beckett stared down at his little girl with awe, and his love for her bloomed in his chest.

Her eyes fluttered open, sleepy and innocent. Then they widened with shock. He silenced her impending scream with a single finger pressed gently over her lips.

'Sam,' he whispered.

Her eyes widened more at the sound of his voice. 'D-d-daddy?'

'Yes, baby.' He smiled. She looked unbearably lovely. She looked perfect.

'You came back.'

'Of course I came back, Sammy. I came back for you. And we'll never be apart again.'

J.T. slipped out of bed and into the pool before sunlight. He swam one hundred laps, twenty-five butterfly, twenty-five backstroke, twenty-five breaststroke, and twenty-five freestyle. The chlorine stung the scratch on his cheek.

At last he pulled himself out of the pool and wiped the water from his skin with his hands. The sun was just beginning to peer over the horizon. He stood there for a moment, watching the rays gently weave into his mesquite tree and illuminate his garden.

He knew what he had to do next. He walked to Marion's room.

Her doorway was open, as he figured it would be. The room was empty, as he'd known would be the case. He sat down on the edge of the bed. He ran his hand over the pillow she must have hugged as she sobbed herself to sleep.

Merry Berry, I am so sorry.

'I should've killed him,' he said in the silent room. 'I should've just killed him.'

He found himself in front of the open refrigerator, staring at four bottles of beer. Corona Extra Gold. Cold and smooth going down. *Takes the edge off – isn't that what you want, J.T.? Something to take the edge off.*

Something to make you forget, because you never mastered denial like Marion did.

His hand reached in. He curled his fingers around the cool neck of elixir. So easy to pull it out. He could be drunk before the sun even got high in the sky.

He thought of Tess, still sleeping in his bed. He thought of the way she'd cradled his head between her breasts and stroked his hair. He thought of the feel of her lips, brushing his temple.

She was a fool, he thought angrily. Hell, maybe they were both fools.

His hand slid away from the beer bottle. He stalked back out to his pool and swam a hundred laps more.

As he walked back to the house towel-drying his hair, he heard the phone ringing. He didn't pay it any heed. Tess emerged from the hall, her footsteps fast and urgent. She'd obviously been searching for him.

Once she spotted him outside, her shoulders immediately relaxed. He didn't smile, but he didn't scowl. He just looked at her in her big, oversize Williams T-shirt. Goddamn, he wanted to hold her.

The phone was still ringing. She finally reached for it.

He stepped into the living room in time to hear her say 'Yes' in a wary voice.

Her knuckles whitened, her body began to sway. Her gaze swept up and her beautiful brown eyes were dilated with horror.

'My baby,' she whispered. 'My baby!'

The phone clattered to the floor as down she went.

He caught her as she fell and wrapped her against his chest.

21

Special Agent Quincy rubbed the back of his neck. It was just after ten A.M. and he'd spent most of the night at the Difford crime scene. In the last three days he'd slept only eight hours and lost five pounds, and he felt it.

'Tell me something good.'

'The Red Sox finally won a game.'

Quincy gave Houlihan a blurry glare. 'Try again.'

'Sorry, that's it. When Officers Campbell and Teitel arrived for their two A.M. shift, they found Harrison shot dead in the car and the safe house empty. Traces of blood on the kitchen floor indicate violence, but we haven't located Difford's body or his car. Samantha and all of her belongings are gone. Also, the gun cabinet was forced open and emptied. We're not sure what all Difford had in there, but he formally checked out a Mossberg 12-gauge shotgun, a Smith & Wesson 9mm, his police issue .357 Magnum, and probably a Smith & Wesson .38 Special. Difford may have kept a few surprises in the inventory as well. Maybe a sawed-off shotgun. You know how cops can be about guns.

'We have Beckett's latent and patent prints at the crime scene, paper towels with makeup residue, a state police uniform, and a state police badge issued to an Officer Travis four years ago. Beckett also left us his wig, nylons stuffed with padding, and yes, two plastic bags filled with neon purple Silly Putty. Then we have his note.' Lieutenant Houlihan's voice grew somber. He said softly, 'Beckett wrote: "Sergeant Wilcox sends his regards." Wilcox has been missing for twenty-four hours now. His wife thought he was on special assignment, we thought he was out sick. There, uh, there hasn't been any sign of his body yet.'

Quincy squeezed his eyes shut and pinched the bridge of his nose where the tension had gathered like a hard knot, pressing against his eyeballs, trying to force them out of their sockets. 'The neighbors? Did they see anything?'

'Saw two cops sitting in an unmarked car most of the evening. One of the officers appeared to be asleep.'

'Estimated time of death for Harrison?'

'Six P.M. Beckett probably shot him beginning of shift, when Harrison first climbed into the car.'

'And you last heard from the watch car at one A.M.'

'Exactly. Difford called in a little after midnight. So sometime between midnight and two A.M. . . . .'

'Wonderful. You call in the National Guard?'

'Are you kidding? If a person can dress himself, I have him looking for Jim Beckett. We've cordoned off a fifty-mile area. Samantha Williams's picture has been sent to every TV station and newspaper in the nation. Soon her picture will be plastered on every milk carton in the goddamn free world.'

'It's a start.'

'We're going get him, Quincy. How the hell is he going to hide a four-year-old girl? No, he finally screwed up and we're going to nail his ass.'

'Humph.' Quincy wasn't convinced. He leaned back and studied the cheap white ceiling, the kind that could double as a dart board and on slow nights, probably did. The inset lights increased the pounding behind his temples. Some days the pressure made him want to flush his whole head down the toilet and yet he still wouldn't give up his job. What kind of sick bastard did that make him?

'Want a few more ideas?' He phrased it as a question because the task force fell under Houlihan's control and Quincy didn't want to appear as if he were taking over. Crossjurisdictional coordination was never easy during the best of conditions, let alone when everyone had been up all night and the case seemed to be unraveling before their very eyes.

'Well, you're the Einstein. If you know the secret formula for catching Jim Beckett, cough it up. Our department can't afford any more fucking nights like this.' Houlihan's voice contained a bitter, rusty edge that they both felt. In Quincy's career, he'd seen eight officers go down and two damn good agents. How many times had he listened to the guns firing their grim salute? It never got any easier. It never got less personal.

'Okay, we know Beckett loves his daughter. We don't believe she's in any danger. So you're right, let's exploit this for all its worth. You have a four-year-old girl to keep happy. What do four-year-olds want?'

'I'm the proud father of two Dobermans, Quincy. What the hell do I know about kids?'

'Hmm, and I can't even handle goldfish.'

'Hold on a sec.' Lieutenant Houlihan opened the door of the office and shouted, 'Rich, get in here!'

The middle-aged homicide detective materialized a few seconds later. He'd also been up half the night, but he didn't comment on it. Like all the task force members, his face was haggard and his shoulders drooped. In the last twenty-four hours they'd seen Lieutenant Difford and Officer Harrison brutally murdered. Most likely Sergeant Wilcox had met the same fate. They were angry. They wanted justice, they wanted revenge. Beckett's chances of being brought in alive were diminishing exponentially – much to Quincy's regret. They still had a lot to learn from a man such as Beckett. Except that the price was becoming too high.

'You got two kids, right?' Houlihan pressed the detective.

'One girl and one boy. Ages three and five.'

'Good. Think like a four-year-old for us.'

'Jesus.'

'You've been woken up in the middle of the night,'

Quincy supplied. 'You're tired and cranky. Beckett probably had to look for a hotel, right?'

Rich shook his head. 'He took Difford's car, yeah? Kids sleep great in cars. We used to drive Shawn all night long when he was teething. It was the only thing that put him to sleep.'

'Shit. So Beckett, with possibly one hour's head start, can drive straight through. What about the morning? By the time she does wake up, she's going to be scared, uncertain, cranky . . .'

'Happy Meals,' Rich supplied without hesitation.

'What?'

'Greatest form of bribery on the planet. Kids are unhappy or whining, take then to McDonald's. Is Beckett a cook?'

'No, he's a chauvinist pig.'

'Well, kids aren't really into restaurants, especially four-year-olds. Check all the fast-food places. She'll need to eat, and any kid worth her salt will want to eat at McDonald's or Burger King or a place like that. Those commercials really brainwash the little guys.'

Quincy nodded. 'There you go. Let's get a map, plot out just how far he could get in one night of driving, and canvas fast-food joints with her picture. I can get the field office to help.'

'Works for me,' Houlihan said curtly. Rich was excused. 'I want the airports on alert too. LaGuardia, Logan, JFK, etcetera. Can you arrange it?'

'He won't try to leave the country yet.'

'How can you be so sure?'

'Tess is still alive. He won't leave until he's gotten her.'

'Come on. How's he going to track down Tess with a four-year-old?'

'I imagine he has a plan.' Quincy leaned forward. 'Airports are alerted, Lieutenant. The international departure gates have had Beckett's picture ever since he escaped. We can get them Sam's picture too, but I don't think he'll fly the coop yet. Sam was step one. Killing Tess Williams will be step two.'

'Then he'll leave?'

'I don't know.'

'You don't know? You're the expert and you don't know?'

Quincy remained silent for a moment, giving Houlihan a chance to take a deep breath and pull it together. When the lieutenant had succeeded in fisting his hands down by his sides, Quincy tapped his computer. 'Remember the pattern –'

'For chrissake, screw the pattern! He's doing it personal now, not by the numbers.'

'He's doing both. Think, Houlihan. He uses the first letter from the place he leaves the bodies to play his little games. Two guards in Walpole, W. Shelly Zane in Avon, A. Harrison and most likely Wilcox in Springfield. *S, Was. Jim Beckett was* . . .'

'The best.'

'Number one. Here. Supreme. It could be many things. The point is, the phrase is unfinished. And we still haven't found Difford's body. My guess is that he'll drop it somewhere else for another letter. Perhaps he's done the same with Wilcox's body – we won't know until we find it. But Beckett is still engaged in his little game, and he finishes what he starts. Maybe he'll complete it out of the country. Maybe he'll take a year off and then do it. But he'll kill again. Until we find him, he'll pursue Tess Williams and he'll pursue others.'

The silence stretched out long. Houlihan's jaw was so tight, Quincy could hear the lieutenant's teeth grind with frustration. Quincy didn't say anything. Any comment now would merely light the lieutenant's fuse. He sat back and waited it out.

'I offered her police protection,' Houlihan said abruptly, his voice tight. 'She turned me down. She won't come in.'

'Tess Williams?'

'Yeah. Difford left her contact number in a safety

deposit box. That way if anything happened to him, we could notify her. Difford liked to think of all the angles, plan for all contingencies.'

'Beckett probably knows where she is,' Quincy said quietly. 'He must have gotten the safe house information from Wilcox. He'll have used the same tactics on Difford.'

'Yeah. What a way to go.' Houlihan swallowed thickly, then made a big production of squaring his shoulders. 'I gave it to her straight. I offered her what I could. She told me the police had done quite enough already –'

Quincy winced.

'She would handle things her own way.'

'Oh, God.'

'She's been training with a mercenary.'

'You're kidding.'

'Nope. She's gone vigilante.' Houlihan tried to force a laugh. 'Can you blame her?'

Quincy shook his head tiredly. 'Let's just hope she doesn't do anything stupid.'

'This is stupid.'

'You don't have to be here.'

'Tess, think about it a minute. Beckett kidnaps your daughter. So what do you do? You return to his backyard. What do you think he intended?'

Tess stared stubbornly out the window. It was after midnight and they were on the Mass Pike, headed toward Springfield. Few cars were on the road. The moon was weak and further obscured by a steady drizzle. The windshield wipers offered a rhythmic, *thump thump, thump thump*, otherwise the rental car was quiet.

J.T. was tired and grim at the wheel. He already missed the sun and the desert. Six hours ago he'd been wearing a T-shirt and admiring his garden. Now Rosalita tended his villa and Glug while he and Tess landed in a state so damn cold, it was inhospitable.

J.T. didn't like Massachusetts. Boston had strong ethnic populations from all over the world – Irish, Italian, Chinese – but everyone still had to answer the same three questions to consider themselves a true Bostonian: Did their ancestors get off the *Mayflower*? Did they go to Harvard? Did their family personally know any of the Kennedys?

Fail that and forget it. You could live in Boston until you were a hundred and fifty and you still wouldn't be a Bostonian.

'You said Beckett loves Sam, right?' J.T. continued pressing. 'So she's not in immediate danger.'

'Not in immediate danger? For God's sake, she's been kidnapped by a sadomasochist serial killer who rapes and strangles women as a hobby. How safe can she be? He'll never hit her, but he's on the run. What if the police corner him? What if there's a shootout? Dear God, what if there's a shootout?'

'Tess –'

'No.' She shifted away from him. 'I don't want any platitudes.'

'Oh, dear, what will I say now? Listen to me and pay attention. By your own admission, you are Big Bad Jim's prime target. And you've just traveled within striking distance.'

'The police think he knows how to locate me in Arizona anyway.'

'Yeah, but with a four-year-old girl, it's going to be a little difficult for him to get there. Dammit, Tess, you're doing exactly what he wants.'

Tess simply shrugged. 'Jim's a resourceful man. He would have found a way. Now we do it my way.'

'You're not ready for this.'

'Oh? And at what point is someone ready to take on Jim Beckett? After they've been a homicide cop for ten years, twenty years, thirty years? Oops, I'm sorry. He killed them too.'

J.T.'s grip tightened on the wheel. She'd been withdrawn, sarcastic, and bitter ever since getting the news.

So far she'd been everything but afraid. That was a bad sign. Fear served a purpose; it helped keep people safe.

'Let me drop you off at a hotel,' J.T. tried again. 'I'll check out the safe house and see if there's anything to be learned. If there's a trail, I'll find it. We'll go from there.'

'No.'

'So eager to be part of the action?'

'My daughter, my ex-husband, my problem.'

'Your death.'

Her jaw clenched.

'Tess,' he said quietly. 'How long do you plan on punishing yourself?'

'What?'

He took the exit for Springfield. 'You heard me. There's more on your mind than Jim Beckett, and, honey, you'd better get it out. Because you take him on with a chip on your shoulder and he will eat you alive.'

'I don't know what you're talking about.'

'You're angry.'

'He murdered my friend! He kidnapped my child!'

'Not at him. You're angry with yourself.'

'And why would I feel that? Because I left my daughter alone to be taken? Because I left the state so Difford could get killed instead of me?'

'Because Samantha was kidnapped while you were screwing a former mercenary and playing family counselor to siblings only Manson could love?' he finished for her. 'Come on, Tess. Get it out, get it all out. Hit me if you want. Hit yourself. Then pull it together. Because I'm not letting you out of this car until I know your mind's one hundred percent on the matters at hand. You're worthless otherwise.'

'Dammit!' she cried. Then she did hit him. In the shoulder, hard. Next she hit the dash. Three times. He could still feel her frustration and rage.

'I should've stayed with Sam,' she whispered miserably. 'I should've stayed with my daughter.'

'Then you'd be dead too. You wanted change, Tess.

246

This is it. Stop being the martyr and learn to be the cavalry.'

Neighborhoods appeared around them. He knew they were getting close. In a low voice Tess directed him to the former safe house. Most of the neighborhoods appeared older, comprised of one-story ranch-style homes with two token windows, one token chimney, and not much else. Like growing up in a cereal box, J.T. thought.

He turned down another street. This late, there was no one around. Cars slumbered in driveways. Houses hunkered down on their foundations. Not even a porch light offered a ray of comfort.

He looked over at Tess. She was very pale.

'I can still take you to a hotel.'

'Fuck you.'

'Oh, yeah, Tess. You're tough.'

She scowled, then pointed to a house tucked between two others. Yellow crime scene tape encircled it like a garish boa.

J.T. parked the car next to the curb. He looked down the block just in case an unmarked car was watching. Nothing. Of course the action here had already come and gone. The crime lab chemists had probably spent a solid day here, analyzing the scene, dusting for prints, cataloguing evidence. Dogs had been brought in to locate Difford's body, which Tess said they still hadn't found. Now the real police work would be performed in the lab, the house just an old monument to the violence.

J.T. and Tess had come for that testimony. They needed a starting point to track Beckett, and his last crime scene seemed as good as any. Maybe it would tell them something, maybe it wouldn't.

J.T. opened the door and stepped out into the stunningly cold fall night.

'Christ,' he muttered. 'Give me a cactus any day.'

He jammed his bare hands into his front jeans pockets and hunched lower in his leather bomber jacket. Tess was already climbing out of her side of the car, much more suitably attired.

'Stay here.' He stepped up onto the sidewalk.

'No.' She closed the car door and squared her shoulders.

He didn't feel like arguing. He walked right over to her and pinned her against the car with his body. His dark eyes bore into hers, harsh and impatient.

'I'm the professional.'

'I'm the client.'

'Tess, you'll only make a mess of things. Now, get back in the car.'

She stared at him mutinously. 'He already has Sam. How much messier could it get?'

'A lot,' he said bluntly. He pinned her in place and leaned closer. She didn't shrink or cower. Her brown gaze remained steady. God, she'd learned. A regular hellion these days. Marion would be proud. He said, 'Beckett isn't a hay bale, Tess.'

'I know. I felt some pity for the hay bales. I don't feel any toward Jim.'

She pushed against him hard, but his body didn't budge.

'In the car.'

'Nope.'

She pushed again, and while he was steeling his body against that feeble effort, she ducked beneath his arm. Step, twirl, and she was free, striding beyond his reach with a grim smile.

'You have to admit, I'm getting a lot better.'

He scowled. 'It's not a game.'

He wanted her in the car. He wanted her someplace where he wouldn't have to worry about her.

She headed toward the front door. 'Do you really think he's here? He already has what he came for.'

'I don't feel like taking any unnecessary chances.' He briefly debated knocking her out cold and stuffing her into the trunk until it was over. It would serve the fool right.

248

'He has Sam,' she said flatly. 'He'll have to stay with her in the evening.'

'Or find a beautiful blonde to watch her for him.'

She paused. He caught a slight tremor racking her frame. But Tess brought her chin up stubbornly. The wind stirred behind her, bringing him the scent of China Rain. The moon highlighted her sable hair and caressed her heart-shaped face.

'Christ,' he muttered, and turned away. She looked beautiful, precious, and he didn't want to see that – not knowing what he did to beautiful, precious things. Thirty-six years old and his life was still locked in the same old patterns, spiraling toward the same bitter end. He hated that. 'You got your gun?'

'Yes.' Now she sounded shaken.

'Get it out.'

'You think he's in there?'

'Get out the damn gun. You wanna play soldier? Soldiers do not question orders. You do as you're told when you're told. Is that clear?'

'Yes, sir.'

'You'd better believe it.' He took out his gun and removed the safety. Cocked, locked, and ready, the only way a marine made an entrance. 'Follow me and do what I say. Don't make any noise, don't leave my side. Disobey me once and I'll shoot you myself.'

'Yes, sir.'

'You know what a clock is?'

She gave him an exasperated look that clearly stated she knew what a clock was.

'Good.' He ignored her attitude. 'Anything happens, this is how it works. You're responsible for the six to twelve position, I'll cover twelve to six.'

'You mean . . . you mean shooting, don't you?'

'Well, you can shake his hand if you want to, but I wouldn't recommend it.'

'Okay, okay,' she said hastily. Her uneasiness had returned. Then she cleared her face and set her shoulders, the good little soldier. She was killing him.

'The car,' he attempted one last time.

'No.'

'Stubborn ass.'

'Yes. Are we going to talk all night, or do this?'

'Fine.' He sounded angry and couldn't help it. 'But don't say I didn't warn you.'

'Don't worry, I give you full permission to engrave "J.T. was right" on my tombstone.'

'Gee, thanks. I look forward to that.'

He looked back at Tess one more time. Her hands were trembling slightly, but she was holding the gun the way he'd taught her.

J.T. gave up on indifference.

Okay, God, he bargained shamelessly in his mind. *You got Marion. You got Rachel. You got Teddy. The colonel's prostate cancer was a nice poetic touch, but thirty years too late. Give me Tess. Just give me this one.*

Then I'm willing to call it even if you are. It's a helluva deal.

He received no answer but then he never had. He smiled grimly.

'We're going in. *Semper fi.*'

J.T. entered first, his back pressed against the entryway wall, his arm making smooth, level sweeping motions as he pointed his gun at each shadow. His left arm was cocked back, beaming a small flashlight into the entryway. He looked like Rambo.

She felt like the halfhearted understudy.

J.T. slid around the corner and she followed quickly, focusing on taking quiet, shallow breaths. The hallway was long and dark and seemed to bisect the house as a main artery. Her nose twitched. She recognized the scents from years before. The pungent odor of chemicals sprinkled and sprayed onto carpets, the oily residue of fingerprint powder clogging the air. The distant rusty scent of something she didn't want to contemplate. Crime scenes had their own distinct fragrance of old violence and fresh chemicals. It made bile rise in her throat. She swallowed it back down.

J.T. turned right and led them straight into a tiny kitchen. Dishes were still stacked in the sink and a newspaper was open on the kitchen table, giving the eerie feel of life interrupted. The vinyl floor, however, no longer looked like a kitchen floor. Huge sections had been ripped up, cut out, and sent off to the state crime lab. Most likely they were being analyzed for blood.

J.T. opened the lower cupboards and swept the dank depths with the penetrating flashlight beam. The light came up, washing over an old countertop, now coated in luminescent chemicals.

The beam continued relentlessly. The walls glittered as the light picked up various residues. As he glanced up, he saw the flashlight illuminate dark dots arching across the ceiling like a rainbow. The spray pattern. Indicating a beating with a blunt wooden instrument. Like a tree limb or mop handle or baseball bat.

She was having a much harder time breathing. She squeezed her eyes shut and pictured Sam. *You're doing this for your daughter. You will be strong for your daughter.*

'Hold it together,' J.T. growled in her ear. He moved into the living room.

After another deep breath she followed. There was less disturbance here. The furniture looked like it had been hastily rearranged by cops looking for evidence. Random squares of carpet had been cut up and sent off to labs. It was obvious, however, that the main action had happened in the kitchen. The living room just got the residue.

'Stay here,' J.T. said curtly. 'I'll check out the rest of the house.'

'What about my six-to-twelve responsibilities?'

'The wall is the only thing holding you up. Let's not push it.'

He slid down the hall without another word, taking his flashlight with him. She gripped her gun tighter in her sweaty palms. Carefully she eased away from the wall. She wasn't going to be sick, she wasn't going to faint, she wasn't going to be scared. She was going to be strong, she was going to be tough.

Jim walked up right behind her and popped the plastic bag over her head.

'Theresa,' he whispered in her ear. 'I see you answered my invitation. And it looks like you brought me your mercenary to kill.'

J.T. had just opened the last dresser drawer in the spare room when he knew he was no longer alone. Tess? She couldn't move that quietly. These were the steady steps of a professional.

Beckett. How?

He tightened his finger around the trigger of his 9mm and rolled up on the balls of his feet just in time to hear the telltale whistle of a bat whizzing down. He leapt to the side and fired twice. The bat crashed into the dresser.

J.T. pivoted, tried to aim, and received two sharp blows to his kidneys for his efforts. His gun went flying. He lashed out with his foot and heard the grunt of Beckett receiving the blow.

Whirling his head around, J.T. spotted his gun. He lunged. Simultaneously Beckett lifted the bat.

Roll and fire, just like a shooting drill, except Beckett wasn't a cardboard target and the stakes were real.

His finger pulled back sharply, one, two, three, and through the ringing in his ears he heard Beckett's sharply indrawn breath. The bat, however, rose again.

J.T. moved but not fast enough; the bat caught him with a solid crack against his forearm. His fingers went immediately numb, then flared red hot with pain. The gun dropped from his lifeless hands.

'Shit.'

The bat rose.

There was no more time for thinking. Now it was

about adrenaline. It was about rage. And J.T. felt a whole lot of it well up inside him.

His lips curved back in snarl. He held his wounded arm against his ribs and kicked hard with his left leg. He connected solidly with Beckett's kneecap, hearing the other man's winded grunt and feeling the blood lust grow.

He lashed out again, stomping a rock-hard stomach. Quick pivot and turn, and he smashed his foot into Beckett's upper arm. The bat dropped to the floor. J.T. closed in for the kill.

Just as he lunged forward, however, Beckett hooked his feet and he flew through the air. He landed hard, his hands too numb to catch him. The oxygen left his lungs in a painful whoosh, his chest filled with fiery red ants. His eyes saw spots and his bruised hip roared with pain.

He kept moving, instinct yelling *roll roll roll or die.*

He staggered to his feet, trying to sight Beckett. The world spun sickeningly. He couldn't get his balance. He couldn't find his gun.

Shit, he was in trouble. *Focus, dammit, focus.*

His blurry gaze finally found Beckett, a tall, pale shadow that looked alien and ghostlike. It took J.T. a minute to understand why. Beckett was hairless, no head hair, no eyebrows, no nothing. His eyes seemed to have receded in his face, smaller and more penetrating without brows to highlight and soften. A serpent's head, that's what it looked like.

The two men stared at each other.

J.T. held his arm against his side. Blood trickled down Beckett's shoulder.

Beckett moved. He clenched his teeth in blatant frustration and leapt for the window. J.T. lurched after him.

At the last minute, however, Beckett turned, one foot swung over the windowsill.

'Theresa,' he said simply. 'By now I wouldn't think she has any oxygen left.'

J.T. halted.

Beckett smiled. 'You fool. I had her for years. I can tell you, she's not worth it.'

'You're dead.'

'She's mine. Help her and you become mine too. Just ask Difford when you see him again.'

Beckett slipped out the window, and there was nothing J.T. could do that wouldn't cost Tess her life. He recovered his gun from the floor, and with his left arm clutched against his ribs raced for the living room.

Tess was handcuffed to the coffee table with a plastic cooking bag plastered against her skull.

J.T. unsheathed the knife from his ankle, slit the plastic bag, and peeled it back from her face. Her head lolled to the side, her pale skin tinged with blue.

'Tess, Tess, come on, come on!'

Her head fell to her chest.

He slapped her hard and was rewarded by a sharp intake of breath. She was alive. He'd screwed up, but somehow she was alive. He rocked her against his chest. He cursed his own stupidity. He got down to business.

They had to leave. Now.

'Jim,' Tess whispered hoarsely. Her eyes were glazed.

'He left. But he might come back. Can you walk?'

'I tried to shoot him. I raised my gun, but–'

'Shh, pull yourself together. Come on, Tess.'

He raised the coffee table, slid the other half of the handcuffs free, and dragged Tess to her feet. She leaned against him heavily, still gasping for air.

'Okay. You breathe. I'll run. Here we go.'

He pulled her out the front door, and the night slapped them like a vengeful woman, cold and stinging against their cheeks.

Run, it seemed to hiss in their ears.

J.T. didn't argue.

'He's dead.'

Marion glanced up from the fire, her cheeks unusually rosy from the mesmerizing flames. She sat on the edge of a white leather stool. Italian leather, very good.

She'd picked it out herself and the couch and recliner that went with it. They fit the living room well, a minimalist motif of white leather and frameless glass. She'd always liked this room in her upscale Virginia town house.

After the warm earth tones and vivid greens and reds of Arizona, however, she suddenly found the white overwhelming. And she resented that fiercely.

'Did you hear me?' Roger stood stiffly in the doorway, as if he couldn't decide whether it was safe to enter or not. She looked at him coolly, not giving him the slightest expression that might aid his decision.

She knocked back the last of the brandy she'd been sipping. 'I heard you.'

'I thought you were going to be by his side.'

'Obviously I didn't make it.'

'Are you all right, Marion? You don't seem . . .' His voice trailed off. His face held genuine concern. She hated that.

'Go back to your cocktail waitress, Roger. I don't need you here.'

For a change, he didn't listen to her. Instead, he stepped into the room.

She arched one fine brow. 'Why, Roger, did you grow a spine while I was away?'

His face spasmed, revealing the direct hit. 'I know this has been rough for you, Marion,' he tried valiantly.

'Spare me.'

'I know you must hurt a lot right now. I can't be your husband anymore. I'm sorry. But I thought . . . I thought I might still be your friend.'

'Why would I need a friend?'

'I know you loved him,' Roger whispered hoarsely. 'I loved him too, Marion. He was my friend, my mentor . . . I already miss him. I can't imagine how much you must hurt.' The emotion welled up in his face. Before he controlled himself, she saw the glint of honest tears in his eyes.

She stared at him blankly. She should be crying too.

She should feel sadness, grief. But she felt nothing, just ice, flowing through her veins and freezing like a solid mass in her stomach. Ever since two nights ago, ice was the only emotion she could find.

Because sometimes when it cracked, she glimpsed things she didn't want to know.

Roger stepped forward. He looked handsome and distinguished in his suit, the crystal chandelier reflecting off his fine light brown hair and elegant patrician features. He'd been born with a silver spoon in his mouth and was the epitome of grace, refinement, and class.

The first time she'd seen Roger, she'd been dressed in a flowing white gown and slowly descending the grand curving staircase of her parents' house to make the dramatic entrance for her eighteenth birthday party. Roger had been standing by the colonel's side in full military dress uniform, looking at her mesmerized while the chandelier glinted off the medals on his chest. Her gaze was supposed to sweep the whole room like a duchess granting royal privilege. Instead, she'd simply stared at Roger. She'd thought he was a prince coming to carry her away.

If he put his arms around her now, could he make the images go away? Could he save her from the ice that was consuming her?

I am lost inside myself and no one can hear my cry.

'Marion –'

'Go home, Roger. I don't want you here.'

'You shouldn't be alone –'

'Go home, goddammit! Go home or I will call your sweet little cocktail waitress and tell her just how strong and brave you really are! Get out of my home. Get out of my living room. Play the grieving protégé on your own time!'

He looked stricken. She took a step forward and he shrank back. His face became shuttered, his eyes accusing, and he didn't have to move his lips for her to know what he was thinking.

256

Cold Marion, unfeeling Marion, frigid Marion.

And for her part she remembered life after the storybook wedding. She recalled the time she'd been in the bathroom, washing her face, and he'd slammed open the door, stepped into the bathroom, and in front of her startled gaze lowered his zipper and pissed in the toilet. He'd stared at her mutinously. '*After five years of marriage, we ought to be at least comfortable enough to take a leak in front of each other, Marion. I want that kind of closeness!*' She'd just stared at him, unable to keep the horror and disgust from her face. He'd never done it again.

'All right,' he now said stiffly, retreating to the door. 'I'll leave, if that's what you want.'

'How many times do I have to say it?'

He opened the door, then paused long enough to shake his head. 'You've always been remote, Marion,' he said quietly. 'But I don't remember you as being so cruel.'

'I'm just getting wiser.'

'Don't get too wise, Marion. You don't have that many friends left – just Emma, whom you despise, and J.T., whom you hate.'

'Emma is insane and J.T. is a drunk. I don't give a flying fig for either of them.'

'J.T. is a drunk?'

'Absolutely,' she said coolly. Goody Two-shoes Roger always had been fascinated by her brother and even more fascinated by J.T.'s obvious disdain.

'Is that why he didn't come back?'

'I'm sure of it. You'll have to come to terms with it, Roger. My brother is no longer some dashing rebel. He's just an alcoholic. And wherever he is right now, I'm sure the tequila is golden.'

22

The motel room was brown, shit brown. Brown floor, brown beds, brown curtains. Not even a traveling salesman would like the room. Tess thought it was fitting.

J.T. was fetching ice. She stood alone in the middle of the room with her arms wrapped around her middle. She could hear a faint ringing in her ears. When she inhaled, her throat felt scratchy and raw.

She'd called Lieutenant Houlihan and told him what had happened. The APB had been updated with the information on Jim's recent sighting, and local search efforts intensified. The lieutenant wanted her to come in. She didn't see what that would accomplish. They would put her in a house. She'd sit and wait as she'd waited two and a half years ago. The mouse pinned by the cat, living day in and day out waiting for him to finally pounce. She just couldn't do it anymore.

You were going to be so tough. Instead, you walked right into Jim's trap.

She found a thick wool sweater in her bag and pulled it out. Her hands were trembling so badly, it took her a few tries to get it on. She could still hear her teeth chattering with the unrelenting chill.

Where is Samantha? Is she asking for you right now? Is she curled up, wondering why you haven't come to save her?

Why didn't you save your daughter?

The night was too dark. The room was too empty. The truth came crashing down on her and there was no way to escape it: She had failed her daughter.

J.T. walked into the room. The slamming of the door sounded loud in the silence. 'You okay?'

'No.' She sounded raw.

'Have a glass of water.' He stuck the plastic cup into her hand without waiting for her argreement. 'Drink it up. Pull yourself together. We need a new plan.'

She looked at him at last as he sat down by a warped brown table. He'd bought cigarettes while fetching the ice and now he lit one up. He used only one hand. The other remained tucked against his ribs.

'You're hurt.'

'I'm fine.'

'Your arm.'

'You know how to set a bone fracture?'

'Not really. My father always took my mother and me to the emergency room so we could tell naive interns that we'd fallen down the stairs.'

'Well, we're not going to any emergency room. I'm fine.'

She looked away. The acrid smell of cigarette smoke stung her eyes. She could feel the hot, salty knot of tears in her chest, but she couldn't cry.

Samantha. Difford. How much are you going to let Jim take from you?

'I shot him,' J.T. said at last.

Her eyes widened.

'Jim and I had a little get-together in the back bedroom. He brought his bat, I brought my gun. Next time I'm leaving the 9mm at home and bringing an AK-47.'

'Is he seriously wounded?'

'No.' J.T. sounded furious. 'Probably just a flesh wound. He sure as hell didn't slow down much.'

'I don't understand why he was there,' she murmured. 'Why did he come back and where was Sam?'

'He came for you, Tess. He planned it like a two-for-one sale – get his daughter, kill his ex-wife.'

'Where did he come from?' she whispered. 'One moment I was all alone, and the next . . .'

J.T.'s jaw tightened. 'I screwed up,' he said tersely. 'Didn't secure the perimeter, didn't scope out the full house before leaving you behind. I didn't really expect . . . Well, I screwed up. It's that simple.'

'You didn't know.'

'I should've.'

'What do we do now?'

'Sleep. Eat. Regroup in the morning.'

The room drifted into strained silence again. She snapped on the TV to fight it. The first image she saw was Sam's.

'Samantha Williams was kidnapped late last night from a police safe house in Springfield. Two officers were killed by her father, convicted serial killer Jim Beckett, who is considered armed and dangerous. Samantha is four years old, wears a pink winter coat, has long blond hair and blue eyes. Anyone with information on Samantha can call the hotline listed below.

'Once again, Jim Beckett is considered armed and dangerous and should *not* be approached. He frequently disguises himself as a police officer or security guard. Police are currently combing the area with the aid of the FBI and the National Guard. Beckett escaped three weeks ago from the maximum security block of Walpole after killing two corrections officers . . .'

Tess couldn't stop staring at the screen. It showed one of Samantha's preschool pictures. She was looking over her shoulder with a toothy smile, her blue eyes bright, her blond pigtails curly. Tess fell to her knees.

'Let it out,' J.T. said quietly behind her. 'Let it all out.'

She couldn't. She couldn't cry. She couldn't yell.

What are you going to do, Theresa? Fight me? We both know you're too weak for that.

'Pull it together, Tess,' J.T. said more sharply. 'Take a deep breath. Focus on the carpet if it helps.'

You're weak, stupid. You couldn't even stand up to

your father. What did you do when he hit your mother?
Watch? And what did you do while he hit you? Wait?

'Tess! Dammit, don't do this!' J.T. grabbed her shoulders and shook her hard.

For a moment she lolled like a rag doll. She couldn't find her strength. She had no mass, no muscles, no bones. She had no spirit.

'Tess?' J.T. whispered roughly. 'Sweetheart, please . . .'

The dam broke. She began to sob, her throat burning, her shoulders heaving. So many tears. J.T. sat down beside her on the ugly rug. He wrapped his good arm around her shoulders and cradled her against his chest. She cried against his T-shirt, big, messy tears that soaked through to his skin and made her feel worse. He stroked her hair.

'Shh. Shh. I'll help you. We're going to find Sam, sweetheart. I promise you, we'll find Sam.'

She cried harder. He rocked her against him.

'It's okay, honey, it's okay. I know. I know.' He kept murmuring against her hair. She pressed her shivering body against him.

Hold me, hold me, hold me. Don't ever let me go.

'I know,' he whispered. 'I know.'

'We should ice your arm.' It was an hour later. She'd sobbed, J.T. had smoked. Now they both sat on the edge of the too-soft bed, looking worse for wear. 'Can . . . can I look at it?'

He shrugged and pursed his lips around the thin white cigarette. The pungent smoke stung her eyes.

'Can you stop smoking?'

He arched one dark brow.

'In return for my health services,' she negotiated.

'I thought you didn't know much about first aid.'

'I know better than to smoke, so I'm obviously more qualified than you.'

He didn't give in right away, but after a few moments

he ground out the cigarette. 'Self-righteous Tess,' he murmured.

She ignored his comment and sank to the brown carpeting before him. His knees parted, allowing her closer. His thighs brushed her shoulders. She placed her fingers on his arm and heard his harsh breath.

She had told him the truth earlier. She had no idea what she was doing. In her mother's house she'd learned to put makeup over scrapes and bruises, not Bactine. She'd learned to mend broken bones with carefully scripted lies to health care professionals. She'd learned how to pretend most of the beatings didn't hurt.

Now she examined J.T.'s injured limb helplessly. His left forearm appeared furious – beet red, swollen, and hot to the touch. She risked a glance up, her fingers still resting delicately on his skin. His face had gone pale. Sweat beaded his upper lip. She could tell he was biting the inside of his cheeks to keep from making a sound.

'I think you need a real doctor,' she said quietly.

'Do what you can, Tess. Or I'll fix it the old-fashioned way.'

'Amputation?'

'Bourbon.'

'Oh.' She poured ice into a towel and placed it to bring the swelling down. He could wiggle his fingers a little, but not a lot. Did that mean it wasn't broken, just badly sprained, or did that mean something worse? She had no idea.

Finally she gave him a couple of aspirin from her purse.

'Two? My arm's been pulverized by a baseball bat and you hand me two aspirin?'

'You're right.' She doled out six. He swallowed them as a single handful.

She sat on the edge of the king-size bed, her knees not far from him. They had been through a lot, but neither of them knew how to put it into words. She'd slept with him, but she didn't know how to ask him to hold her.

She'd cried on his shoulder, but she didn't know how to offer him comfort.

'Are you going to stare at me all night?'

'Maybe.'

'You're giving me the jitters.'

'Why did we come to a hotel? Why didn't we go straight to the police?'

J.T. was silent for a moment. 'Because they're the police.'

'You don't trust them?'

'No, I guess I don't. Big Bad Jim seems to know how to run circles around them. We're better off on our own.'

'Your arm is busted, I almost died. Care to say that again?'

'And we both lived to tell the tale. So far that puts our records way ahead of the police.'

'J.T., he has my daughter.'

'We'll find him.'

'How?' She could hear the hysteria in her voice. 'Place an ad in the yellow pages? Read tea leaves?'

'I don't know.'

'*You don't know?*' She was screaming at him now. She didn't mean to scream.

'Tess, I'm not fucking Superman! I don't have all the answers. I'm making it up as fast as I can.' J.T. slammed out another cigarette and promptly snapped it in two. 'Shit,' he said, and reached for another. 'What time is it?'

'Three A.M.! He has had my daughter for over twenty-four hours. Twenty-four hours and we have nothing!'

'We know he's in the area. We forced him to take a risk returning to the crime scene. Sooner or later he'll screw up.'

'Oh, that's a fine strategy. The police have been using it for the last three years with such success as well.'

'Fine, Tess.' Now his voice was cold. 'What do you suggest?'

'I . . . I . . .' She didn't know. She just wanted Jim dead. And she wanted to hold Samantha in her arms again.

She closed her eyes. She took a deep breath and raked her hand through her hair. Suddenly she was too tired to think. The pain ran too deep, sapped all the strength from her until she was simply a hollow husk. Her daughter was out there alone. She was sitting in a cheap roadside motel, not knowing what to do. Her head hurt unbearably and J.T. was right, he was not Superman. She was foolish and silly to expect so much from him.

You have to learn to stand on your own. You have to be strong. You have to pull it together and get your daughter back.

She stood and held out her hand. 'Come to bed.'

J.T. snarled, 'Well, sweetheart, I do try hard to be accommodating, but even my talents are limited by the loss of an arm.'

'I didn't ask you to fuck me,' she said bluntly. 'I know you're not angry enough to do that.'

His black eyes widened, then narrowed dangerously. 'If I screw you out of anger, what makes you so hot for me?'

'Lust. Pure lust. Isn't that what you want to hear?'

He didn't reply. And he didn't accept her outstretched hand. She shook her head, disgusted with them both. Why couldn't he understand that for a woman like her, there was no such thing as simple lust. Even when she wished there was.

She grabbed his right hand because she knew he'd never take hers, and with a fierce jerk she brought him to his feet.

He towered over her, his face no longer passive and no longer unreadable.

'I changed my mind,' he murmured. 'I'm angry enough after all.'

'Like hell.' She pushed him back on the bed. 'You're going to lie there, keep that ice on your arm, and do exactly as I say.'

She placed both her knees on the bed, the mattress sagging dangerously. J.T. was still watching her through heavy-lidded eyes. She reached across to the bedside lamp and snapped it off.

'I prefer seeing,' he commented.

Her breasts were brushing his chest. She drew back carefully, not wanting to prolong the contact but not wanting to disturb his arm. 'Sleep.'

'Sleep?'

'It's as good a skill as any, remember?'

'Only until eight A.M.'

'Fine. Only until eight.'

'He's gotta have someone watching Sam,' J.T. was insisting. 'A relative we don't know about. An old friend. An unwitting accomplice. He couldn't just leave her alone to return to Difford's house.'

'I don't know,' Tess said. She was straddling his lap, examining his arm. It looked even worse in the morning light. Now he couldn't move his fingers at all.

'Think, Tess.'

'I have thought about it! I'm telling you, his family is dead, he never had friends, just associates, and now there's no logical person for him to turn to. On the other hand, he picks up women like that.' She snapped her fingers. 'Maybe he has a steady girl these days. I don't know.'

'Where did he hide last time?'

'I don't know.'

'He disappeared for six months and the cops still don't know how?'

'I'm sorry, J.T., but once he was caught, he didn't exactly volunteer all the information. That only happens in the movies.'

'Where did they search last time?'

'In the beginning, everyplace, just like they're doing now. His picture was posted, a hotline established. They issued a warrant throughout New England. As time wore on, however, the task force grew smaller, the effort less intense. Police departments don't have the budget to maintain that level of manpower and diligence for six months.'

'Which Jim knows. So he waited, the number of officers working the case slowly dwindled down, and soon there's you, sitting in your old house with only a couple of cops working each watch shift.'

'We weren't even sure he'd come back,' she whispered. 'Quincy just thought it was probable.'

J.T. was silent. His skin was an unhealthy color. His forehead felt like he was running a fever. 'He could do that again, you know.'

'He has Samantha.'

'Exactly. An even better reason for him to lie low. He has a place – maybe a person. Let's just assume that for now. He used it last time he disappeared and he's using it now. You're right. He keeps a low profile, and six months from now the task force will be half the size. They'll start thinking he slipped through the net unseen, men will get called onto more active cases. Yeah, if he can be patient, it can work.'

'Then we find him,' Tess said simply. 'I'm not leaving Samantha in his possession for six months or a year.'

'I'm not arguing. But we have to have a starting point. We need information.'

Tess took a deep breath. 'You're absolutely right, J.T.'

The tone of her voice gave her away. He was immediately shaking his head. 'You can lead a horse to water, Tess, but you can't make him drink.'

'I'm not playing with a horse. I'm talking about you and your sister and my daughter, who needs you both!'

'Trying to play matchmaker?'

'I'm trying to do what's best for Samantha.'

He stiffened, letting her know she'd struck deep. He rolled off the bed and stood, putting plenty of space between them. 'Marion might not be willing to help. Not given the way she feels about me right now.'

'She doesn't hate you any more than you hate her.'

'Get that out of your crystal ball?'

She walked up to him and placed her fingertips on his collarbone. She wasn't willing to accept his distance, and she wasn't willing to let him push her away. 'You were just a little boy, J.T. She must understand that you couldn't have saved her any more than you could have saved yourself.'

'Save her? Tess, she won't even admit it happened.'

'I know. It's not uncommon for incest survivors –'

He flinched at the word, his face shuttering.

'You can't even say it, can you?' she whispered.

'I don't . . . I don't . . . It's an ugly word.'

Her gaze remained on his face, her fingers rubbing his shoulders.

'I still see it all so clearly,' he muttered. His shifted beneath her touch, his body wired with tension. 'She tells me it never happened, but I can still remember every detail of it. All the times he beat us. All the times she stood at the foot of my bed and begged me to save her –'

He pushed away from Tess.

'J.T. –'

'Stop it!' His right hand raked his hair. 'It happened. We grew up in spite of him. And I hope he rots in hell.'

'But you still love your sister,' she said softly.

His hand balled into a fist. His jaw worked. 'Yeah,' he said, staring out the window. 'And she still thinks I'm a loon.'

'I don't think so, J.T. I think she's beginning to think you're right, and that's what scares her so much.'

She took a step toward him, reaching out. He flinched. 'Don't.'

She faltered, stung by the rejection. She forced her hand down to her side, her gaze never leaving his face. He hurt, she knew he hurt. She could see it in the remoteness of his expression. *Let me in, let me help a little bit if I can.*

But he remained unyielding. She didn't know anyone who could be as hard as he could be hard.

She took a deep breath. Her eyes stung.

'All right,' she said quietly. 'I'm going to shower. You do . . . you do what you think is best.'

'Yeah, I'll do that.'

'You're the professional.'

The minute the bathroom door closed behind Tess, J.T. retrieved a cigarette. He paused long enough to open the window and get hit by the solid New England chill. Then he brought the cigarette to his lips, lit it clumsily, and inhaled gratefully.

The open air was cold, the sky gray but bright enough to hurt his eyes. He stood there anyway, squinting, exhaling out the window and smoking the first cigarette down to a nub. Then he lit a second.

And then he picked up the phone.

His finger shook when he punched the number. He told himself it was the nicotine. Marion picked up on the third ring. For a minute he couldn't find his voice.

'Hello? Hello?' She already sounded angry and she didn't even know it was him. He contemplated hanging up, but didn't.

'Hello, Marion,' he said at last.

She was silent. He used the opportunity to drag deeply on his cigarette. On the other end of the line, was she doing the same? That was a pretty picture – a brother and sister who couldn't carry on a thirty-second conversation, but boy could they smoke.

'Are you speaking to me or not?'

'Give me one reason why I should.'

'It's about Beckett.'

'Beckett?' She sounded suspicious. 'What do you want, J.T.?'

'I'm not asking for me, Marion, I know better. Tess is asking. And let's not forget that this is the kind of case that could build a career.' He couldn't keep the edge out of his voice.

'You have two minutes to state what you need, or I hang up.'

'Information.'

'Information?'

'Beckett returned to Mass. He killed the cop who was watching Tess's daughter and kidnapped her.'

'Oh, shit.' For a change, Marion's voice was soft. Her shock sounded genuine.

'I think he has Sam stashed with some friend,' J.T. said quietly, 'but Tess can't think of anyone. The FBI are the ones who've been tapping phones and handling surveillance. Maybe there's something there that will tell us where he's gone, who might be helping him.'

'Maybe.' She was silent for a moment. 'Why come to me, J.T.? Why not just contact the special agent in charge? I could get you a name if you want.'

'Is that what you want me to do, Marion? Contact the SAC?'

This time the period of silence was long. He forgot about his cigarette until it burned down far enough to singe his fingers.

'I'll come,' she said abruptly. 'Where are you?'

'Outside of Springfield in a motel.' He rattled off the phone number, careful to keep his voice neutral. He wasn't sure how to feel yet. Or if he should feel anything. 'Ah . . . give us a call when you land at Logan. I'll give you directions from there.'

'The shuttle flights are steady. I imagine I can be there by midday.'

'All right.'

He waited for her to say good-bye and hang up the phone. Or say she remembered something, maybe the good times. The hot summers they'd spent perfecting cannonballs into the swimming pool, or early evenings when he would watch her ride, thinking she must be the most graceful girl in the world to sit so perfectly on that huge horse.

She said abruptly, 'Daddy's dead.'

'Okay.'

'The funeral will be next Friday. He's being laid to rest in Arlington with full military honors.'

'Huh.'

'Will you come, J.T.?'

'No.'

'Your hatred is that pure, then?'

'Isn't yours, Merry Berry?'

She hung up the phone and the dial tone filled his ear.

He interrupted her shower. She halted, her hands shampooing her hair, her gaze questioning. He took in the sight of her body covered delicately with soapsuds. Her arms had freshly defined muscles, her legs too. He couldn't really remember what she'd looked like that first day anymore. He just saw her now and she was beautiful to him.

His gaze rested on the harsh red line encircling her neck. The ligature line from the plastic bag.

'What are you doing?' Her voice was husky, uncertain.

'Looking for someone to scrub my back.'

'What makes you think I'd do a thing like that?'

'I'm an invalid. You'll help me.' He pulled the shower curtain all the way back, unmindful of the hot water that sprinkled his chest. He placed his right hand on his fly and rapidly undid the buttons.

She remained standing beneath the shower spray, openmouthed and watching as he stripped. He joined her in the tub, his legs cradling hers.

Without asking, he took the soap from her hands. He ran it over her breasts, her flat belly. He felt her skin quiver beneath his touch. Wordlessly he brought the soap up and slid it over the red welt encircling her neck, as if he could erase it. As if any man had that kind of power. Christ, he wanted it. He wanted to make the world better for her, he wanted to give her everything he hadn't been able to give Marion, everything he hadn't been able to give Rachel and Teddy. He'd failed so many times. It scared him to death to try, and scared him even more to leave Tess alone at the mercy of a man like Jim Beckett.

His fingers massaged the red line again. He thought that when he saw Jim Beckett next, Beckett's death would be painful and a long time coming.

Goddammit, let me keep one person safe. Let me help Tess, let me help Samantha. Let me stand up at the plate and finally be a man.

She said quietly, 'You called her, didn't you?'

His thumb brushed again, slow, his silence answering for him.

'J.T., I'm proud of you.'

'I don't need you to be proud of me.' He let the soap go. He looked into her eyes, searching for something he was too afraid to put into words. Her eyes were so large and so clear. Trusting. God help him. God help her.

His fingers slid into the brown thistledown of her curls and found her. She was moist, hot, ready. She arched into him, her hands digging into his shoulders. She whispered his name; the sound alone toppled his control.

She gave him hope. And maybe something more.

She pressed her forehead against his chest as his fingers started to move. 'I know,' she whispered against his skin, 'but I'm proud of you anyway.'

'I want Mommy.'

'I know.' He touched her blond hair lightly where it pooled over the plain white pillowcase. She sank deeper into the pillow, not quite cringing but not quite wanting the contact. After the first big shock of seeing him, she had become worried and anxious. She didn't fight him, but she didn't cling to his hand the way she used to. He accepted that. It had been two years since she'd last seen him, and he hardly looked like his old self.

He continued smoothly. 'As I told you, Mommy's not coming back.'

Sam's lower lip jutted out. Blue eyes became liquid. 'But she *promised*!'

He didn't respond to the whine in her voice. If you reward such behavior with attention, the child never learns. Instead, he said bluntly, 'Theresa lied to you, Sam.'

'Mommy wouldn't do that!'

'Yes, she would. She told you I would never come back, correct?' Samantha nodded miserably. 'She lied, Sam. She lied, but it's okay, because I'm here for you now.'

She cried a little, as if that would refute his words. He remained sitting there patiently. Finally she wiped the moisture from her face, then sighed with a little girl's broken heart. He didn't console her or hold her. He just waited. Within a few weeks Theresa's image would begin to fade in Sam's mind, within a few months her mother would seem like a distant shadow, and within a few years Theresa wouldn't be recalled at all. Starting over again tabula rasa was the glory – the privilege – of youth.

When Samantha was tearless and composed once more, he tucked the covers beneath her chin and patted her shoulder. 'I have a surprise for you,' he said lightly, giving her a reward for handling her new circumstances so well.

'A surprise?' She mused over the matter for a bit. 'Is it *Toy Story*?'

Her eyes were so bright, he felt a pang of regret that he hadn't thought to buy her the movie. He didn't have time to attend to such things now. Last night's unfortunate rendezvous with Theresa had already added days he couldn't afford to his master plan. Also, beneath his long-sleeved black turtleneck, his shoulder throbbed from the bullet wound. He moved stiffly and resented it fiercely.

'It's not *Toy Story*,' he said, his voice tighter.

Samantha cringed and he forced himself to smile. He'd forgotten just how sensitive children could be. The minute he relaxed, so did she. Her eyes grew contemplative once more.

'Did . . . did . . .' Her face grew very bright. 'Did you get me a new brother or sister?'

In spite of himself, Jim blinked his eyes in shock. 'No,' he said slowly. 'Has Mommy talked about getting you a new brother or sister?'

Sam shook her head glumly. 'No, but I've always wanted one.'

He smiled, and for a change the gesture was genuine on his face. From the moment he'd first seen Samantha nestled against Theresa's breast, he'd been enraptured by his daughter. She was half him, half his genes. He could see himself in her bright blue eyes. Already she showed promise of great intelligence and great resilience. Even as a baby she hadn't cried as much as other babies cried. She was better than all that. Sweet, genuine, and strong. She was the better part of him.

'Daddy,' she demanded, impatient now.

That made his smile grow. He was pleased that she'd called him Daddy. 'It's better than a brother or sister. I got you a new grandma.'

'Grandma? You mean Grandma Matthews is here?' She looked very puzzled.

'No, a new grandma. Now you have two.'

She slowly nodded. '*Two* grandmas. When do I get her?'

'In the morning.' He brushed back her hair. 'I have to go away for a while, but you'll meet your grandma when you wake up. She's tall and heavy, and speaks with a light accent I'm sure you'll find funny. Do what she says, Sam. She'll take good care of you.'

Sam didn't look convinced.

His thumb brushed her cheek. 'Do you trust me, Sammy?'

More slowly this time, she nodded.

'Good. I'll take care of everything. In just a few days I'll be back. And then we're going to leave. I think we'll go someplace very warm, what do you think of that?'

'Will Mommy come with us?' she whispered.

'No.'

'Grandma and Grandpa Matthews?'

'No.'

'The . . . the new grandma?'

His eyes grew unreadable. 'Maybe,' he said at last. 'I haven't decided yet.'

Edith had just sat down on her patio with her morning cup of tea and a wool blanket, when Martha's front door opened. For a moment Edith was startled. It was still dark out; Edith had always been an early riser, and these days her insomnia had her up before even the sun. In the first hours of dawn the air in the community was almost normal again, almost peaceful.

But the door opened, and the air was shattered. Edith felt goose bumps rise on the back of her neck. She clutched her warm mug tighter.

Martha stepped out and looked at her from across the way.

There was tension between them. It had been growing ever since Martha's return, taking shape and substance from the myriad small lies that had inexplicably fallen from their lips. It had gained permanence yesterday, when Martha had simply disappeared. Edith had gone over for their nightly cigar and found the house empty. Just empty. Martha didn't owe her an explanation, of course. The woman was responsible for her own life, but the mysterious absence, the undefined disappearance, had dealt the final blow to the fragile friendship between them.

It made Edith think of just how little she knew Martha, just how little the woman spoke of herself. She'd moved into the neighborhood two years earlier, been around for a bit, then hightailed it to Florida with barely a by-your-leave. The phone calls in between had made the absence less conspicuous, but Edith was paying attention now. She was realizing she really didn't know her neighbor at all.

Martha stepped off her patio and crossed to Edith's yard.

Abruptly the hair rose on Edith's arms. The air howled around her ears. She knew without turning that the visions were back, the poor, tortured girls hovering around her patio as if there was something important they had to tell her but death had robbed them of their voices.

The tea mug trembled violently in her grasp, splashing her hands with scalding hot liquid.

'Edith,' Martha said, coming to a halt at the bottom of the steps.

Edith didn't say anything. She just looked at her neighbor.

This close, she could see the subtle changes. Martha's eyes were now dulled by exhaustion and strain. She moved differently too. She walked stiffly, as if her age had caught up to her suddenly and now weighed on her heavily.

'Martha,' Edith acknowledged at last.

'I apologize for intruding.'

'No need.'

Martha squared her shoulders. 'I have a visitor,' she announced. Her gaze met Edith's. It was a touch defiant.

'A visitor?' The hair still danced up Edith's arms with wild electricity. Her chest was beginning to tighten with a familiar pain.

'My granddaughter.'

'You have a granddaughter?'

'From the boy. The salesman who travels.'

'I see.'

'I had to meet him, unexpectedly. Something came up; he needs me to watch my granddaughter.'

'Uh-huh.'

Martha looked at her again. In this dark moment before dawn, her gaze appeared flat, as if she were dead. 'Will you meet her this morning?'

Edith wasn't certain. Finally she nodded. 'If you'd like.'

'If . . . if something should happen to me, will you take care of her, Edith? I would trust you with her.'

Again there was that stare. That only-half-alive gaze.

There was no pleading in Martha's voice, not even fear. It was strangely matter-of-fact, and that scared Edith more.

'Yes,' she agreed softly. 'I suppose. But I'll need the address and phone number of your son.'

Martha shrugged. She said, 'Don't worry. He'll find you.'

23

They met at a small diner, one of those places where people bring their children because the ice cream sundaes are better than the hamburgers, and senior citizens laid claim to corner booths to enjoy the 'two eggs, two strips of bacon, two pieces of toast for $2.22 special.'

Against an unlikely backdrop of a swirling sea of red and blue floral carpet, Marion perched on the edge of a brown vinyl booth and waited impatiently for her brother and Tess to arrive.

One long, slim leg was carefully crossed over the other. Her back was ramrod straight. She hadn't dressed for her surroundings, but had donned a navy blue pants suit trimmed with gold braid around the cuffs and collar. The outfit inspired enough awe to halt a two-year-old, who stared up at her icy, perfect posture as if maybe he should salute. Even her hair was obedient, pulled back harshly into its usual French twist with not a single strand escaping to curl delicately around her cheeks.

She glanced down at the toddler, her blue eyes cold and impenetrable. With a startled squeal he bolted on stubby legs. Marion simply raised her cigarette to her pale pink lips and inhaled.

'Scaring off another admirer, I see,' J.T. drawled, walking across the restaurant to her with Tess in tow. A moment later he leaned against the booth, hip thrust out. A homemade sling decorated his arm.

She exhaled into his face. 'It's a gift.' She looked at

him steadily, waiting to see who would draw first blood.

Tess positioned herself between brother and sister. Marion flicked her a cold glance. 'And you're playing ref?'

'Apparently,' Tess said, but didn't sound happy about it. She had just started sliding into the booth, when Marion shook her head.

'Not here. Too public.'

The cool agent collected her cigarettes and led them toward the back, where the banquet rooms were open and unoccupied. She commandeered the smallest one, closing the door behind them and gesturing to the collection of empty tables.

Tess selected one in the middle of the room. J.T. sat next to her, while Marion took the seat across.

'Nice,' Marion commented, nudging her chin toward J.T.'s sling. 'Making a fashion statement?'

'Beckett.'

Marion arched a brow, stubbed out the remains of her cigarette, and consulted her pack for a second. 'Found him already? Then why do you need me?'

'He found us. Last night.' He recapped events briefly, Tess filling in portions. Marion smoked, nodded, and smoked some more.

When they were done, she split her disapproving gaze between the two of them. Law enforcement never looked kindly on civilians taking matters into their own hands, and Marion was no exception.

'Do you know what happens when you hook up a psychopath to electrodes and tell him he's going to receive a shock?' Marion asked.

'Not really.' J.T.'s tone was laconic. Tess could tell that he already had all defenses up.

Sensing the same, Marion turned her attention toward Tess. She said, 'Nothing.'

'Nothing?'

'Nothing. His heartbeat does not accelerate, he will not sweat. There is absolutely no response, no fear of pain. That is the nature of the psychopath – impenet-rable, cold, and immune to fear.'

She said the words quietly, but Tess already knew what Marion was driving at.

Marion stubbed out her cigarette. 'I pulled Beckett's files as you requested, J.T. I read them myself on the plane. I'm only going to tell you this once – you're in over your head.'

'Thanks. Now tell me what's in the file.'

Her gaze remained on Tess. 'Jim Beckett is a pure psychopath. You survived him once, now you've sur-vived him twice. Be grateful for that, Tess. And let the police hand it – let the FBI handle it – because you won't be so lucky the next time. Beckett isn't someone who's made a lot of mistakes.'

'I don't plan on asking him to dance,' J.T. said curtly. 'And I'm too old for lectures. Trust me just once, Marion. I know what I'm doing.'

Her tight lips said she doubted that.

J.T. gave up with a disgusted shake of his head. 'Fine, we'll skip the foreplay. Tell me where he is.'

Marion lit a fresh cigarette. 'Oh, dear me.' She drew out the words, matching his mood inch for inch. 'I meant to bring the magical map to his hiding place, but I must have left it on the plane. Whatever will we do?'

'Smart ass.'

'I learned it from you.'

'And I'm so damn proud.' His gaze narrowed, pinning her in place. 'His friends and associates. You said he escaped with the help of some prison groupie.'

'Dead.'

'Dead?'

'So he killed the prison groupie. Then he broke into the safe house?'

'No, then he kidnapped Sergeant Wilcox and tortured and killed the man. Two kids found the body early today in the woods. Beckett had covered everything but his hands with rocks. Of course, wildlife had taken its toll on the man's hands.'

'He likes to mutilate people's hands,' Tess whispered.

Marion looked at her curiously. 'It's true. Quantico isn't sure why. Maybe because hands are so personal. Or maybe simply because it makes the process of identifying the body that much more difficult.'

'Have they found Difford's body?' J.T. quizzed.

'No. But they found his car. Twenty miles from Difford's house, so Beckett probably had another vehicle parked there for the exchange. The trunk of Difford's car was soaked through with blood. We're pretty sure he's dead. We're not so sure why Jim has kept the body.'

'Sam?' Tess asked. She couldn't keep the plea from her voice.

Marion looked away. 'Nothing. I'm . . . I'm sorry.'

'He told me we'd see Difford again.'

'What?' Both Marion and Tess stared at J.T.

'Back in the bedroom he said, "When you see Difford again, you can ask him about it."'

'So you think Difford's still alive?' Marion prodded.

J.T. shook his head. 'Too risky, particularly with Samantha around. But Big Bad Jim doesn't do things randomly. He kept the body for a reason. We just have to get better at anticipating him. After all, he does such a nice job of anticipating us.'

'The pattern,' Tess muttered. She felt frozen and numb. They sat in such an ordinary banquet room in an ordinary restaurant in an ordinary town. And they spoke casually of murder, torture, and the best way to use a corpse. This was why Jim played games. Because more than killing, he enjoyed tormenting. Somewhere right now she was sure he was thinking about what he'd done to her life and enjoying every minute of it. She didn't want to give him that satisfaction.

'Pattern?' J.T. quizzed.

'*Was*,' Marion supplied. '*Jim Beckett was* . . . ? Quincy has some theories. Jim Beckett was number one? Jim Beckett was here? Jim Beckett was the best? Whatever. What's relevant is that Beckett forms his pattern based on where he leaves the bodies. Obviously that's why he took Difford's.'

J.T. frowned. 'In other words, he's running out of time.'

Marion looked at him with a puzzled expression. 'How do you get from A to B?'

'Well, he's been killing at each location, right? Now, however, he's . . . recycling bodies, so to speak. Instead of leaving Difford in Springfield with the others, he took the body to a new city, gaining a new letter. Obviously he wants to finish his statement, but he realizes he doesn't have unlimited time. Maybe since he took Sam he's decided he has to wrap things up and get on with it. I thought he would hole up.'

Tess began rubbing her temples. She still couldn't get the pictures out of her mind. Her four-year-old daughter being driven around in a car with Difford's corpse in the trunk.

'Look, Marion, the man must have a hiding place or accomplice,' J.T. continued. 'Surely you guys are looking into it.'

'Oh, no, J.T., we thought we'd just sit back and see how many cops he kills. Of course we're looking into it! But you know as well as I do that the logical starting place for any investigation is friends and relatives. Beckett has none.'

'How can you be so sure?'

'I read the reports, of course! His family is dead –'

'Did they check for death certificates?'

'They're not stupid, J.T.! Yes, they checked.'

'Death certificates can be forged. How thorough was the check?'

For the first time Marion faltered. 'What do you mean?'

'Did they actually call the doctors or hospitals that signed the certificates? Come on, it's one of the most elementary ways to start a new life. Forge your own death certificate, then assume someone else's birth certificate.'

'I . . . I don't know. I'd have to ask.'

'Ask.'

'Well, yes, sir! Even then, J.T., it's hard to believe a member of his family faked their own death so they could hide a killer. Far more likely is that he found a new friend. The man is good with women.' Marion's glaze flicked to Tess.

Tess bowed her head with shame. Yes, she was the Bride of Frankenstein. She'd fed and clothed a killer. She'd even bore his child. Some nights she watched Samantha sleep so sweetly and she wondered if evil could be inherited. No one knew what caused a psychopath. Were they born? Were they made? Could they pass on that cruelty to their children?

J.T. took her hand. 'If he was to find someone else, Tess,' he asked softly, 'what should we look for?'

Tess shrugged. She felt weary again, but she forced herself to function. This was what it was all about. Not giving up. Not letting him win. 'She'll be blond, pretty, no older than early twenties. She won't be a professional or college educated. She could be a waitress, a stewardess, the woman working at the dry cleaner's. Maybe a police receptionist. He would like that.'

'It's tough search criteria,' Marion murmured. 'Not that some police officer wouldn't love the assignment of cataloguing all the young, beautiful blondes in the area.'

J.T. shook his head, then rubbed the back of his neck with his one good hand. 'In other words, we have no leads. How can a man kill sixteen people, kidnap a child from beneath the police's nose, and leave no trail?'

'It's his specialty. He's studied it. He's careful.'

'Discipline is the key,' Tess whispered. Her eyes squeezed shut. She felt so much horror, because she knew the truth. It didn't matter that he had their daughter. It didn't matter that he'd brutally savaged Difford. Jim still wasn't done. 'He'll strike again. He always finishes what he starts. He'll finish the pattern. He'll come after me.'

She saw Difford, telling her everything would be all

right. She saw Sam, asking her why she had to go away, why they couldn't stay together.

She saw herself, standing at the altar, saying I do.

'Tess, are you all right?'

She turned her head slowly. She stared at J.T. She wondered if Beckett would kill him too.

'I . . . I need some fresh air.'

Marion and J.T. exchanged glances.

'Please. I'll be back . . . in a minute.' She pushed herself away from the table.

'Tess –'

She shook her head, ignoring J.T.'s outstretched hand. She made it to the banquet room doors, pushed them open, and plunged herself toward the daylight. The sun streamed through stained glass trim of blue and red.

She saw the reflection on her hands as she leaned against the hallway wall. She thought it looked like blood.

'She doesn't look like she's doing so well.'

'She's tough. She can handle it.' He wanted to sound firm, but he didn't. Offering comfort wasn't his strong suit. And watching Tess suffer tore at him in ways he didn't want to be torn.

He glanced at Marion. She wasn't as calm as she pretended either. Every time she raised her cigarette, he could see her hand tremble. After a moment she held out her pack of cigarettes to him. He accepted, lighting one quickly. They sat there and smoked.

'How are you doing?' he asked at last to cover the silence.

'Just dandy. I'm thinking of suing Roger for all he's worth, and he's worth a lot. Old money. What more can you ask for?'

'Physical harm,' J.T. suggested lightly. 'I'll help you burn down his place if you'd like. I know a thing or two about setting explosives.'

'Really? Hmm, blow him up. Why not? It could be fun.'

'You're a trained professional, Marion. Think of how well you could stalk him. It would be an example for hundreds of women with traitorous husbands.'

The corners of her mouth lifted briefly. J.T. kept his hand on the cigarette so he wouldn't do something so stupid as reach out and take her hand.

'I'm glad you came,' he offered abruptly.

'Why did you ask me to?' Her smile was gone. Now she was cool, but perhaps also a bit nervous.

'Because I needed the information and I knew you could get it.'

'No other reason?'

'No other reason. Why did you come?'

'Because I want to get Beckett.'

'No other reason?'

'No other reason.'

'We're both bad liars, Marion.'

She turned away, but not before he caught the flash of vulnerability in her eyes. The tension in his body increased.

'Next time Beckett will kill you, J.T.' She motioned her head toward his arm. 'Two-handed you couldn't take him on. What are you going to do with one?'

'Fire the gun faster.'

'Don't be stupid. Take Tess and get out of Massachusetts. Special Agent Quincy is one of the best. He'll take care of things.' She paused for a moment. 'I think I may try to volunteer my services. The FBI still balks at putting its female agents on violent crime cases, but my caseload is relatively light right now. I know they need more manpower. Perhaps something could be arranged.'

'You think you can take on Beckett?' He kept his tone indifferent.

'I'm a trained professional.'

'Yeah, Marion, and so am I. But you've been trained to follow rules. Where I've been, there were none.

Beckett knows law enforcement. He can anticipate you guys, think like you guys. On the other hand, he's never met the likes of me before.'

'Oh, yes, J.T. You're just tough shit, and you have the arm to prove it.'

'Both Tess and I walked away alive. That's more than anyone else can say lately.'

Marion shook her head furiously. 'You're so damn arrogant. If you ever met God, the first thing you'd say is What are you doing in my chair?'

'And as long as She got up and handed it over, we'd do just fine.'

'Drop it, J.T. Get out. You're good at running, why quit now?'

His face darkened. 'No.'

'Why?'

'Because I have nothing better to do than piss you off, why do you think? Marion, I took the job, dammit. I'm trying to follow it through. Isn't that what you're always telling me to do? Isn't that what you've always wanted?' He leaned forward abruptly. 'And I *want* Beckett. I want him dead.'

'So you'll know you're the biggest, baddest, toughest thing around?'

'No,' he said, angry enough to lash out with the truth. 'So Tess can sleep at night. So she can have her daughter back. So two people can get on with their lives, because we sure as hell aren't doing a great job of getting on with ours.'

'I don't know what you're talking about.'

He hit the table with his fist. 'Yes, you do, Marion. I know you do. I can see it in your eyes. And I know it's the real reason you came, just like it's the real reason I called you.'

Her face fired to life. It filled with a venomous rage that froze the breath in his lungs. He knew that kind of anger. He knew that kind of hate.

'He left everything to you, you son of a bitch!' Marion hissed. 'He left everything to *you*.'

J.T. couldn't think, couldn't respond. He sat there and took it.

'You hated him. You walked away from him, tossed everything in his face, blackened the family name, and became a first-class loser . . . and he left the bulk of the estate to you! Emma gets a trust fund to keep her shopping until she finally cracks up completely. My *child* gets a trust fund. You get the rest. You bastard. You bastard, you bastard, you bastard!'

Her face was no longer icy, it was haggard and unbearably tortured. J.T.'s hand began to shake. It was out in the open now. And it hurt more than he'd thought.

'I don't want the money. I won't accept it. Take it all.'

'He left it to you, goddammit. The least you could do is accept it!'

'No. He was the bastard, Marion, the fucked-up will only proves it. Take everything. You . . . you deserve it.'

'Don't you mean I *earned* it?'

The world stopped spinning. He couldn't quite grasp all the memories, emotions, and reactions that flooded his head. He whispered faintly, 'So you do remember. You really do remember.'

'No!' she declared immediately. Neither of them believed her.

'Marion . . .' He reached out his hand. She immediately shrank back. 'What he did to you was so wrong,' J.T. whispered. 'My God, he raped you–'

She flinched, but he couldn't stop. It had to be said. He didn't know any other way to move on.

'It wasn't your fault, Marion.' The words tumbled out. He said them almost desperately, not sure how long she would allow him to speak, and having so many things that he just *needed* to say. 'You have to understand that it wasn't your fault. It *wasn't*. He was a sick, twisted man who ruined us both for sport. But he's dead now. He's dead and we're alive and we can get

286

through this. We'll stand together, you and me. Don't you remember?'

He tried to take her hand, but she still wouldn't let him.

'Leave me alone,' she whispered. 'I am nothing like you, J.T. I'm not some drunken failure.'

'When we were kids, Marion, I used to wish I was a girl. You want to know why?'

She stared at him dubiously.

He continued. 'So he would've left you alone. I figured if I'd been born the girl, at least he would've left you alone.'

He looked at her openly, no more wisecracks, no more defenses, no more protection. He couldn't be more honest.

And he saw the ice crack. Marion was gone and Merry Berry sat before him, and she looked so unbelievably lost and so unbelievably alone that tears stung his eyes. *Oh, God, what had the colonel done to them? And why now, even after the man's death, couldn't they make it right?*

'I remember the pillow forts,' he whispered with a voice so hoarse it couldn't be his. 'Tell me you remember the pillow forts. Tell me you remember how we used to throw socks at the maid and she'd throw them right back and we would screech and howl and laugh.'

She shook her head. He could see the tears in the corners of her eyes.

'You would come into my room at night, and we would huddle beneath the sheets with a flashlight to read GI Joe comic books. You liked the character Snake. You thought someday he'd come and rescue us.'

'No.'

'And we were always moving and there were new cities and new schools and new kids, but at least we had each other. You used to hold my hand the first day of school and I would tell you everything would be all right.'

'No.'

'And once I told a school principal that the colonel hit us. And I told the man that the colonel went into your room every night –'

'*No!*'

'And he told me I was a liar and gave me detention for spreading rumors. The colonel beat me so hard, I couldn't sit for a week, and you wouldn't even talk to me. I had no idea what he'd told you or why no one ever believed me. Why someone like Snake didn't come at night and save us.'

'Damn you, damn you, damn you.'

'I hated him, Marion. But I never hated you. You were the only good part of my childhood. The only person who gave me hope. The only one I loved.'

'Shut up!' The tears escaped and trickled down her cheeks. He wanted so badly to touch her. He wanted to wipe away her tears and hold her close, because he could feel the tears in his own eyes and the rage that never quite went away because so much had been taken from them and they couldn't get it back. Now there was only emptiness and rage and an unbelievable hurt he'd never known how to mend.

'I don't want to hear any more!' she whispered brokenly. As he stared at her, she drew the cigarette back up to her lips with a hand that shook so badly, it took her three times to actually thrust the cigarette between her teeth.

'Marion,' he said urgently, 'we have to talk about this.'

'I . . . I can't.'

'Merry Berry –'

She leaned over, her blue eyes desperate and pleading. 'Jordan Terrance, if you ever loved me, then you will swear to me now that you will never bring up Daddy again. Swear to me!'

He shook his head.

'Swear to me!' she demanded fiercely.

'And that will make it go away?'

'Swear!'

He shook his head again. It didn't deter her. He pleaded with her. It didn't matter. She was adamant, and he felt too much guilt to fight her. She won. 'All right, Marion. All right.'

She released her breath, leaning back with a shaky sigh.

'I'm not like you,' she said at last. 'You did the right thing, J.T. Leaving him. Hating him so purely. I . . . I can't. It's all twisted inside me and . . . I can't make head or tail of any of it. I used to think I was so strong, but maybe I'm not strong at all. Maybe I just can't handle it.'

'You've made it this far. Talk to me. Trust me that much –'

Her head turned slightly. Her eyes were filled with guilt and anger and pain. He began to understand just how much he'd failed her all those years ago.

Oh, God. 'Marion . . .'

She looked away. He heard the sound of Tess's footsteps behind them, and with a blink of an eye Marion's expression shuttered. His sister was gone and only the cold, composed FBI agent remained. They'd grown up in a household filled with masks and where everyone was a quick-change artist. Some habits couldn't be broken.

'You swore,' Marion reminded him under her breath. 'I'll hold you to your word.'

Tess arrived at the table. She stated without preamble, 'I have a plan.'

She planted her hands on the table. 'We'll take it back to where it all started. Williamstown, the old house. We're going to give Jim what he wants more than anything. We're going to give him a second shot at killing me.'

24

'Mr Dillon, this is going to hurt a bit.'

'No kidding.'

The doctor gripped the fingers of J.T.'s injured hand and tugged hard. Tess heard the grind, then crack, as the bone snapped into place. J.T. paled, the pain blinding, but he didn't say anything. His eyes remained expressionless on the far wall as Tess winced for him.

The doctor finished inspecting the freshly aligned bone while Tess and Marion waited in metal chairs. Marion wouldn't look at her brother. She stared at everything else in the tiny room – the mechanical bed, the tray of tools, the X ray of his left arm lit up on the wall, the countertop covered with swabs, tongue depressors, and a blood pressure cuff. When the doctor forcefully aligned her brother's arm, Marion flinched. Otherwise she sat quiet and motionless, as if she weren't even in the room.

Tess recognized the signs. Marion felt her brother's pain and resolutely shut it out. J.T. felt his pain and her pain and resolutely shut them both out. Tess wondered how many times they'd gotten to practice this drill growing up and figured it was more than a few. She had her drills too, the distant place in her mind she hid in so she wouldn't hear the sound of her father's hand smacking against her mother's cheek, or feel her husband's body laboring above hers.

The past crept in on people in the most insidious ways.

The doctor finished drying the special polymer blend that now wrapped from beneath J.T.'s elbow to his palm. J.T.'s fingers stuck out ludicrously from the white prison. The polymer substance was waterproof so he could swim. Other than that, his arm was pretty much out of commission. The doctor finally handed him a sling.

'Give it six to eight weeks to mend, then you'll be good as new.'

'Uh-huh.'

'You don't have to wear the sling, but I'd use it the first couple of days to keep your arm fully immobilized so the fracture can begin to heal.'

'Uh-huh.' J.T. tossed the crumpled sling onto the floor and let it lie.

The doctor frowned. 'No running or undue activity until that cast is off. Fall or jar that arm again, and you'll have a serious break.'

'Uh-huh.'

The doctor looked even more uncomfortable. 'Any questions?'

J.T. stared at the man for the first time. Tess saw the doctor recoil instinctively. She didn't blame him. J.T. looked demonic.

'Treat a gunshot wound in the last few days?'

'Pardon?'

'Treat a gunshot wound? Probably to the shoulder. Man's bald, doesn't even have eyebrows. He would be hard to forget.'

The doctor glanced over to Tess and Marion as if pleading for help. Marion flashed her FBI creds.

'Answer his question.'

'Ah . . . no. Honestly, no. I can ask around though, if you'd like.' The combination of Marion's coolness and J.T.'s fierceness made him suddenly eager to please.

'You're telling the truth?'

'Mr Dillon, I'm a doctor, not a felon.' The doctor sat up a little straighter, reclaiming his dignity.

J.T. shrugged and hopped down. 'If you say so. How much do I owe?'

While the doctor continued blinking his eyes, J.T.

unclipped a thick wad of bills from his pocket and began counting out the hundreds.

In the parking lot of the doctor's office Marion said good-bye. She'd agreed to talk to Special Agent Quincy about Tess's idea, though Tess could tell the blonde had her doubts about the wisdom of Tess serving as bait.

Tess wanted her to run it by Quincy. Maybe he'd take it more seriously if he heard it from a fellow FBI agent.

Marion crossed to her car. Her gaze flicked to J.T. twice before she finally opened the door.

'Remember,' J.T. said tersely. 'You can call – anytime.'

Marion hesitated, then nodded.

Tess heard J.T. release the breath he'd been holding. He watched his sister drive away, his eyes hooded.

'You okay?' she asked quietly.

'Just fucking dandy.'

'I thought as much.'

He climbed into the passenger side of their rental car. Tess got into the driver's seat and started the engine. She wondered if he would offer any information, or make her pry it out of him with a crowbar. She suspected the latter.

'You're sure you're all right?'

'I don't want to talk about it.'

'Maybe you should.'

'Lay off, Tess.'

She couldn't though. 'I want to be there for you, J.T. The way you're there for me.'

'When Marion becomes a serial killer, we'll talk.'

'That's not funny.'

'No, I suppose it's not.' His gaze went out the window. 'Just drive, please. I appreciate your offer, but for now, just drive.'

She gave in. Thirty minutes later she pulled into the motel parking lot, turned off the engine, and got out of the car. She'd made it two steps across the parking lot when he finally spoke.

'I'm going for a drive.'

'J.T., that's a lousy idea.'

'Tough. I'm doing it anyway.'

She turned on him. 'And what am I supposed to do? Sit around and knit? Wait for Jim's next attack all alone? Some bodyguard you are!'

'You're right. Get in the car.'

'What?'

'Get in the car. Or get left behind.'

He was already sliding behind the steering wheel. Clearly the matter was no longer open for discussion. She stalked over to the passenger side, sat down hard, and glared at him mutinously.

'You can't drive, you have only one arm!'

'You're probably right.' He started the engine. He looked at her long enough to smile grimly. 'Fasten your seat belt,' he drawled, then slammed the car into gear. He roared the car through intersection after intersection while she gripped the dash with both hands.

'Slow down! For God's sake, slow down!'

'Scared, Tess?' he murmured, turning and staring at her as a sharp curve appeared in the narrow back road. 'Hell, you're planning on taking on Beckett. My driving oughta be boring compared to that.'

'The corner, the corner!' she screamed.

He smiled at her and jerked the wheel, sending her careening against the door. 'No problem.'

Her heart beat rapidly in her chest. She could taste the sweat beading up on her upper lip. She understood what he was doing now, and that he wouldn't slow down. He was angry, and angry J.T. could be juvenile, selfish, and dangerous.

'I'm not going to change my mind, J.T. And I'm really tired of games.'

He didn't reply. His jaw set, his biceps bulged as he corralled the speeding fury of the automobile and bent it to his will. A dirt road appeared to one side, looking bumpy and forgotten. Maybe meant for tractors or heavy pieces of equipment that traveled at five miles per hour.

Tess squeezed her eyes shut.

Pedal to the floor, J.T. attacked the road. The car hit a bump squarely and for three seconds they were airborne. The vehicle hit the dirt hard, shocks groaning, car doors rattling, trunk heaving. Tess felt her teeth grind and her bones crunch. Beside her, she heard J.T.'s breath and knew it had hurt him as well.

She opened her eyes and whirled on him.

'Enough!' she cried. 'Stop this idiocy now! Right now!'

Just like that he slammed on the brakes.

The car came to a heavy halt. Unprepared, Tess landed harshly against the dash, but J.T. didn't apologize. He yanked open his door and rocketed from the vehicle.

Tess scrambled to follow, having no intention of backing down now.

Dust still swirled around their feet, the crisp fall chill immediately bracing their skin. She saw no house, no vehicles. Just flat, barren fields that were beginning to frost over, and the distant promise of mountains.

J.T. stalked around the car, his eyes boring into hers.

'You won't serve as bait,' he declared. 'I forbid it!'

She opened her mouth to argue, but he stormed right up to her, backing her up against the car, trapping her with his body. He smiled, but it wasn't pleasant.

'So eager to die, Tess?'

'No,' she said breathlessly. Her hands were pinned to her sides by his body. She jerked them free and planted them against his chest. If he wanted to fight, she'd fight. She'd learned to give as good as she got.

'You're not going to do it,' he said curtly.

'Yes, I am.'

'There's a flaw in your plan, Tess – a man like that isn't afraid of pain. If he attacks, the only way to stop him will probably be to shoot him. And then what, Tess?'

'He'll be dead.'

'And Sam? What about Sam? With him dead, how are you going to find your daughter?'

'I . . . I –' She didn't know. 'I'll make him tell me where she is,' she said stubbornly. 'I will.'

'Dammit!' he roared. 'I won't let you do this!'

'Like hell!' She heaved with her hands, trying to push him away.

He pushed in closer, his eyes dangerous. 'Attacking an injured man, Tess?'

'Whatever works.' She wiggled her hips, determined to break his hold. It was useless.

'This injured man is trying to save your life!' he snarled, leaning closer, his breath hot against her cheek.

'Save my life? What do you care about my life? You haven't even acknowledged its existence for the last two hours!'

'Feelings hurt? Because I didn't flatter you or gaze longingly into your deep brown eyes?' Abruptly his right hand slid down her sweater and cupped her breast. He knew her body too well. One flick of his thumb and her nipple grew hard. She resented him doing that to her. She arched helplessly into it anyway, wanting him to touch her again.

'I thought of you,' he whispered. 'I thought of your breast in my mouth. Your hands in my hair. I thought of bending you over backward and fucking you. Is that what you want to hear? Is that romantic enough for you, Tess?'

His hips rotated against her suggestively. She bit her lower lip, hating him for making her want him and treating it as if it were nothing.

'Damn you,' she whispered.

For his reply he caught her lower lip and sank his teeth into it. Her hands uncurled on his chest. Her fingers dug into his shoulders, drawing him closer while her mind screamed white-hot fury and called her a fool.

She yanked her head. 'Stop it. I'm not your toy!'

'Could've fooled me.' His thumb began a more

insistent pattern around her taut nipple. Her back arched into it.

'It doesn't matter,' she said hoarsely. 'I'm still going to set the trap. I'm still going to do exactly as I planned. If you want to be angry, fine. If you want to torture me until then, fine. But I know it means nothing to you, and it changes nothing!'

He swore. Then he kissed her hard. It was an eating kiss. His tongue plunged in, hot and thick and filling her. She accepted it greedily, her hips pressing against his groin, feeling his growing hardness. He ground into her and she met him halfway.

Then abruptly he pulled back. She cried out her disappointment shamelessly, her hands reaching for him. In a smooth movement he grabbed her shoulders and spun her around. She landed facing the hood with his breath hot against her ear. His hips rotated suggestively against her buttocks.

'Unbutton your jeans,' he whispered. 'Do it for me now.'

She shook her head but her hands were on her zipper. His fingers curled around the thick denim and tugged it down the minute she unzipped the fly.

She felt the cold winter air against her exposed hips. She felt him push up her sweater, her hands planted on the trunk of the car.

He thrust his foot between hers, parting her legs, pulling her hips closer. It was crude and coarse and she arched her back, her eyes already shut as the anticipation swelled in her veins.

'I'm not going to let you bait Beckett,' he growled.

'You can't stop me,' she murmured, and parted her legs farther.

'Goddammit,' he swore, and thrust hard. She cried out as he penetrated. 'I'm going to save you,' he ground out, his hips already moving. 'Dammit, I'm going to save you. I'm going to save you!'

'You can't,' she whispered, but then she couldn't

296

think. The air was cold and crisp, his body hard and hot.

The tempo increased and her ears knew only the sounds of her thundering pulse and his grunting breaths. The feel of him sliding inside her, deeper and deeper. The joining of him with her. The realization that it might mean little to him, but it meant everything to her. It would always mean everything to her.

'Goddamn the colonel!' he whispered abruptly. 'Goddamn Jim Beckett. I won't let them destroy another. I won't let –'

His voice broke into a garbled cry. He thrust hard, pouring into her just as she cried out her release.

Then she whispered his name and knew in her heart it was too late for sanity. She understood his anger, she understood his fear. She understood his need. She'd gotten under his skin and seen all the good he couldn't acknowledge, the fear he tried to hide, and the loneliness he pretended didn't exist.

She loved him.

Much later, when the sun was gone and a fresh moon flirted with the sky, they checked into a new motel room. J.T. was silent, as he'd been all afternoon. After dropping her bag on the floor, Tess handed him her bottle of aspirin. He shook out eight and popped them at once.

Tiredly he began to strip off his clothes. She watched, wordlessly.

'You're making me self-conscious,' he muttered.

'I'm just admiring. Has anyone ever told you that you're beautiful?'

'The stress has fried your brain.'

'I mean it, J.T. You're beautiful to me.'

He turned away and climbed into bed. She removed her clothes and joined him. They'd already spoken to Lieutenant Houlihan. There was no sign of Jim, no sign of Sam. Somewhere out there her daughter slept alone.

Was she well cared for? Had she been fed? Did Jim read her stories before tucking her into bed?

Tess couldn't stand the distance anymore. J.T. was the one who played tough. Tess knew she was overwhelmed and frightened and near despair. She curled her naked body spoonlike around his, though she knew he resented the contact.

He stiffened. She held on anyway, pressing her cheek against him.

'She's starting to remember,' he said abruptly.

Tess stilled, then stroked her fingers down his shoulder in silent comfort. 'You'll help her.'

'She made me promise never to mention him again.'

'Give her time. Sooner or later she'll need to talk about it. She'll come to you, and you'll be ready.'

'Rachel used to tell me that I had to let things go. That I held on too tight.'

'Maybe.'

'I failed her, Tess. You should've seen the look in her eyes . . . I didn't even know how much I'd failed her until I saw her memories in her eyes.'

'Shh . . .'

He didn't say anything for a long time. Then abruptly he rolled onto his back. She couldn't see his face in the darkness, but his fingers touched her cheek softly.

'Don't do it.'

'I have to. Everyone has fought the battle but me. Everyone has paid the price but me.'

'So that's when you'll be happy? When he finally kills you?' His voice was tight, his muscles tense to the touch.

She opened her mouth, then closed it again. 'I don't want to talk about it anymore.'

'Well, I do. Go away, Tess. Go hide out in some hotel in Arizona and I'll pretend to be you in the house.'

'You're injured.'

His muscle spasmed and she knew she'd inflicted an immeasurable blow to his masculine pride. 'Don't you trust me, Tess?'

She pressed her cheek against his shoulder. She threaded her fingers through the dark hair on his belly. 'It can't be just you, J.T.,' she whispered, 'trying to save the world. No one is that strong. It will be you and me together in the house. I'll be bait, you be ready to catch the rat.'

'I won't have you die on me.'

'I won't.'

'I'm so tired of them dying on me.' His voice was hoarse.

She held him closer. 'I love you,' she whispered.

Neither of them spoke.

Edith sat in the living room of Martha's house, holding a cup filled with black tea and watching Martha's granddaughter read a book on the couch with Martha sitting beside her.

The living room really wasn't much. The sofa was old and threadbare and had probably been purchased from Goodwill. Like the other few pieces of furniture, it reminded Edith of the clothes Martha selected – old, eclectic, and mismatching. There weren't even pictures on the walls. Edith had never noticed that before. In the whole house there wasn't a single picture or framed photograph.

Edith forced her gaze back to the little girl. Her name was Stephanie, and she seemed to be a somber, quiet child. She wore a thick sweat suit with a baseball cap covering her hair and eyes. Her face nagged at Edith mildly, as if she'd met Stephanie before. Of course, little kids had a tendency to all look alike to her.

She focused on examining her tea as Stephanie continued reading the story of Cinderalla out loud.

Edith was just picturing the pumpkin stagecoach in her mind, when the chills swept up her arms.

She looked up and wished she hadn't.

Girls, so many girls. She'd never seen so many at once before. Here in this living room their features were so clear, she thought she could reach out and touch them.

How could Martha not see them? How could Stephanie talk of mice turning magically into footmen while a dozen ethereal shapes swarmed around them, naked and ashamed?

Her chest hurt, the pressure squeezing her ribs like a vise. She opened her mouth. She tried to yell at them to leave her alone; she was just an old woman and she didn't know what they wanted.

Then she realized that they weren't looking at her, not pleading with her with their tortured eyes. Instead, they stared at Martha and Stephanie, and their distress was plain.

Edith bolted upright. She spilled her tea across her lap, not noticing the burn.

'Martha!' she gasped. 'You're in danger! Horrible, horrible danger!'

Stephanie stopped reading and looked at Edith with wide blue eyes. Martha raised her head more slowly.

'Stephanie, please go to your room.'

Stephanie got up quickly, looking relieved to escape. Then Martha turned to Edith.

'How do you know?'

'I see things,' Edith confessed in a rush. She'd never said so out loud before. It eased the pressure in her chest. She said more firmly, 'I see the dead.'

Martha's eyes widened. Edith waited to see shock, disgust, or even a faintly repelled look. Instead, Martha's gaze grew sharp and intensely curious.

'You see the dead?'

'Yes.'

'Do they talk to you?'

'No, they just appear, so tortured, as if there's something they need me to understand.'

Martha leaned forward and clutched Edith's hand. Her grip was surprisingly strong.

'Tell me,' she whispered. 'Tell me everything.'

In the bedroom Samantha took her ear away from the door. She'd been trained how to dial 911 and give her full name, address, and phone number. But she didn't have a phone in this room and she no longer knew her address or phone number. She wasn't sure what she was supposed to do now.

Finally she walked over to the bed she'd been given just a few days ago.

She sat on the edge and stroked her dolly's hair. 'It's all right,' she told her baby. She patted the pretty pink doll again. 'Mommy will come. Mommy will come and everything will be all right.'

25

The police were trying to make up for past mistakes. Now the officers filing in for the briefing had to show their badges at the door. All three task force leaders stood next to the receptionist, personally identifying each man. With this system it took forty-five minutes to assemble the group.

Tess sat at the front of the room, J.T. beside her. Marion sat toward the back and Tess was still trying to decide if the distance was intentional. For the past twenty-four hours Tess and Marion had hammered away on Special Agent Quincy and Lieutenant Houlihan until they agreed to Tess's plan. Last night Tess felt triumphant; finally something would happen. This morning she watched the news, saw her daughter's picture flash across the screen once more, and simply felt terrified.

'All right, people,' Lieutenant Houlihan said, 'listen up.'

Quincy strode into the room, looking harried, and Houlihan scowled. Quincy did a small double take, and instead of walking to his chair in the front of the room, promptly took a seat next to Marion. Houlihan got on with it.

'As you know, we have formulated a new strategy for catching Jim Beckett. In the front of the room here, we have Beckett's ex-wife, Tess Williams, whom many of you know from before. Two and half years ago she agreed to sit in her house and wait for Jim Beckett's return. We agreed to protect her and catch her husband. We didn't fulfill our end of the deal so well. Now she has volunteered to do the same once again, and, people, this time we're going to get it right.

'We have three teams in this room. I've already briefed your supervisors, who will cover the details with you later. This is what you need to know now. Task Force A will continue canvassing for Samantha Williams and Jim Beckett. I know the hotline is still getting hits. Plus, it has been suggested that you follow up on the validity of Beckett's family's death certificates. You're moving from an eight-hour to a twelve-hour shift–'

There were a few tired moans.

Houlihan continued ruthlessly. 'Yes, people, your life sucks. Next, Teams B and C are assigned to Tess Williams with everyone rotating eight-hour shifts. You have three main objectives: Scout and secure Williamstown, watch the safe house, and remain mobilized for a full-fledged assault. Officers will be deployed in pairs. Some of you will walk beats, others of you will keep watch from unmarked cars. We will have ten officers deployed at all times. The FBI will coordinate surveillance and wiretapping. Also aiding you will be the SWAT team. We can't keep them on full alert indefinitely, but they have agreed to give us three snipers to cover the rooftops. As you will read in your reports, that's how Jim Beckett entered the house the first time around. This time we're not going to give him that chance.'

A hand came up in back. It was an older detective who'd worked the task force two and half years before. 'With all due respect, Lieutenant, we can't maintain this forever. Last time we also started out ultra alert and ultra ready. But six months later we were down to two men watching the house and no SWAT support. How's this going to be any different? We got budgets, we got constraints. And Beckett knows it.'

Houlihan nodded. 'Good question. We might as well cover it now. Special Agent Quincy . . .'

Houlihan stepped aside and Quincy walked up to the

front of the room. He didn't look at J.T. or Tess. In his dark blue suit he appeared composed and distant. Tess had spoken to him numerous times; now, as before, their lives were intimately intertwined. But he still refused to call her by her first name, and he rarely spoke to her about anything outside of business.

His job had taught him dispassion well. The things that horrified her were commonplace to him. The questions she found intrusive were merely business. His job took him outside the world of civilized people, and she didn't think he could find his way back anymore. She respected him immensely and worried about him frequently.

He began as he always began, without preamble. 'We don't believe we'll have to wait long for Beckett's attack. We believe he is beginning to decompensate.'

'English, please,' Lieutenant Houlihan muttered. 'We're not the ones with the Ph.D.'

'Jim Beckett's beginning to fall apart,' Quincy said bluntly.

Disagreeing murmurs broke out. The man had killed three officers in twenty-four hours. That didn't fit their definition of someone falling apart.

Quincy held up a silencing hand. 'Hear me out. A psychopath is a complex creature. In many ways, however, we can compare him to a particularly bad child.'

More grumbles. Quincy remained patient.

'You've heard the tapes. You know Jim Beckett considers himself to be a man of unprecedented control. "Discipline is the key," that's what he likes to say. However, he's wrong. He is driven by a compulsion that not even he can explain. On the one hand, he considers himself outside the boundaries of society – that is his neurosis. On the other hand, deep down, like any person, he has a need for limits. As he gets away with murder, he tries even more daring and dangerous stunts. Not just because of ego, but because some part of him *wants to be caught*. Like the child who evolves from petty tantrums to small crime to get a parent's attention, Beckett will commit riskier and riskier murders seeking that barrier.

'That is the psychological component of his decompensating. Research also indicates there is a physiological component, but we don't understand it as well. The act of murder appears to release chemicals in the brain. Murderers talk about a feeling of euphoria similar to a runner's high. Before a murder they are tense, wound, overwrought. Afterward they are relaxed, calm, and settled. Over time, the desire, the *need* for this euphoria begins to drive the killer. We see shorter periods of time between killings, cycle times going from six months to *six days* to, in the current case of Jim Beckett, *six hours*.'

The room grew quiet.

'In most cases the organized serial killer begins to demonstrate more and more of the traits we associate with a drug addict. One, he's no longer so composed or calm. Physical health deteriorates. The chemicals released in the brain and constant adrenaline rush interfere with his ability to function. Like someone mainlining cocaine, he stops sleeping, foregoes food, and neglects personal hygiene. Second, his murders become more rash and desperate, the junkie needing his fix. They also become more brutal; the killer goes from carefully orchestrated murders to a blitz style of attack – hit and run. Third, the use of alcohol and drugs generally increases as the killer seeks substitute highs.

'In short, the killer becomes thoughtless and vulnerable. We have seen the pattern in Kemper, Dahmer, Bundy, and numerous other killers. And we are seeing this pattern in Beckett. Observe.'

Quincy waved his hand and the lights dimmed. He turned on an overhead projector and a time line appeared on the wall. It was marked with red lines, then blue. The blue lines leapt up uncontrollably at the end of the graph.

'Before going to prison Beckett killed ten women over

sixteen months. This is indicated by the red lines, starting with the birth of his daughter, and ending eight months before he was caught. The blue lines indicate postprison behavior. He's now killed six people in less than four weeks. First he killed two corrections officers. He was quiet for three weeks. Then suddenly, in four days, four people died.

'Not all these deaths were necessary. Shelly Zane was his accomplice and would've continued to aid him. His penetration of the safe house could've been done with less violence. Originally his pattern was one body per letter. For example, he killed one woman in Clinton, Massachusetts, for the letter C. Now he's killing multiple people at a location. Two corrections officers in Walpole for the letter W. Both Wilcox and Harrison in Springfield for the letter S. Basically he's gone into a mode of extreme overkill.

'Also, he's no longer sleeping. Observe the last four days and the distances between the crime scenes. First he killed Shelly Zane in the early morning, dumping her body in Avon, Connecticut. Then he drives up to the Springfield area. He kidnaps, tortures, and kills Wilcox eight hours later. Now he must drive to his hiding place, probably outside the Springfield area, as we've turned the immediate vicinity upside down. He has to steal a police uniform, buy his disguise. Then he must assemble everything. Make the phone calls to cover his tracks, etcetera. Then he has to drive back to Springfield as Officer Travis. By six in the evening the next day he surprises and shoots Harrison. Then he has to stay awake in the unmarked police car. One A.M., after thirty-six hours without sleep, he attacks Difford. Then he kidnaps Sam. Now he must run all night. He's carrying around Difford's corpse, and Difford is not a small man. Maybe he does get to sleep a few hours in the early morning while Sam sleeps. But soon she's awake and now he must entertain his daughter. He's gone over forty-eight hours on minimal sleep, and instead of going to bed that night, he returns to the

Difford crime scene. He attacks Ms. Williams and Mr Dillon, and he sustains a shoulder wound. Once again he must drive back to his hiding place, wounded and having gone fifty-six hours on almost no sleep. Samantha will be awake soon, keeping him up for another day.

'He still has Difford's body, and he still has some sort of plan.'

Quincy looked at Tess. 'I believe it's all aimed at getting you, Ms. Williams. His rage is getting high, his blood lust outweighing his control. If he can find you, he'll move. Your idea to serve as bait is most likely the best we can do. Sooner or later there is going to be a confrontation. It's better that it be on our terms than on his.'

The room remained hushed. Tess felt that silence echoed inside her. She nodded slowly.

Abruptly a phone rang. People looked around, shaken and confused. After a moment it became apparent that the ringing was from the back of the room.

'My cell phone,' Quincy murmured. His briefcase was sitting back there. He nodded toward Marion, who picked up his phone and answered it.

She frowned, then covered the receiver with her hand.

'It's a Lawrence Talbert requesting "Coroner Quincy."'

Quincy froze. He didn't say anything, and then Tess understood. It was him. It was Jim. Holy Mother of God, it was Jim.

Suddenly Quincy was gesturing wildly and officers scattered from their seats. Trace the call, trace the call, she watched their mouths cry silently.

Marion walked slowly to the front of the room and handed the phone to Quincy. Her face was calm, controlled. Tess's fingers dug into J.T.'s thigh.

'Hello? Who is calling, please? Dammit, I know it's you.'

Quincy's gaze went to the ventilation grate high up in

the wall. 'No, wait, I don't understand, tell me more. I don't have tools –' His voice was growing frantic, urgent. His knuckles had gone white on the phone. 'Give me a minute. I just need to get a screwdriver. I'm an agent, not a handyman. Wait, I didn't hear you. Can you repeat that? There seems to be interference on the phone –

'Goddammit!' Quincy cried. Beckett had hung up, and in a rare display of rage Quincy hurled the phone across the room. It hit the far wall hard and shattered.

'Son of a bitch, son of a bitch,' Quincy was murmuring. His head was down between his knees. He was breathing hard, as if he'd run a long race. Sweat beaded his face.

He straightened slowly and looked at the faces staring back at him. Then he turned toward the ventilation grate.

'Would somebody get me a screwdriver, please.'

Nobody moved. They just stared up at the grate in the high wall. Tess felt the hysteria bubble up in her throat. No place was safe. No place could remain untouched. Jim went anywhere. He contaminated everything, like a pestilence. She felt the contamination in herself, way down deep. She understood that like Quincy, she'd traveled too far outside the bounds of the civilized world and she'd never find her way back.

'Look at me.' J.T. was before her. He'd stood, and now his hands gripped her shoulders. She managed to bring her gaze up and meet his hard, dark stare. 'Come on. I want you out of the room.'

Someone had handed Quincy a Swiss Army knife with a screwdriver. He stood on a chair before the grate.

'No,' Tess told J.T.

'Dammit, don't subject yourself to this. It's what he wants.'

'I can't leave.'

'Tess, dammit –'

'What if it's . . . Sam?' Her voice was so hoarse, she

barely recognized it. She hadn't realized her true fear until she spoke the words out loud. Now the rushing filled her ears and she thought she might faint.

The grate came off. She remained sitting there, transfixed.

'Focus on me, Tess. Focus on me.'

The smell hit her first. She gagged. Spots appeared before her eyes. There were tears on her cheeks.

Dimly she heard Quincy say, 'Well . . . we've found Lieutenant Difford's head.'

One of the officers led them to the main room. J.T. went off to fetch them both cups of coffee. Tess remained standing in the middle of the room, letting the reassuring noise of talking people and jangling phones sink into her.

The room had high ceilings and not many windows. Once there must have been cubicles, but they'd all been taken down and replaced with long tables. Operators sat elbow to elbow at computer terminals, logging calls on the hotline and jotting down notes. The phones never stopped ringing.

Someone had posted black-and-white copies of Samantha's picture along the wall. Her smiling, innocent face ringed the room and reminded them why they were there, why they were keeping the hours they were keeping.

Tess wanted to touch the photographs, stroke her fingers down the pale cheek, as if that would bring her daughter back to her.

It was odd to stand in the middle of such activity and yet have nothing to do with it. Once Tess had thought all this was focused on her. Now she knew better. If she ceased existing tomorrow, Jim would still kill and the law enforcement bureaucracy would still churn, trying to catch him.

J.T. returned and shoved a lukewarm cup of coffee into her hands. Quincy was on his heels with Marion.

'Why don't we go into one of the interview rooms,'

Quincy suggested. 'Lieutenant Houlihan will join us shortly.'

He ushered them back to a small room with a two-way mirror. It held a single card table and two metal folding chairs. With a murmured apology he went off to find three more chairs.

'How are you holding up?' J.T. asked.

She took a sip of coffee before replying. 'As well as can be expected.'

'He does it just to rattle your cage.'

'Then he's good at rattling cages.'

He stood close. She knew he was waiting to see what she wanted. Did she need to wrap her arms around him? Maybe press her cheek against his shoulder. She thought about it, but she didn't think there was any comfort that he could offer that would blot the picture of Difford's severed head from her mind.

It'll be all right, kid. I'll take care of Sam. Houlihan and Quincy will catch Beckett. It'll be all right, kid.

Quincy returned with the chairs and they all took seats. Moments later Lieutenant Houlihan joined them. His face was still gray and his forehead lined with frustration, anger, and pain.

'No blood,' he said without preamble. 'The head was cut off immediately after death, frozen to slow decomposition, then left in the ventilation shaft. You can access the shaft via the roof. Son of a bitch must've crawled in the morning we were all still at the crime scene and left his little present.' Belatedly he glanced at Tess and Marion. 'Sorry,' he muttered.

'It's okay,' Tess said as she gripped her cup more tightly. 'I'm getting used to these conversations.'

'How did he get Special Agent Quincy's cell phone number?' Marion was eager to establish that she was part of the law enforcement group and not some weak-kneed female observer. 'Surely your number is unlisted, sir.'

'Difford had it,' Quincy said. 'Wilcox too. Beckett either found it on their persons or asked them for it.'

That made everyone in the room visualize just how he would 'request' information, and they all shifted uncomfortably in their chairs. Tess found herself looking at J.T. again. His gaze was locked on the far wall, but she could see that his jaw was tight. He wouldn't worry about himself, it wasn't his nature. But she imagined he could vividly picture Jim Beckett attacking either her or Marion. She had made that horror part of his world. It seemed so blatantly unfair.

'Why just the head?' she asked after a moment.

'I don't know,' Quincy replied.

'Scare tactics,' J.T. stated. 'Demoralize the troops.'

Quincy frowned but didn't argue. It was obvious the straightlaced agent didn't approve of a mercenary.

'He still has Difford's body,' Marion pointed out.

'Perhaps,' Quincy shrugged. 'No one's checked the trunks of their cars.'

They all fell silent, and the air was heavy and strained.

'Do you think you should also be under watch?' Tess spoke up softly. 'You keep saying I'm the target, but he's focused on most of the people who helped catch him before. That was me, Difford, and you, Quincy.'

'It bears consideration.'

'What if he uses the safe house as a ruse? The police are watching me in it, so he seizes the opportunity to get you. That would be something he'd do.'

'Absolutely.' Quincy thrummed the table with his fingers. 'I'll be in the surveillance van with Lieutenant Houlihan for most of the watch. They can guard my back.'

'Snipers?' J.T. quizzed. 'Three's nothing for a town.'

'Williamstown is small,' Lieutenant Houlihan interjected. 'You can walk from one end of it to the other in just twenty minutes. Basically it's a collection of old buildings that make up Williams College, with some historic storefronts for the tourists. Tess's house is on Elm Street, ten minutes from Main Street. The whole block is old, restored row houses. We'll position the snipers on the corners, providing aerial coverage of the street.'

'One corner will be uncovered.'

'True, but visibility is pretty good. We'll put one guy mid-block on the right with the other two on the left-hand corners, forming a triangle around Tess's house. It should keep the roof clean.'

'And the officers on duty?' J.T. persisted skeptically. It was obvious he didn't think much of the police or their efforts.

'We'll have a main surveillance van, two unmarked cars, and three pairs of cops walking the city. It's a college campus with a lot of young coeds. We'll warn everyone of the danger and maintain a strong police presence throughout the campus. Williams College security and the local police will also provide regular patrols.'

'Uh-huh. Won't a surveillance van parked outside the house be a bit obvious?'

'It won't be on Elm. Arnold, Hall, Maple, and Linden all intersect. We'll pick one of the streets as a starting point and move around between them.'

'Why are you so sure he'll come?' Marion pressed no one in particular. 'It's the way you caught him the first time, so he knows it's risky. Two, it doesn't fit his pattern. JIM BECKETT WAS HERE or JIM WAS NUMBER ONE makes sense. JIM BECKETT WAS W? I don't see how it can fit.'

'He'll come,' Tess said.

'Because he's deteriorating?'

'Because he always finishes what he starts,' Tess murmured. 'Always.'

Marion sat back. 'I guess I just don't understand that kind of anger.'

'You can't,' Quincy spoke up. 'You're a woman.'

When Marion tried to protest, Quincy waved her down tiredly. 'I'm talking statistics, not chauvinism. Most serial killers are male. Maybe part of it's hormones, but certainly it's also behavioral. When men get angry, they are taught to lash out at others. When women get angry, they are taught to turn in on themselves. Quite simply, your mothers torment you and you become alcoholics or anorexics or suicide risks. You don't become killers.'

His gaze slid to Tess. He spoke matter-of-factly.

'Beckett will come, Ms. Williams. And when he does, it will be bloody.'

Marion waited for her brother and Tess to return to their motel before she made her move. It was after six, but the war room showed no sign of slowing down. Phones were ringing, operators answering. Lieutenant Houlihan was yelling at some young officer while simultaneously crunching Tums. The mood in the building was stark.

She kept walking, looking for a vacant interview room or forgotten corner. Instead, she ran into Officer Louis, a straw-haired kid who looked too much like Richie Cunningham for his own good. He spotted her coming, froze, and gulped noticeably.

She'd run into him earlier that day. Perhaps someday he'd be a good police officer, but personally she thought he had the spine of a jellyfish. In turn, he seemed to view her as the human equivalent of a black widow spider, waiting to seduce him into answering her questions, at which time she would calmly bite off his head to complete the mating.

'I'm looking for Special Agent Quincy.'

Officer Louis couldn't get the words out. He backed against the wall and pointed down the hallway. Shaking her head, Marion walked past him. His sigh of relief was audible.

She found Quincy sequestered in his own little space, surrounded by crime scene photos. He didn't look up right away. She used the opportunity to glance at the color photographs. They didn't appear to be from Jim Beckett's files. Most of these victims were middle-aged women. They'd been carved up brutally by a serrated knife.

Quincy sifted through them one by one, as though he were shuffling a deck of cards. At long last he sighed, shook his head, and finally set them down, clearly not having found what he was seeking.

'Another case, sir?' she asked respectfully. She'd automatically assumed a cadet's stance, legs apart, shoulders square, hands behind her back.

'Santa Cruz,' he muttered, his gaze still on the photos. 'Can you believe that at one time Santa Cruz was the serial killer capital of the world with three active murderers? Now we have another there. It makes you wonder what's in the water.'

He pushed back from the rickety table. Marion could see the exhaustion deeply stamped into his face. His hand was rubbing the back of his neck.

'And her?' Marion asked, suddenly feeling too unnerved to state her real purpose for finding him. She gestured to the framed portrait of a smiling brunette.

'Oh, her? My wife. I mean ex-wife.' He smiled ruefully. 'Divorce came through a few weeks ago. I guess I'm still adjusting. I've always traveled with her picture, you know. Set it up in every cheap motel and overheated police station in the country. Now I find I can't work without it. Silly, isn't it?'

Marion shifted, even more discomfited by this personal insight. 'Not really, sir. My . . . uh, my husband and I recently split as well. After ten years. It's a big adjustment.'

'Hard to be married and be an agent.'

'That's what everyone says.'

He smiled. 'It is a platitude, isn't it?'

'I don't know, sir.'

They drifted into silence, but it was too unsettling for both of them. 'What can I help you with, Agent?' Quincy asked briskly.

'I . . . I want to speak with you about my role in this case.'

'Your role? You're not even officially on this case, Agent. So far your involvement is due to circumstance, not assignment.'

'I understand. I would like to change that if it's possible. I've been interested in this kind of work for a long time.'

'I pulled your file.'

Marion waited patiently.

'You have a good record. Seems that you can be rigid at times, but you keep a cool head and have above-average analytics.'

'Thank you, sir.'

'But from what I could tell, your experience is in white-collar crimes, mostly bank frauds –'

'There have been some homicides,' she interjected. 'Deals gone bad, informants who were found out, that kind of thing.'

'But always in conjunction with a fraud case.'

'Dead is dead, sir. They were connected with our work, crime scene came under our jurisdiction, and we got to figure out who killed them.'

'The Investigative Support Unit is different, Agent. It's all we do. A typical cop may see a gruesome murder two or three times a year. They might see a serial killer once in their *career*.' Quincy gestured to the pictures spread out on the table. 'This is all I see. One hundred and fifty cases of killing, rape, child molestation, and kidnapping. I deal only with the extremes, day in, day out. On the road, in the office, this is it.'

'I understand.'

'I would be lying if I said it didn't get to you.'

Her chin came up. 'I think I can handle it, sir.'

'I don't think you know what "it" is.'

'Is it because I'm a woman?'

'Don't insult me, Agent.' His voice held clear warning. She persisted anyway.

'You talk statistics, sir. Well, the Bureau statistics show that female agents are disproportionately assigned to white-collar cases and not homicides.'

'That's the Bureau. We have female profilers in the Investigative Support Unit – and they're damn good. And you're not them, Agent. They paid their dues. They served as cops, forensics pathologists, or criminologists. They all joined with extensive homicide experience. If you're serious about the ISU, talk to your director about getting on some different cases. Prove yourself in the kiddie pool before you jump into the ocean.'

'I have this opportunity now.' Her voice was steady but her eyes burned. She was being put in her place and she hated it. Sometimes it seemed her whole life had been spent being put in her place by men who should've known better. Who should've trusted her more.

'I have some ideas,' she persisted.

'Agent –'

'Just hear me out. I looked at Jim Beckett's file. I've spoken to Tess Williams at length. I think it's clear, I think it's obvious, Jim Beckett must have an accomplice. You said he can't go long without female companionship. Tess also stated that he charms and seduces women as a hobby. I think there is someone helping him with everything, someone who helped him two and a half years ago, when he disappeared for the first time. And I think I may know how to find that person.'

Quincy appeared skeptical but he didn't interrupt.

She kept talking before she lost her courage. 'Let's assume for a moment that the woman isn't a random stranger but someone he's known for a while. That means he would need to maintain the relationship even while in prison.'

'Shelly Zane was his only visitor ever logged.'

'Yes, but what about *called*? I checked with Walpole. Beckett was a model prisoner. He didn't have any disciplinary tickets written up, and as a "ticket free" maximum security inmate, he was entitled to four phone calls a month, up to thirty minutes apiece.'

'I know, Agent. And as you must have found out from Walpole, those calls are monitored. Prisoners must file all numbers with security to be approved. They don't even get to dial. The guard brings the phone down to the cell, plugs it in, places the phone call, and then passes the phone through the window for the inmate to pick up. A four-digit security code has to be entered for any number to go through, so the prisoner can't try to covertly hang up and dial a different number. Any sign of two-way calling, and the phone automatically disconnects. The system is pretty rigid, and we checked Beckett's numbers. He called Shelly Zane about twice a month and his lawyer for the other calls.'

'I know, sir,' Marion forced herself to say patiently. 'I did look into the matter. I know two-way calling shuts off the phone, but what about call forwarding?'

'Who would forward a call for a prisoner?'

'Shelly Zane.'

Quincy was silent for a moment. Then he blinked his eyes. 'I don't know if Zane has call forwarding.'

'She does. I checked. She used it a lot. In the last two years calls were forwarded to two hundred and forty-seven different numbers. I compiled a list.'

Slowly Quincy nodded. 'We should look into that. We can ask Houlihan to have Task Force A start in on it immediately. They could use a few good leads.'

'Thank you, sir.'

'You can sit in the surveillance van with Houlihan and me,' he said abruptly. 'If there's action, you'll see it.'

'What about assisting Team A?'

'That would be stepping on the team leader's toes, Agent. First thing you learn in crossjurisdictional investigations – don't step on local law enforcement's toes.'

Marion knew a lecture when she heard one. 'I would like to sit in the van. Thank you, sir.'

'Then it's settled. You may not agree, but even being invited to take part in surveillance on this kind of case is a huge responsibility. Don't blow it.'

His tone was curt and dismissive. His attention was already returning to his gruesome stack of photos, and it was clear he didn't want to speak to her anymore.

She nodded her head once and left. Her throat was thick with frustration. She had wanted more. More praise for her ideas, more inclusion into the male-dominated world of violent crime. More recognition that she was smart, savvy, and capable. Instead, she'd been dressed down as thoroughly as any rookie, then tossed a bone to keep her from whining too much.

She thought Quincy was wrong. She had her own opinions, her own ideas. And she was suddenly sick of spending her life playing by other people's rules.

Opportunities were not given. They were made.

She knew how she would make hers.

The phone rang in the motel room. Tess snatched up the receiver.

'Yes?' Her voice was hopeful. Lieutenant Houlihan had told her he would call if they learned anything about Sam. Tess had been staring at the phone for the last two hours as the sun had sunk, the room had darkened, and she and J.T. had become too weary to even snap on a light.

'Oh, hi, Marion.' Her shoulders slumped. 'No, we're fine here. It's just a motel, you know how motels are. It does have a pool, so J.T. got to swim. I don't think it helped much. He's about to wear a hole in the carpet. Do you want to speak to him?'

J.T. halted mid-stride. The look on his face was wary and torn.

Tess held out the phone to him. Marion's answer had equaled his expression. At least they were both trying.

'Hello?' J.T. said carefully. 'No, it's fine. Tess is playing solitaire, I'm going insane. The usual.' He nodded his head and just listened for a bit. 'He wasn't the right one for you,' he said finally. He sounded awkward. 'You'll . . . you'll find someone else. Someone better. It's tough. I know. But there are other fish in the sea, you know?' His gaze rested on Tess.

After another few minutes he said good-bye and hung up. He resumed pacing immediately.

'Is she okay?' Tess asked quietly.

'The divorce papers arrived today. Her housekeeper called her with the news.'

'Oh,' Tess said with feeling. 'That must be very difficult. Especially now, with everything else going on.'

J.T. nodded, but she couldn't read his expression.

'It was good that she called, J.T. She's reaching out to you.'

'Yeah.' He was silent for a moment. 'I'm not good at this.'

'You're doing fine.'

'I don't know what I'm supposed to say.'

'No one does. Have you ever tried explaining to a four-year-old that her father's an ax murderer? In the end, we all make it up as we go along.'

'Huh.' He still didn't sound happy. She got up off the bed and went to him.

The moonlight slashed across his face, shrouding his eyes in shadows. She touched his shoulders, then his cheek. She moved until her body was brushing his. His face was hard, his chin and jaw sculpted with resolute lines. He looked strong, and suddenly she needed that strength.

She wrapped her arms around his waist. 'Hold me.'

'I'm not . . . I'm not . . .' His arms went around her. He held her, but a part of him remained out of reach.

She drew back and took his hand. 'Let's go to bed.'

He simply stood there.

'J.T., this is our last night together. Tomorrow we're in Williamstown. I know you want me to do it differently, I know you're worried the worst will happen. I made my decision. I accept that risk. And I know I have this night and I would like to spend it with you. Can you give me that much?'

He couldn't find an answer.

Her face was pale and ethereal, her eyes huge, luminescent, and knowing. He thought if he remained silent and distant long enough, she'd give up and storm away. He'd forgotten just how well she'd learned to fight. She wrapped her arms around his neck. She pressed her slender body against his.

He wanted to be cold. He wanted to be unfeeling.

Her lips feathered over his gently, and he succumbed. He slanted his mouth and devoured her.

She haunted him and he didn't want to be haunted. She consumed him and he didn't want to be consumed. The emotions rolled over one another, churning his blood. He kept hearing Marion's voice, the thin thread of vulnerability beneath her dispassionate words, the unspoken need he didn't know how to address. He kept seeing Tess, her eyes dilated with horror as the ventilation grate came off and revealed once more what Jim Beckett could do.

Marion and Tess. The women he loved, the women he was so sure he would fail. The women he wanted to hold close and the women he wanted to push away because he couldn't stand his own weakness. He couldn't stand the fact that Tess was right and he couldn't save the world all by himself or make it a better place.

Tess pulled herself closer to him, fragile and strong, needy and giving. He kissed her senselessly, trying desperately to overpower his desire, to crush true emotion beneath the leaden weight of pure lust.

He dragged her down onto the bed. He tasted the sweetness of her skin and inhaled the soft, secret scent of her body. He felt her rose-petal skin and unending warmth.

She thought he and Marion were the tough ones – she didn't understand. The fire that had forged them had made them too brittle. Tess was the one who'd emerged as true steel.

He gave in to the pull of her fierce embrace and the whispered urgings of her lips.

Suddenly their lovemaking became urgent and fierce, a war fought amid tangled sheets. She rolled him onto his back and straddled him shamelessly.

'I love you, J.T.,' she whispered. 'I love you.'

Finally she moved. Tears glittered on her cheeks. She cried and she rode him and she let him see her cry as she did so. He couldn't look away.

'Don't do this,' he muttered. 'God, don't do this to me.'

She kept moving. Suddenly his right hand was at her hip, his fingers digging into her flesh, his strong arm setting a furious pace. His heels dug into the mattress, giving him leverage as his hips thrust up hard. She had wanted to consume him, but now he consumed her because she was killing him with her silent tears and he didn't know what to do.

Her head fell back, her climax long and racking and ripping his name from her lips. He didn't relent, moving, moving, moving, and spiking her back up. He thrust harder, sweat building, teeth bared.

The climax eluded him. Fine tension corded his neck and rippled his body with unbearable pain. He wanted, he needed.

He didn't know anymore. The emptiness was endless and he was dying and she was the only person who could save him and he didn't even know how to say the words.

He rolled her over harshly, his body still joined with hers, and fucked her hard. She gasped. He couldn't stop. The release was so close, but he couldn't find it. He couldn't embrace it, he couldn't welcome it, because he knew when it came it would be like a spring rain and smell of the roses that reminded him of her.

'I love you,' she whispered against his sweat-soaked torso. 'I love you.'

And he climaxed with a primal yell, his semen ripped from him and pouring into her.

He collapsed over her, shaking and trembling and fallen apart. She held him close, then stroked his hair.

'I know,' she whispered. 'I know.'

Later, the sheets tangled around their legs, the sweat drying on their bodies, he said, 'I loved Rachel.'

'I understand.'

'She died.'

'I know.'

'I never told her that I loved her.'

'I'm sure she knew.'

'But no one ever told her. Not her parents, not the colonel. Not me.'

'But you showed it to her, J.T. That matters more.'

His head turned toward her. His fingertips brushed her arm. 'Sometimes I hate you.'

'I know,' she told him honestly. 'That's how I know that you care.'

In the morning the thin rays of a weak sun rapped at the window, illuminating the room in shades of misty gray. Tess crawled out of bed first, entered the bathroom, and closed the door without looking back.

He waited until he heard the scouring sound of the shower. Then he reached over to the nightstand and found his pack of smokes. His hand was trembling, making it difficult to get one out. Finally he dragged a cigarette to his lips, lit it with a plastic lighter, and inhaled deeply. He leaned back onto the bed, staring at the ceiling and watching the rolling smoke slowly dissipate as it rose through the early morning air.

Alone, he had no more pretensions. He hadn't been the kind of brother he should've been. He hadn't been the kind of husband he should've been. His life had started with pain and he'd been adding layers ever since.

Tonight a new layer would be spread. He wanted to get this one right. He was afraid the beast in his belly would keep that from ever happening. He had too much anger in him. He wasn't good at leaving it behind. He understood all that and wondered if understanding it really made a difference.

His lips formed the words soundlessly three times before he trusted himself enough to add voice. Finally he whispered, 'I love you too, Tess.'

And a second later: 'Jim Beckett is a dead man.'

26

'Well, here it is,' Marion announced. She gestured to the house Tess had lived in for four years, her entire married life. The house had been sold two years earlier, but the police had commandeered it. The owners had been forced out with their furniture and the house hastily filled with garage-sale rejects.

Tess found the decor as dismal as her mood.

In the living room to her left, a sloping blue love seat had been stuck in the middle of the brown carpet. Dark brown shelves had been hastily erected and stuffed full of used paperbacks. An old TV sat on a coffee table with a more modern-looking VCR. The metal desk lamp perched on the fireplace mantel provided the only light. Stairs were straight ahead. The small brown kitchen to her right. Upstairs was the master bedroom and two extra rooms. She hated to think what kind of furniture was in them.

'The kitchen is fully stocked,' Marion said. 'You also have a TV, bookshelves, and so forth. It'll be just like before –'

'Solitary confinement,' Tess stated.

Marion glanced at J.T. 'Not quite solitary.'

J.T. didn't look at either of them. He prowled the living room perimeter, peering through the front bay of windows.

'We've been talking on and off over the police scanners,' Marion continued. 'Not too many conversations, but enough to give the general idea that a "special package" is arriving in Williamstown and should be "handled with care." Quincy is confident that Beckett monitors the police scanners. Sooner or later he'll hear the chatter and make his plans.'

'Which roofs have the snipers?'

Marion pointed them out for J.T. 'One across the street with a clean line of fire on the front door. Other two on the corners of this side of the block.'

'Lots of chimneys and fancy archways. What are the chances of a clean shot?'

Marion shrugged. 'Depends on where Beckett stands. Either way, they'll see him coming and the rest of us will mobilize.'

'Huh. Windows wired?'

'All wired. Bug in every room.'

'The bathroom?' Tess asked. Now she was beginning to remember all the details her mind had conveniently blanked from the last time. She'd hated last time.

'*Every* room. This is your life, right?'

'Lucky me.'

'You need anything, just speak up loudly. We'll be monitoring you from the van at all times.'

'I guess this means no sex,' Tess said. She was struggling for control.

'Only if you want an audience,' Marion said expressionlessly. 'Any questions?'

'Did you pull sewage maps of the area? What about manholes, any underground systems?'

'J.T., we know what we're doing.'

'I don't want to see any utility trucks in the area. No cable company, no phone men, no electric company. Call and tell them to keep out or I'll personally give their driver the message. It's too easy for Big Bad Jim to use something like that.'

'We won't even permit door-to-door encyclopedia salesmen,' Marion assured him.

'Huh.' J.T. turned to Tess. 'Fine with you?'

'Just dandy.' She forced a smile to take the sting from the words. It didn't work. She still felt like a rat in a trap.

She glanced at Marion. 'Any news about Sam?' she whispered, though she knew there wasn't.

'Not at this time.'

'Difford's body?'

'Nothing.'

J.T. shook his head. Marion scowled. 'The task force is working very hard, goddammit. We'll let you know as soon as we get a break. Now, if you'll excuse me, I have some loose ends to attend to. I'll return by sundown.'

Marion headed for the door. J.T. followed, catching up with her in the doorway.

'How are you?' he asked before he lost his courage.

She didn't answer right away. 'Fine.' She glanced toward Tess, then looked at him. 'Congratulations.'

'For what?'

'She's a strong woman, J.T. I'm happy for you.'

He scowled, then gave it up. 'Yeah. She is. Thanks.' He looked away for a moment. The sky had become unbearably bright and clear. 'She deserves better,' he said.

'You're not so bad.'

'Not so bad?'

'Not so bad.'

'Marion . . .' His throat constricted. He couldn't say the words. It wasn't the way things worked between them. He settled for brushing her arm lightly. 'Keep me posted about the stuff with Roger, okay? I'm not the best at saying the right things, but I know you loved him, Marion. I'd like to help. You know, if I can.'

Marion looked at the floor. 'J.T., you know those mean things I said about Rachel?'

He nodded. He remembered each and every one of them.

'I sent her to you,' she confessed in a rush. 'She came to me looking for help. And I – I just couldn't help her. I looked at her, and I wanted her to just go away. I couldn't even bear to look at her. Just this poor slip of girl, and I couldn't even look at her. Stupid, wasn't it?'

She shrugged. He began to hear the things left unsaid.

'I gave her your name. I told her you would help. I knew . . . I knew you would have the guts to do what I couldn't.'

'You did the right thing, Marion. Thank you.'

'Good,' she said quietly. She sounded better. 'I wanted you to know.'

'I'll be there for you, Marion. When you're ready.'

She smiled again, faint and tremulous. Briefly she touched his face.

'I know.'

She left.

He turned back to Tess.

She still stood in the middle of the living room, looking ragged from her sleepless night. Her thumbnail had gone to work on her other fingers. She didn't seem to notice.

He walked toward her and brushed her mangled fingernails. She flinched, looking chagrined.

'Got your gun?'

'Yes,' she said, clearly startled.

'Want to practice now? We can do some shadow targeting without bullets.'

Her relief was palpable. 'All right.'

He nodded, already reaching for the 9 mm holstered against the small of his back. He had a .22 around his left ankle and a hunting knife strapped against the inside of his left forearm cast.

He was ready.

Tess retrieved her gun from her purse.

'We're ready, Tess. We'll get him.'

Tess just smiled. 'That's what Difford used to say.'

'Yes, I understand the doctor is dead. We just need some way of verifying this death certificate. Yes, ma'am, twenty years is a long time ago. Do you have copies in the hospital files? Or maybe a nurse or someone else in attendance at the time still works at the hospital. Yeah, I'll hold.' Detective Epstein rolled his eyes. He hated this kind of grunt work.

Jim Beckett's foster parents had been dead less than ten years, so verifying their death certificates hadn't been tough. They'd gotten lucky with his birth father – a police officer who'd arrived at the traffic accident twenty years ago was still on the force. He confirmed James Beckett had been DOA, a victim of a four-car pileup.

Verifying the death certificate for Mary Beckett was more difficult. The doctor who'd signed the original certificate was dead and the hospital bureaucrats had bigger matters than hunting down records on someone who'd died twenty years earlier.

The person came back on the line. Detective Epstein stopped twirling his pencil.

'Archives? What do you mean by archives? In a *separate* storage facility. Well, sure I understand the volume of records you must have. Is there a system? Can you send some exhausted intern to search? Well, ma'am, I'd send an officer, but you're not really going to let us paw through your records unattended, are you? That's what I thought. So what time is good for you? Yeah, an hour it is.'

He hung up the phone and rubbed his eyes. Technically his shift had ended two hours ago. It was about to extend for several hours more.

Night was falling soon. The first night with Tess Williams in her old house, and Team A was feeling the pressure. If they could find Jim or Samantha Beckett ahead of time, they'd save everyone a lot of trouble. There were twelve of them working now. Epstein had taken over confirming the last death certificate. Four officers were hunting down the numbers Shelly Zane had forwarded calls to over the last two years. Eight officers still reviewed the hotline logs, following up leads, chasing down ghosts. Shit, this case was killing them all.

Epstein had known Difford. He'd respected the

lieutenant very much. Once they'd gone to a Red Sox game together. Difford had been one of the few locals who'd remained loyal to the Red Sox even in the rotten years – the long, long periods of them.

Epstein picked up his jacket. 'Andrews, you available?'

'Only if I have to be.'

'You have to be. Grab your coat. We have an appointment.'

'Where to?'

'A storage facility. We have a haystack to search for a needle.'

'Jesus, Epstein. You sure know how to show a guy a good time.'

Marion sat in the middle of the floor in the office she'd borrowed. She was surrounded by a sea of maps, all wearing different shades of pastels. She had New England maps, Massachusetts maps, Berkshire County maps, and Williamstown maps. They frolicked around her, holding the secret to long life.

She'd been staring at them all day, and now her vision was blurred. She was also having difficulty concentrating.

For no good reason she remembered being seven years old and ducking with J.T. behind a sofa cushion as Melhelia, their maid, launched another sock grenade over the defensive perimeter of decorative pillows.

J.T. was laughing. Merry Berry was giggling. It defied the imagination.

She shook her head. She blinked her eyes three times, then popped them open and focused on the maps. She didn't want to think of herself or long-ago days. She didn't want to think of the shadow that hovered behind the laughing Merry Berry, the dark shadow that tinged the edges of all her memories, even the good ones.

She wanted to think of Beckett. She wanted to crawl behind his eyes.

'We have more in common than you can imagine,' she muttered. 'Ice. It's all about ice.'

No empathy, no compassion. Just the cool practicality and efficient ruthlessness of immoral genius. No restraints, no boundaries. If you could think of it, you could do it.

She stared at the maps harder, willing the dispassion in her blood. Focus, focus, focus.

A knock sounded on her office door, making her flinch. She scowled, rubbed the back of her neck, and pulled herself together.

'Come in.'

A secretary cracked open the door. 'Roger MacAllister on line one for you.'

'Tell him I'm not available.'

'He's called several times now, Agent.'

Marion turned to the Williamstown map. 'Tough.'

She ran her finger down the streets, trying to see the small, quaint town the way he saw it. Trying to know it as he knew it.

Jim Beckett was number one. Jim Beckett was here. Jim Beckett was *here*.

She stared at the map harder and at Tess's house, which she'd marked with an X.

'Oh,' she said at last, the pattern clicking in her mind. '*Oh*.'

Eight p.m. The sun was down, the streetlights on. In the generic white van Lieutenant Houlihan and Special Agent Quincy sat in silence. The snipers were in place on the roof, woolen mittens pulled over their hands for warmth. At the end of the block a young college girl in black tights, black boots, a short red skirt, and beige barn jacket arrived home with her backpack, opened her front door, and stepped inside.

At six o'clock the tiny residential block had showed signs of life. Now things were settling down. The few families who lived there were eating dinner. The college students had already departed again, heading for a

Friday night of college entertainment. Houlihan didn't imagine they'd see much more traffic until one or two A.M.

Linden Street was a quiet place.

The radio crackled briefly to life. Patrol teams Alpha, Beta, and Omega all reported in. So far, no signs of Jim.

'Get ready for a long week,' Houlihan muttered.

'Where's Agent MacAllister?' Quincy asked.

'I don't know. She's your agent.'

Quincy looked at his watch again and frowned. 'I wouldn't have thought she'd blow it this early on,' he murmured. He went back to staring out the window. He hated stakeouts.

Houlihan finally picked up the cell phone and checked in at headquarters. 'Any news?' he asked the sergeant in charge.

'No, sir.'

'What about Team A? Have they found any leads on Jim or Samantha?'

'No, sir.'

'All the death certificates are confirmed?' Houlihan pressed. He was damn tired of hearing 'No, sir.'

'Yes, sir.'

'I thought they had a lead?'

'I just spoke with Detective Epstein himself. Hospital archives revealed a copy of Mary Beckett's death certificate. His family is dead, sir. If someone is helping him, it's someone we've never heard of. They're still working on the phone list.'

'Just wonderful.' Houlihan grumbled a bit more, then hung up the phone. Quincy remained silent.

They stared down the street. Waiting.

Marion changed clothes. She pulled on a pair of designer jeans, a peach silk turtleneck, and a cardigan of hand-woven Irish wool. She left the cardigan unbuttoned so she could reach easily for her gun.

The clothes were much nicer than what a college

student would normally wear, but at a glance they would do.

She pulled the first pin out of her hair. Then the second, then the third. The pale gold locks uncurled slowly, as if they were afraid of the unexpected freedom. She picked up a brush and worked on her hair until it gleamed.

She had no bangs and no natural wave. Just fine flaxen strands that reached the small of her back. She added a headband and thought she looked like Alice in Wonderland. Perfect.

The clock glowed 8:30 as she pulled on her gray wool overcoat. Her shoulder holster fit comfortably. Around her ankle she had a .22.

She took out her FBI shield and studied it one last time. Fidelity, bravery, integrity, it said. *I do solemnly swear that I will support and defend the Constitution of the United States against all enemies, foreign and domestic . . .*

She placed the shield on the middle of the bed. There was one last matter to attend to. She kept the note simple:

> J.T.
>
> *I do remember the pillow fort and the GI comic books and the night we cried because Snake still hadn't come to take us away. Sometimes I still dream of the colonel and he is always standing amid the flames of hell while little demons flay his skin. I watch from outside the intense heat and I always think, it's not enough. There is nothing that would ever be enough.*
>
> *You were right to remember, but I need to forget.*
>
> *Remember me young, for both of us.*
> *Merry Berry*

She left the pad sitting next to the phone. She added two extra clips to her coat pocket.

Head high, shoulders square, she left the room and didn't look back.

Edith sat on her front porch, hugging her old hunting coat closer to her. It was cold, colder than it should be.

She'd thought that after telling Martha about her visions, everything would get better. They'd spoken of it frankly. Martha was afraid of her son. She thought he may have done some bad things and that's what the dead girls were trying to tell Edith. Tonight Martha would bring little Stephanie over to Edith's while she went to the police.

Edith had agreed. They were taking action. They had a plan. The visions should go away.

But as she stood on the front porch, her chest had that too-tight feeling and goose bumps were already prickling up her arms. As she stood on her front porch, she knew that she was scared. Very scared.

Martha appeared in her driveway again. She was loading up the trunk of her car. She'd been loading it for a while with luggage and bags of supplies. Edith had no idea how Martha had ended up with so much stuff.

Martha disappeared back inside her home. She no longer moved stiffly. Now her strides were long and purposeful, almost jaunty. Their plan had had a euphoric effect on Martha. Edith suspected it would only be temporary. Thick shadows circled Martha's eyes and her gaze had that too-bright look of someone who wasn't sleeping at night.

Edith felt another chill and rubbed her arms again. The girl drifted back in front of her – the one with a butterfly tattoo. Edith shook her head. 'I'm doing what I can. Now go away. Find the light, do whatever it is you people do.'

Martha reappeared, Stephanie's hand tucked in hers. They crossed the yard, then Stephanie's small hand was ceremoniously transferred to Edith's age-spotted grip. The little girl didn't appear happy, but she didn't complain. Beneath the brim of her everpresent baseball cap, she wore the resigned expression of someone who'd gone through all this before.

Edith thought she was very strong for a four-year-old.

'If all goes well, I'll have a restraining order by morning,' Martha said.

'How will a restraining order protect you from Jim Beckett?' Edith grumbled.

Martha instantly stilled. She looked at Edith very carefully. 'How do you know about Jim Beckett?'

'I –' Edith's mouth worked soundlessly. It was one of those things she hadn't known she'd known until she'd said the words out loud. 'I just . . . I just do.'

Martha nodded, but there was something new in her expression. Something that made Edith stand very still. Beside her, Samantha had stopped breathing, also sensing the danger.

The old woman and child stood together very quietly.

Slowly Martha nodded. Slowly she stepped back.

She finally climbed into the car and shut the door with a bang. The shakes hit Edith in a rush; suddenly her whole body was trembling.

She looked down at Stephanie, subdued Stephanie, whose hair was as golden as any of the faded girls haunting her porch. She looked at the old brown Nissan now pulling out of the driveway.

And suddenly the visions cleared her porch. They leapt into the car, crowded into the car with their long blond hair and silent, somber faces. They were crying and keening, tearing at their hair, spilling out of the car. Begging for help.

Edith dragged her eyes away, feeling the pain once more in her chest. Needle-sharp pain. Horrible pain.

Her gaze went to the back of the car, pulling down the street. Her gaze landed on Martha's too-white hair, and she knew. She knew why the visions had started appearing. She knew why they grew worse when Martha was in the room. She knew why Martha's face was too smooth and her hands too strong and her shoulders too broad.

Martha wasn't Jim Beckett's mother. Martha was Jim Beckett.

The brake lights suddenly glowed bright red. The beat-up car halted in the middle of the street.

And she knew that Jim Beckett knew that she knew.

She grabbed Samantha's hand tightly.

'Run, child, run,' she commanded, and yanked her off the patio. 'Run with me!'

Tess pulled away from the window. She turned toward J.T., who sat in the reclining chair, twirling his hunting knife around his fingers.

'You all right?' he asked.

She said simply, 'Nightfall.'

27

Marion walked down the streets of Williamstown without fear.

She'd scouted them out earlier, matching buildings to the street map she'd burned into her mind. Houlihan hadn't lied – Williamstown was small. Settled in 1753 as West Hoosuck, the town was nestled in the Berkshires with a 450-acre campus. Land sprawled around the town, undulating green fields broken up by impressive gothic churches built from stone. White-trimmed brick buildings added prestigious touches. The mountains towered in the horizon.

The heart of Williamstown, however, contained no more than a few square miles. From Marion's location off central Hoxsey Street, she could walk to Tess's house on Elm in twelve minutes. She could run there in six. The centralized collection of shops, dormitories, and houses made it the ideal setting for a hit and run. And the steady traffic of bundled-up college students and tourists made it easy to blend in.

She could understand why Jim Beckett would allow himself to be lured back to this town.

She lingered on Hoxsey Street. The science compound loomed to one side, a dark mass of shadowed buildings where old pine trees sheltered a zigzagging maze of walking paths. The other side of the street began with the beautiful redbricked Spencer House, one of the many fraternities lining Main Street. The rest of the street was occupied by old, traditional homes that had been subdivided into apartments for the Williams students. The student infirmary marked the end.

It was only nine-thirty, and the street witnessed steady traffic flow. Students traced the walking paths that began one block over on pulsing Spring Street and carried them through the science compound, across Hoxsey Street, and down the row of fraternities. Tonight students walked briskly and in groups. Obviously they'd paid attention to warnings of a possible escaped murderer in the area.

Marion urged them on mentally. *Run and run fast. You don't want to meet Jim Beckett tonight.*

Jim Beckett was here.

She turned the phrase over in her mind again and again, and that was the only one that made sense. 'Jim Beckett was the best' was pejorative; he'd say 'Jim Beckett *is* the best.' Same with 'Jim Beckett was number one.'

Jim Beckett was here. The statement was as arrogant and childish as the man. It fit him.

Tonight – or maybe tomorrow night, or the one after it – he would come after Tess. But he would also finish his pattern. He always finished what he started. He didn't have time to do it anymore with city names. But he could use street names.

Tess lived on Elm Street. That supplied one of the *Es* in *here*.

But to start he would need the letter *H*.

Marion pivoted and walked down the other side of Hoxsey. It would end here.

She veered away from the main street, following one of the footpaths through the science compound. Gravel crunched beneath her feet as she walked.

A group of four students passed by her and faded away.

A blue-suited security guard approached, gray hair protruding from beneath his cap. His generous middle jiggled like Jell-O.

She shook her head, tucking her chin against her chest for warmth as she trudged on. Another retired policeman who'd become a rent-a-cop. Slow, out of shape, and absolutely no match for a man like Jim Beckett.

Out of the corner of her eye she saw the guard's head come up. His face was lined heavily. He had jowls.

Less than twelve inches away from him, she finally noticed his eyes.

Bright blue eyes.

Ice.

She reached for her gun. And he lunged forward.

'Where's Marion?' J.T. grumbled. He paced back and forth in the kitchen, where Tess was trying to keep busy by making chili. She was stirring the beans obsessively and adding chili powder with a heavy hand.

He glanced at the clock for fourth time in five minutes.

Only 9:35. And they were already going nuts.

'Maybe she's still at the office.'

'Maybe.' He could feel the tension rising inside him. Jungle drums with a jungle beat. He couldn't stop pacing.

He picked up the phone and called in. Lieutenant Houlihan picked up the secure line on the first ring. 'What?' the lieutenant demanded sourly.

'I thought Marion was coming back to the house one more time.'

'She seems to have changed her mind.'

The statement irritated J.T. beyond reason. 'Put her on the phone.' His tone was curt.

'Can't.'

'Can't?'

'She's not here. I don't know what the deal is. Last we heard, police team Alpha saw her walking down Hoxsey Street. She must have had some last-minute things to do. It's going to be fun watching her try to explain it to Quincy. He really doesn't look happy.'

J.T. frowned harder. 'Why would she be walking around? That's not like her.'

'Don't know. It's been a tough week.'

'Yeah, well, Marion isn't exactly weak in the knees.'

'J.T., she's not under my jurisdiction. She was supposed to be here by seven. It's now 9:38, and last we knew she was walking through Williamstown in an overcoat and casual clothes. The officers said they almost didn't recognize her with her hair down.'

'*What?*'

Warning bells were already going off in his mind. He didn't want to believe them. 'She was wearing jeans and her *blond* hair was down. Would you say she looked like a college student? Like a young blond coed?'

There was a stunned pause. Then, 'Oh, shit.'

'You idiot,' J.T. swore, and suddenly he was so angry and so terrified, his hand shook on the phone. 'Can't you see what she's doing? Damn you! *And damn her!*' He didn't wait for a reply. He slammed the phone down and grabbed his gun from the small of his back.

Tess was staring at him, her hand frozen on the wooden spoon protruding from the pot of chili.

'Lock the door behind me,' he ordered curtly. 'Don't move, don't blink, don't open the fucking door for anyone. For *anyone*. Do you hear me!'

'Y-yes,' she whispered. He was already running toward the door. 'Wait! You can't –'

It was too late. He was gone.

'Damn!' Houlihan grabbed the van door. Quincy's hand shot out and stopped him.

The radios were crackling to life around them. The snipers reported J.T. running from the house. Team Alpha was responding to reports of a disturbance at the Student Union.

Things were heating up.

'Stay smart,' Quincy warned. His grip relaxed a fraction, but not his gaze. 'Team Alpha will check out the disturbance. Can we move Team Omega to the last reported sighting of Marion?'

Houlihan made a fist, then released his breath with a sigh. 'Yeah. Yeah, we'll do that.'

'Can you handle surveillance alone?'

'What?'

'The van, can you handle it alone?'

'Sure I can –'

'Good. Ms. Williams is alone in the house now, Houlihan. That's not acceptable. I'm going over.'

Houlihan gave it some thought. His nerves were strung too tight. Hell, all of their nerves were strung too tight. And now they had an agent going AWOL and her mercenary brother following suit. Everybody wanted to know what the hell was going on and what the hell to do. Now was not the time for panic. Beckett was right, after all. Discipline was the key. Houlihan took a deep breath and said, 'Remember, Beckett has the guns he stole from Difford's safe house. You got a vest on?'

'Yes. I'll watch from inside the house. You keep control from the outside.'

Quincy pulled out his 9 mm and took off the safety. From the drawer in the specially equipped van he pulled out two more mgazines and slipped them into his pocket. He nodded to Houlihan one last time, then stepped out of the van.

Houlihan closed and locked the door behind him. He was now alone. His eyes chased down all the shadows. He sat down lower in his seat.

It was 9:41 P.M. and his team was fractured.

It wasn't good.

In the war room an operator waved her hand for the sergeant. She put the caller on hold and said to him, 'I have a woman on the line who insists she knows where Jim Beckett is.'

'And where is that?'

The police operator sighed. In the last few weeks she thought she'd heard it all. By the time this gig was up, she would have no more faith in man's intelligence. 'The woman claims her next-door neighbor his Jim Beckett. Her next-door neighbor, the sixty-year-old retired woman from Florida.'

'A sixty-year-old retired woman is Jim Beckett?'

'Yes, sir.'

'Of course, what was I thinking? Why are you wasting my time with this?'

'Because the woman also claims she has Samantha Williams with her right now. She says she's calling from a gas station, Martha is going to hunt them down at any time, and she's scared for herself and for Samantha. I can hear sounds of traffic in the background and what sounds like a child crying. She says she's not hanging up until we send over the cavalry, and I believe her.'

The sergeant motioned for the headset. He put it on and took the caller off hold. 'Hello? This is Sergeant McMurphy. Who am I speaking to? Edith? Edith Magher? How can I help you, Edith?'

He was frowning. Edith Magher. Why did that name sound familiar? He glanced at the log sheet while she babbled in his ear about dead girls haunting her porch and her sixty-year-old neighbor who liked to smoke cigars and was too big and too strong and had too blue eyes . . . .

He didn't see her name listed on the log sheet. He flipped the next page, going back a few days. He could hear a child sobbing quietly in the background. The woman kept telling her everything would be all right. And then she started talking about the dead girls climbing into a brown Nissan and Martha/Jim Beckett driving away. But Martha/Jim knew that Edith knew. Sooner or later Martha/Jim would come get them.

The sergeant's gaze fell on the list of phone numbers Team A was tracking down. Suddenly the name blazed out at him. Edith Magher. Shelly Zane had forwarded calls to her seven times in the last two years.

The sergeant grabbed the operator's shoulder so tightly, she winced. He pointed furiously at the screen. 'Where's the location of the caller listed on this damn thing? I need the location and I need it now!'

Beckett trapped her arm first. Marion didn't panic and

she didn't struggle too hard. She let him drag her behind the trees, where they were further isolated, while her mind formulated her best plan of attack. He thought she was helpless. She wasn't. But she didn't want to give away the game too soon. With a man like Beckett, surprise was everything.

She raised her foot and slammed it down hard on his toes. He jerked away, but the motion unbalanced him. With a quick twist she slipped out of his grip, leaving him holding just her coat.

She spun to face him, bringing her gun out of her holster, but he caught her squarely on the chin with a single fist formed by knitting together his two hands. Her head cracked back.

Move through the pain, she ordered herself. She drew out her gun and he nailed her forearm with the billy club. Her fingers went numb. The gun dangled, and for a moment she thought she was going to lose it. The gun would fall and she would be helpless.

Don't drop your weapon.

She grabbed it with her left hand and got off three awkward shots.

He dropped low, then rushed her. He plowed her back against a hulking tree, knocking the air from her gut. She responded instinctively, hammering down on the back of his neck with the butt of her gun. He grunted and squeezed harder, two years of weight lifting in a prison rec room giving him incredible strength. His shoulder pressed into her diaphragm, squeezing her lungs, killing her.

She couldn't shoot him. She couldn't get her hands to function. White dots were appearing before her eyes. She tried to bring up her knee. He blocked it effortlessly. She pulled at his hair and the wig came off in her hand.

The world began to spin. Her chest burned. Her body cried out for oxygen. Tree bark dug into her back. There were so many ways to suffocate a person. She'd forgotten about that. What a thing to forget.

J.T., I'm so sorry.

With her last sane thought she fired the gun again, alerting the world to her position. Then she clawed at Beckett's shoulder, searching for his old gunshot wound.

It didn't matter.

Beckett counted off eight more seconds, then her body went limp.

He let her slip to the ground, stepping back and staggering drunkenly for a moment. The back of his head continued to throb from her blows. When he tried to focus on her, he saw double.

He didn't have time for such weaknesses. Discipline is the key.

He raised his baton and got it over with. One two three. After a bit of practice a man became efficient about these things.

He ran, stripping off his guard's uniform as he raced through the trees. Act one was over. On to act two.

J.T. heard the gunshots as he raced down Main Street. He veered onto Hoxsey, rushing through students, who were suddenly stopping, eyes wide.

'Move, dammit!' he cried. 'Outta my way!'

He knew the minute he'd found her, because people mingled around the entrance to the shadowed footpath, not quite sure what Bad Thing had happened and not quite willing to step forward and find out. They craned their necks from the relative safety of the lit sidewalks.

J.T. swung his cast-covered arm like a bat, forcing his way through.

'Cop!' He lied baldly. 'Someone dial 911!'

'Some guy went crashing through the trees,' a kid volunteered.

'He looked like a campus guard.'

'Stupid campus guards,' another student murmured. 'Probably shooting at a rat.'

'Or his big toe.'

J.T. raced forward. Passing the fifth tree he saw her,

her long, golden hair spilling out from behind the tree trunk. Darker red strands were slowly mingling with the gold.

'No! No no no no no!' He fell to his knees. He grabbed her hand. Then he grabbed her shoulders and clutched her against his chest. Her head rolled lifelessly forward, her lashes still against her cheek, pine needles tangled in her hair.

So much blood. Her skull fell apart in his hands. He tried to hold it together. To put her back together again. And he willed her to survive as he'd willed her to survive every day when they were children.

Pillow forts and GI comic books.

Live, live, live.

Horseback riding and swimming suicides.

Don't leave me don't leave me don't leave me.

Standing at the foot of his bed, begging him to save her.

Don't let me fail you a second time.

'Damn you!'

Beckett moved fast through the shadows. He came at last to a thick hedge and stopped to regroup. His breath was coming out in sharp gasps, forming puffs of steam in the cold night air. He could feel blood on his cheeks, and the back of his skull was swollen and tender.

These things were not supposed to happen to him.

The euphoria was dimming. Beneath, exhaustion threatened to crash his system. He shook his head, fighting it.

He had the letter *H*. He was fulfilling his plan.

Some adjustments would have to be made. Edith knew his true identity and had Samantha. He'd debated giving chase, but couldn't possibly kill an old woman in front of his daughter, so he'd let them go for now. Later he would show Edith what happened to women who crossed him. Then he would simply reclaim his daughter from the police. He'd done it before, he could do it again.

343

Theresa was still in the area, and that's what mattered. They'd buzzed about her enough on the police scanner and he understood that he was invited to join them.

He was looking forward to seeing her again.

He smoothed a hand over the navy blue suit he'd worn beneath the guard's uniform. From the pocket he produced four towelettes and used them to wipe the thick makeup from his face, wincing a little as the soap stung the scratches along his jawline. Next he pulled out a pair of glasses and a short dark wig.

Then he unbuckled the sawed-off shotgun he'd strapped beneath his arm. Difford's gun cabinet had been a gold mine.

He was ready.

Tess turned to Quincy. 'Ten o'clock,' she whispered. 'Where is he?'

'Any sign?' Quincy asked over the walkie-talkie.

'Unconfirmed,' Houlihan answered. 'There's a report of another disturbance on Hoxsey, the sound of gunfire. Team Omega is almost there –' Crackling interrupted. A new voice came on.

'This is Sniper A. It's ten o'clock-check time. I have visual of B, but no reports on C. Please confirm.'

Houlihan's voice crackled again. 'Sniper C, come in. Sniper C, come in.'

The radio was quiet.

'Sniper C?'

More silence. Tess and Quincy exchanged glances.

Houlihan's voice was strong. 'Do we have visual of Sniper C?'

'This is Sniper B. I'm looking across the street now. I see Sniper A standing in the west corner. I do *not* see Sniper C in the east. I repeat, I do *not* see Sniper C in the east. Please confirm, Sniper A.'

'This is Sniper A. I don't have visual, sir. Requesting permission to check it out.'

'Permission denied,' Houlihan said flatly. 'Hold your

position. I'm calling in SWAT. I repeat, stay at your points, I'm calling in SWAT. We are now in status red. I repeat, status red.'

As Tess watched, Quincy calmly took out two extra clips of bullets and placed them on the table beside him. He raised his 9 millimeter and pointed it at the door. 'Do you have a gun, Ms. Williams?'

'Yes.'

'Now is the time to take it out. Please remember, he's here to kill. There will be no negotiating on his part and there will be no leniency. Do you understand?'

'I understand,' she said. 'I won't hesitate.'

'Good.'

'Sir, let us take her. Sir, you have to let go now.'

J.T. stared at the man dully. He was wearing a paramedics uniform and holding a red medical kit. Behind him sirens whirled red and garish.

'I'm holding her together,' he said hoarsely, not relinquishing her.

'I know, sir,' the young man said gently. He could tell that the woman was dead. 'That's our job now. Someone said you were a cop.'

Slowly the words penetrated. J.T. looked down at Marion. Her head lolled against his arm. The loss inside him was too great. He couldn't measure it. He couldn't put it into words. He couldn't feel it, because when he did, it would bring him to his knees.

He placed his baby sister in the paramedic's arms. 'I have to go. Take good care of her for me, please. Just . . . please.'

He began to run.

Behind him the paramedic shouted at him to stop. He didn't listen.

The darkness in him had grown a voice. And now it screamed at the top of its lungs, *Kill Jim Beckett, kill Jim Beckett, kill Jim Beckett.*

He ran like a man possessed, and blood lust lit his eyes.

'Sir, sir!' The walkie-talkie blazed to life. 'This is Team Omega. We have a hit on Hoxsey. I repeat, a woman is down on Hoxsey, same MO. Beckett is in the area!'

Tess put her head between her knees and started taking deep breaths. Quincy's radio seemed to dance with a hideous cacophony of reports.

'This is Team Alpha. Repeat, Team Alpha. We are on the roof, east corner. There is no sign of Sniper C –'

'This is Team Omega. Officer down, officer down. Repeat, Agent MacAllister is down –'

'Shit!' Quincy's fist hit the table. Tess jumped.

'Suspect is reportedly dressed as a security guard. Last seen headed north. We are in pursuit. Requesting full mobilization –'

'SWAT team has been mobilized. They are in transit –'

'Officer down, officer down! This is Team Alpha, from the east corner. We have found Sniper C. Dear God, sir, we have found Sniper C –' From the background there came the sound of retching. 'Requesting backup, requesting immediate backup. He's on the roof. Shit, I think I see him. He's on the fucking roof! The roof, the roof!'

Over the airwaves Quincy and Tess heard the sound of men running.

'Hold positions, hold positions!' Houlihan screamed. 'I said, hold your fucking positions!'

Gunfire exploded across the radio. The sound of a man's hoarse cry. 'Difford. OhmyGod, ohmyGod! Jesus fucking Christ!'

Houlihan was now yelling at the top of his lungs.

'What is going on out there?' Tess cried.

'I don't know,' Quincy said.

His face had gone pale. His gaze settled on the ceiling.

J.T. rounded the corner. He heard shooting and drew his gun. He heard a man's cry. He was still too far away to see anything. He just heard the sound of all hell breaking loose. Three blocks to go, two.

The doorbell rang, followed by immediate pounding.

'Ms. Williams, open up. Detective Teitel, Massachusetts State Police. I've been sent to stand guard.'

'Stand back,' Quincy told Tess.

He didn't have to convince her. She clung to the wall, her .22 held before her in a shaky hand.

Quincy approached the door, keeping to the side. 'I want to see your badge,' he called out.

'Okay.'

Quincy stepped up to the peephole.

The shotgun blew the door apart and hurled him across the room.

Screaming filled the room. It took Tess a moment to realize it was her own.

J.T. rounded the corner. Black-clad men swarmed the rooftop, screaming at the top of their lungs. Sirens split the air behind him. An ambulance roared toward him and he barely jumped out of the way.

He twisted his ankle and went down hard.

More gunfire split the neighborhood. A shotgun blast.

He staggered up and continued running.

Kill Jim Beckett. Kill Jim Beckett.

'Hay bales, hay bales!' Tess cried. She pointed her gun and tried to remember her stance.

Jim pointed his shotgun at Quincy, slumped on the floor.

'I'm going to kill you, Theresa,' he said calmly. 'The question is, how many police officers will you take out with you?'

Tears streaming down her cheeks. *Don't hesitate. Don't hesitate.*

Quincy moaned. There was blood on his face, pieces of wood embedded in his skin. But she knew he was wearing a bulletproof vest, which would have spared him the worst.

Jim pumped the chamber.

J.T.'s form filled the doorway. Tess couldn't stop her gaze from flickering there. Jim turned and calmly pulled the trigger.

'*No!*'

The shotgun blast burst her eardrums. J.T. fell back into the sidewalk. Down he went, arms splayed like a cartoon character's. Because the violence never ended. For her it just went on and on and on.

She pointed her gun, squeezing the trigger. Jim grabbed the .22 from her hand and pistol-whipped her hard. She fell to her knees, clutching her cheek.

'We do it my way.' Grabbing her arm, Jim dragged her upstairs.

Fresh blood stained his shoulder red. Had she hit him? She couldn't think anymore. Her cheek was on fire from the blow, and ringing filled her ears. The madman was winning. Jim had gotten control.

No! Goddammit, no!

She kicked out at the back of Jim's legs, aiming for his kneecap. He twisted away. She knitted her fingers of her free hand into a shovel and went after his kidneys. He slapped her across the face. She bit his shoulder, then tore into his ear.

'Fuck!' He flung her from him so hard, she hit the wall and fell to the floor. Even then she staggered up and aimed a kick toward his groin.

Fight, fight, fight. She fought.

And Jim Beckett rose in front of her as an enraged beast. He threw aside the shotgun. He grabbed her shoulder and yanked her toward him. She hit his clavicle with the heel of her hand. He grunted with pain.

Then he wrapped his hands around her throat and squeezed.

She fell to her knees. She struck out futilely. She thought she heard groaning downstairs and she struggled to buy time. She didn't want to die. White

348

lights appeared in front of her gaze, but she refused to give in.

She'd fought too hard, come too far to fall to Jim now. She would win, goddammit. She would win.

Jim smiled cruelly. His hands tightened their grip.

J.T.'s chest was on fire. When he drew in a deep breath, his insides burned beneath his Kevlar vest. He was pretty sure he was dying. The stars looked too bright above him and the pavement was too cold beneath him.

He kept thinking he was supposed to ask for Merry Berry, then memory hit him hard.

He struggled upright. He heard the smack of flesh hitting flesh. He hated that sound. Tess . . .

Furious, he staggered to the shattered doorway, his left hand barely holding his ribs together. He grabbed the doorway for support, and wooden slivers drove into his palm.

He used the pain to anchor him.

The colonel had raised a son who could walk two miles on a broken ankle. That's a man. Be a man. Fight like a man.

He found the hunting knife strapped inside his cast and advanced for the stairs.

Sirens wailed behind him. Men were still screaming. Someone was yelling about the front door.

Let them all come. Let them all fucking come.

Beckett saw someone out of the corner of his eye. He dropped Tess and reached for the shotgun. He didn't see the knife hurtle through the air, until it drove through his shoulder.

He stared at it without comprehension. J.T. had arrived on the landing.

With a roar he charged.

He caught Beckett around the middle, and they went down with a crash. Something warm filled J.T.'s mouth. He opened his lips, and blood spilled down his cheek. The rusty flavor made him angrier.

Beckett fisted his hands and drove them into the small of J.T.'s back. J.T. got a fresh mouthful of bloody bile. He reared back and caught Beckett beneath the chin with his head. Then he reached up for the handle of his knife and gave it a twist.

Beckett staggered back with a sharp cry of pain. Vaguely J.T. was aware of the thick shadows beneath the man's eyes, the gaunt lines of his chin. Beckett had lost twenty pounds since his prison break, and he looked it.

He didn't feel it though. He felt only the heady thrum of adrenaline in his ears. The sirens, the screams, the noise. It fueled him.

He grabbed the baton he'd strapped inside his arm and started swinging.

J.T. leapt out of the way the first time. He rolled the second. The third swing cracked him on his already cracked ribs. The pain rocketed through him beyond description or color. He fell to his knees.

Above him the baton rose again. He could hear the whistle. Feel the draft.

He commanded his body to roll. One more time, closer to the stairs. His muscles took a long time responding.

The baton whistled down.

And the shotgun blast sent Beckett halfway across the second-story landing. Tess stood with the gun in her hands and the powder staining her cheeks. She pumped in another cartridge.

A low, wet groan escaped Jim's lips. As J.T. lay there, his eyes barely able to focus, he watched her walk over to him. There were no tears on her cheeks. No emotion in her eyes. Her face was pale, her face was calm. He thought of Marion as Tess pointed the shotgun at Jim's fallen body and pulled the trigger.

Through the haze of dissipating smoke, her brown eyes met his.

'It's over,' she whispered hoarsely, shotgun against

her shoulder. 'Massachusetts might not believe in the death penalty, but I do.'

Jim didn't move again. Tess let the gun slide to the floor. She cradled J.T.'s bloody head on her lap and waited for the police to make it up the stairs.

Just south of Lenox, the cop turned his wailing car into a gas station. A backup patrol car came to a screaming halt behind him.

The woman who was about to pay for her gas stared at them. The man who was unscrewing the gas cap of his Mercedes stopped. The two young kids who were out looking for a good time hunched down lower and wondered if they'd hidden the marijuana far enough beneath the seat.

The cops searched for the pay phone.

An older woman with a somber face and liver-spotted hands appeared from around the side. A little blond girl clung to her neck. She looked at the policemen somberly.

'Edith?' one of the officers asked.

She nodded and he approached the pair slowly, since the girl was obviously scared. The girl perfectly matched the posters all over the war room. He knew. For the last few nights, the officer had gone to bed so tense, he'd dreamed of that face.

'I want my mommy,' she whispered in a tiny voice.

'I know, sweetheart. You're Samantha Beckett, aren't you?'

She nodded slowly, her grip still tight around Edith's neck.

He gave her a reassuring smile. 'It's okay. We're gonna take you to your mommy, Sam. We're gonna take you home.'

Epilogue

The new arrival caused a bit of a stir.

She stood in the doorway of the Nogales bar with the long, slender lines of a beautiful woman. Male heads turned instantly, some ancient instinct coming alert. Cue sticks halted before cue balls. Beer mugs paused before parted lips. Predatory gazes cut through the thick miasma of cigarette smoke and lingered on the simple white cotton dress that brushed down her figure and flirted with the tops of her knees.

She stepped into the bar.

Her steps did not invite interruption. She had a target and headed straight for it. Observant gazes plotted the trajectory and ran ahead of her to see who the lucky man was. The minute they figured it out, the gazes quickly hurried away.

If she could tame him, she was welcome to him. The rest of them had already learned to get out of his way – and they'd each learned that lesson the hard way.

He was hunched over a tumbler of amber liquid. His blue cotton shirt was rumpled and hung over faded jeans. His black hair had gone a long time without being cut. His lean cheeks were thick with unshaved whiskers.

Some of the women had found him handsome. He hadn't appeared to find them to be anything at all.

He came day in and day out. He drank. He played pool. Then he drank some more.

Now the mystery woman arrived beside him. She slid onto the ripped vinyl stool. She gazed at him quietly. He didn't look up.

She said matter-of-factly, 'I love you.'

He raised bleary eyes. They were bloodshot and shadowed enough to indicate he hadn't slept in weeks. It had been a month since she'd last seen him. The police had brought her Sam. Beckett had been carted off to the hospital and pronounced DOA. J.T. and Quincy had been hospitalized for broken ribs, and in J.T.'s case a punctured lung. She'd visited the hospital every day for a week. He'd lie there silently the whole time, not responding to her voice or her presence. He'd looked half dead, and at times she wondered if he wished that he were.

Then one day she'd shown up and he was gone. He'd dressed himself in his bloody clothes and walked out the front door. There had been nothing the hospital staff could do to stop him, and nobody had seen him since.

Difford's body was recovered from the rooftop, where Jim had placed it as a decoy after he'd killed the sniper. A store mannequin's head had been attached to Difford's neck. Tess had attended the memorial service for the lieutenant and the sniper. Following Difford's wishes, his body was cremated and his ashes scattered over the Atlanta Braves spring training field in Florida.

Two days later Tess had attended Marion's funeral, where Marion was laid to rest next to her father in Arlington. J.T. still hadn't show up. It was as if he'd fallen off the face of the earth. That's when Tess had known he'd returned to Nogales.

'What are you doing here?' His voice sounded hoarse, either from whiskey or tobacco or disuse. Maybe all three. His fingers picked up a cigarette case. He didn't open it, he just twirled it between his fingers. It was the cigarette case that had belonged to Marion.

'You shouldn't be here,' she said.

His gaze slid down her body, then dismissed her. 'Too virginal. I'm not interested.'

'I'm not in the sinning business.'

'Well, I am.'

'Come home, J.T.' She touched his cheek lightly. His

beard was so long, it was silky. She reacquainted herself with the line and feel of jaw, the fullness of his lips. She ached for him. She looked at him and she hurt. 'Tell me how to help you.'

'Go away.'

'I can't.'

'Women are always trying to change a man. You think there's something more inside us, and frankly it's just not true. I am what I am.' He jerked his hand around the bar. 'Honey, this is me.'

'You are who you are. But this isn't it. This is you drunk. I've seen you sober. I care for that man an awful lot. I think that man is one of the best men I know.'

His gaze fell to the table and the tumbler full of amber liquid. Shame stained his cheeks.

'I'm haunted,' he said abruptly. 'Like an old house. I close my eyes and I see Rachel and Marion again and again. Sometimes they're happy. Sometimes they're sad. There's nothing I can do about it. I reach out my hand to them and *poof*, they're gone.' He opened his palm on the counter and flung the emptiness into the air.

Tess didn't know what to say. She wasn't an expert on how to heal. She did the best she could. She kissed him. And he didn't taste of whiskey or cigarettes. He tasted suspiciously of apples.

Her gaze went from him to his glass to him. He sat stiffly while she sniffed the contents.

'Apple juice?'

'Yeah.' Shame infused his cheeks again. 'I tried whiskey. I truly, truly did. And every time I raised the glass, I just saw Marion shaking her head at me. Christ' – he hung his head – 'I'm a teetotaler!'

'It's okay,' she assured him, stroking his hair. 'It'll get easier. It will.'

He didn't look convinced. Her fingers traced the beard on his cheeks, the purple puffiness beneath his eyes, the fullness of his lips. 'J.T., I love you.'

He groaned like a trapped beast. His eyes closed. 'Why can't you just go away? Why can't you just leave

354

me alone? You killed him, you survived, isn't that enough for you?'

'I don't want to live in the past.'

'I can't escape it.'

'You can, it's just going to take a while.' She gave up sitting beside him and slid onto his lap. In this bar few people noticed. His thighs were hard and masculine beneath her, the denim of his jeans soft and worn. She kissed his lips, then his cheek, and then the scar on his chest.

She rested her head against his shoulder, and after a heartbeat she felt his arms slide around her waist. He buried his face in her hair.

And after a ponderous moment his broad shoulders began to shake.

'Tell me,' she commanded softly.

'I love you. Christ, I love you.'

And he was dying and there was nothing for him anymore. No place he could go where he didn't see Marion lying in the dirt, no room to sit in where he didn't see Rachel waving to him and blowing a kiss as she got into her car, and Teddy's little arm waving in the backseat. He wanted to find them each again. He wanted to hold them in his arms and whisper, Please, please be happy. I love you, I just wanted you to be happy. I love you.

Remember me young, for both of us.

He raised his head. There were tear tracks on his cheeks. He didn't care anymore.

'Make me whole. I want to be whole.'

She pressed his face against her throat and stroked his hair. She smelled of roses. He inhaled deeply and felt the scent finally soothe his shattered senses.

'Come on. It's time to go home and meet my daughter.'

He kissed her. He held her close.

And he let her take him home.

Later, almost twelve months after that bloody night, he

had the dream for the first time. Marion and Rachel were in a field of wildflowers, wearing white dresses and whimsical summer hats. Teddy picked daisies at their feet, his chubby hand filled with the flowers. They were talking and laughing, enjoying the day.

J.T. stood at the edge of the field, invisible to them and unable to touch. They spread out in the field and opened their arms to the sun.

It was a ridiculous dream, he thought upon waking. But he held it in his mind anyway.

He liked to remember them laughing, he liked to remember them happy. In the end maybe that was the most any of us can do – remember the ones we loved the way we loved them.

He rolled over and curled his arm around his wife's supple waist.

'Bad dreams?' she murmured sleepily.

'No.'

'Okay. Stop hogging the covers.'

She drifted back to sleep. He pulled the covers over her shoulders, then settled her against him. She whispered his name and even in her sleep returned his embrace.

available from
THE ORION PUBLISHING GROUP

☐ **The Perfect Husband** £6.99
LISA GARDNER
978-0-7528-1430-8

☐ **The Killing Hour** £6.99
LISA GARDNER
978-0-7528-5903-3

☐ **The Other Daughter** £6.99
LISA GARDNER
978-0-7528-3707-9

☐ **Alone** £6.99
LISA GARDNER
978-0-7528-6515-7

☐ **The Third Victim** £6.99
LISA GARDNER
978-0-7528-4483-1

☐ **Gone** £6.99
LISA GARDNER
978-0-7528-7808-9

☐ **The Next Accident** £6.99
LISA GARDNER
978-0-7528-4826-6

☐ **Hide** £6.99
LISA GARDNER
978-0-7528-8201-7

☐ **The Survivors Club** £6.99
LISA GARDNER
978-0-7528-4963-8

All Orion/Phoenix titles are available at your local bookshop or from the following address:

Mail Order Department
Littlehampton Book Services
FREEPOST BR535
Worthing, West Sussex, BN13 3BR
telephone 01903 828503, *facsimile* 01903 828802
e-mail MailOrders@lbsltd.co.uk
(Please ensure that you include full postal address details)

Payment can be made either by credit/debit card (Visa, Mastercard, Access and Switch accepted) or by sending a £ Sterling cheque or postal order made payable to *Littlehampton Book Services*.
DO NOT SEND CASH OR CURRENCY.

Please add the following to cover postage and packing

UK and BFPO:
£1.50 for the first book, and 50p for each additional book to a maximum of £3.50

Overseas and Eire:
£2.50 for the first book plus £1.00 for the second book and 50p for each additional book ordered

---

BLOCK CAPITALS PLEASE

name of cardholder ....

address of cardholder ....

....

....

postcode ....

delivery address
(if different from cardholder)

....

....

....

postcode ....

☐ I enclose my remittance for £...........................

☐ please debit my Mastercard/Visa/Access/Switch (delete as appropriate)

card number ☐☐☐☐☐☐☐☐☐☐☐☐☐☐☐☐☐☐

expiry date ☐☐☐☐   Switch issue no. ☐☐

signature ....

prices and availability are subject to change without notice